Clay Engle's Arsenal Stories

# Battle Zone Wilkes-Barre

Clay Engle

authorHOUSE®

*AuthorHouse™*
*1663 Liberty Drive*
*Bloomington, IN 47403*
*www.authorhouse.com*
*Phone: 1 (800) 839-8640*

*Published by AuthorHouse 06/11/2018*

*ISBN: 978-1-5462-4612-1 (sc)*
*ISBN: 978-1-5462-4611-4 (hc)*
*ISBN: 978-1-5462-4610-7 (e)*

*Library of Congress Control Number: 2018906811*

*Print information available on the last page.*

*Any people depicted in stock imagery provided by Getty Images are models, and such images are being used for illustrative purposes only. Certain stock imagery © Getty Images.*

*This book is printed on acid-free paper.*

This book is dedicated to my daughters, Olivia and Marissa—I love you both—and to Rebekah Zurn. You mean more to me than you know.

This book is also dedicated to all of those who did not believe.

# AUTHOR'S NOTE

If you live or ever have lived in Wilkes-Barre, you might wonder about some of the details in the story. For example, in the novel, the North Street Bridge and Veterans Bridge are next to each other, when in the real world, one replaced the other, and New Public Square is next to Old Public Square, when really, there is only one Public Square. I did all of this to expand the city, including placing the canal, railroads, and boulevards next to each other, when they were basically in the same location at various times in history.

"Felt like Nero"
was originally published by
Iliad Press in 1996,
in the book Perspectives.

*Achtung*! *Achtung*, citizens of Wilkes-Barre! Because of the actions of the United States, Wilkes-Barre has been chosen as the location of the first of many battles in your country. We are like the werewolves of old. Though the head of our leader has been removed, we are still a deadly threat. Guten Tag is fully prepared to cause the death and destruction of all those in our way. We intend to bring America to its knees, and your blood will write the first chapters in this war!

—Heinrich Waffen

# PRELUDE 1

# April 1988

A warm spring wind rustled through the siding of John Lanesra's house as three pebbles struck the bedroom window of his son, Michael. The distraction kept Michael from completing his homework assignment, the last sixty pages of *The Silmarillion* by J. R. R. Tolkien, something he should have finished a week ago. He'd lost the book on the bus but had been lucky enough to get it back during yesterday's ride home.

The light from his room had been on for quite a while, as the time approached three o'clock in the morning, when another volley of pebbles struck. Michael mumbled to himself, marked the page, and leaned over to glance out the window. In his backyard, waving back at him, was his longtime best friend, Mitchell "Mitch" Lewis, whom he had known most of his life.

As Michael opened the window, Mitch said, "Come on out!"

Shaking his head, Michael peered out at the darkness beyond and said, "Do you have any idea what time it is?"

"No," he answered, "but get down here quick."

Squinting slightly, Michael noticed Mitch was kind of squirming and bouncing around, and he asked, "What's wrong with you? Why are you so jittery? You need to go to the bathroom?"

"No, it's better than that," Mitch answered. "So hurry up."

"Hold on," Michael said. He pulled his head back in and closed the window.

*I wonder what he wants at this time of night*, he thought, slipping on his socks. *I bet he didn't even start reading this book yet and wants me to give him answers so he doesn't have to.*

Quietly, he made his way past his parents' bedroom and down the back steps to the kitchen, where he turned on the lights and opened the door. Expecting Mitch to push past him and run to the downstairs bathroom, Michael opened the door and said, "Go on, and use the one next to the washer."

"What? I told you. I don't need to go to the bathroom," Mitch said, stepping inside. "I do, however, need to borrow one of your forks."

"A fork? At this time of night? What are you up to?" Michael asked, angered and trying not to yell. "You're not high, are you? If my father comes down here and sees you, he'll kill both of us."

"It's important," Mitch answered as he started to squirm again.

"You're not high, are you?" Michael asked again, looking at his eyes. "It's after three, and I still have to finish that book for English class tomorrow—today."

"Something happened to me on my way home from school yesterday," he said, shaking his head.

"Yeah, you missed the bus again and had to walk home," Michael said, remembering how a few of their classmates had laughed as the bus pulled away.

"You make it sound like a bad thing," he said, grinning. "I took a shortcut and got lucky—well, not that kind of lucky. I got superpowers."

"You are high. You'd better go before I wake up my father. I'm going back to bed." He pointed toward the back door. "You got superpowers from something you took. Now, go home. I'll see you in school."

"No, listen. I climbed over a fence that I didn't know was electrified, and something strange happened to me," Mitch said, smiling as he recalled the sensation from touching the fence.

"Somehow, when I grabbed the fence, the electricity didn't harm me. It changed me, and I absorbed it."

"Yeah, it fried your brain," Michael said, reaching for the door and expecting Mitch to take the hint and leave.

"No, I made it over the fence and outran a security guard," Mitch said, trying to find the proof on his shoes.

"What did you step in?" Michael asked, looking around the kitchen floor for anything brown.

"Nothing," he answered. "You're not listening to me."

"I'm not. I think you're twitching 'cause you took something," Michael said. "And I've got a book to finish for class in the morning. Speaking of which, did you read any of it yet?"

"Give me a few minutes to prove it to you," Mitch pleaded, clasping his hands together in a begging manner.

After pausing for a moment, Michael replied, "Okay, five minutes."

Just then, a black cat walked into the kitchen, looking nothing like an ordinary house cat. It appeared to have had its share of fights. Both boys stopped and looked at it. As it stopped and returned the gaze, looking each of them over, Michael grabbed it just as it was about to lick its paw.

"Hey," he said, picking the cat up. "This thing yours?"

"Nope," Mitch said, shaking his head. "By the way it's purring, I'd say it was yours."

"Mine? My father hates cats," he replied, gently tossing it out into the backyard. "He'd strangle me if he saw that in here."

"So you going to give me that five minutes?" Mitch asked, returning to the reason he was there.

"Yes, I said I would," Michael answered, wanting the situation to be over already.

"Good. Then give me a fork," he said, holding out his hand.

Giving him a look that said, "Come on," Michael replied, "You know where they are."

As Mitch reached for the handle of the silverware drawer, the same black cat jumped up onto the picnic table in the backyard and peered in through the window. Neither saw it, but the cat appeared to be interested in what was going on inside.

Watching as he took one of the forks out of the drawer, Michael realized quickly what his friend was about to do. Shaking his head in opposition, he said, "You know I'm not going to let you stick that in the socket, right?"

"Come on, Mike. How long have you known me?" Mitch asked as he bent back the middle prong of the fork. "I've never been high before and don't have any plans of starting."

"You know I'm not going to let you shove that fork in the socket, right? My father isn't going to kick my ass for your stupidity," Michael said, folding his arms. "While we watch the house burn."

Smirking, Mitch replied, "Stop me if you can."

Cracking his knuckles, Michael felt one punch ought to do the job.

Mitch took a few steps back, smiled, and asked, "Ready?"

Shaking his head, he said, "If you wake my father, he's going to kill both of us, and then I'm going to kick your ass!"

"So then step out of the way," Mitch said, eyeing the wall socket behind him.

Michael locked his eyes on Mitch and nodded that he was ready.

"This is for your dad," Mitch said, whirling around quickly and shoving the fork into the socket behind him, which was just above the can opener on the counter.

The electricity surged through the fork and caused the lights to flicker and dim. Michael stood surprised as he watched the expression on his friend's face; it showed no sign of pain. Instead, Mitch looked as if he were benefiting from the electricity, and Michael wasn't sure what to think.

Mitch pulled the fork out of the socket, tossed it to Michael, and watched as Michael dropped it the instant he felt the heat.

"How long does it take to get to my house from here?" Mitch asked. Then he answered, "About forty minutes?"

"Yeah," Michael said, guessing.

"I'll bet I can call you from there before you can get to bed," Mitch said, turning and reaching for the kitchen screen door.

"I'm not waiting for you," Michael said, glad the strange episode was finally over and he could return to reading.

"I'm not expecting you to," Mitch said. "I'll call you from my house before you can shut this door, turn the lights off, and get upstairs and into bed."

"Deal," Michael said, watching as Mitch stepped out into the yard.

Five minutes and thirteen seconds later, Michael was pulling the sheets up around him. He was about to mumble a comment, when he heard the phone ring.

*I guess Mitch really does have superpowers*, Michael thought, laughing softly as his father answered the phone.

Michael walked into class and almost tripped several times as he tried to navigate through homeroom to his seat while struggling to read the last few pages of the book. Just as he sat down, Mitch walked into the room. He acted as if he were a new man, and his smiled seemed to show it. The only person not looking was his best friend, who struggled to finish the last ten pages of the reading assignment.

Mitch sat down just as a hand gently touched Michael's hand.

Jumping up, Michael yelled, "Mitch!"

"Mr. Lanesra, is there a problem?" the teacher asked, seeing him spring up out of his seat.

Feeling embarrassed as he sat down, he replied, "Um, no."

Mitch put the book back on his desk and said, "Wasn't me, Romeo. By the way, your dad wasn't too happy answering the phone last night."

Glaring at Mitch, the girl off to his right said, "Sorry about that, Michael."

Rubbing his hand where he'd felt the static shock, he looked at Becky and replied, "Oh, hi."

Becky was in every one of Michael's dreams; she had been there since he'd first met her in second grade. He could recall countless arguments and fights with the other boys in his class when they made comments about her or disagreed with how beautiful he thought she was. However, as much as Michael Lanesra fantasized about Becky Carlin, he never had the courage to ask her out on a date.

"Anyway, I've something I wanted to ask you," she said, leaning closer to him.

*If I finished reading this book*, he thought as he looked at her and calmly asked, "What's that?"

"Out," she replied, keeping her eyes locked on his. "On a date."

Those words closed *The Silmarillion* for the rest of the day. It no longer mattered if he finished it; everything in the universe stopped when she spoke those words.

"What are you doing this weekend?" Becky asked as Michael pushed the book away.

"Um, nothing," he replied, unable to think.

"Would you like to go ice-skating?" she eagerly asked. "I can pick you up."

Not comprehending what she'd just said, Michael asked, "Are you asking me out on a date?"

"Looks that way," Mitch said, interrupting.

Giving him a cold glare, she said, "How else are we going to ice-skate?"

"What about Shane?" Michael asked, referring to the guy he thought was her boyfriend.

"It's over between us," she answered. "Besides, I haven't been with him since you took first place at state finals."

"That's right," he said, recalling. "You were cheering the loudest, which pissed your brother off."

"I think he was jealous you won, especially by the way you beat the other guy so easily," she replied. "Besides, my brother only went to the meet just to watch you lose. I'm glad you disappointed him."

"So am I," he said as she smiled.

"What time do you want to go skating?" she asked, changing the subject back to their date.

Trying to think, he just shrugged.

She took out a pen, wrote her phone number on his hand, and said, "Call me tonight."

A month passed. Michael had become one of the happiest men in the world, all thanks to the time he spent with Becky. At the same time, Mitch was surprised when he agreed to become his crime-fighting partner. After taking a few days to practice, they decided that night was going to be their first night as Wilkes-Barre's newest superheroes.

"That's the odd thing," Michael said as they walked into Mitch's bedroom. "Every time we touch, I get the slightest tingle of static electricity. Maybe that's what love is supposed to feel like."

"I bet she's got some kind of electrical power," Mitch said. "Maybe I should date her."

"Maybe I should give you a fat lip," Michael said, dropping his gym bag onto the floor.

"Okay, okay," Mitch said, trying to avoid an argument. "Do you have a name picked out?"

"Name? What do I need a name for?" Michael asked. "You think we're going to see some major action tonight?"

"Who knows? We might even run into Quarrel," Mitch replied. "For a superhero, she's one fine-looking woman."

"Probably married and definitely older than you," Michael replied. "She's a pro. What would she want with us?"

"Once she sees how I look in this costume, I'm telling you—she's going to want a piece of the Stingray," Mitch said proudly as he pulled his costume out of the closet.

Michael tried not to laugh when he saw the flashy, disco-looking red-and-gold costume Mitch was going to wear while fighting crime. "Stingray?" he said. "You're not going to wear that out, are you?"

"Wait till you see the mask," Mitch said, eager to show him.

The moment Michael saw the mask, he wondered if he should reserve a seat at the circus. *Maybe by me telling him this, it will make him change his mind. On the other hand, what if I caused him to hate being a superhero so much that he turned to crime as a way to get revenge?*

"So what do you think?" Mitch asked, laying the mask next to the rest of the costume. "Seriously."

After hesitating, Michael answered, "I guess I'll have to get used to it."

"Cool. So now you need to pick out a name," Mitch said, looking at the gym bag on the floor. "Let me see your costume."

As he unzipped his gym bag, Michael said, "You know I don't have any superpowers, right? You told me to use my wrestling skills to fight crime, so I thought about it and picked the name the Biting Rat."

Looking over the blue-and-orange wrestling sweat suit Michael pulled out of his bag, Mitch said, "What! You can't. That's not a superhero name. The Biting Rat? Come on. You can't be serious. That sounds so stupid."

"I told you I didn't have any powers, and you said to use my wrestling skills, and that's what I did," Michael said. "So I named myself after the greatest wrestler of all time: C. C. Champs."

"You named yourself after him? King Rat?" Mitch said. "The guy who bites the head off of a rat to start every one of his matches? What are you going to do when the press finds out that you named yourself after a devil worshipper?"

"I can't name myself after a wrestler, but you can name yourself after a fish?" Michael argued. "In a disco outfit?"

"I guess we'll have to see who the world thinks is better: the fish in the disco outfit or the wrestling rat!" Mitch shouted.

"I intend to make my actions speak louder than my words," Michael said. As he proceeded to get dressed, he mumbled, "Wrestling Rat."

The sun set over Wilkes-Barre as its two newest superheroes, Stingray and the Biting Rat, made their way to the playground behind Mitch's house. As the two climbed over the fence and into the bushes, Michael hesitated, realizing that people would see him dressed like this. Mitch had superspeed and wasn't worried if people caught sight of him as he ran.

"We need to get past them without being seen," Mitch said, acting as if he knew what he was doing.

"Why?" Michael asked. "Are we on a covert-ops mission? I thought we were superheroes. Why are we hiding?"

Unsure how to respond, Mitch remained quiet.

"Well?" Michael said, waiting for a response.

"Well what?" Mitch asked, getting annoyed.

"What do we do?" Michael asked, leaving the choice up to Mitch. "Hide here and wait?"

"You're leaving the choice up to me?" he asked, surprised.

"It's your idea," Michael answered. "So why not lead? Just don't expect me to be Biting Rat the Boy Wonder."

For the next few minutes, the two of them hid in the bushes, laughing, arguing, and making noise. As the kids left the basketball court, they kept looking in their direction to see if they could locate the origin of the noise. Once they finally left and the sky was filled with night, the two heroes made their way through the vacant park.

Thirty-nine minutes later, they arrived in town, where no one greeted them or looked upon them with awe and curiosity. Those passing by in their cars taunted them and laughed at them.

Standing on the rooftop of the United Penn Bank building was the reason they didn't give up and retreat to their homes to hide in their bedrooms. She was looking down on them.

The strawberry-blonde woman dressed in blue and yellow, known to the world as Quarrel, had been fighting crime in the city of Wilkes-Barre for the past three years. She spent the majority of her time stopping petty thieves, though on occasion, she had run-ins with more skilled criminals.

Watching the city of Wilkes-Barre from above, she paid no attention to Mitch and Michael as they looked up, expecting to see a sign of approval. The only thing she had in common with Mitch was that they were both sapient dominant—the term for those born with superpowers.

Besides the two new crime fighters seeking to follow Quarrel, two others lurked nearby, dressed just as out of context with their surroundings. They weren't criminals who'd crossed paths with her previously and come back for revenge. Their intent was to replace Quarrel, for they believed they were better. They went by the names of Crimson Falcon and Thunderflex.

"Those are the villains," Mitch said, pointing at them as they stood in front of the United Penn Bank.

"They're what?" Michael said, confused as to how Mitch had come to that conclusion.

"Bad guys," he answered. "I mean, look—they're standing in front of a bank in costumes. How much more obvious do they have to be?"

Taking a closer look at one of the costumed strangers, Michael thought, *That's Becky.*

"Why are they waiting in front of the bank? Wouldn't they break in the back way, through the alley?" Michael said, squinting for a better view of the girl he believed was Becky Carlin.

"Because they're lookouts for the rest of the gang," Mitch replied, guessing.

"Lookouts?" Michael said, wondering how he'd come up with that theory. "Quarrel's on the roof. Don't you think she'd know what was going on right under her own nose?"

"Yeah. She's on the roof, but maybe she sees us down here and knows we can handle it," Mitch said with a wink as he tapped the side of his head.

"I think you've lost it," Michael said, shaking his head. "You make it sound like we've been doing this for years and that we're pals with her. Take a good look at those two. Tell me who they are."

Deciding he could use his superspeed to get a better look, Mitch nodded and took off running. Unfortunately, his shoelace came untied, and he collided violently with a trash can just a few feet away from the two he was trying to investigate.

"What the hell?" the guy dressed in the crimson costume with a black trench coat said, seemingly startled.

"Oh, my God!" the girl standing next to him in green and silver said, jumping back.

Mitch mumbled as he rolled around in pain, while Michael ran as quickly as he could to get to his partner's side. As he got closer, Michael could see he was right: it was Becky. She was with her older brother, Greg Carlin.

Remembering Greg's personality and attitude, Michael quickly changed his mind. If anyone was going to go down the path of crime, it was Greg Carlin. He was a talented wrestler, but he'd never had the opportunity to further that career at a college level because his mother had run off after his father died in a mining accident.

Leo Carlin had been a mine inspector for more than forty years, and on the day he planned to retire, the other inspectors went on strike. Since it was his last day, Leo chose not to strike, even though he agreed with everything the others were fighting for.

A few of them became convinced he was a sellout and should be made an example of. They attempted to scare him by sabotaging the elevator, but a rare earthquake in the Wilkes-Barre area made matters worse. Thanks to that 2.1 quake, none of the conspirators were ever charged with the crime.

Greg and Becky buried their father the day of Greg's high school graduation, and when he and Becky returned home, they found the goodbye note their mother had written before she left. After his tears dried, Greg quickly came to the realization that he was the sole adult in the house and would have to care for his sister, even though she was only two years younger than him. College was no longer on the agenda, and his future as a wrestler was out of the question.

Now he needed to search for a means of income to support his sister. Keeping her safe and putting food on the table were his main concerns. The day he learned about Becky's abilities, the idea came to him. The final piece was seeing Quarrel on the front page of the *Wilkes-Barre Record*. He decided they too would become superheroes.

Greg's wrestling skills and Becky's unique ability to store static electricity in her aura and release it as a quick burst of electricity when she flexed would make them Wilkes-Barre's first crime-fighting team. However, they didn't intend to fight crime for free. Greg hoped to use the money they earned to go to college, and the rest would be Becky's to do with as she pleased.

Reluctantly, Becky agreed to go along with her brother's idea, but she hoped someone with knowledge of sapient-dominant powers would take notice and offer to teach her how to use them. There was no other way for her to find someone like that; the newspapers and phone books remained quiet on the subject. She hoped that by getting out into the public and using her powers, she might get lucky.

Now Michael was standing face-to-face with the woman he would be spending tomorrow night with again. It was going to be their seventh date, provided she didn't intend to do him serious harm.

"Flex!" her partner yelled, moving quickly to her side. "We're under attack!"

"Attack?" Michael said in a surprised voice as he looked at the man he suspected was Greg Carlin.

Judging by the way the falcon was sewn onto the hooded crimson sweatshirt, Michael could see it hadn't been done professionally. Recalling that Greg was an Atlanta Falcons fan, he was confident Greg was the one who'd sewn it on. If it hadn't been him, then it must have been his sister.

"Who the hell are you?" the Crimson Falcon said as Michael knelt down in front of him to help Mitch.

Ignoring him, Michael spoke to his partner instead. "You okay?"

"Hey, I'm doing the talking here!" the Crimson Falcon said loudly as nearby people began to gather.

People waiting close by for the final buses of the day had heard Mitch collide with the trash can and believed it was an explosion of some kind. However, when they saw Mitch lying on the ground in pain, dressed strangely, they wondered who he was and why he was dressed in such an odd way.

"Yeah, so what?" Michael said loudly as he continued to assist Mitch.

"Yeah, so what?" the Crimson Falcon repeated, getting in Michael's face. He kneed him hard in the midsection. "I'll rip that mask from your face!" he yelled as Michael moaned and almost fell over.

*Been waiting for this for quite some time*, Michael thought, charging him head-on. *Never thought it would be in this manner.*

Michael slammed into him and knocked him into the bank wall. They fell hard to the ground and immediately started wrestling. For the next few minutes, the two tossed and flipped each other as if they were still back on the high school wrestling team, though this time, it wasn't to impress the coach.

As the two threw each other around, Becky made her way over to Mitch, who was holding his right arm and was in pain. The moment they came in contact, her body gave off a slight burst of electricity. To his surprise, Becky's shock seemed to increase the healing of his arm. Instead of taking weeks, the healing took minutes.

"Are you okay?" she asked a second time as his hearing returned.

"Um, yes. Yes," Mitch answered slowly as he looked over his arm.

"That was a terrible crash. Are you sure you're not hurt?" Becky asked, putting her hand on his shoulder.

Feeling the electricity running through his body, Mitch replied, "Nothing us superheroes need to be concerned with."

"Is that what you're doing out here?" she asked, looking over what Mitch called a costume.

"What? Super heroing?" Mitch asked, keeping calm while focusing on his healed arm.

"Yeah, you're not the only ones out here"—she paused— "super heroing."

"Guess not," he said, realizing he had been wrong about their intentions. Looking over at Michael, he knew he had to break up the fight.

"Stop this!" Becky demanded, pulling her brother off of Michael. "We don't have to do this. They're not the enemy. Come on. Let's leave them be and get out of here."

"Next time," Greg replied, climbing off of Michael.

Grabbing Michael by the shoulder, Mitch yelled, "Come on! Let's get out of here before the cops show up!"

A few blocks later, Michael pulled off his mask and said, "I've had enough of this crap." Tossing it into a nearby trash can, he continued. "This was a ridiculous idea, and I don't want to be part of it anymore! If you want to continue this goofy crap, do it by yourself. Don't try talking me out of it. I'm going home to soak in the bathtub and forget about this."

"You're serious," Mitch said in a surprised voice as he stopped dead in his tracks. "Aren't you?"

"Yes, the whole idea was stupid right from the start," Michael answered as he began to outdistance Mitch.

"I think you're just jealous of the powers I have," Mitch remarked. Then he thought, *Besides, I'm not the one with the black eye.*

Becky Carlin stepped out of the shower at five thirty and proceeded to dry her long, curly blonde hair. As the heat dried her hair, she couldn't help but think of how foolish she felt. She and Greg had wasted the entire night standing in front of a building in downtown Wilkes-Barre, waiting for a crime to be committed. Making Thunderflex a household name was a bad idea, and from that moment on, Becky was going to start doing the right thing.

*Leave crime fighting to Quarrel*, she thought. *She can have the soreness and pain of stopping a crime. I don't want it. Not that Greg is going to like the idea, but I'm going to find something I can be happy with. He's also not going to be thrilled when I tell him about my date with Michael. Then again, they already slapped each other around, so what's left? Another round?*

A little less than an hour later, Becky parked in front of Michael's house. The rumblings of nervousness in her stomach made her hesitate to get out and approach Michael's door.

*Get a grip on yourself, Becky. It's only Mike. You saw him last night, running around in blue and orange, just like you were,* she told herself as she took a deep breath and stepped out of the car.

What worried Becky the most was running into Michael's bald, menacing-looking six-foot-five father. She hadn't done anything wrong to get on the man's bad side; it was just that his overall appearance made her think otherwise. Each step toward the door was slower and smaller than the last, until finally, she was standing in front and knocking.

As the door opened, Becky's heart jumped into her throat. She'd expected to see John Lanesra looking back at her. Instead, it was his son, the man she'd come to see, and her nervousness turned to a smile.

"Becky," Michael said, catching the scent of her perfume as he stepped out onto the porch next to her. "How are you?"

"Ready to spend the evening with you," she answered as she took his hand.

"Ice-skating? We've seen all of the new movies," Michael said as she led him to her car.

"Ice-skating? When did you learn to do that?" she asked, teasing.

"About fifteen minutes from now," he replied, opening her door.

Greg Carlin's old, beat-up white pickup truck was parked at the end of the street. He'd followed his sister there to his sworn enemy's house and watched as she picked him up. The cheap whiskey that he'd paid double for was making all of his decisions. He followed them to the Kingston Ice-Skating Rink. Greg intended to put a stop to this.

Several other soon-to-be losers around his age had offered to join Greg on his stakeout, but his hatred for Michael was at its strongest when he was alone. The more he thought about Becky being with that guy, the more he saw his dreams of being a superhero fading fast.

Whether or not she had the desire to continue didn't matter. Greg was older and worried his sister would tell Michael about his plans to be the Crimson Falcon, and superhero or not, he wanted his identity kept secret.

Twenty minutes later, Becky pulled into the parking lot. They were discussing their biology homework and Mitch's outrageous plan to get out of dissecting a frog. Neither noticed Greg's white truck pull in right behind them. As they walked across the parking lot, they saw Greg stagger out toward them.

"Get away from my sister!" he yelled. "Becky, get in the car!"

"You're drunk!" Becky yelled, moving away from him.

"And I'm the boss. It's my right," he said, locking eyes with Michael. "What's up, sport? Do you want to go another round, or was last night a good enough lesson?"

Stepping in front of Becky, Michael smiled and replied, "Come see!"

Greg smiled, took one long final drink, and dropped the empty bottle. He took two steps toward Michael and was met by a right cross that knocked him to the ground.

"Yesterday was a fluke," Michael said, not waiting for him to stand. "No more silly costumes to hide behind. Your sister is with me; I'm not going to hurt her. But after tonight's date, she's going to stay at my house until you get that alcohol problem of yours taken care of."

"That's my sister! My parents are gone, and I'm in charge! You're not taking her home!" Greg said as Michael's fist grazed the side of his left cheek.

"I'm not going to stand for this, Greg. Now, get out of here. You're drunk!" Becky yelled, pointing to the road. "Go home before the cops arrest you."

"Arrest me? Becky, we were a team—you know, the Crimson Falcon and Thunderflex," he said. "I can't be arrested. Superheroes don't go to jail."

"Come on, Mike. Just walk away," Becky said, turning toward him and the entrance to the rink.

"Don't do that!" Greg yelled, reaching into his jacket pocket. "I didn't want to do this, but you leave me no choice!"

"Greg!" she yelled. "Where did you get that? Put that away, and get out of here! You're so screwed if the cops get here."

"Hey, I'm the Crimson Falcon," he said, waving the gun. "I don't run from the cops. I'm a superhero."

"Like hell you are," Michael said, grabbing for the gun.

As the two of them wrestled for control, people began to gather around. Some were inches away and thought of jumping in to break up the fight, but none of them made the move.

*Bang.*

The bullet tore through Becky's left leg, knocking her to the ground. Michael heard her scream and fought for control of the gun. Pushing him, Greg managed to make a feeble attempt to throw it away.

"You shot my sister!" Greg yelled, enraged by what had just happened.

As drunk as Greg was, his anger at what he'd caused pushed him to hit Michael with more force than he expected. A green Ford Bronco with the passenger door open became Greg's next weapon when he slammed Michael's head into it a few times. The woman it belonged to did nothing more than scream and swear she was calling the police.

After throwing Michael into the backseat and slamming the door, Greg said, "Go ahead, lady. He's the criminal. Tell them the Crimson Falcon caught him."

Moving fast, Greg picked up his screaming sister and put her into his truck. He climbed in quickly, started the truck, and pulled out. Realizing Greg was getting away with Becky, Michael ignored the throbbing in his head and rushed out of the Bronco. The last thing he saw was Greg throwing him the finger and driving off.

*One chance*, Michael thought as he started running.

The way out of the parking lot was in the opposite direction, but Greg would have to come his way to take Becky to the hospital.

*Thank God the North Cross Valley Highway isn't finished yet*, he thought, running as fast as he could.

Even with his head pounding, Michael was able to reach the road just as Greg approached. Had it not been for Becky kicking and screaming, Michael might have missed them; instead, he was lucky enough to grab on and climb into the back. However, with all of the junk and truck parts scattered about, it wasn't an easy ride.

As the truck pulled out into traffic, Michael knew that whatever happened that night, things were going to be a lot different for the three of them. Greg was going to be arrested before the night was over; Becky was going to need a place to stay; and whether his parents liked it or not, she was going to live in his house.

The thought of her living with him ended when Greg slammed on the brakes, and Michael crashed into the back window. It was the first time Greg noticed him; however, he had his sister's bleeding, kicking, and screaming to deal with. There was also enough traffic on the North Street Bridge to keep Greg from flying across it and reaching the General Hospital.

From the top of the Wilkes-Barre Coal Exchange Building on the corner of South River Street and Market, Stingray stood looking out over the Susquehanna River and Kingston beyond. He had just finished his patrol of the Wilkes-Barre side of the river and was looking to check the outlying area. Moving along the edge of the rooftop, he was about to make his way down the fire escape, when he caught sight of Greg's erratic driving.

Returning the binoculars to his utility belt, he said, "Probably just a drunk driver, but I still need to check on it. People's lives could be in danger."

It had been twenty-four hours since the Biting Rat and Stingray had gone their separate ways, but Mitch was determined to make it on his own as a superhero. If his best friend didn't want to do it, that only meant he wouldn't have to share the spotlight or the fame he expected would come.

*Feeling kind of drained, but my speed is still holding up*, Mitch thought, moving quickly down off of the fire escape ladder. *Can't juice up now. That'll have to wait until I deal with this problem on the bridge.*

Reaching the sidewalk, Mitch looked out at the traffic in front of him. Timing his first step, Mitch took off running, and he easily made it through the traffic and had no problem making it to the North Street Bridge.

Stepping onto the bridge, he saw two men spring from the truck and start fighting. Stopping to identify the men, Mitch recognized one to be Michael, but Michael wasn't in costume, and he wondered if he was right.

*What's he doing out here?* Mitch thought as he stumbled. Almost tripping over his own feet, he had no choice but to grab the bridge to keep from falling. Regaining his balance, Mitch felt weak, as if he had gone days without any food or sleep. He had drained all of his energy—a sensation he'd never felt before.

*Come on. Keep going*, Mitch told himself. *Now is not the time to drop. Mike needs your help.*

Pushing himself to keep moving, Mitch looked to see who Michael was facing off against. When he caught sight of Greg's face, he knew he couldn't stop, and he moved as fast as he could to intervene.

"Mitch, what are you doing here?" Michael yelled while dodging an oncoming motorcycle.

Turning to look, Greg recognized Stingray from the night before and managed to hit him in the stomach while still maintaining his focus on Michael. In Mitch's weakened condition, the blow only added to his need for sleep or a quick jolt of electricity. With Michael stuck in the center of the bridge, avoiding cars, Greg continued his attack on Mitch.

The truck wasn't going anywhere. Becky had been fighting with her brother the entire time. To keep her from jumping out of the truck, Greg had handcuffed her to the door. Her constant kicking had caused Greg to lose control and crash into the side of the bridge.

The force with which he'd hit the railing had left the passenger-side wheel hanging over the Susquehanna River. With the way Greg was slamming Mitch into the truck, little by little, the vehicle was moving toward the water below.

"Get off him, asshole!" Michael yelled, tackling Greg. "It's you and me!"

Mitch took a step toward Michael, but his head started spinning, and he had to lean up against the truck. He felt it move. Jumping back, he looked at Michael, at Greg, and then at the traffic piling up as the other motorists tried to see the fight. He heard approaching sirens.

*Good, 'cause I need a break*, Mitch thought as he let out a sign of relief. *But I can't show any kind of weakness.*

"Mitch!" Michael yelled as he and Greg rolled around, still punching each other. "Get Becky! She's still inside the truck."

"Becky?" Mitch repeated in a surprised tone. At first glance, he didn't see her. She was lying down on the floor mat, semiconscious due to the loss of blood. When Mitch stepped up and opened the door, he saw Becky handcuffed to the door.

"Now comes the hero part," Mitch mumbled to himself. Then he looked back and said, "I've got her, Mike."

Pushing the door open all the way, Mitch saw the truck begin to rock slightly. Doing his best to convince himself he could do this, he slowly entered the truck.

"Becky," he said, moving closer to her.

As she lifted her head, the truck teetered.

"I'm here to help you," he said as the noise of the truck moving sent a shiver up his back. He turned to Michael. "We've got a problem! Becky's handcuffed to the door!"

Greg heard him yell and laughed. He had the upper hand and didn't care. He still believed he was the Crimson Falcon, and he was going to get out of this situation and be the hero.

All of that changed when he threw Michael against the truck, and it disappeared from view.

Feeling the truck move from its position, Michael jumped up and cried out, "Becky!"

Seeing the truck slide forward, he attempted to grab it, but he missed and hit his face on the sidewalk as the truck plunged into the river. Not waiting to see the splash, Michael sprang up, ran toward the Wilkes-Barre side of the river, and started wading out.

He could see the truck bobbing up and down in the water, and he started to swim, but due to all of the rain in upstate New York, the river was high. With each stroke toward the truck, he called out to Becky and Mitch. Swimming became harder and harder in the strong current, and before he knew it, he was fighting for his life.

The next thing he knew, he was on the shore several yards from where he'd started. Coughing up river water, he looked up to see standing over him Wilkes-Barre's only successful superhero: Quarrel.

"You could have drowned out there," she said. "What were you thinking?"

"What was I thinking?" he repeated, sitting up. "You're the reason for all of this shit! My friends are dead because of your damn superpowers—because they wanted to follow in your footsteps!"

# PRELUDE 2

Five years after the death of his girlfriend and best friend, a lot had happened in Michael's life. The summer of his graduation, he learned his mother, Elizabeth, had cancer, and six months later, she was gone, leaving Michael and his father alone.

Being an only child meant Michael didn't have to care for any younger siblings. However, after Elizabeth's funeral ended, John's journey from loving husband to helpless alcoholic began the instant the beer bottle touched his lips. Each drink took him further and further from the life he and his son once had.

Just like Greg Carlin, Michael never had the opportunity to go to college. The family's money put his mother to rest, and the remainder went to the bar with his father. After his failed attempt at being the Biting Rat, Michael returned to the streets of Wilkes-Barre late at night—not as a superhero but as someone walking to clear his mind.

He never set out to do anything other than find his father. However, John Lanesra had enemies and debts, so finding him wasn't Michael's only problem; getting him home safe and sound was the bigger challenge.

One on one or even two on one, Michael had few problems. Groups of men and trouble outside of the bar forced Michael to carry weapons. During the day, when he wasn't searching for his father, he taught himself how to use those weapons including his mantis poles, none of which had a trigger.

For the first year, all Michael did was search for his father and get him back home. Never once did he run into Quarrel. He wasn't sure what he would do if he saw her. With the way things had ended the night his friends had died, Michael might have fought her, especially during those rare moments when he was in an alley fighting for his own life. After a while, he came to be known as the Man in the Purple Hood, and a few people even gave him tips on things that might be of interest to him.

In the beginning, Michael showed no interest and did little to follow up on any of the tips; he just wanted to get his father home and out of trouble. However, the more he thought about it, he realized that acting on those tips would get some of the problems off of the streets, and that was how Michael took on the name Hooded Justice.

Michael didn't consider himself a superhero in the sense that Mitch had envisioned. As Hooded Justice, Michael never sought the publicity and popularity he would have worked toward as Biting Rat. He focused on his father as the only person in need of saving and in no way sought to stop a robbery, help an old lady cross the street, or that type of thing.

Little by little, that changed. He was keeping other people in the city safe from the same problems. In his mind, it was all part of the same problem: people needed to be watched over in a way that the Wilkes-Barre police couldn't.

The times were changing, and as Michael stood looking at his newest costume creation and the old purple hood next to it, he recalled his conversation with Mitch.

"Stingray. That's the name I chose," Mitch had said, although the costume he'd designed didn't match the name in any way. "How about you?"

Michael had replied, "The Biting Rat."

However, the black costume with the yellow trim topped off with a light brown trench coat wasn't the one he'd worn when he'd chosen that name. That costume had been blue and orange—nothing more than a gym suit. The weapons he'd taught himself to use over the past nineteen months were now attached to a weapons belt he wore around his waist.

This time, when Michael responded to Mitch's question, he looked into the mirror at his reflection and replied, "The Arsenal, Mitch. I'm the Arsenal." Recalling the phrase spoken by the angels in the book of Revelation, he added, "Come and see."

As the clock struck midnight, Arsenal made his way across the Wilkes-Barre canal loading docks toward center city and the downtown section. Originally built to move freight to the rest of the world, it was used for recreation and public transportation. A security guard was supposed to be patrolling the area and the docks, but drugs and prostitutes kept him from making his required rounds.

"Here it is, lady," the taxi driver said, pulling his boat up to the dock.

Turning toward her, he remembered she was deaf, so he said it again as he pointed out that this was her stop. She looked up at the street sign: North Hampton Street Canal Stop. She signed, "Thank you."

Guessing at what she'd said, he nodded in reply and took the money she handed him. He then stood up and helped her out of the boat; once she was on the dock, he returned to his seat and drove away.

To help increase travel on the canal, Wilkes-Barre's city council had awarded Posten Taxi, one of Northeast Pennsylvania's oldest cab companies, the sole contract to operate on the city's waterways. It had taken several months to get the project up and running, but the service slowly had seemed to find its own niche in the city's transportation system.

During the warmer months, most of its service consisted of taking people to the parks located on the shores of the river from the Pittston and West Pittston area in the north and Nanticoke and West Nanticoke area in the south. Eventually, service was planned to stretch north into Tunkhannock and Sunbury in the south, where the river split into the West Susquehanna branch of the river.

The woman who'd just gotten out of the boat had used the taxi for the first time to get home from the Nanticoke Area Nursing Home, located half a block away from the river. She didn't have enough money to take a traditional taxi, so one of her coworkers had suggested she try the cheaper water taxi. It would drop her off in downtown Wilkes-Barre, not far from her home, the Center Main Street Apartments.

All she needed to do was walk a few blocks, no more than ten minutes, which she hoped would be easy and trouble free. That hope faded away when she heard, what sounded like a whisper, "Hey, baby, can I give you a ride?"

She barely heard the words, but a voice within told her to keep walking. She hoped the driver would get the message that she wasn't interested and drive off.

*Where is Quarrel?* she thought, rushing through the alley to reach the main street. *Somebody please help me.*

But her prayer was not answered. On that night, Quarrel would not be there to save her. Three steps later, she was out of the sight of the stoned security guard and on her own as the white van caught up and saw her looking.

"Get in the van!" the driver ordered as the window rolled down.

She tried to move past him and reach the street, but reading his lips and getting in the van wasn't going to happen.

She tried to speak, but no words passed her lips, and she knew there was no chance he'd understand her signing.

Knowing she was attempting to communicate with her fingers, the driver knew he had an easy mark. After stepping out of the van, he turned to block her and noticed a golf ball roll to a stop at his feet. He picked up the ball and looked it over as he said, "Get in the van!"

"The ball wasn't a gift, scumbag," a voice declared. "It's a calling card!"

The foot that hit the driver knocked him into the door so hard that the window shattered, and glass covered him as he fell to the ground. Had the woman been standing closer, the knockout kick wouldn't have been possible, and the man who'd performed it would have had to resort to a different striking method.

Seeing the black mask and brown trench coat, she knew that whoever this person was, he or she was not Quarrel. The large metal poles protruding from the coat's sleeves were another sign. As the stranger got to his feet, he jerked his wrists, and the poles retracted. Turning toward the woman, he reached into his trench coat pocket and took out a pen and tablet. He wrote out the question "Are you okay?" and showed it to her so she could read. She answered by nodding as she smiled.

"Who are you?" she asked as she touched the yellow cloth of his costume and caught a glimpse of the weapons.

Opening his coat, he pointed to the triangular symbol on his chest and replied, "The Arsenal."

He picked up the golf ball and showed her the word *Arsenal* as he handed it to her. She read it, smiled, and then, with her fingers, signed, "Thank you."

He walked her out of the alley and then over to a police car parked at a stoplight. He waved his arms to get noticed, and the female cop stepped out of the car. She reached for her weapon.

Officer Val Stein had grown up in the poorer section of Wilkes-Barre, spending most of her days running from trouble or getting into one form of it to stay out of another. Gradually, Val managed to get better and better at staying out of trouble, until she was able to find extracurricular activities at school that kept her out of it altogether.

One was basketball. She worked hard and got a scholarship to college, where she studied criminal law. Shortly after graduating, she joined the police force, and after six years, she was still keeping the city of Wilkes-Barre safe.

"Keep your hands where I can see them!" she yelled, coming fully out of the car. "Step away from the girl!"

"Relax. It's not like that. She's deaf and wants to report a crime," Arsenal said, holding his hands up.

"Who are you?" Val asked, keeping her eyes on him. "Stay where you are!"

"Arsenal," he replied, knowing the name wouldn't go over well.

"So, then you're carrying weapons?" she asked, stepping away from the car.

"Are you going to inquire about me, or are you going to find out about her crime?" Arsenal asked, pointing back toward the alley. "Her attacker is back there. But I wouldn't ask the stoned security guard with the hooker sitting in the green Chevy Camaro; he's not securing anything on those docks."

"There's a security guard back there?" she said, surprised, and she called for backup.

"Well, I'd call him a drug addict," Arsenal replied as the deaf woman approached Val. "If you can't speak sigh language, you'll need my tablet."

"Who are you?" she asked again as Arsenal tossed his tablet and pen to her.

"I already told you," he answered. "I'm only doing this to fill in for a friend."

"Who are you working with? Quarrel?" she asked, keeping her eyes on him as she picked up his tablet.

"No," he answered. "Stingray."

"Stingray?" she repeated. "I'm not familiar with that name."

"Yeah," Arsenal said, pointing toward the skies, "that's because he's up there."

Tilting her head, she asked, "In the air?"

"Stingray walks with the angels," Arsenal answered, looking up the street at the approaching police cars.

"You mean he's dead?" she asked as she too looked back. "Did this happen recently?"

There was no reply. When she turned back, Arsenal was gone. In his place was his calling card: a golf ball with his name printed on it.

A little more than an hour later, Arsenal was moving along the dark sidewalk near the Wyoming Valley Sanitation Plant, heading toward the Breslau Bridge, which was undergoing major road repairs. He'd received a tip about a big-time drug deal involving Raphael and an out-of-town gang.

Raphael was the leader of the city's Spanish gang, which operated in the Hanover Township and Lee Park area. His gang was one of the problems Arsenal and his father had to deal with whenever his father journeyed to that region of town, all because John had been brave enough to watch the back of a friend and pull him out of a fight with a kid named Diego.

The gang was getting things together and waiting for members to show at the far corner of the Lee Park Greyhound Racing Track. Originally, the track had been used to race horses when it was constructed back in 1896, but it had gone out of business in 1931 due to the Great Depression.

Ten years later, new investors had reopened the track, and it had remained open until the early sixties, when plans to build a newer, state-of-the-art facility at the other end of town had emerged. Lee Park had been put on the sales block with the plan to use the money to finance the new track.

When the new owner had bought it, he'd renovated the park to race greyhounds. Wilkes-Barre had become the only city in Pennsylvania to have both types of racing in the same city. For the past nine years, Raphael's gang had done business there, taking bets and having their girls work the parking lot, bars, and surrounding area.

Arsenal's top priority was getting Raphael and his gang off of the streets, something he hoped would start that night on the Breslau Bridge, where even with a fear-inducing name and an interesting collection of weapons, he was still outmatched. Among all of his weapons, he carried no guns.

Raphael and his men were meeting a group of investors from out of town. They were interested in hiring Raphael's gang to work as bodyguards for something big that was going to happen in Wilkes-Barre. What that big thing was, Arsenal's informant didn't say, but it was going to be big, and the world was going to take notice.

*Lucky my father's at home in a wheelchair with a broken leg*, he thought. *One less thing I'll need to worry about tonight. Hopefully Judy, the nurse who stops in to check on him, keeps coming back. She's someone I wouldn't mind getting to know. But for now, I need to stay focused on the business at hand.*

Returning to the reason he was out there, Arsenal spotted two from Raphael's gang; they must have been part of the advance team. They stepped from the car and walked a few feet up the road toward the bridge, and once they were sure everything was clear, they returned to the car and used the radio to contact Raphael.

Ten minutes later, Raphael and the rest of his gang drove up Fellows Avenue toward the bridge, ready to do business. Unknown to them, Arsenal was climbing the steel-framed bridge, preparing to thwart whatever they had planned. As for the other gang, Arsenal's informant didn't know anything about them other than they were from out of town, possibly as far away as Philadelphia.

*Maybe they're trying to bring in some new drug*, Arsenal thought, kneeling down to hide in the shadows. *As soon as I get some money, I need to invest in night-vision goggles.*

After discussing a plan, Raphael and his men pulled out their guns and approached the bridge. Whatever they were discussing, Arsenal couldn't hear well as he silently moved out to the center of the bridge.

The men on the other side of the bridge wore black business suits. They looked as if they were Mafia or some group similar in nature. One of the men in the lead was carrying a black briefcase, which Arsenal believed held either money or the new drug they wanted to hit the streets of Wilkes-Barre.

*I'm going to bet that's the key to what's going on*, Arsenal thought, keeping his eyes on the briefcase.

Arsenal crouched on the bridge, listening to what the men were saying as the rain fell harder and harder. Moments later, two of Raphael's men began shouting, and Arsenal could hear them over the storm.

"No! I swear to God, Tito!" the short gunman said. "That's the guy who raped my sister."

"He's from out of town, Rico. That's not the guy," Tito replied.

"The way my sister described that fat mother," Rico said as he shook his head slowly, "that has to be him."

Tito didn't react; he just stood there and watched as Rico pulled out his gun and took aim. Raphael hadn't heard the conversation as he and two of his men walked toward the center of the bridge. They were approaching the construction equipment, when the first shot rang out.

Jumping behind the bags of cement, Raphael looked back, puzzled, as he tried to figure out who was shooting and why. Raphael pulled out his own gun and opened fire while ordering both men to go back and find out what had gone wrong. Neither of them got more than a few steps before being killed.

*This is out of control*, Arsenal thought, hoping no stray bullets were bound for him.

Crawling along the top of the bridge and climbing down onto the road wasn't a good idea. At any given moment, he could be shot. As each second passed and more of the men below opened fire, Arsenal knew he couldn't stay there much longer.

*The briefcase*, he thought, trying to see it below. *No, just get out of here.*

Without hesitation, Arsenal walked across the steel beams and jumped into the river. Just as he hit the water, the sky lit up as lightning streaked across it, and the shooters managed to get a glimpse of him, but they were too caught up in the fight to react.

# CHAPTER 1

# September 28, 1991

It was just like any other Thursday morning. It was eight forty-five on a beautiful September day with few clouds blocking out the sun. Downtown Wilkes-Barre was filled with people of all ages, shapes, and nationalities scattered about, going on with their daily lives. Schools and colleges had been in session for almost a month; buses, taxis, trolleys, and boats on both the canal and the river helped them move about.

Wilkes-Barre was the only American city to modernize and include its canal in the local transportation system. There were several docks in the downtown area where one could catch a water taxi and travel via the canal or river as far down as Nanticoke and West Nanticoke or up to Pittston and West Pittston. Originally built in the 1800s, the canal had been restored and updated several times, most recently after the 1972 Hurricane Agnes flood.

Nine bridges spanned the Susquehanna River, bringing people in and out of the city via all recognizable forms of transportation. The Market Street, Veterans, and North Street bridges connected the city to Kingston, Wilkes-Barre's unofficial other half. The North Cross Valley Expressway reached into the cities of Plains and Dallas, while at the southern end, the Carey Avenue and Breslau bridges brought people in from Larksville and Plymouth. The South Cross Valley Expressway connected the city to Nanticoke, West Nanticoke, and lower Plymouth.

Routes 115, 309, and 315 ran through the city at various locations, as did Interstate 81. Wilkes-Barre, Pennsylvania, Coal, North Main, Central Main, South Main, Mundy, River, Blackman, and Scott were the main streets within the city's borders. Butler, Coal, and South Street bridges stretched across the center of the city and brought people into the downtown region.

The Pennsylvania, Central New Jersey, and Lehigh Valley railroads ran through the city, with both passenger and business service available. Their tracks ran through the outskirts of downtown and were parallel to the two boulevards and the city's waterway.

The Wilkes-Barre canal system connected to the Susquehanna River, one of the largest rivers in the United States. On the other side of the city stood Wilkes-Barre, Bear Creek, and Palooka Mountain, named after Joe Palooka, a character created by cartoonist Hamm Fisher, who lived in the city.

Julius Arbinovawitz had been a police detective for more than fifteen years, and he'd spent the last three in Wilkes-Barre. He'd been born forty-three years ago in New York City. Two years ago, he'd decided on a change of scenery and moved to Wilkes-Barre. There, he'd become interested in the superheroes popping up and begun taking notes for a private file he was compiling on them.

Currently, the only official superhero operating in the Wilkes-Barre area was a woman known as Quarrel. In the past several months, a few others briefly had made names for themselves before fading away. On the other side of the law were the criminals, enemies of his, with the assassin sisters Slaughter and Massacre at the top of the list. That was a separate list he frequently carried and used on the job to bring criminals to justice.

Unlike the fictional Batman and Commissioner Gordon friendship, Julius had only met Quarrel on a few occasions and seen her in combat half as many times. As far as he knew, she'd been born a sapient dominant with the power to create an energy bow and the ability to shoot energy bolts. She'd selected the name Quarrel, believing it sounded better than the White Arrow, Arrow Girl, or Energy Arrow.

She mainly operated alone, although from time to time, she was seen working with a group of BMX stunt riders. Whether Quarrel was related to or romantically linked with any of the bikers, Julius never investigated. Most of the file consisted of newspaper clippings and notes handwritten on small bits of paper. It was a project he'd begun out of curiosity.

Pulling onto the North Street Bridge, Julius thought, *With the fairly peaceful stretch going on in this city, I wonder if she decided to pack it in.*

*Boom!*

The force of the blast sent river water shooting up into the air like a Yellowstone geyser, knocking leaves from several riverfront trees on both shores. The boats in the river felt the force of the explosion. Two small rowboats flipped, and waves were sent through the river in both directions. The seven people now in the water, fighting for their lives, were the first victims of the newly formed whirlpool.

In the seconds it took Julius to reach the walkway, the whirlpool had stretched to nearly the base of the bridge, just below his feet. It was a growing threat that showed no signs of stopping or slowing down. Julius knew he had to act fast.

*Was that the bridge?* he wondered, feeling the vibrations. Clearing the bridge was now a top priority.

"Come on! Everyone off the bridge!" he yelled, pulling out his badge. "We've got an emergency in the water. I need everyone to please evacuate the bridge as fast as possible!"

Few heeded his words. They continued watching what was unfolding below. He pulled out his pistol, though he wasn't sure it was the right thing to do, and fired three shots into the air. "Now, people! Everyone off the bridge. It's going to collapse!"

Pushing past the people, Julius moved farther up the bridge, repeating his commands and hoping they would listen this time. Several more onlookers did as ordered, but no sooner had they pulled out into traffic than others took their places.

The Wilkes-Barre Courthouse district consisted of four buildings, including two located next to each other on the riverfront. The third was located in Old Public Square, and the fourth was the Max Rosenn Courthouse on South Main Street. The main courthouse, the Luzerne County Courthouse, had been built in 1909 alongside the canal and trolley tracks.

The trials under way that day were disrupted and quickly canceled, as the blast blew out windows and knocked paintings and people to the floor. Those inside the building concluded that something serious had happened outside at the gas company. The choice was made to end the day's events and evacuate until the cause could be determined. Then they stepped outside and followed the other onlookers and curiosity seekers to get a look at what had happened in the river.

Parking his car a block away was Elliot Breckenridge, the man most expected to become the next Wilkes-Barre chief of police. With the current chief on leave while recuperating from a heart attack, Elliot had taken over. He'd joined the force in 1963 after returning from Vietnam, where he'd served as an observer prior to America's actual involvement. In returning to small-town America, he'd hoped he'd never see anything like that again, but that day would change all of that.

*All this chaos. Is this Wilkes-Barre or a battle zone?* Elliot wondered, seeing the large crowd. *Must get these people out of here. We don't need all these people blocking the investigation. Need to find out who or what caused this.*

Making his way through the crowd, he caught sight of Julius Arbinovawitz talking to two other patrolmen. Just as they turned to leave, Elliot called out to him.

"Something exploded in the river," Julius replied. "I didn't see any boat debris. My guess is it was underground, because we got a whirlpool. I'm trying to get as many of these intersecting streets blocked off as possible, but we don't have the manpower to pull it off."

"That'll change," Elliot answered. "What were they doing down there to cause an explosion like this?"

"I don't know, but it's near the base of the bridge. If that bridge goes, I'd say at least a hundred people could die."

"I'll contact Kingston; we're going to need help on this," Elliot said, running his fingers through his hair. "We need to get this area cleared on both sides of the river. And no boats in the water except for emergency rescue."

Ninety minutes later, Elliot had the permission of the on-duty gas company supervisor to set up camp there to deal with the whirlpool. A tent was erected, and tables were brought in for engineers and city council members to accommodate all of the calls in and out of the area.

One of the important men not there was Lt. General Mason Colts, who was currently in Washington, DC. He was in charge at the Kingston Armory, which was located less than a mile away across the river. He had lobbied to turn it into more than a recruiting office, and though it was in the city of Kingston, it was active in Wilkes-Barre politics and linked to Dyna Cam Industries.

Returning to the command post, Elliot watched as the Bell phone repairman finished his work on the phone. "Just give me five minutes, and I'll be done here," he said, cutting a red wire. "Have you guys figured out how to fill that hole and what caused it in the first place?"

"No," Elliot answered, shaking his head as he watched the man work.

"I have an uncle and two cousins who work in the mines. Two of them are at Loomis, and the other's in Pine Ridge," he said, placing the cover on the phone. "All set."

Lester O'Keefe had been on the phone with various officials, discussing what he'd learned about the explosion. One of his biggest fears was that a shaft under the prison would cause the ground to collapse. The explosion had occurred just as he was walking in to begin his day. His only thought had been the execution scheduled for later that afternoon. Marshal Kadfeller had been found guilty years earlier of murder. He'd killed everyone on a bus filled with children by setting it on fire.

The man of the cloth there that day was Father Bradley Brock. He was the unofficial top-ranking priest in the city, a position he used to sit in on all open-to-the-public government meetings and offer advice to all those who sought it. He also spent a lot of time in poorer neighborhoods, where he tried to teach peace and love instead of violence.

He had been the man Marshal Kadfeller asked for when his execution was less than six months away. Bradley was to be there that night to read him his last rites and pray as his life ended by lethal injection. Afterward, he was to contact the family and let them know of Marshal's death.

With his jet-black hair and goatee to match, Bradley Brock looked more like a villain out of *Flash Gordon* than a man of God. He was the brother of Dyna Cam Industries president Kyle Brock, a man he'd had no contact with until recently because first, Bradley was twenty years older than Kyle, and second, Kyle was suspected of being a crime boss.

When Bradley reached the office, Lester put the phone down and said, "We're on lockdown until further notice. The governor said so. He intends to contact Mason Colts, and once martial law is imposed on the city, he'll get the prisoners moved to Dallas and other places."

Nodding, Bradley said, "I'll go talk to the guards and keep fears among the prisoners from escalating."

Just up the road and outside of the prison were two men Elliot was expecting to see. Shelton White had been working for the *Wilkes-Barre Record* since 1965, when he'd become the first black reporter in the city. Working to prove he belonged with the paper, the first major story he'd covered was the White Cross Discount Drug fire.

In 1972, during the Hurricane Agnes flood, Shelton nearly had died by jumping from a helicopter into the water to save a drowning pregnant woman who'd fallen in when the roof she was on collapsed. He'd gained national attention when it was discovered later on that her family was linked to the Ku Klux Klan.

The other man was Corman First, who'd served in the United States Marines and retired at the age of forty-two to enter Wilkes-Barre politics. Thanks to his family connections, he'd been hired as the bodyguard to Mayor Hart IV, and he'd quickly become known as the vice mayor of Wilkes-Barre.

He'd been walking away from his car, when an explosion had thrown him down the street as the windows from the Wilkes-Barre Bottling Plant Museum had shattered and sent shards of glass everywhere, cutting into the right side of his face.

The man he was about to speak with hadn't fared as well: Shelton's leg had broken when he was thrown into a fire hydrant. The blood oozing from his face didn't help his appearance. Shelton screamed out from the pain as he tried to stand. Elliot and a few police officers were the first to reach him.

Seeing the remains of the colliery, Corman asked, "What the hell is going on? Are we under attack? This can't be an accident in the mine; it's got to be something else."

"I don't know," Elliot replied, seeing the fire burning what remained of the colliery. "But the army will be here soon, and we'll get answers."

The Dorrance Mine had been in operation for more than a hundred years, and as part of the mining industry, it was one of the major employers in the city. The major event of the morning didn't happen when the explosion took place in the river; it began hours earlier when a group of nine masked men made their way onto the site.

The older, unarmed security guards were no match for the gun-toting terrorists, who executed anyone they saw. They then took the bodies deep into the mine, where they set the explosives to hide the crime.

Pointing up the road, Corman replied, "Dorrance was just hit. I don't think it was just another explosion in the mine; this seems like a strike. Are we at war with the Russians?"

"As far as I know, we're not," Elliot answered, looking at the burning colliery and then back to the river. "But this is the second explosion. This kind of shit shouldn't be happening here. It's freakin' Wilkes-Barre, not the United States capital!"

*Boom!*

The command post was now gone. In its place was a massive fireball that shot up into the sky. All of the men were thrown to the ground as the heat made them think they were going to die. The rumbling they felt afterward made them think it was an earthquake.

Elliot propped himself up on his elbows. He was about to speak, when he saw the Brominski Courthouse spread out all over the street. Hearing the North Street Bridge collapse into the river, he concluded that World War III or not, Wilkes-Barre was under attack.

# CHAPTER 2

The water splashed against Arsenal's mask as he came to. His face was up against large rocks somewhere downstream in the river. The bad taste of the water in his mouth left him spitting to get as much of it out as possible. Pulling the soaked mask from his face, he stood up and noticed the briefcase lying in the water next to him.

Surprised to see it, he quickly pulled it out and looked it over. He pushed on the levers, and his eyes almost popped out of his head when he saw how much money was within.

"Holy wow!" he yelled, smiling.

Looking around to see if anyone had heard him yell, he knelt down, pulled off his gloves, and grabbed a stack of money. He didn't count it; he just put it to his ear, flipped through it, and smiled.

"So that's what it sounds like when they do that," he said, putting the money back in the case.

Looking at the scenery, he tried to determine where he had washed up. Arsenal knew he was downstream, but he wasn't sure how far from Wilkes-Barre he was. The next thing he needed to do was reach the nearest road, which he suspected would be Route 11, since it followed the river all the way down to Harrisburg.

"Why do I feel like this is going to be one hell of a walk home?" he said, climbing onto the rocks. Stepping onto the dried mud, he pushed through the weeds and high grass. He could hear the sounds of several large trucks on the road up ahead. Crossing his fingers, he hoped that the road would be recognizable and that he wasn't very far from home. With the sun just coming up, Arsenal wondered what had happened when he'd hit the water and how he hadn't drowned.

"Somebody upstairs must be watching out for me," he said, taking one last look back at the river.

After squeezing the water out of his mask again, he slipped it into his trench coat pocket and did the same with his gloves. He then set the briefcase down, buttoned his trench coat, and set out for the road several yards up ahead.

*Yep, it's going to be a long walk home,* he thought as he pulled the hood up over his head. *It's not going to be easy, but I'll figure out what to do with this money and take care of business at home.*

The business he was referring to was his father, John Lanesra, and his addiction to alcohol. Alcohol made his father a completely different man, and in less than three years, it had changed their relationship, putting his son back on the city streets as Arsenal.

By the time Arsenal arrived at home, it was almost fifteen hours later. As fit as he was, his body ached from all of the walking he'd done and the briefcase that was going to change his life. The hardest part was stopping in the woods near his house to change out of his costume. As tired and exhausted as he was, he was tempted to just wear the costume inside the house, but he didn't. With his luck, his father would have been sober and waiting up for him.

Just as expected, John was awake and semi-sober, watching television, but for the first time in a long time, John wasn't drinking beer while watching it. He held a bottle of 7UP, and in his other hand was the remote for the television. He was flipping between stations.

"Where have you been?" his father asked, turning toward him. "There was some kind of explosion near the courthouse. Two buildings collapsed, and the North Street Bridge is in the river. They said there are at least three dead or missing."

"What?" Michael said, stunned, turning to look as he listened to Susan Brock's report. "In Wilkes-Barre?"

*When did this happen?* he thought. *Was I in the river during all of this?*

Trying to think of any friends he knew who might have been in that area, he drew a blank. He was tired and needed to get to bed, but this matter couldn't wait. As grungy and dirty as his costume was, Michael knew he had to investigate.

*The briefcase*, he thought. *Just put it upstairs, and head back out. If I weren't so damn tired, I'd jump out the window.*

Then his body reminded him of the pain and soreness he felt. If he sat even briefly, he would most likely pass out.

In the short amount time he'd been wearing the Arsenal costume, he never had been able to get it on in less than twenty minutes. Stepping out of the woods and onto the trail, Arsenal returned to the dirt road formerly used by the railroad companies until the line was disbanded and the tracks were used to aid the war effort during World War II.

Originally, the tracks had led to the Blue Coal Company, located at the base of the mountain in Ashley, where coal mined in Mineral Springs had been shipped out to the rest of the world. That particular mine had closed in 1955 and switched owners, until Dyna Cam Industries had bought it in 1985. It was supposed to be turned into a research facility, but to that day, nothing had been done to achieve that goal.

Arsenal had passed by that collection of old buildings quite a few times, never giving much thought to the place being anything more than a refuge for the homeless and drug addicts. There was still a fence surrounding the complex. As a kid, he'd thought of sneaking in and taking a look around, but he'd never gotten around to it.

Looking over it and the Arena Hotel Golf Course, Arsenal thought, *Not tonight. I've got to get down to the river and find out what happened. On the other hand, if I cut through there, the Hollenback complex is almost right next to it. I can check those out and then follow the creek to the river and not have to worry about being seen. Even though the Springs mine is closed, they used the North Wilkes-Barre Mine to cause all that shit to happen beneath the river. Just about half of Wilkes-Barre is over a mine; if they plant another bomb like that in one of these two shafts, they could possibly destroy a lot of homes and businesses. Wilkes-Barre Township High School is built over a mine; according to Mr. Daru, the back few feet of the science room is tilted because of the mines below.*

Moving quietly through the shadows, Arsenal noticed that other than the few still-working streetlights and the severely rusted fence, there was no security in the complex.

*Of all the land that Dyna Cam owns, I'm surprised this place isn't in better condition. It's not like they don't have the finances to do it; they're the world's largest camera maker,* he thought. *I wonder if they're in some kind of financial trouble. On the other hand, what would a camera maker need with an old mine?*

In that section of Parsons, Mineral Springs, Hollenback, and Pine Ridge were all mining operations working in the same general underground area. Mineral Springs had gone out of business, but Hollenback and Pine Ridge were still operational and pulling the same amount of coal from the earth that they had decades ago. Even though Mineral Springs was defunct, with Dyna Cam Industries owning the mine, there was always a chance the mine would eventually reopen.

The light from the lantern pushed the darkness back far enough for Wes to see the dug-out cavern that stretched out before him. It was a route dug out long ago, and it no doubt warmed thousands of homes somewhere in the world. However, thinking about the historical aspect of the mine wasn't something Wes was interested in, nor was it the reason he was there.

The large puddle that spread out before him was bigger than anything he'd ever seen. He could tell there was a slight descent in the shaft, because the water was deeper a few steps ahead and closer to the ceiling. Rainwater often found its way into the mines, and as he realized that, he concluded that being down there was looking like a bad idea.

Pushing on, Wes lifted the lantern up to chest level and stepped into the water. If that mine was going to be the next attack site, then a little bit of water shouldn't be something to worry about. He couldn't report back to his superiors and tell them he was afraid to get wet, so he waded through the thirty-foot-long puddle, which never got deeper than a few inches above his knees.

Even though the mine hadn't been worked in decades, there had been a recent inspection of the shaft. Wes was well aware of that because he'd paid the inspectors well for the map and entry to the shaft.

*Cliff, buddy, you could have warned me about the water,* he thought, reaching into his backpack and pulling out a detonator. *Let's hope that's all he forgot to mention.*

After checking around for a dry, level place, Wes set up the first bomb. Setting the timer for an hour would give him more than enough time to get out and drive away. He was going to bring that shaft down, just as he'd orchestrated the chaos at the river.

However, unlike that eye-catching event, Mineral Springs was going to be a lot less dramatic. They'd planned this second act to add to the fear and let the inhabitants of the city know that all of Wilkes-Barre was a target, no matter what section of the city they were living in.

Wes pulled the map of the mine out of his pocket. He saw that it ran under the Arena Hotel and down into the East End section of the city; however, that section appeared blocked off. The other shaft ran underneath Parsons. Originally, he'd intended to level the hotel and destroy the roads leading to the Wyoming Valley Mall and shopping district, but Parsons also held a lot of homes, and he knew that could be just as deadly. With Scott Street in ruin, there was only one other way in: through North End, near the golf course.

Also located in Parsons, not far from the Mineral Springs Mine, was the Hollenback Mine. According to Cliff, there was a narrow connector route built in case of an emergency. Either company could use it to get out quickly, but just like the shaft under the hotel, it was nearly impossible to get through thanks to age and decay.

*And I already set the first detonator,* Wes thought. *Got to stick to the plan. Eddie O'Hare's body isn't going to be pulled out of the river, and neither will mine if I screw this up.*

Eddie O'Hare was the only casualty Wes's team had suffered during the opening attack at the river. He'd failed to make it out of the shaft on the other side of the river when he'd run back to get his personal gear, swearing all the way that it was irreplaceable.

Wes thought of resetting the detonator, but he had a ride waiting above for him and a meeting to attend on recruiting a few other local gangs.

However, with the way things had gone with the Lee Park Spanish gang the other day and the lost briefcase, Wes wasn't sure he was ready to lose another chunk of money that wasn't his.

This meeting was going to take place at the Laurels, a group of skyscrapers built in the Wilkes-Barre Township section near Ashley. Originally built to house all of the people who lost their homes when the underground mine fires ruined the land back in the early 1960s, it was now home to the biker gang the Diamond City Riders, who owned and operated the Diamond City Scrap Yard, the largest scrap yard in Luzerne County.

Arsenal climbed through the time-worn, rusted fence and looked at the long, graffiti-covered wooden building in front of him. He didn't know what its original purpose had been, but he noticed several sets of unusable rail tracks coming from it. The empty beer cans, broken bottles, and mixture of other trash that filled the rotted, partially burned coal cart and surrounding area were signs it wasn't useable for anything other than trash collection.

At first sight, Arsenal knew there was no chance that place would ever reopen without a total overhaul of the entire complex. Even though Mineral Springs had been closed decades ago, the Arena Hotel complex was next door, and he didn't want to be stopped there. Maybe nothing was going to happen, but Wilkes-Barre was under martial law, and he wasn't prepared to outrun the police, especially as tired as he was.

As he moved about the area, he noticed a white van parked near the road, which looked abandoned. The instant the lights flashed, Arsenal was surprised, and he briefly assumed it might be some type of security.

*Can't be for this place. Maybe it's for Scott Street,* he thought, thinking of the road behind the van. *No, that can't be. It's not a police van, and besides, they wouldn't flash the headlights like that; they'd just step out of the car and tell me to put my hands over my head and not move.*

Slowly, he approached the van, not sure what to expect. The driver's door opened, and a middle-aged man stepped out. He remained behind the door, which hid his face, as he realized he'd signaled the wrong man.

"Who are you?" the man asked, stepping back into the darkness.

"Who are you?" Arsenal said, stopping. "What are you doing here?"

*Whoever this guy is, he's definitely not with the police. This guy is probably just waiting for his buddy to come back from puking or taking a piss*, Arsenal thought, trying to get a better glimpse.

He had no luck. Whoever the guy was, he had enough smarts to keep out of the light, which led Arsenal to conclude something criminal was transpiring. He was slowly reaching for a weapon on his utility belt, when Wes came up from behind and knocked him to the ground.

Rolling onto his back, Arsenal came face-to-face with Wes, not knowing who he was. Since he was the one wearing the mask and costume, he would be suspected of being the criminal. Arsenal didn't plan to stay around to speak with the police. Whoever this guy was, Arsenal knew he didn't belong at the gate of an abandoned mining complex.

"Who is this guy?" Wes called out to his partner. "Another idiot looking to make a name for himself?"

"Leave him. Let's get out of here," the man replied, starting the van.

Stepping past Arsenal, Wes stopped and thought, *Don't kill this guy. He's masked. Let the cops think he's behind this.*

As Wes turned around, Arsenal got up and hit him with a kick to the chest, knocking Wes into the fence. After getting to his feet quickly, Arsenal hit him in the jaw with a left hook. Out of the corner of his eye, he saw the other person move as if he were going to intervene.

The first bomb Wes had set detonated and threw both men through the air. Wes ended up inside one of the old buildings. Arsenal hit the fence and fell on his face as the ground disappeared several yards in front of him.

Doing the equivalent of a push-up, Arsenal was struck by a burst of electricity that kept him from moving.

Thinking Arsenal was dead, Wes made his way out of the building and past the still-forming crater to the van. Just as he slammed the door, his partner fired at Arsenal a second time.

A white sphere that appeared in the air kept his strike from hitting Arsenal. Had it reached him, Arsenal surely would have been killed right there, but the sphere absorbed the electricity. The second explosion reminded both men that they needed to flee the area before they were killed.

"Come on! Let's go!" Wes yelled as his partner got back into the car.

As they pulled out onto the road, large segments of the ground began to vanish. The hole stretched to the houses, and as they reached the entrance to the supply company, three houses fell in. The van reached Denny's a moment later as the third bomb added to the carnage and took down even more homes, destroying everything up to the beginning of Mill Street.

After that explosion, the sphere lowered itself and began healing Arsenal. A white beam shot out of the sphere and spread to cover Arsenal. It enabled him to get up. Suddenly, he heard the screams of the people at the Arena complex, and as he stood, he saw the crater in front of him expanding.

*This doesn't look good*, he thought. *Better get the hell out of here before I end up missing.*

Pondering if he should stick around and give assistance, Arsenal could hear sirens approaching. He knew Parsons would be there soon, and East End would be coming in from the other direction. The police would quickly follow, and as tired and exhausted as he was, Arsenal didn't want to confront the police.

He felt the costume meant he should stay to help those injured and trapped in the turmoil, but he knew he needed to get rest. A fall into the river, a fifteen-hour walk home, and now this—if Arsenal didn't get rest, he wouldn't make it.

Looking to the sky, he prayed for all those suffering, and five steps later, Arsenal collapsed. Had it not been for the white sphere, Arsenal would have remained there.

# CHAPTER 3

With soreness in his body and flashbacks in his mind, Michael sat up in bed. He wanted nothing more than to go back to bed, but that day, he needed to get out and start a new chapter of his life.

Scratching his oily, dirty hair, Michael looked down at the pile of dirty, wet clothes that made up his Arsenal costume. Along with getting his life ready, he needed to wash and dry the costume and get a shower in before he left for the day. He reached down, grabbed a piece of the pile, and dropped it into the laundry basket with some other articles of clothing.

Reaching back under the bed, Michael pulled out the briefcase. He opened it, and the moment he saw all of the money, a smile spread across his face. Taking out a stack, he noticed they were all hundred-dollar bills.

Stopping to figure out how much money he had, he said, "That's got to be close to a million dollars—enough to do what I want and then some."

After putting the money back in the briefcase, he put the case under the bed and went back to putting the rest of his costume into the basket. Forty minutes later, Michael went downstairs and checked on his father, put his clothing in the wash, and headed upstairs to stretch and plan. Shortly after that, he put the clothes in the dryer and headed for the shower. When he came back down, his father was there, waiting for him.

"I talked to Mary this morning," his father said as Michael stopped on the third step.

As Michael looked down at him, his father continued. "I'm going to go stay with her. You're going to need to find a place to live, because I plan to sell the house. With all of the crazy shit going on in Wilkes-Barre, I don't feel safe here anymore! Even when you're here. Hell, last night, after you had to go out, more bombs went off—this time, five minutes from here. Right down that dirt road, they blew up the Mineral Springs Mine, and where were you? The city is under martial law, and you had to go out. You'd better not be dealing drugs or some other kind of shit."

Deciding not to respond, Michael continued up the stairs to shower. He didn't like what he'd heard, but then again, now he didn't have to tell his father he was leaving; his father had beaten him to the punch. There would be no more walking the streets of Wilkes-Barre all night long to search for his father, and he had more than enough money to be out on his own without having to worry about struggling or suffering.

As he dried from his shower, he went over the list of things he wanted to accomplish.

*Eat, open new bank account, get newspapers, and start looking for a new place to live,* he thought as he got dressed. *Maybe even buy a place to live.*

From Michael's backyard, he couldn't see the destruction he was in the middle of, but once he reached the top of the tree-covered culm-bank hill, he walked a hundred yards to the right and got a fairly good view.

Glancing down at the black gym bag he held in his right hand, he thought, *This isn't over yet. I'm going to run into you again, and I'm taking you down. This won't last much longer.*

Via the trail behind his house, it took fifteen minutes to reach the mall and shopping area. It was a route that almost everyone took to get there. Day or night, work or pleasure, no matter the weather, the trail was quicker than the thirty- to forty-minute walk around, and in the winter, the trail was unofficially the best place to go sleigh riding.

At the other end of the trail were McDonald's, Franklin's Family Restaurant, Pizza Hut, and Toys "R" Us, and on the other side of the street were the Wyoming Valley Mall, a movie theater, and many stores and places to eat. His first destination was the United Penn Bank.

Ever since Judy Monteno could remember, her parents had practiced magic, and as she'd grown, she'd followed in their footsteps. Her uncle Ramsey also had taken the time to teach her a great many things, and by the age of eighteen, she'd learned all she could. Her parents had died three months later in a plane crash. The money she'd gotten from their insurance policies had paid off the house, taken care of the bills, and paid for her to become a nurse.

Judy had been the nurse taking care of John Lanesra, and she'd often flirted with his son, Michael, who was five years younger than she was. He was either too shy or just not as interested, but she hoped she could make him see things differently. All of that changed when John called her to say he wasn't going to need her services any longer. Judy was heartbroken. She was never going to see Michael again, and she hoped shopping would make her forget her sadness.

Ever since the death of her parents, Judy had used her magic to watch different people in and around the city of Wilkes-Barre. Oddly enough, she hadn't seen any of the people involved in the attack on the city. However, she didn't think she could stop them. That task, she knew, would fall to the masked man she'd discovered one night. Ever since then, she'd used her magic to view Arsenal.

Getting out of her car, Judy realized she'd parked at the wrong end of the mall, but she decided it wasn't a big deal; she had the extra time. Now that she didn't have to go care for John, she thought about finally getting her hair cut.

*If I called and asked for Michael, I wonder if he would be interested in a movie*, she thought, grabbing her purse and entering through the newly built food court.

*Hopefully, that sale isn't over at McCrory's*, she thought, making her way through the food court.

Just as she stepped in front of the United Penn Bank door, she almost walked into the man she'd been thinking about.

"Michael," Judy said, surprised, coming face-to-face with him.

"Hey. Hello," Michael replied, moving away from the door. "How are you?"

"I'm doing okay," she replied. "More free time now that your dad isn't going to need me."

"Yeah, sorry about that. He's kicking me out too," Michael replied. "Now I've got to find a place to live. He's moving in with his sister and selling the house."

"Well, good luck," she said, giving him a quick surprise hug.

"Take care, Judy," he said, hugging her back. "It was nice seeing you again."

Watching as Michael walked away, she told herself it was her last chance, and she shouldn't let it slip away.

"Michael!" she called out. "Do you want to hang out?"

Turning back toward her, he smiled and said, "Yes."

He hadn't expected the invitation, and it changed the rest of his day. He no longer worried about how his life would end up. If he played his cards right, he might end up with a girlfriend. Judy was one of the first people he'd thought of when he'd climbed out of the river.

"Which one do you like?" Judy asked, holding up a blue dress in her left hand and a brown dress in her right.

Looking at each of them and then at her, he answered, "I like the blue one. It matches your eyes."

Smiling, she returned the brown dress to the rack and said, "I didn't think you ever noticed my eyes."

"I notice a lot of things," Michael answered, shrugging. "With all of the things going on, I didn't say anything, but now that I'm out on my own, there's a lot less pressure."

"What kind of place are you looking for?" Judy asked as they walked up to the register. "I know that you don't have a job, but if you want, you could move into my place for a while until you get on your feet. I've got a couple of extra rooms you could use—that is, if you don't mind living with an older woman."

Laughing as he caught her wink, he thought, *If I don't mind living with an older woman? I never paid any attention to that. The question is, would she mind living with Arsenal? How do I tell her about my other identity or the money I found?*

As he thought that over, she asked, "Do you want to put your bag out in my car instead of carrying it around the mall?"

*I guess this could be considered our first date*, he thought. He shrugged and replied, "Sure."

They spent the next hour and a half talking as they walked around the mall, shopping and getting to know more about each other. The walk through the bookstore caught them both by surprise. She showed him books on magic and explained which ones were fake and which held the most promise. She was surprised by how well he was listening.

"How did you learn so much about that?" Michael asked. "I never thought that stuff was real."

He walked her over to the other side of the store, picked up a copy of the King James Version of the Bible, and said, "This was the last book that I read—twice."

"Really?" she asked, not believing him. "What's your favorite passage?"

"Job 29:17: 'I break the jaws of the wicked and pluck the spoils from their teeth,'" Michael answered. Then he added, "And Job 20:24: 'He shall flee far from the iron weapon when the glittering sword is drawn out of his gall.'"

"You don't look like the kind of person who would read the Bible," she said. "Do you go to church too?"

"No. Well, not on a regular basis," he replied, putting the book back on the shelf.

Checking the time on her watch, Judy asked, "Do you have a lot of stuff to move?"

"Bed, dresser, and small stuff," he answered. "I've got some money to rent a van. One stop ought to get it all."

"Do you want to go get it now?" she asked. "I mean before U-Haul closes. It's right across the street. How long do you have to move?"

"I've got to be out by the end of the day, so that would be a good idea—to go get it over with," Michael said, wondering if he would need to go get some money or if what he had in his pocket was enough.

"Do you need any supplies?" Judy asked minutes later, walking into the U-Haul rental storeroom. "Boxes, tape, or safety wrap?"

"Nope, everything is taken care of," Michael answered. "Except for the truck."

Standing behind the counter was a middle-aged man who looked as if he could have been Danny DeVito's twin brother. Noting the heavy scent of stale cigarettes and yellow teeth, Michael hoped that if this were true, he kept up on his appearance better than this guy. Running his fingers through his half-balding, greasy hair, the man gestured for them to hold on while he finished his conversation on the phone.

As they waited for the man to hang up, they couldn't help but overhear fragments of his conversation and laugh as they wondered what he was discussing. Whatever it was, the guy sounded as if he were trying to con somebody out of something to get a bigger cut.

Judy turned to wander the aisles and watched as Michael looked around, trying to remain patient. Stepping to the back of the store, where she couldn't be seen, Judy used her magic to help things along.

"Charley? Charley?" the clerk said, looking at the phone receiver and shaking his head. "I don't believe it."

"Lose the connection?" Judy asked, walking back to Michael.

"Yes," he answered, hanging up the phone. "Just when I was about to close the deal. So how can I help you folks?"

"I need to rent one of those small trucks out there," Michael said, pointing out the window.

Nodding, the man said, "Let me guess. Just got married?"

"Close," Judy quickly replied. "Moving in."

"Lucky man," he said with a big smile and a wink. Then he asked, "Been together long?"

"No, actually, we've been friends for a while, and I'm renting a few rooms off of her," Michael answered, wondering if he should have said that.

"Wow," the man said, stunned. "You mean you two aren't … I would have thought you two were a couple."

"Nope," Judy said, "but you never know what tomorrow will bring."

Changing the subject back to the business at hand, the clerk asked, "Which of you will be doing the driving?"

"I will," Judy replied, taking her identification out of her purse.

As the man took the information he needed for the paperwork, his mind began to wander. *But what would she do with a middle-aged man? How about a night out on the town and hot, passionate sex afterward? I could call off work tomorrow and maybe even the day after.*

"That will be twenty-nine ninety-five. Just sign there at the bottom, and you'll be the proud renters of truck number twelve," he said with a smile as he winked at Judy and returned her identification.

As she signed the paper, Michael reached for his wallet and caught sight of the clerk writing something on a slip of paper. Not putting anything to it, he took out three ten-dollar bills as the man slid the note across the counter.

"Are you going to read the note that he slipped you?" Michael asked as she got into the driver's side of the truck.

"You saw that?" she asked, smirking.

"Yeah," he answered as he got in. "I wonder if he does that with all of the women who go in there."

"Probably does," she replied, starting the truck. "How many do you think accept his offer?"

"Every unattractive, desperate woman," he answered, looking out the window.

Taking his hand, Judy said, "Not in a million years. I think your life is going to get better."

He didn't realize how close she was sitting to him. As he turned to answer her, she kissed him. The next thing he remembered was Judy pulling up in front of his house. As for whatever happened during the twelve-minute ride, Michael's mind was blank.

"Where are we?" he asked, not paying attention to where she was parking.

"Your house," she answered. "I had to go the long way to get here. Scott Street is blocked off because of what happened last night. Hopefully they catch whoever is behind all this."

Caught completely off guard, Michael replied while opening his door, "That happened last night? I totally forgot about it. Now, with any luck, my father will be sleeping, and there won't be any trouble, especially since you're helping me."

"Don't worry. I won't let him get to me," she said, stepping out of the truck. "Remember, I used to take care of him."

Wiping his sweaty palms on his jeans, he looked over the house he'd grown up in. Judy took his hand and said, "One room, right? In and out.

Don't worry; it will be over quick, and you won't have to come back here again."

He nodded in reply and squeezed her hand slightly, and they walked up to the front door. In the twelve steps it took to get there, Michael saw his entire life unfold: playing in the front yard, taking Easter pictures at the side of the house with relatives, and then, finally, driving off with Becky Carlin.

In the driveway, he'd learned to ride a bike and had his first crash, which had resulted in a broken leg and a ruined brand-new gas grill for his father. All of that seemed like a different life, one that had occurred when his mother was still alive, when they were still a family.

Everything was there—memories of more enjoyable times long ago, of different times in his life building up to the night with Mitch at his back window. The superhero he'd become because of that night and the woman whose hand he was now holding were going to be part of his new, better, brighter tomorrow.

Entering the living room, Judy saw nothing had changed since the last time she'd been there. The words she'd spoken to Michael, she now repeated to herself: *One room. In and out. Quick and easy.*

As they made their way up the stairs, John wheeled into the room. "Judy, what are you doing here?"

"Hello, John," she replied, stopping on the stairs. "Michael asked me to give him a hand with moving."

"Did he find a job?" John asked. "Kind of hard to pay bills without one."

"I'm sure he'll do fine," Judy replied as she continued walking up the stairs.

"Lazy bastard can't get anyone but my ex-nurse to help him move!" his father yelled as beer cans crashed to the floor. "Does your job know that you're here, Judy?"

She was about to turn around and argue with him, but Michael grabbed her and motioned for her to keep walking. He could see her face was starting to turn red, and he kept hold of her hand until they reached the top step.

"I'm sorry for that," he said as they stood close together. "One room. In and out. I'll make it up to you later."

Nodding, she smiled, and they walked into his bedroom. He sat her down on the bed as he said, "This is all I've got. As you can see, a lot of it's packed. I knew this day was coming, and I got ready for it."

*So did I*, she thought, though they weren't referring to the same thing.

He turned to close the door, and Judy took off her shirt.

It took them an hour longer than planned to get everything out of the room.

Neither of them spoke as they pulled up in front of Judy's house. As Michael got out of the truck, he came face-to-face with a black cat. It was a typical-looking male black cat with nothing special about it; however, the moment Michael first looked upon it, for some reason, he recalled the black cat from the night Mitch had shown up to tell him about his superpowers.

"Shadow," Judy said as she saw him sitting on the third step. "I hope you like cats. I've had Shadow almost three years. That's when I took him in."

Leaning over, Michael began petting the cat, and as Shadow purred, he replied, "Yeah, I guess so. I've never had one."

*Good*, Judy thought. Then she said, "He's my familiar."

"Familiar?" he repeated, confused. "What's that?"

"In magic, it's an animal that you build trust with and use while practicing magic," she answered. "Not that I expect you to understand that."

"No, I think I've got it," he answered. "Maybe you can give me a private demonstration of your magic sometime."

Smiling, she replied, "We'll see about that."

They walked to the back of the truck, and Judy unlocked it and lifted the door. Michael climbed inside and picked up his first box, which was filled with a few random books he found interest in. Taking a book off the top, he propped the box on his left leg and said, "See? I've read a book or two on magic, so I'm not that much of a novice."

"That's good to hear," she said, reaching for the keys in her purse. She thought, *Maybe this is something we can work on.*

"We'll go in, and I'll show you what rooms you can use. If there's anything in there we can move it out," she said, taking the box of books.

"Sounds like a plan," Michael said, taking another box of books and following Judy to the front door.

As Judy opened the door, she realized she'd left a few private things out. She'd never thought she'd have the man of her dreams in her house, and now that he was there, she knew she'd have some explaining to do. She had more than twenty photos of Arsenal in action scattered across the coffee table.

There was no way she could grab all of them without him seeing. Her only option was to leave them out and hope he didn't figure things out. Luckily, all of the pictures she had of him undressing weren't down there. Now that she had the real thing, she would need to get rid of them quickly.

As he walked in and spotted a picture near the coatrack, she knew it took him by surprise. She could see the color drain from his face, and as he turned to her with his mouth open, she said, "Do you like him? I'm a huge fan."

Still unable to speak, Michael looked at the picture again and then at Judy, shook his head, and returned to the truck. Looking at the pictures, Judy smiled. She followed him out. For the rest of the time, Michael had a puzzled look on his face, appearing as if he were mentally lost. Judy wondered if she should tell him she knew his secret, but she decided against it.

"I take it you're not a big fan of Arsenal's?" she asked as she took a bag full of clothing.

"No comment," he answered. He wanted to turn around and say, "I am him," but he didn't know how. "But if he stops by, you won't even know I'm here. I like to do a lot of walking."

"Michael," she said, "you live here too. You won't have to leave when I have company. Besides, I don't think I'll have that kind of company. I prefer the company I've got. Come on. I'll show you around the house."

As they walked upstairs, Michael took one final glance at the last Arsenal picture and wondered how she'd been able to get that shot at night without him seeing her.

*That was right before I helped that deaf woman,* he thought. *Maybe she knows a reporter, but that would mean I made the newspaper.*

Reaching the top of the steps, Judy pointed to the front of the house and said, "There are two rooms you can have—and this little half room on the other side of the bathroom, which is right there."

"Okay." Michael nodded as he looked in the other direction, toward Judy's bedroom, at what appeared to be a balcony.

"That's my bedroom, and the attic is where I practice my magic," she said, leading him into her room. "I like to sit out here at night and watch the view of the city."

"Sounds like a good idea," Michael said as she opened the doors and led him out.

Looking down into the yard, Michael guessed that it must be about thirty feet to the ground, but the alley alongside of it would make it easy to come and go as Arsenal.

*So far so good*, he thought. Then he asked, "How long have you lived here?"

"All of my life. I graduated from Meyers High School in 1986," she answered, leaning up against the railing. "My parents died in a plane crash a few years ago, and they left all of this to me."

Seventy minutes later, Michael had carried in the rest of his bed, and Judy closed up the truck. Checking the time on her watch, she said, "I'm going to take this back before they close. Are you going to be all right by yourself?"

"I should be," he answered, walking the headboard toward the house.

"There are towels in the bathroom, if you want to take a shower," she added. "I'll be back in half an hour or so. And don't worry. I'm not interested in the clerk."

Michael entered the house, closed the door, and carried the headboard up to the larger of the two rooms. After placing the headboard against the wall, he walked over to the window and watched as Judy drove away.

*Wow*, he thought. *Could this day get any better? Money and a beautiful girl.*

After watching as she disappeared from view, Michael picked out a change of clothes, his radio, and a cassette from a local Wilkes-Barre band that had made it big called File Horse.

"A little 'Sympathy Cathedral' sounds good right now," he said, thinking about one of his favorite songs off the cassette.

As he looked through his clothing, Shadow hopped up onto the dresser. Watching as the cat climbed into the dresser and inspected the clothes he had placed there, Michael said, "Hello, Shadow."

As expected, the cat didn't respond; it simply glanced up at him as it purred. He added, "I hope my moving in here isn't cutting in on your sleeping area. Well, don't worry; you can still sleep in here anytime you want."

Whether or not the cat understood him, Shadow curled up near the door and laid his head down.

Sometime later, Michael stepped out of the shower and realized he'd left his clothing on the dresser next to the cat. Turning off the radio, he reached for a towel, but there weren't any there. Looking in the mirror, he scratched his head. Using his old T-shirt, he dried himself off as much as he could, and then he quietly made his way down the hall.

"Terrific," he said as he walked into his new bedroom and saw Judy standing by the window.

Looking at him, she smiled and said, "You left your clothes in here."

"You're out of towels," he said as she tossed him his underwear.

"Oh yeah, that's right. Today was supposed to be laundry day," she said, looking away as he slipped on his underwear. "Sorry about that. Are you hungry?"

"A little," he answered, reaching for a T-shirt. "What do you have in mind?"

"Would you like to go to Q's for dinner?" she asked, tossing him his socks.

"The new restaurant by the mall?" he asked. "I've never been there, but sure, I'd love to go."

"They serve nothing but Mexican food," she said. "I've never had a quesadilla before."

"I think that's all there is on the menu," Michael said, recalling what the Q stood for.

"Are you ready?" she asked as she parked.

Looking at the crowded parking lot, he answered, "Ready and hungry."

"Good. So am I," she said, opening her door and stepping out.

Michael did the same, and she walked around the front of the car toward him and slipped her arm around his waist.

"I like the way this is going so far," she said as he put his arm around her shoulders.

"Dream come true," he replied, thinking about how he could tell her his secret.

As they reached the door, a hostess greeted them. "Welcome to Q's. Party of two?"

"Yes," Judy answered, watching as the girl took two menus off of a pile.

"Smoking or nonsmoking?" the hostess asked, looking out into the dining area.

"Non," Judy answered, looking toward the salad bar.

"Okay," she said. "Please come this way."

As they followed behind, she led them to the seventh booth and placed the menus on the table. As they sat down, she said, "Enjoy your meal."

Pulling the menu toward him, Michael said, "I've got to go to the restroom."

Nodding, Judy replied, "I think I'm going to check out the salad bar."

A few minutes later, they both returned to the table, but their seats had been filled by a man and woman. They were left puzzled and wondering.

"Excuse me. You don't remember me, do you?" the man asked, looking up from Michael's seat. "You look lost."

Taking a longer look at the man, who appeared to be about his age, Michael replied, "Nope, can't say that I do."

"What's wrong?" Judy asked as she walked up to him.

"They gave our seats to somebody else," Michael said, looking at the man and his date.

"Do you want to leave?" Judy asked, pulling her keys out of her purse.

Michael was about to answer, when the man stood up and said, "No, wait. Perhaps you could join us."

Michael looked at Judy as the man's blonde girlfriend said, "Yeah, come on. It won't be that bad."

"If you can't figure out how I know you, I'll buy you dinner," the man said, offering the seat next to him.

After thinking for a moment, Michael sat down next to him and said, "Deal."

"Hi," the man said to Judy. "I'm Ron Powers, and this is my girlfriend, Karen Whitehal."

*Karen Whitehal. Where do I know that name from?* Judy thought as she smiled and sat down next to her. Then she realized. "Are you the Karen Whitehal who won gold medals at the Olympics in '80 and '84?"

"One and the same," Ron answered. He turned to Michael. "So how about you? How come you didn't wrestle at the Olympics in Seoul?"

"I think you've got me confused with somebody else," Michael answered. "I haven't wrestled since high school."

"The Grappling Assassin," Ron said, recalling. "Isn't that what they called you?"

Looking at Karen and then at Judy, he continued. "In tenth grade, there were only two wrestlers in our weight class who were undefeated since beginning wrestling at the YMCA. We met for the first time in tenth grade, in the gold-medal round. No offense, but I was the best in the state. Your boyfriend put thirty points on the board against me. I don't know what you were trying to prove, but that was one hell of a statement you made."

"Wow, so you were that good," Judy said, surprised.

Smiling slightly, Michael answered, "I remember now. I beat you all three years. How come you didn't wrestle last month?"

"I never went to college," Ron answered, looking at Karen. "Too many things changed in my life."

"Too many deaths ended my career," Michael answered. "Two friends died a few months after state finals, then cancer took my mom's life ninety days later, and my father ended up an alcoholic."

"Wow," Ron said. "I'm sorry to hear that. I think the world missed out on two great wrestlers. So what kind of work do you do now?"

"Nothing yet, but I'm looking," Michael answered as the waitress returned.

"Can we get a few more minutes?" Karen asked. "Our friends just arrived."

"Sure, I'll come back," the waitress replied, and she walked away.

"What kind of work are you looking for?" Ron asked. "Karen and I are starting our own security business."

"Yeah, and with all of the trouble going on in Wilkes-Barre, this is the perfect opportunity to," Karen added. "I don't know about you, but I'd like to catch the person responsible for all of this."

"I think it's going to take more than a security guard to do that," Judy said as she looked over her menu. "I think you'll need an Arsenal."

"Just someone with a vigilant eye who isn't afraid to speak up," Ron replied. "Somebody must have seen something. For an event of that magnitude to have happened in downtown Wilkes-Barre, people were either paid or forced to keep quiet. The security of the everyday, average man, woman, and child must be worth fighting for."

"Sounds like something Quarrel should be taking care of," Michael replied. "Not that I've seen or read about her recently."

"Exactly," Karen said. "For all we know, she could have been killed. If she doesn't show up, there's no light on top of the police station to signal her."

"Besides, it seems like there's more than one person behind this—at least that's what Karen and I are thinking. So that means there would have to be a team of people out there investigating," Ron said, looking at each of them.

"No offense, but you sound like somebody I once knew," Michael said, thinking back to the night Mitch had died. "A superhero named Stingray wanted to make changes like that, but in the end, his lack of experience killed him."

"Stingray?" Ron said, unfamiliar with the name. He looked at Karen.

"His real name was Mitch Lewis. He wanted to fight crime in Wilkes-Barre just like Quarrel. He drowned in the Susquehanna River while trying to save my girlfriend, Becky, from her older brother, the Crimson Falcon."

"Michael," Judy said, surprised, "I never knew."

"Crimson Falcon?" Karen said, shrugging. "I've never heard of him either."

"Do you remember Greg Carlin?" Michael asked. "He graduated a year ahead of us. I ended up breaking all of his records. He thought he could use his wrestling skills to replace Quarrel as the top superhero in the city. Neither of them was good enough back then. Whoever is behind this terror spree is more than security-guard-style justice can handle."

"I got to learn a little more about you tonight," Judy said as they walked up the steps to Judy's house. "And I like it."

Faking a yawn, Michael replied, "Yeah, and I never thought I'd run into Ron Powers again, let alone have him offer me a job like that."

"Are you going to take it?" she asked as he yawned again.

"I don't know if that's the right job for me," he answered as they walked inside. "I'm going to go to bed. I'll let you know in the morning."

After closing the door, she turned on the light, gave Michael a long hug and a kiss on the cheek, and said, "Well, sleep tight. I'm going up to the attic to practice my magic."

They walked up the stairs together, and then Judy turned toward the attic stairs as Michael walked down the hallway to his room. Listening for her to close the door, Michael did the same, and he reached for his black gym bag.

*It seems like more and more people want to do the superhero thing,* Michael thought. *Let them follow in Quarrel's footsteps; I'll make my own path. Speaking of which, should I take that job? If I do, does that mean a different secret identity, or do I tell Ron and Karen I'm Arsenal? And if so, does that mean I'll have to tell Judy as well?*

Ninety-three minutes later, Michael Lanesra was completely dressed as Arsenal and walking the streets of Wilkes-Barre. His intent was to make his rounds and be home to Judy three hours later, which meant taking a quick check of the still-closed-off courthouse area and then the Scott Street region. As he made his way over the hill toward King's College, a few drops of water fell from the sky.

As he glanced upward in an attempt to see how bad the rain was going to get, flashing police lights caused him to stop and look back. Stepping from the car was the police woman he'd seen a few days ago. As she approached, he tried to recall her name.

"Busy?" she asked, looking into his trench coat.

"Searching for those responsible for all of this death and destruction," Arsenal answered, looking down at the blocked-off area and the crews working to stop the whirlpool still swirling in the river.

"Having any better luck than we are?" Officer Stein asked as she too glanced back.

"Would you be upset if I said no?" Arsenal asked as more raindrops fell.

Joking, she remarked, "No supercomputer back at the base?"

"No," he answered. *Only a very beautiful woman.*

"So having a badge is no different than having a secret identity," she remarked. "We're both clueless on how to stop this thing."

"But I didn't give up on trying to save this city," he replied. "I've been talking to a few people about expanding my search."

"What do you mean?" she asked. "You getting help? Quarrel?"

"Nope," he answered. "Never met her, and haven't seen her either."

"New recruits?" she guessed.

"Yes," he answered as the sky opened up. The rain fell harder and quicker.

Rushing back to her squad car, teasing, she asked, "Can I give you a ride home?"

Laughing, he replied, "You can't; it's a secret."

Watching as she drove off, Arsenal thought, *I should have stayed in with Judy and waterproofed my costume.*

The walk back to his new house took longer than expected, which he suspected was due to the hard rain weighing down his already heavy costume. He looked around as he stepped into the alley. The wind began blowing harder, and he moved into the darkness, realizing he'd forgotten to ask Judy for a key.

"Should have thought this out better," he whispered. "I'm going to need to find a place to hide this completely soaked costume, provided I can get into the house."

Crossing his fingers, he reached the front door and slowly turned the handle. To his surprise, the door opened, and he quickly said to himself, "I love you, Judy."

Standing there in the doorway, he looked at the carpeting and wondered how he was going to get to his bedroom without leaving a puddle of water behind with every footstep. He closed the door quickly, undressed, carelessly packed the costume into the black gym bag, and carried the bag up to his bedroom.

"Damn," he whispered, realizing he hadn't put his bed together. Dropping the bag inside the door, he whispered, "Oh well. Guess I'll be sleeping on a mattress without any sheets."

After changing into a dry pair of underwear and a T-shirt, Michael lay down on the mattress. Sometime later, as he rolled over, he felt a blanket being pulled up against him and an arm slipping around his waist.

# CHAPTER 4

A little more than a year ago, Karen Whitehal had been in love and on her way to marrying her longtime boyfriend, Jeff Mathers. She had known Jeff for most of her life, and she looked forward to spending the rest of it with him. She had just won her last Olympic gold medal a few years earlier, proving that at the age of nineteen, it was still possible to be the best in the world. However, unknown to Karen and the rest of the world, she was sapient dominant.

Her dream life went out the window when Jeff met a mysterious man by the name of Mr. D. He offered Jeff a job that filled his head with fantasies and promises that corrupted him. Though no testing had been done on Jeff, Mr. D. was able to determine that he too was sapient dominant. He guaranteed that the job he offered Jeff would bring out his powers and unique abilities.

To increase his ability to do the job, Mr. D. had Jeff study martial arts, which activated his dormant powers. Unknown to D., anger and rage were side effects of Jeff's powers. Without the proper training to control them, they pushed Jeff down a twisted path that caused him to become the criminal Mass Execution.

As the training and teachings went on, D. became interested in Karen joining the group. He was familiar with her gymnastic abilities and believed they would work well with the group he was planning. In the course of turning him down, Karen met a man expected to be another possible recruit: Ron Powers. All of that changed when Ron came up on the losing end of a fight with Jeff. From then on, Mr. D. no longer had interest in him as a member.

In the end, Jeff and Karen were no longer together, and the police were seeking Jeff for murders they suspected him of. She fled with Ron Powers to Wilkes-Barre, keeping a vigilant eye in case Jeff or Mr. D. returned. By moving downriver to the bigger city, they hoped they could hide in plain sight, all the while training and teaching each other.

Both were familiar with Quarrel, the hero who had been patrolling Wilkes-Barre for the past several years. She wasn't a top-tier, larger-than-life hero whom everyone knew. She did what she could with the limited resources she had, and just like Ron and Karen, she wasn't doing it to gain a cult following.

Ron and Karen knew the city was large enough that they didn't have to compete with Quarrel or try to replace her, as Greg Carlin had intended to do. It was a security job, and with terrorists running rampant in the city and nobody able to catch them, they felt that adding Michael would be a good choice. However, if they'd paid more attention to the newspaper, they would have heard of Arsenal and what he too was trying to do.

The afternoon September sun was beating down on Ron as he finished doing his last set of pull-ups, when Karen walked up to him.

Dropping down from the pull-up bar, he looked at his watch and said, "It's almost three. Are you going jogging with me?"

"No," she replied, handing him a towel. "I've got a few errands I need to run."

"Do you want me to go with you?" he asked while drying his face.

"No, I'll be fine," she said as he slipped his T-shirt back on.

After giving her a quick kiss, he whispered in her ear and began jogging down the road.

*I wonder what Mike's answer is going to be*, Ron thought. *Is he going to be interested in this line of work? I mean, I didn't exactly come out and say, "Do you want to join my superhero group?" And am I asking him to join for the right reasons? Will he follow my lead, or will there be a lot of arguing? What kind of name is this group going to have? Maybe the Knight Shift. I just hope we don't run into any serious trouble our first night out. Explaining it to Judy won't be easy. If Mike does agree to join, then we'll have to find a time and place to practice so everything goes as smoothly as possible.* He reached the trolley tracks that ran parallel to the canal. *With the way Wilkes-Barre seems to be under attack, I don't think that's going to happen. We're going to see some kind of serious action sooner rather than later. I just hope we're up to it. I also hope Karen's ex isn't involved in any of this—or that freak doctor who was trying to recruit us.*

As he made his way along the trail, Ron noticed a white van parked along the side of the road, and he wondered if it might have been abandoned. He made his way up the steep embankment and reached the road several minutes later. He saw someone sitting in the passenger side.

Cautiously, he approached the door and was surprised to see an elderly man inside. As the man turned toward him to speak, Ron noticed he was wearing the clothes of a priest and said, "Hello, Father. Do you need any kind of help?"

Startled at first, he stuttered as he replied, "No, I'm fine. Thank you, my son. My driver has gone to the nearest pay phone to call for help. All is well; you've no need to worry, though I am grateful in this day and age for someone like you. It is very rare."

"You're right about that," Ron answered, seeing a man approaching. "This must be your driver."

"You need something?" the man in the black leather coat asked in an angry, tough-guy tone.

Sizing the man up, Ron knew he didn't pose much of a threat. He was curious why a priest would travel with a thug like him.

"Relax, Wesley. The man was just offering his assistance," the priest said. "He was just offering to help us in our time of need."

"Yeah, well, thanks," Wesley replied. "But help is on the way. One of the guys from Diamond City will be out with the truck in about twenty minutes."

"Well, Father, I'm off," Ron said, walking past Wesley. He started jogging.

Upon returning to the trail, Ron soon came upon a fairly deep swimming hole with a Tarzan swing connected to one of the larger trees. Seeing that neither was being used, he turned toward the creek and headed for the swing. Timing his steps, Ron jumped and reached for the rope. He caught it and swung out over the water. It snapped.

He splashed down into the five-foot-deep water as he laughed. Looking up at the other end of the rope, he wondered how long it had been there.

Scanning the area, he decided that would be a good place to relax, swim, and screw off for a few minutes before his jog back home.

"Get that sweated up jogging?" Karen asked as Ron, still visibly wet from the creek, walked into their apartment. "Or was it raining?"

"I'll have to take you to where I was," he answered, pulling off his T-shirt. "Nice, quiet place, but it's in need of a new Tarzan swing."

Watching as he took his sneakers off, she replied, "But you're going to need to take a shower and get cleaned up for tonight. I've a surprise for you."

"Surprise?" he repeated, wondering. "Any clues?"

"Nope, but I know you'll definitely like it," she answered, following him down the hallway to the bathroom. "Meaning the faster you get in and out, the faster you'll find out what I got you."

Thirteen minutes later, Ron opened the bathroom door and almost tripped over the gift in plain brown wrapping paper. On top of the package was a note that read, "Put this on."

Untying the yellow string, he saw a black leather trench coat on top of a pair of black steel-toed work boots, black gloves, dark green spandex pants, and a hooded long-sleeved shirt.

*I love it*, he thought as he began dressing.

A few minutes later, Karen yelled, "Does it fit?"

"Like a glove," he replied, all smiles.

Peering out into the hallway, he saw Karen walking toward him wearing her long pink bathrobe. He asked, "How about you? Where's yours at?"

Coming to a stop, she pulled open her robe and said, "I'm wearing it."

She'd chosen red and blue for her costume. The colors were split, with red in the front and blue in the back. Across the center of her chest was a large white star, and on each of her hips was a star that stretched the length of her leg.

"I added the stars to represent the gold medals I won," she said, twirling around. "So I picked the name Star. What do you think?"

"Star, huh?" he said. "What about masks?"

"Check your right pocket," she replied. "Did you think up a name?"

As he pulled out the mask and looked it over, he replied, "Yes, I'm thinking Power of Justice." He slipped his arms around her waist. "I love you. Thanks for the gifts."

"I love you too, Mr. Justice," she said. Then she asked, "Are you ready to make your debut in Wilkes-Barre?"

"As ready as I'll ever be," he replied, and they kissed.

"Good," she said with a sly smile. "Because I got tickets to the Savoy Theater in town to see *Romeo and Juliet*. It starts in ninety minutes."

"Ninety minutes, huh?" he said, looking into her eyes. "I can sit through that."

"Good, 'cause we're going to meet Mike and Judy there," she said, stepping away from him. "So take that costume off, and get ready."

"You think he likes *Romeo and Juliet* as much as I do?" he asked, watching as she stripped.

"Who knows? Maybe the two of you can sit and complain about it," she said, stopping to wait for him to start taking his costume off.

***

"The costumes add a nice touch," Ron said as they walked down the street. "And the romance was even better."

"Yes," she said, "quite memorable."

"This night is going to be memorable in more ways than one," Ron said as they approached the crowd in front of the Savoy Theater.

"Evildoers beware!" Karen said, joking.

Just then, Ron spotted a blond-haired man in a limo who looked out at him as the car passed by. He got only a brief glimpse through the tinted window before the man pulled his face back into the darkness within the car—but not before Ron recognized him.

Nudging Karen, he asked, "Hey, did you see that?"

"No," she answered, looking toward the road. "Why?"

"I just saw Kyle Brock drive by in that limo," he said, pointing.

"Well, yeah, he lives and works in Wilkes-Barre," she said. "Why wouldn't you see the president of Dyna Cam Industries driving down the streets of Wilkes-Barre? I think I see Mike and Judy up ahead."

After waiting a moment, he added, "Well, of course you do, dear. They live in Wilkes-Barre. Why wouldn't you see them?"

"Ha-ha, very funny," she said, squeezing his hand as they picked up the pace.

They were a few feet away, when Judy turned around and saw them. She waved them over, and the four friends made their way inside. In the lobby, they made their way over to a display set up along the wall. It featured pictures of all of the legendary performers who'd played there, including a director who'd lived and worked in Wilkes-Barre nearly a hundred years ago named Lyman Howe.

"I remember him," Judy said while reading over the plaque of his career on the wall. "I read about him back in school. He was a silent-movie producer. I never saw any of his movies, though, if they still exist."

Looking at the different pictures on the wall, Karen said, "He worked for a movie studio over in Forty Fort. I know where that place is, but I never knew he worked there, let alone that it was in business that long."

Ron said, "There are even pictures up here about Mayor Hart IV's great-grandfather Daniel Hart: 'Mayor Daniel L. Hart graduated from Wyoming Seminary. He was a three-term mayor, serving from 1919 until his death in 1933. He defeated Republican Charles Loveland three times in a row. Prior to his political career, Hart was the manager of the Wilkes-Barre Music Hall and wrote sixteen original plays and musicals, five of which were staged on Broadway. Turning his career toward politics, Daniel was elected treasurer, and in 1919, he became mayor of Wilkes-Barre. He was a leader in progressive urban planning and established the city's park system. His beautification programs resulted in a new Market Street Bridge and Kirby Park.'"

"An actor and a politician," Michael said. "The Ronald Reagan of his time."

"Kirby Park is that old?" Karen said, surprised. "I would have guessed it was opened in the fifties or later."

"Nope," Michael answered with an image in his head. "It was 1924. It's written in stone at the old front entrance. Back then, you used to be able to drive through the park."

Glancing up at the night sky, Ron and Michael stepped out of the Savoy Theater with their girlfriends trailing behind. The women were discussing the parts of the play they'd liked the best. Neither of the men were thinking about that; both were visualizing what they'd be doing shortly.

"So did you think about my offer?" Ron asked as they stopped at the corner.

Thinking, Michael replied, "Give me your number, and I'll give you a call in the morning."

"She said that to you?" Judy asked, taking the car keys out of her purse. "Do you think that's what he meant when he asked you to do security? He wants you to become a superhero with them?"

"Looks like it," Michael answered as he helped her with the door. "I wonder what gave them the idea they could do this line of work."

"Who knows what makes people do what they do?" she answered as he got into the car.

"I knew someone else who had the idea to make a career out of this, he answered, "Let's hope it goes better for them than it did for Mitch Lewis, the Stingray."

# CHAPTER 5

Ben Ostren stood in front of the bookshelf, looking at the piece of wood he'd discovered a few years ago. It was lying out in the open on the ground in the woods. He'd been there several hundred, if not thousands, of times prior. As he picked up the fifteen-inch-long fragment of wood to look it over, he knew that it didn't belong.

*I still believe the ark is up there*, he thought, gazing out at the mountains several miles behind his house. *Or at least it passed by here as it sailed.*

He was referring to the biblical ark that Noah had built to survive the flood—the one everyone knew was somewhere on Mount Ararat in Turkey, on the other side of the world. Except he'd had the fragment of wood he'd discovered tested, and he'd been told it was the only known piece of gopher wood in the world, or it was a hoax, because there were no other pieces like it for a true comparison.

Sadly, as incredible a find as it was, nobody believed him or came to investigate his claim. Thus, the wood sat on his bookshelf, out in the open where everybody could see it, but nobody believed it except for Ben. Even after he'd discovered more and proved to the world that it really was gopher wood just like the testing said, not one reporter had come to talk to him.

At the age of twenty-one, Ben had done more adventuring on Wilkes-Barre Mountain than anyone else in the entire Wyoming Valley currently or throughout history. There was nothing he hadn't seen, and there was no rumor he had not investigated. The only time he'd found exactly what he'd set out to find had been a buried treasure. Back in the late 1800s, two men had robbed a train on its way to Wilkes-Barre from Hazelton.

The money never had been recovered, and the two men had claimed they hid it, but they'd never said where. Almost a hundred years later, Ben Ostren had followed the train tracks and the clues, and three days later, after searching, he'd found the money, which, at current value, had been more than $3,000.

Other than that, Ben had chased every legend without being able to prove any of them. Twice, he'd almost drowned while investigating the cement plug in the Susquehanna River. It had been used to fill the hole caused by the Knox Mine disaster. He'd attempted to swim down and do an inspection, believing there was more to the disaster than the mining accident. His sources told him something else had taken place in that shaft: an explosion. None of the survivors had mentioned an explosion, and he believed they'd been paid not to.

He dressed for that day's adventure up the mountain, which was going to be a normal stroll through the woods. However, as he listened to Wilkes-Barre Network News talk about the attacks in Wilkes-Barre, he changed his mind. The city of Wilkes-Barre had come under attack by unknown forces, and nobody knew why. Nobody had come forward to take responsibility.

*They've got to be stopped*, Ben thought. *This town can't handle stuff like this. People are going to flee in droves if this isn't stopped. Half the town is under martial law, and the military is already out patrolling the area. Where's Quarrel when you need her? Maybe this town needs a little more than that.*

After slipping on his green camouflage pants, he picked up one of his comic books off his desk and said, "Shockwave—that's what this town needs. That kind of hero would get to the bottom of this easily!"

Crime fighting was a profession Ben had thought about, but he'd never had the time to really look into it, let alone design a costume and think of a catchy name. Besides, it would just get in the way of his adventuring, although Dr. Walter Straub, the secret identity of Shockwave, was an archeologist. On the other side of the coin, he knew his longtime live-in girlfriend, Michelle O'Rourke, wouldn't go along with it.

Michelle had been given the opportunity to live with Ben and his mother more than fifteen years ago after her parents had died in a car accident. She and Ben had been best friends, and the Ostrens had agreed to take her in when none of her family stepped up to do so. Unofficially, they'd been dating since they were fourteen, but Mrs. Ostren hadn't figured it out until the night of their high school prom, when she'd caught them kissing.

That day, Michelle wasn't going to be home until five thirty or six, when she got off of work. For the last year and a half, she had been working at a retirement home in Plains, doing the laundry. She would come home, and the weekend would be theirs, regardless of the martial law imposed on the sections of the city in the attack zones.

As far as Ben was concerned, he was going to have the mountain named after him—he just needed to give the world a reason to do so. He'd been up there so many times he practically knew where every rock and tree was located. Rumors of investigations of Hoffa, Elvis, and little green alligator men had become part of the legend he was trying to build.

Along with going over the mountain, Ben had been under it several times. His adventures had brought him into closed abandoned mines to get answers he still hadn't found. Ben was also one of the only people to see the underground Wilkes-Barre Township mine fire up close and in person.

*If whoever is responsible for this gets into the old Red Ash Mine, they could do a lot of terrible things to that mountain—to my mountain,* he thought. He slipped his Rambo hunting knife onto his belt. *Not that I think this will do anything to stop men with guns, but it's better than nothing.*

After filling his knapsack with the usual items, Ben made his way down to the kitchen to pack two canteens filled with water, three apples, and a pack of lime Life Savers. Stopping at the back door, Ben mentally went over his checklist. He dropped the backpack and returned to his room when he realized he hadn't packed his soon-to-be-filled fifteenth journal. If W-BNN came around to interview him on his career, he'd be ready with all of his notes.

A short time later, Ben was making his way through the large sewage tunnels passing underneath Interstate 81. The tunnels had been his sole means of crossing the highway since he'd discovered the three of them more than a decade ago, when he was thirteen.

At the other end of the tunnel was a trail: to the left, it took one around the mountain to the mini waterfalls known as the Seven Tubs Nature Area, and to the right, the trail led to the dumping area that Ben called "the stove graveyard." Just beyond that were the houses of Wilkes-Barre Township.

Thinking over which route to take, Ben decided on the third choice: he'd go straight through the woods, past old mining routes and lost sections of Laurel Run, to the top of Wilkes-Barre Mountain.

*Head up there first, and look down over the city. Hope for peace and no more devastation, and hope there's nothing suspicious taking place on my mountain*, he thought. *Shockwave—why do I get the feeling that's where I'm heading with this—taking on that role to protect the mountain and the city? Am I superhero material?*

Pushing through the woods, Ben caught sight of what looked like an albino raven. Slowly, he reached into his backpack for his binoculars and camera. No sooner had he gotten them out than the bird took off. Something was coming fast.

As he turned around to see what it was, a large buck charged past, knocking Ben over.

"Wow, that was close," he said, getting to his knees. "Wonder what that was all about."

The answer came in the form of barking dogs a hundred yards away. They were approaching fast.

"They're coming this way," Ben said, grabbing his stuff. "Time to run."

Ben ran up the hill, but the seven dogs were faster, and just as he reached the open field, he knew the dogs were coming for him. Reaching the old mining track and level ground, Ben pushed himself to run faster. He managed to get a few yards' distance only to have the dogs quickly reclaim it.

*This ain't going to last*, Ben thought as he pondered dropping his backpack to lighten the load.

Off to his right was the steep field he'd just come from; turning in that direction, he knew he'd fall in no time if he continued straight on. The steep cliff on the other side didn't look like an intelligent option, but it was all there was.

Ben thought, pushing himself, *They're coming fast.*

The large white birch tree growing out of the side of the cliff saved his life. He hit the tree and, ignoring the small branches digging into his face and hands, felt the tree bending. Coming to a stop on the edge of the trail, the dogs watched and barked as Ben tipped farther from their drooling jaws.

Giving them the finger as the tree continued to bend, he mumbled, "Where did wild dogs come from in this day and age?"

Before he could come up with an answer, the tree snapped, and Ben hit the ground twenty feet later. Landing in the soft mud, Ben was grateful he didn't break anything. He slowly stood up. Looking up at the dogs, Ben walked over to a large rock and sat down to think.

"Well, at least I'm not lying here in severe pain, counting out the painful moments left of my life as the dogs chew on my body," Ben said sarcastically, reaching into his backpack for a canteen.

Placing it to his lips, Ben noticed something strange about the large, dried-up thorn bushes behind him. After taking a quick drink of water, Ben stood up and took off his backpack as he looked around the small, quasi-circular fifty-foot area. Taking a closer look at the dead thorn bushes, he wondered how they were growing there. It was the only spot down there where the sun didn't appear to shine.

Reaching over to touch the bush, Ben was shocked when his hand passed through it. Confused by what he saw, he tried it again, and the same thing occurred, leaving him wondering what was going on. The same thing happened when he attempted to touch another part of the thorn bush.

"An illusion?" he said, surprised. "I've been all over this mountain. Where did this come from?"

Stepping into the location where the illusory thorn bush was, Ben reached out to touch the stone behind it. He knew that some of it had to be real, because he'd just been running for his life across the top of it. He tried not to smile; he knew he was onto something there, and whatever it was, nobody was supposed to find it.

After feeling real stone a foot above his head and two feet on each side of him, Ben started moving into the concealed opening. Never once did he think he was investigating something long lost by the mines. He knew what kind of technology they used, and this was in no way part of it. He couldn't help but conclude it was something out of that world.

Ben rushed back to retrieve his backpack, took out his flashlight, and returned to the cave.

"And not a single miner has ever been in here," he said as he scanned the walls for any signs. "At least a hundred years of digging in this mountain, and I'm the first one in here. Of course, how else would it be? That's if this is that old. After all, there aren't any footprints in here. But why is this all here in the first place? Who did this, and why? I'd like to think aliens because of the illusionary bushes. Judging from the way the gopher wood thing came to pass, the press might think I've gone nuts. After all, that was the last press conference I had."

Several steps later, Ben found odd markings and symbols on the walls, along with a straight line drawn in the dirt. Kneeling down for a better look, Ben quickly reached for his journal and a pen so he could start the tedious task of copying everything.

As he copied the three hundred symbols, he tried to figure out what language he could identify them as being similar to—Choctaw, Ojibwe, Apache, or Lakota. Besides the mountain, Ben's second favorite spot was the local library. He knew he'd be there tomorrow, trying to figure out what he was reading now.

*Better than nothing, I suppose*, he thought as he started on the second row of symbols. *Hopefully this won't be hard to decipher tomorrow. It's looking more and more like it's going to be from a local Indian dialogue.*

Joking, he said, "It's probably going to read, 'Teedyuscung was here,' or 'Lenape forever.'"

Teedyuscung was an Indian who'd lived in the Wyoming Valley and declared himself king of the Delaware. He'd spent most of his life trying to bring about a permanent Lenape-Delaware home in the area. All that had ended when he'd taken part in the Treaty of Easton, which had forced them to give up all claims to Pennsylvania lands. On April 19, 1763, Teedyuscung had fallen victim to a fire when an unknown person or group burned his cabin in the middle of the night.

The sun had gone down more than a few hours ago. Ben had discovered another way out, and he took notes on getting back. While crawling out, he noticed a second illusion covering the exit. This one was in the form of a large, round rock. Like the previous illusion, this one surprised him because it was out in the open, and nobody had found it until Ben crawled through it.

The walk home took Ben fifty minutes longer than expected due to his looking over the symbols he'd copied. As he walked, he thought about the illusions covering both openings and was still puzzled as to who'd placed them there. Stepping up to the side porch entrance, Ben put the tablet into his jacket, and he walked inside.

His mother was sitting in the living room at the game table, working on a puzzle. Without looking up, she knew it was her son, and she knew where he had been.

"Michelle is looking for you," she said, focusing on the finished picture on the box.

Nodding, Ben walked over to the kitchen sink and washed his hands.

His mother asked, "What did you find this time?"

"Something I can't explain yet," he answered, reaching for the towel. "I mean, I know what it is, but I don't know why it's there—yet."

"Sometimes I think you go up to that mountain to search for your father," she said, watching as he put the towel back on the rack.

Chet Ostren, Ben's father, had last been seen on October 9, 1977, by his wife and son just prior to taking his weekly walk along Old Bear Creek Road. Originally, that road had connected to Mundy Street prior to Interstate 81 being constructed in the late 1950s. His father had been one of the last people to walk the road on its last official day before being closed.

His father had lived in the only house to have been demolished by the highway, and he'd often walked the road to reminisce. Almost twenty years later, Chet had gone for that same walk and never returned home. His green Chrysler had been found parked on the side of the road with no signs of forced entry.

A few weeks later his father's left shoe, a pocketknife, and the bones of his right wrist had been discovered lying on the shore of a nearby swimming hole. Even though the Seven Tubs Nature Area had been there since the Ice Age, it had not yet been recognized as a state park. Bernard Paulides, a private investigator passing through the area, had taken an interest in the case and said he had been investigating cases like that throughout the country.

"You were where?" Michelle asked as he pulled out his journal.

Flipping through the paper until he came upon the symbols, he answered, "I found an old Indian cave—one I don't think anyone has been in for quite a long time."

"On the mountain," she said while folding a few sweaters. "Again."

"Yes," he replied. "Where else do I go?"

"Where else do I go?" she repeated, turning toward him and taking the tablet. "You didn't happen to see Mokele Lembe up there again, did you?"

Mokele Lembe, according to legend, was supposedly a dinosaur that lived in the African Congo. As long as the villagers in that area could remember, witnesses had been circulating stories about a dinosaur-like creature called Mokele Lembe. No modern-day pictures or sighting of the creature had been reported, until Ben Ostren had seen it. Not only had he seen Mokele Lembe on Wilkes-Barre Mountain, but he claimed he'd had a lengthy discussion with it.

He laughed. "I didn't see him this time, but he's been up there before. You're not upset with me, are you?"

"You know, I think I'm the only woman on Earth who doesn't have to worry about her boyfriend cheating on her with another woman," she said, slipping her arms around his waist. "It's Wilkes-Barre Mountain that gets me jealous."

It was a little after midnight when Ben woke up, unable to sleep. Rolling over, he scratched his head and sat up. It was time. As tired as he should have been, it was time for Ben to take his walk to nearby Turkey Hill for his nightly bottle of soda and whatever he was going to surprise Michelle with.

"It's that time," Michelle said, knowing where he was going. "From the mountain to your lover to the darkness, the circle never ends."

Leaning over, he kissed her cheek and said, "You're welcome to come."

"Nope," she mumbled. "Some of us have work in the morning."

"Do you want anything?" he asked as he reached for his camouflage pants.

"Just you back in here with me," she replied, pulling the covers up. "Quickly."

"I'll be back soon," he said, grabbing his boots and jacket.

For almost as long as Ben had been going up to the mountain exploring, he'd been taking late-night walks to nearby Turkey Hill, mostly to clear his mind. He also claimed it helped him sleep better when he went back home to bed. Unlike Michael Lanesra, Ben didn't go out there for anything other than the walk and a bottle of soda. Without knowing, Ben had, a few times in the past couple of years, chatted briefly with Michael about sports and tavern locations.

Sometimes he would spend time talking to the clerks behind the desk, since he came in every night no matter the weather. On the rare holiday nights when Turkey Hill was closed, Ben would go to the soda machine across the street at Hollenback Park, in front of the fire station.

Stepping out into the cool night air, Ben zipped his coat about a third of the way and began walking down the street. Slipping his hands into his jacket pockets, he found a rolled-up comic book—it was the Shockwave comic from earlier in the day. Often, Michelle would do this, placing a comic book in his jacket as a reminder to pick things up. That night, however, the comic book would give him a different idea.

"Well, Dr. Straub, it appears today I found a mystery," he said, as if his comic book idol were here with him. "And this one is a little different from the others. There was an illusion blocking the entrance, and that's something I've never encountered. What do you suggest?"

Not expecting an answer, Ben continued his walk while thinking about the illusions and the symbols he'd copied. Later on, in the day, he'd walk back down to the library to research his discovery. Afterward, he would be on the phone with his cousin Jason to get ready for a weekend on the mountain with the girls, the usual third step in all of this would be pacing the car and going.

Stopping to tie his shoe, Ben looked back and was surprised to see a black cat following behind. The moment Ben began walking again, so did the cat, and the distraction ended up being the reason he was caught by surprise and lying with his face pressed in the dirt.

"Keep your ass on the ground!" Power of Justice demanded, staying above Ben.

"Someone wearing the same clothing was seen robbing this store," a female voice said. "You didn't forget anything, did you?"

"Quarrel?" Ben said, knowing that was not who it was. "You'd better give up smoking; it's ruining your voice."

"You're a funny guy," the female said, coming up from behind. "Let him up. The cashier said it was a short black man with a camouflage jacket."

They allowed Ben to stand.

*Superheroes,* he thought. He said, "When did the police change their uniforms?"

"We're not cops," the male in the green costume said.

"No, they're on the way," the female with stars on her costume said. "Let's hope you weren't with that guy."

"Rob this place? I come down here for my nightly walk," Ben answered, slipping his hand into his pocket. "How about you two? Aren't there enough heroes in this town?"

"It's a big place," the male said. "I'm Power of Justice, and that's my partner, Star."

"Power of Justice and Star," he repeated. "Catch any of the terrorists yet?"

"No," Star answered. "We're working on it, but people like you ought to stay inside, where it's safe."

"Safe? Safe from what?" Ben asked. "They're blowing up mines. I could be sleeping in my bed and wake up in a hole covered with two tons of dirt, halfway to China."

"What's your name?" Power of Justice asked, folding his arms.

Gripping the comic book in his pocket, Ben replied, "Shockwave."

"Shockwave?" Power of Justice said. "That the name you were born with?"

"Nope," he answered. "In costume, I don't wear a mask. I conceal my true identity."

*If they can do this, then so can I,* he thought, still clinging on to the comic.

"Shockwave," Power of Justice said, not believing what Ben had said. An unmarked police car pulled up next to them.

The car came to a stop, and Julius stepped out. He looked over the three of them and said, "Brings the count up to five now." He shut the door and stood in front of them.

"Five?" Power of Justice said. "Robberies?"

"Nope," he said, touching Power of Justice's trench coat. "Superheroes. It's like an epidemic. Bombs are going off in town; there's mass destruction, chaos, and carnage all over; the river is gushing into the unknown below the city; and now we've got common everyday people running around in trench coats and camouflage, trying to do a better job than paid, trained professionals. So, tell me—what exactly happened here?"

# CHAPTER 6

*The Wilkes-Barre skyline has never looked so good. Going to take one last look around for anything suspicious. Ron and Karen are going to take over and fill in nicely, I hope. Make sure nothing's going to blow up. If I'm lucky, I'll catch whoever is behind this. That'll be a good way to end my career as Arsenal,* Michael thought, making his way along the canal and railroad tracks, heading into the center of town.

*You know, I've never gone up onto any of these roofs,* he thought, looking over the group of buildings in front of him. *Like all the big-name superheroes do to check out the city from above.*

After making a quick scan of the area, Arsenal found a way to get up onto the rooftops, and five minutes later, he was looking down South Main Street. From what he could see, nothing appeared to be out of the ordinary; Wilkes-Barre was going to have a much-needed peaceful night.

When he turned in the other direction, that changed. Taking out his binoculars, he said, "Something's burning. Out of all of the buildings in this city, this has to be the one on fire, and it certainly isn't going to be an easy job to put out."

The largest building in downtown Wilkes-Barre and all of Luzerne County was by far the Public Square Plaza Hotel, which was two and a half times the height of any of the other buildings in the region. Jason Winfield and his three brothers—Tyson, Isaac, and Boris—had made their fortunes in the coal-mining industry and designed and built the hotel in 1925. They'd made their fortunes from 1883 to 1936, and the Winfield Hotel was the sole project they'd worked on together.

In 1940, Jason had died from a heart attack, and Boris had been killed in a train accident while returning to the city from Philadelphia. A few months later, the last two brothers had sold the hotel to Casper

Vandermark, who'd owned it until 1976, when it had been turned over to the city of Wilkes-Barre and had officially become known as the Public Square Plaza Hotel.

As Arsenal approached the front entrance, a large doorman said, "You're not permitted in here! There's no costume party here. Take the show elsewhere."

"I'm not here for a show," Arsenal replied loudly. "There's a fire up on one of the floors. You'd better get the fire department down here."

"Get off the property," the doorman declared, stepping in closer to Arsenal. "Or else!"

"Get out of the way. I don't have time for this crap," Arsenal said, attempting to step around him.

Putting his hand on Arsenal's shoulder, he said, "Don't touch the door!"

The doorman squeezed Arsenal's shoulder and pulled him back in his direction. As Arsenal reacted, the doorman grabbed his other shoulder and then, spinning around, pushed Arsenal out toward the street. Catching himself before he fell, Arsenal regained his stance and turned to face his new opponent.

"There's a fire in there!" Arsenal yelled again. "If you're not going to let me in, then contact the front desk, and tell them to call the fire department."

"I'm not doing shit!" the doorman declared. "Now, get off the property!"

"You've been warned," Arsenal replied, moving quickly and hitting him with a kick to the stomach.

Due to the bulkiness of the man's coat, the kick didn't do as much damage as expected. It only angered the doorman, who was already in a bad mood after being forced to work on his off day instead of celebrating with friends who'd come to town for his birthday.

The next thing Arsenal knew, a second doorman coming to the aid of the first struck him from behind and knocked him to the ground. Arsenal didn't get the chance to get up, as they stood there stomping him. Rolling over onto his stomach wasn't a good idea, except it would enable Arsenal to use his mantis poles.

He extended his right arm, and the mantis pole shot out and caught the first doorman underneath his jaw. Falling backward into the trash can, the doorman grabbed at his jaw as he felt blood in his mouth. Spitting it to his left, the doorman got back to his feet just as Arsenal jumped up. The second doorman stepped back, rethinking his choice to attack the masked man. Arsenal didn't stop and let him go long enough for his mantis pole to strike him in the back of the knees, knocking him down.

"Gentlemen, if one person dies in there because you impeded my work," Arsenal said, stepping back with his mantis poles still extended, "I'll hold you personally responsible, and neither of you will survive my vengeance!"

"Let him pass," the second doorman said, holding his hands up, "and call the police in case any shit starts."

The first doorman didn't respond. He reluctantly opened the door, and the small crowd inside came in their direction to see the fight outside. Arsenal walked through the open door, retracted his mantis poles, and calmly said, "Your hotel is on fire. Please call the fire department and exit the building."

Mumbling, the people in the crowd looked at each other and then at Arsenal. He was telling them they were in danger, and had it not been for the attacks in the city earlier in the week, believing him would have been a little harder. As some of them pondered his words, Arsenal looked around for further assistance.

"Who's in charge here?" Arsenal yelled, pushing through the crowd. "There's a fire in here, up on one of the floors, and I need the fire department called immediately!"

"Help me!" a man cried out as he fell down the stairs.

Instantly, the people turned away from Arsenal and rushed to help the man. Just as the nearest three people reached him, there was an explosion inside the elevator. As the smoke and dust seeped out, somebody rushed to the front desk and made the call.

Knowing he couldn't calm all of those people, Arsenal left the man in the care of the others. Then he headed up the stairs to investigate the explosion and discover if the fire was related to the other attacks in the city.

When he reached the third floor, Arsenal searched the walls for the fire alarm and then quickly pulled it. The instant the alarm sounded, people began stepping out of their rooms and looking up and down the hallway. Some, out of instinct, headed for the lobby, while others wondered if it was a prank when they saw the costumed figure moving about in the hallway, banging on doors.

Responding to a comment an elderly couple had made, Arsenal said, "Well, go complain at the front desk, and stay down there because the hotel is on fire."

Seeing a large group of people gathering at the elevators, Arsenal shouted for them to take the stairs because the other elevator had crashed in the lobby. When the doors to the elevator opened, he had to fight to keep from being pushed inside with the crowd. Forcing his way out and hearing the door close, he hoped they would make it down without a problem.

The next five floors weren't as bad; the people had heard the alarms and didn't put up as much resistance. Fewer and fewer people seemed to resist and hesitate as Arsenal told them the alarm wasn't a drill. However, at the pace he was going, he knew he'd have to move a lot faster if he was going to get more of the hotel cleared.

*Thank God they're finally starting to get the message*, he thought, reaching the elevators at the other end of the hallway.

Coming to a stop, Arsenal heard the hotel's main fire alarm activated. He breathed a sigh of relief; he no longer needed to go floor to floor, pulling them. Forcing his gloved fingers between the two doors took longer than he expected. Only after he took a hunting knife off of his belt was he able to pry the doors open easier.

With the doors open, Arsenal looked in and found the service ladder. Slowly, he made his way inside and started to climb. Concentrating on going up instead of down made the climb a little easier, and then, as odd as it was, he began singing to keep his fears in check.

By the time Arsenal reached the thirtieth floor, the smoke was beginning to get to him. With his gloves still off, he touched the door to check for heat. After concluding the doors were safe to open, he used his knife to pry open the doors, and as he entered, he realized the smoke was only getting worse. The only thing making him feel good was the fact that he didn't see any flames.

Either all of the people were suffering from smoke inhalation, or they already had evacuated the floor. With visible smoke in the air and nobody coming out, Arsenal started kicking in the closest doors and making noise to warn the people.

"What are you doing?" a man yelled upon seeing Arsenal barge in.

Judging by the way the man was standing, Arsenal easily determined that the man had had too much to drink. He answered, "The hotel is on fire. You need to get out."

Reaching for Arsenal's trench coat, the man replied, looking down to see if he was wearing his shoes, "I know you. I know your kind—put a mask on and save the world. Superheroes like you are a dime a dozen back where I come from."

Curious as to which superheroes the man was referring to, Arsenal was tempted to inquire, but he knew it would only distract him from what he needed to do. Even if only a minute, he could use the time to get somebody else to safety. After escorting the man to the stairs, Arsenal returned to check the rest of the floor.

The third door on the thirtieth floor flew open as Arsenal yelled, "Is anyone in here?"

With heavier smoke filling the room, Arsenal was about to return to the hallway, when he heard somebody nearby coughing. Kneeling down, he could barely see the figure underneath the bed.

He motioned for her to come out, and she nodded as she asked, "Are you an angel? Mommy won't wake up. You took Daddy after the car accident. If you're taking Mommy, please take me too, because I don't want to be left alone."

Thinking over what she'd said, he replied, "No, I'm not an angel. I'm Arsenal, and I'm here to take you and your mommy to safety. Where is your mommy?" As she climbed into his arms, he asked, "The other bedroom?"

Coughing, she nodded, and he went in to find her.

Despite the training Arsenal had put himself through, as good as he thought it was, he wasn't prepared for any of this, but he knew he couldn't make two trips. The blonde woman lying on the bed looked to be in her mid-thirties, about his height, and maybe 130 pounds or so.

After setting the girl down, he lifted her mother into his arms and slowly pushed his legs to a standing position. Once he had a good hold of the woman, he instructed the girl to climb onto his back.

"Close your eyes, and don't let go," he said, slowly turning around and heading out of the room.

Each step was harder than the last, and it seemed to take forever to reach the hallway. The smoke filling the room only added to the difficulty of getting them out. The fifteen hardest steps he had to take finally brought him to the hallway. He'd just moved past the door, when he heard a loud crash as fire from above brought the roof down into the room.

The girl screamed but didn't let go as she forced herself deeper into Arsenal's neck. With the fire just a few feet away, he knew he had no choice but to push himself to move faster. He'd just made it to the stairwell, when he saw two firemen approaching.

"Where are you coming from?" one fireman inquired, taking the woman from Arsenal. "Is it as bad as it looks from the street?"

"The floor right above us," Arsenal replied as the other fireman took the young girl.

*From the street?* Arsenal thought. "I just got these two out, when the roof collapsed."

"Well, let's get the three of you to a safer location," the lead fireman said, turning to go back down the stairs.

They followed his suggestion, but they'd taken no more than a few steps, when the wall just above the next landing exploded, sending debris down toward them. A large portion of the wall struck Arsenal in the chest, knocking him down several steps.

"Thank God for chest armor," he said, brushing the small bits of debris off.

Wiping the blood from his mouth and spitting out the rest, Arsenal slowly got to his feet only to collapse back down briefly as he struggled for air.

"Come on," the second fireman said as he slipped an oxygen mask over Arsenal's mouth.

After taking a few deep breaths, Arsenal gave a nod, and the group moved. They entered the twenty-fourth floor, and another fireman approached him.

"Tony, what happened up there?" he asked, talking to the lead fireman.

"Explosion brought the fire out into the stairwell," Tony answered. "Whoever this guy is, he rescued these two on twenty-seven."

"Let's get back down to the command post, alert the captain, and get a crew up here," the head fireman said, looking over Arsenal's weapons.

The command post, as it was referred to, was set up ten stories below, on one of the safer levels. The paramedics and fire captain were located there, and plans to stop the fire were unfolding. It was also the place where Arsenal assumed he would be able to tell the captain the situation, after which he would go home, leave it up to the professionals, and retire like he planned to.

"Who are you?" the tall black man in the open fireman's coat asked, approaching Arsenal.

Just from his appearance, Arsenal knew the fireman had to be the captain, and he answered, "Arsenal."

"Should have known by the weapons you've got hanging from your belt," the captain replied. "What do you know about this fire?"

"Don't know how it started, but I got here an hour ago, I'd say. After a fight with the two doormen, I got up here as quickly as I could to do what I could to help. I managed to alert several floors that there was a fire and rescue that woman and her daughter," Arsenal replied, pointing toward the woman.

Seeing him point in her direction, she asked the paramedic who he was, and afterward, she inquired about meeting him to show her gratitude. Believing his job was done, Arsenal proceeded to make his way toward the stairs to return home, when the paramedic approached.

"The woman you rescued would like to speak to you," he said, looking back toward her.

*Wonder what she wants*, Arsenal thought as he scratched his head through his mask and made his way over to her.

"You know, when they told me I was saved by someone wearing a mask, my first thought was I had been saved by a compassionate thief," the woman said as Arsenal stopped in front of her. "I saw you standing there and knew it had to be you."

"It's what I'm here for," he said, and he thought, *One final act of goodness.*

She stood and gave him a hug as she said, "Thank you."

"Like I said, it's my job," he said, helping her to sit down.

"A superhero in Wilkes-Barre—I never would have figured on that," she said. "Only one question: Where's your cape?"

Laughing, he replied, "They went out of style some time ago—1950s-style trench coats are in fashion again." He reached for his weapons belt, took out one of his golf balls, and handed it to her.

She asked while reading it, "What's this?"

"My calling card," Arsenal answered. "Something to remember me by."

Stepping away from the woman, Arsenal took a quick look around the entire area and saw firemen rushing in every direction, doing their best to bring about a quick end to the inferno. With his work done, he thought about taking his costume off and leaving it behind as he made his way toward the stairs, but something kept him from it.

The blast that knocked him to the ground and left the floor in turmoil changed his plans. No longer was he a few steps away from quitting; he was thrust back into the center of it all as he rushed back to help as many people as possible.

He heard gunshots on the stairwell he'd planned to use. In the back of his mind, he kept reminding himself how close he was to getting injured. Retirement was definitely out of the question now; he had to help those people as well as find the assassin and arsonist before the situation became worse. He could have tried to contact the police, but by the time they got the proper gear on, the culprit would have gotten away. Arsenal knew it was all up to him. Whether or not he liked it, retirement wasn't moments away.

"What the hell are you doing?" the captain yelled, seeing Arsenal going through the reserve gear.

"You heard the gunshots. I can't go up there without this gear, and we can't wait and hope the police will get here in time," he answered. "There's no choice."

"The police are right outside the building," the captain said as he grabbed hold of the oxygen tank.

"They're not suited to fight crime in an inferno. We'll all be dead by the time they get up here," Arsenal said. "So help me put this on!"

Realizing he was right, the captain changed his mind and assisted Arsenal. While he did so, he informed Arsenal of everything he needed to know to use the equipment properly.

"Make sure you get this bastard," the captain said as Arsenal pulled the oxygen mask down over his face.

Giving him a thumbs-up, he replied, "His ass is mine!"

# CHAPTER 7

The new motorcycle of Quarrel sped down Interstate 81 at speeds well over the limit. She had been Wilkes-Barre's sole true superhero for the past several years. The criminal element she'd faced never had amounted to anything of the caliber that was attacking the city now. There were exceptions, such as Slaughter and Massacre, two trained assassins she'd faced off against several times in the past.

Taguchi Soto had come the closest to eliminating Quarrel. Soto had taken her to Japan and forced her to become a slave, hoping she'd bear his children. In the end, she'd been able to get free and take control of the situation, which had ended with Taguchi's death.

No sooner had the motorcycle cleared airport security than she noticed the fire in Wilkes-Barre. The bike had been registered to Susan K. Thomas, the name she was born with. She hadn't taken the name Quarrel until she'd discovered she was a sapient dominant. Her unique ability allowed her to create a bow and arrows out of light energy.

From as far away as the Wilkes-Barre and Scranton Airport, the fire from the hotel was visible, and Quarrel knew that was the first place she was going. Having been out of the country, she had limited knowledge of the attacks and didn't know how bad the situation was.

By two thirty, she was speeding down Scott Street, and the Public Square Plaza Hotel was only a few blocks away. The hotel, which now looked more like a giant candle, attracted people like insects. They were blocking the streets to watch. The closer she got, the more people she saw crowding the streets. Some were praying the fire wasn't connected to the previous chaos that had struck the city, while others worried it would spread.

"What is this—a superhero convention?" a cop asked, seeing Quarrel get off her bike. "Where have you been?"

"Hey, Frankie, it's been awhile," Quarrel said, taking her helmet off. "Been busy in Japan. What's going on here?"

"A fire broke out a little before midnight. Some guy using the name Arsenal got into a fight with two doormen before he was able to get inside," he answered, glancing up at the burning floor of the building.

"Arson Al?" she said, imagining a guy with a flamethrower. "Doesn't sound like a superhero kind of name. Is he the one behind all of the fires in the city?"

"No," he said. "Arsenal, not Arson Al. He started patrolling the city a few weeks ago. Just another masked man attempting to take your spot at the top."

"Boy, you get kidnapped and taken to Japan for a few months, and somebody tries to muscle in on your territory," she replied, looking around. "Did he make it out, or is he still inside?"

"Black-and-yellow costume with a brown trench coat," Frankie replied, trying to locate him in the crowd. "Don't see him."

Noticing two others in costume standing across the street, she asked, pointing, "Who are they?"

"I've no idea," Frankie answered. "Like I said, it's a superhero convention down here. You're not thinking of going into that, are you?"

"No, I'm not fireproof," she answered, walking toward the two heroes.

"Who are you two?" Quarrel asked, stopping in front of them.

"I'm Star, and he's Power of Justice," Star answered, tilting her head toward her partner.

"Were you two in there?" Quarrel asked, watching as three firemen rushed past.

"No, it was out of control when we arrived," Power of Justice replied, "so we ended up doing crowd control."

"Do you work with Arsenal?" Quarrel asked, "or are you two a team?"

"No, we never met him," Star answered, shaking her head.

"You're not going in there, are you?" Power of Justice asked, watching as the fire danced up the side of the building.

"No. Out of all of the powers I have, being resistant to fire isn't one of them," Quarrel answered as a helicopter landed in the middle of the street. "What's with the helicopter?"

"It's been bringing people down from the roof," Power of Justice said as he too watched.

"Quarrel!" the pilot yelled, motioning for her to come over. "We need you up on the roof!"

"Guess I was wrong," she said, looking back at them. "I'm probably going to need some help up there, and you two are the only others in this business I'm aware of."

They looked at each other and followed Quarrel over to the helicopter.

"I hope you are ready for this," the pilot said as the three heroes climbed in.

"As ready as I can be," Power of Justice said, gripping Star's hand nervously.

Seeing him do that, Quarrel asked, "Do you two know each other out of costume?"

"Yes. Why? Is that a problem?" Power of Justice asked, looking at Star.

"No, I think it's a good thing because you'll make sure nothing happens to each other," she answered, thinking back to when she'd had someone like that.

Seconds later, the helicopter landed on the roof, and the three heroes leaped off and were surprised to see the people weren't fighting to get in the helicopter; the scene was orderly and calm. They were being assisted by a man dressed in camouflage who Power of Justice immediately recognized from earlier that night.

"Now, that's a surprise. I figured there'd be nothing but chaos up here," Quarrel said to the man in the camouflage.

"The fire is at least twelve floors below; they're safe for now," the man answered as the people filled in.

"What are you doing up here?" Power of Justice asked, looking at him.

"The same thing that you are," he answered, "Just call me Shockwave and let's get these people down to safety."

"Please help me. My stepbrother and his granddaughter are trapped inside," an elderly woman pleaded, grabbing Power of Justice by the arm.

"What floor are they on?" Power of Justice asked, trying to appear anxious to help.

"Fifty-nine," she answered, trembling.

"We'll find them," Star said, helping the woman into the helicopter.

"Are we ready for this?" Quarrel asked, looking to the group for an answer.

Power of Justice turned to Star and said, "If you don't want to go in, I won't force you."

"I didn't put this costume on just to wait outside. Hot and deadly or not, I'm going in," she said bravely. "For all I know, this might be linked to our past. My ex-boyfriend and the Designer could be involved in this."

"I hadn't thought about that. I just don't want to see you get hurt," Power of Justice said, worried.

"Since when did you become resistant to fire? You could get just as injured as me. If you don't want to go in, I won't force you either," she said, reminding him that he could suffer as well.

"Look, I'm not thrilled about going into this oven. I don't want to go in either, but we're here, and we're heroes. We didn't do this to get our faces in the paper. At least I know I didn't," Quarrel said. Then she added, "I don't know about the three of you."

"Neither did we," Star said, looking to her boyfriend.

Turning to Shockwave, Quarrel asked, "Who's the Designer?"

"I've no idea," he replied, shrugging, "Never crossed paths with him."

"Here it is—floor fifty-nine," Quarrel said as she checked the door. "Coast is clear."

They stepped out into the smoke-filled hallway and immediately began checking the rooms for the two people they'd promised to find.

"Anyone in here?" Power of Justice yelled, opening the door.

"Yes! Please don't leave us! I'm blind, and I think my grandfather had a heart attack," a woman pleaded, reaching out for them.

"We won't go anywhere without you," Quarrel said, taking her hand.

"He's breathing, but he won't be if we don't get him out of here," Power of Justice said, checking his pulse. "I think I can carry him out." He lifted the man.

"Are you with the fire department?" the woman asked, curious who they were. "You can't leave without finding my step aunt."

"She's okay; she's the one who told us," Quarrel said, escorting her.

As they made their way down the hallway, Star stopped at a door and said, "Did you hear something?"

"Hear what? We checked all these rooms earlier," Power of Justice said, continuing toward the roof.

"No, I heard it too," the blind woman said, looking toward the door.

"We don't have time for this," Power of Justice said nervously as his fear started to get the best of him.

"You don't. This man needs to get fresh air. I'll check it out and meet you up on the roof in a few seconds," Star said, checking the door and slowly opening it.

"Karen, wait!" Power of Justice yelled, not wanting to split up.

"Get him to the roof!" she yelled, stepping into the room.

Power of Justice looked at the door and then at the man and knew he had to get him to safety. Once there, he would move fast to return for Star, provided he wasn't too late.

"Okay, I heard you in the hall. Where are you?" Star said, entering the room and looking through the quickly thickening smoke. "Come on out."

"Mommy?" a little child cried.

*Mommy?* she thought, putting her hands over her mouth to try to breathe easier.

Kneeling down, Star looked under the bed and saw nothing. She sprung up, took five steps, looked into the bathroom, and pushed the door open all of the way.

Without seeing anyone, she said, "Come on! Let's go."

A chubby boy opened the shower curtain and ran into her arms. Pulling the boy up toward her chest, she returned to the hall. Just as she did so, Power of Justice appeared and took the child.

"Thank God I found you," Power of Justice said, wanting to hug her.

"Yeah," she said. "Let's get out of here."

# CHAPTER 8

Judy sat on the couch, curled up in a blanket, with all of the lights off, relaxing and eagerly awaiting Michael's return. Out of curiosity, she turned on the television with the hope of finding something to help pass the time.

"This is Susan Brock of WDAU News, reporting to you live from the Public Square Plaza Hotel, which, as you can see, is an inferno. Just about every fire company in the area has been called in to deal with this. The fire is reported to have begun somewhere between the twenty and thirtieth floor of the hotel and was noticed shortly after midnight. Assisting the police and paramedics are Wilkes-Barre's superheroes Quarrel, Star, Shockwave, and Power of Justice, and from what I've been told, there is a fifth hero inside. Fire Chief Adams said he was battling the arsonist. Right now, standing next to me is Lieutenant Colonel Mason Colts from the Kingston Armory. He's been overseeing the military presence in the city since the destruction of the North Street Bridge and the courthouse earlier in the week."

As a cameraman turned his camera toward him, Mason gave a nodded response as Susan continued. "Do you think this fire is in any way related to the two earlier attacks Wilkes-Barre suffered?"

"Currently, we can't be sure," he replied. "We won't know anything until the fire has been put out and the fire marshal can get inside and determine the cause. But until somebody comes forward and takes responsibility for this, there's no way to be sure if the incidents are related."

Judy's heart skipped a beat. Of all of the things she'd done to pass the time, the one that brought Arsenal to her hadn't been on the list. She wasn't using her magic to watch him; she'd figured it would be a quick and quiet patrol of the city. Waiting for him on the couch with a smile had seemed more appropriate than spinning spells to watch over him on his final night.

Now it appeared to have been a mistake that could cost her the man of her dreams. Countless cantrips and incantations ran through her mind as she rushed up the stairs to the attic. If Arsenal was going to make it through this and return home to her safely, he was going to need her magic to help him through the chaos he was caught in.

As Judy stepped into the attic, Arsenal made his way deeper into the inferno.

*I wonder if this is on the news, if Judy's watching this. Baby, if you can see me, get me the hell out of this. I'll never leave your side again,* he thought. *I promise.*

"Who are you talking to?" Chief Adams asked, overhearing his conversation through the radio.

Realizing he wasn't thinking but talking to himself, Arsenal replied, "Just praying—that's all."

"Good idea," the chief answered. "You've been up there for more than fifteen minutes. If you can't find him, then get out of there. The place is surrounded; he won't get away."

That night was supposed to be the night he retired and started a new life in a house with Judy, where he knew there would be lots of love and no anger. With the money he'd found the other night, he and Judy wouldn't have many financial problems to worry about and could possibly work toward starting a family. His father wanted nothing to do with him and had left the city after all Arsenal had done for him.

"Being a hero," a voice said from somewhere within the flames.

Spinning around quickly, Arsenal expected to be face-to-face with the arsonist, but he was left staring into the flames and dense smoke.

Shaking his head to try to focus, Arsenal realized he wasn't thinking but talking to himself. But if that were the case, then there was somebody else in the fire, watching. Or could it be that he was just confused and in need of a retreat?

There was still time to exit that madness and walk away. However, during the split second needed to contemplate that thought, Arsenal took another step and felt a slight popping sensation against his right ankle. The explosion knocked him off his feet and sent him sailing down the hall and crashing into a wall not yet burning. Getting up slowly, he tried to contact the chief, but the radio was dead.

His only answer came in the form of a set of large hands coming out of the smoke and grabbing him. One of the hands hefted him high into the air, and the second struck him in the face, cracking his oxygen mask. Choking from the small amount of smoke seeping in through the mask, Arsenal kicked the arsonist hard in the chest as he struggled to breathe.

Laughing as he shrugged off the attack, the arsonist said, "You made a mistake in trying to stop this. It's just the beginning; all of Wilkes-Barre is going to burn. Too bad you won't be around to see it!"

Forcing his words out, Arsenal replied, "If I'm not getting out of this, then I'll drag your ass to hell with me."

"Consider this to be your funeral pyre," the arsonist declared, charging at and tackling Arsenal.

Flailing his arms wildly, Arsenal desperately tried to grab something to avoid falling back into the fire. In the brief moment it took to respond, momentum would have pulled him in anyway. Crashing into the burning wall, Arsenal could feel the fireproof fabric of his suit tear slightly in different places, and immediately, he felt the heat and knew the situation was about to get worse.

The arsonist fared no better; a section of the wall and burning cinders managed to get inside his fireproof clothing. Crying out from the pain, the arsonist tried to get the clothing off and douse the burning he felt, giving Arsenal the opening he needed.

Using the wrestling moves that had left him undefeated in high school, Arsenal used the arsonist's own weight against him and brought him to the ground. As soon as the man hit the ground, Arsenal turned to leave and increase his chance of survival. He didn't get more than a few steps before a burning board struck him on the shoulder, spinning him around and brining him to his knees.

Dropping the piece of wood, the arsonist then kicked Arsenal in the face, shattering his oxygen mask.

Gasping for air as he staggered backward, Arsenal tried to gain distance as he saw the entire floor collapse not far behind the arsonist.

Flames covered most of the room, making it impossible for Arsenal to get any substantial amount of air. He knew he needed to get out quickly.

He'd left his weapons behind in his black gym bag so he could move quicker and be less encumbered; now it looked as if that hadn't been a wise choice. As the arsonist leaned in, Arsenal tried kicking him in the stomach only to discover he was out of reach. Catching Arsenal's foot, the arsonist yanked on him and easily lifted him into the air. Turning slightly, he threw Arsenal into the fire behind them. Falling to the burning floor, Arsenal struggled to breathe as the fire started to consume his gear.

"This is just a little glimpse of the burning you'll receive in the afterlife, hero," the arsonist said as Arsenal fought for his life. "Heaven isn't part of the plan."

With his life fading fast, Arsenal knew he wasn't going to live longer than a few minutes. Using all of his remaining energy, he dove at the arsonist as the ceiling collapsed around them.

The intense heat and flame took away his senses, and Arsenal knew he was dying; nothing was going to change that. Then he saw a strange purplish figure standing ahead of him. The figure appeared to be human, though Arsenal couldn't make out any recognizable features. Arsenal got the impression it was observing him.

"You want me to heal him? Is this what my afterlife is supposed to be—helping this freakin' guy out? Well, who was there to help me? Where was my aid when I was taunted by the world for my oddly colored purple skin and high IQ?" the figure screamed, looking to the ceiling. "Answer me!"

"This was all discussed before; an agreement was reached between you and those I represent. This was how it was presented and accepted. Do not change the contract to which you are bound! Arsenal must live! Things have already been set in motion, and evil will win if you do not do your agreed-upon part! If that becomes the road you choose, then you will feel my wrath; I've worked too hard to fail this far along. I've come too far in the universe to have you wreck it all and have to start anew again. Now I leave you to do your part. If you flee before that is accomplished, I will kill you, no matter what psionic discipline you elect to use as defense," the other voice said, though Arsenal couldn't see who was speaking.

"My task at hand?" the purple figure said in a cold, uncaring way. "Why do I feel I got the short end of the stick?" Sensing Arsenal's heart was still beating, he said, "He's not even dead yet, though he is fully cooked."

With the same helpless luck that had allowed him to see the purple figure, Arsenal forced out the words "Help me."

"Don't rush me," the figure replied calmly. "All things in due time. For now, just shut up and die!"

The instant the figure told Arsenal off, Judy's magic informed her that he was gone. There was nothing she could do to save him. Or was there? Uncle Ramsey had taught her a lot about the craft, and now was the time to find out if that knowledge would pay off. After pacing the room and drying the tears in her eyes, Judy called for her familiar.

Shadow gave no reply. The magic she'd bestowed upon him that enabled him to answer was silent. She knew the cat wasn't dead; she could still sense his presence through her magic. Whatever he was doing, it kept him from responding.

Using magical phrases she'd never thought she would speak, Judy vanished from the room and reappeared just behind a fire truck located not far from the fire. If the spell had brought her there, then that was where her familiar was.

"Hey," Power of Justice said, tapping Star on the shoulder, "isn't that Judy?"

"Yeah, it is," she answered. "Wonder what she's doing down here."

"Who's Judy?" Quarrel asked, seeing a woman dressed in black trembling.

"A friend," Power of Justice replied, approaching her. "Judy, what's wrong? Why are you down here?"

Turning as she heard her name called, she looked at the man in the green costume, confused, and asked, "How do you know me? Who are you?"

"Do you work in there?" Power of Justice asked, wondering why she was there. "Where's Michael?"

"No," she answered as she began crying. "He was inside."

"Michael," Star said, recalling his name. "Inside? Where is he?"

Nodding, Judy sat down on the curb.

Breaking the first law of being a superhero, Star removed her mask and sat down next to Judy. She said, "It's me—Karen."

Turning, Judy embraced Karen and said, "Michael's in there somewhere."

"Did he work there?" Quarrel asked, kneeling down in front of her.

"No," she answered, hesitating. "He's Arsenal."

"Michael?" Power of Justice said, shocked. *He is Arsenal?*

"I'm sure he got out," Quarrel said, trying to comfort her.

"No. He didn't. I saw it," she said. "He was fighting the man who set it."

"How do you know?" Shockwave asked. "There are no cameras in there."

"I practice magic," she replied. "I know I can help him. I just have to get to him."

Thinking, Quarrel looked the others over and said, "Well, people, one of us has fallen, and he needs our help to bring him home. I know we're all basically new to this line of work, and none of us really knows each other, but we need to come together as a team. If you're not in, leave now. I've never met Arsenal, but I won't leave him inside either."

"I haven't met him yet, but I don't intend to leave him either," Shockwave said, folding his arms.

"Count me in," Star said, looking at her boyfriend.

"Then it's settled," Shockwave said, stepping up to Judy. "You've got our help."

# CHAPTER 9

On August 7, 1970, Michael Lanesra was born at Wilkes-Barre General Hospital. During the same time, at the other end of town, in Mercy Hospital, Jonathan David Beighn came into the world, weighing in at a little less than six pounds. Physically, he grew to be a normal-looking boy.

Mentally, it was an entirely different story. Jack, as he came to be known, by the age of five, was smarter than anyone in the country. A select few children were educated enough to skip a grade; Jack, however, managed to skip the first three grades and started his schooling in third grade. Due to an educational jump of that size, Jack made no friends.

Most young boys were playing sports and exploring their backyards as they engaged in imaginary adventures. Jack was not one of them. His idea of entertainment was increasing his knowledge of the world.

By the time he was eight, he was able to read and write in German, French, and Spanish as well as speak in sign language. Chinese, Polish, Latin, Russian, and Arabic came in that order over the next several years. His plan was to become the world's first official person to read, write and speak every language of the world.

Both parents were shocked and confused by Jack's superior intellect. He was their only son, and they wanted him to be smart—but not like that. They were puzzled as to where he'd gotten his intelligence from; neither side of the family had anyone with an intelligence of that kind. Neither of his parents was close to being in Jack's league. They weren't dummies, but his level of genius made it look that way.

By the age of fifteen, Jack was so smart that he began skipping school because he felt it was holding him back. He'd go to the library and pick out college-level stuff to read, which usually included advanced science and mathematics. The number of languages he spoke fluently was up to twenty-three, including Hawaiian and Ojibwe.

He also believed he'd discovered the final answer to Pi, but he wasn't interested in informing the world at the moment. He planned to work on more important things, such as a cure for stupidity and ignorance.

He didn't like school because he had become smarter than anyone else in the school, including the teaching staff. Furthermore, Jack's skin had begun taking on a slight purplish hue, and the children had given him the name Kidneybean, a name he hated.

To his face, others still called him Jack, though the small circle of friends he had dropped to zero. His mother noticed his skin discoloration and immediately took him to the family doctor. Evolution was the problem, the doctor claimed; Jack was sapient dominant.

However, whenever his parents became upset with him, the same name used by his schoolmates was now used at home. Getting away was all that Jack thought of, but as to where he could escape to he wasn't sure.

There was one place Jack felt would help: the local cemetery. The doctors didn't know what was wrong with him, and he wasn't sure if he could die—not that committing suicide was ever on his mind; he just wanted to fit in. Then he figured others would taunt him just as much in the afterlife.

He was on his way home from a nearby park, where he'd been lucky enough to have the opportunity to talk to a young girl named Judy. She didn't live far from him, and he was curious why he had never seen her at school. He'd wanted to talk to her more; however, her uncle had arrived and said she had to leave because it was time for her studies. Jack hoped to see her again, but he knew they'd met only by luck in the first place, and he would most likely never see her again.

"Judy," he said, skipping down the street. "Her name is Judy."

Suddenly, a sharp pain in the back of his head stopped him in his tracks. It was as if a radio had been turned on within, and the volume was up all the way. Many people seemed to be talking loudly in his ears at the same time, yet when he stopped to look around, there was nobody near him.

Voices and thoughts continued to bombard his mind as he screamed and dropped to his knees. That was only the beginning; within minutes, Jack could hear the entire world shouting in his mind.

"Turn it off!" he screamed, putting his hands over his ears.

Nothing happened. For the next few minutes, the onslaught continued, and then there was total silence, as if every sound ceased to exist. Confused, Jack wondered what could have been the cause. His answer came when he realized the new sensation had to be connected to the strange color of his skin. It was another ability proving he was sapient dominant and pushing him further from humanity.

As he got to his feet, his head throbbed. He told himself to focus, and slowly, he staggered home. What should have taken him fifteen minutes took Jack well over an hour, and he found he was able to pick up a conversation that had taken place a few minutes ago between his mother and stepfather.

Tim Chide had been Jack's stepfather for the past three years. His father, Ronald, had left one night after an argument with Jack's mother. He'd gone out to take his usual walk and been killed on the side of the road. A truck had lost its brakes, slid on the ice, and killed him instantly. A few months later, Jack's mom had met Tim at a local bar, and the two had been together ever since.

To provide for his family, Tim worked as a motorcycle repair man at the Diamond City Garage. He spent much of his free time attending motorcycle rallies and socializing with the biker gang that operated out of the garage. However, living in Wilkes-Barre meant having to drive to the larger rallies held out of the state. Most of the time, Tim went whether or not Jack or his mother objected, because alcohol had come to mean more than his family.

That particular Friday was no different, the only exception being that his newly rebuilt motorcycle wouldn't start. The rally was going to begin the following morning about three hundred miles from there, and unless he fixed the problem, he was going to be walking. The motorcycle had run last night; the test drive he'd taken around the block hadn't shown any problems. The bike had appeared to be in perfect working order.

Convinced that Jack's mother, Helen, was to blame, Tim marched up to the bathroom, where Helen was taking her daily hot bath. No sooner had the door opened than the room filled with yelling and screaming. Before Tim realized what was happening, the radio fell into the bathtub. The electricity that coursed through Helen's body killed her instantly. Immediately, Tim attempted to pull the plug and drain the water only to be electrocuted the moment his hand touched the water.

Tears dripped from Jack's eyes as he followed the vivid dream to its end. Could it be real? That would mean Jack's purple skin wasn't his only evolutionary difference. He possessed the gift of precognition, and from what Jack could guess, he'd also had his first telepathic experience, neither of which fit the nickname Kidneybean.

It was just more reason for him to want to get away, but where could a freak like him go? After thinking, he decided there was only one place to go: home. Shrugging off the entire experience as his imagination gone wild, he hoped that by going home, he could rest, and it would all go away.

But that wasn't to be. Jack got to his front door and heard his stepfather stomping hard up the stairs as he called out for Jack's mother.

"Helen!" Tim yelled, reaching the top step.

There was no reply. He turned right and walked down the hallway, disappearing from Jack's view as the lights in the house began to flicker. It was the vision unfolding before him. Cursing himself, he ran up the three steps to the porch and entered the house; two strides later, he reached the staircase as fast as he could only to get there too late. Tim grabbed the radio and died along with Helen by electrocution.

Entering the bathroom, Jack saw the water spilling out across the floor. He tried to stop, but momentum kept him going, and he died in the water with his mother and stepfather.

The next thing Jack heard was the voice of a woman. She seemed to be speaking as if she were doing some kind of ritual. At first, he ignored her, because after all, he'd just died. The sensation of being electrocuted was still fresh in is mind. Or was it?

There was something else, yet he couldn't remember it—a voice, a black cat, some strange place, and a pact. Speaking of strange places, this was not his body. Who was Michael Lanesra, and why was Jack there? "Immortality," someone said. The person told him he was going to be part of a link, and together they would be immortal.

*Who, and why?* Jack was supposed to be dead. Was this the afterlife? Or maybe it was just some bizarre dream. Jack needed to know. The decomposing body he was now residing in was definitely not his. It didn't feel right, and he didn't like it. He wondered what he'd gotten himself into.

Using powers he was confident he hadn't possessed moments ago, Jack used his mind to enter the mind of Michael Lanesra. More than a trillion images ran through Jack's mind, and in an instant, he knew Michael's entire life history, including how he'd burned to death in the hotel fire. He knew about the woman he was deeply in love with, who was using her magic to resurrect him at that moment.

*Judy*, he thought to himself—the girl he'd seen yesterday in the park.

A lot of time had passed since that yesterday. Judy looked to be at least ten years older and he couldn't remember what had put him there, but if he was going to be in the body of Michael Lanesra, at least he got to have the prettiest woman he'd ever seen by his side.

*But am I going to have to be Arsenal?* Jack thought to himself as he listened in on what Judy was saying.

Trying not to laugh, Jack said to himself, "She's trying to resurrect me. I'm already here."

With the aid of his powers, Jack used his astral form to project his mind into the air above Judy. The room had a wooden floor and seven bookshelves filled with books of various sizes, all on the subject of magic. While looking around, Jack also peeked into Judy's mind and learned she had been a practitioner of magic since she was seven years old.

Her parents had practiced magic as well, but they'd given it up to raise their daughter. Judy had learned almost all of her skills from Uncle Ramsey, and on the day she'd talked to Jack, magic had been the reason for her leaving. Since that day, Judy had become one of the best in the land.

It would have broken her heart if he'd told her he was immune to what she called magic, though Michael, on the other hand, was not. The resurrection spell she was now performing had been successful in returning the person to life; he would be bound to her until the end of time.

Because they were already in love, Arsenal could have no interest in any other woman; he was all Judy's—at least while Jack was in control. Currently, Arsenal was dead. His body was now Jack's property, and until he used his powers to restore Michael to life, he was going to do what he wanted and have no worries at all.

*Resurrection is a powerful thing,* Judy told herself as she recalled the warning in the spell book written in her uncle's handwriting. Still, she had to try; she was in love and had no intention of letting a thing like death get in the way of her feelings.

She took out a satchel filled with a rust-colored powder and began spreading the powder out across the floor in a perfect circle. As she did so, she chanted in an odd voice, which Jack assumed was a magical tongue and part of the ritual.

The incantation wasn't the actual resurrection spell but a spell needed to keep anything non-worldly from getting in and creating havoc or entering Arsenal's body. Screwing up and allowing a demon to possess his body would have been far worse than failing to bring Arsenal back. A demon set free in a city where chaos was already running rampant would be a disaster.

Her contacts, most of whom had been allied with her now deceased uncle Ramsey, had promised to aid her by watching the various eldritch planes of existence. She had been practicing magic for quite a long time and considered herself lucky because she'd never made any powerful magical enemies, which could have made this ritual impossible.

When she completed the circle, she and Arsenal were in the inner part, protected. If anything had intended to intervene, it would have had to come in before she'd dropped the last of the powder.

Looking at Arsenal, she leaned in close and kissed him softly on the lips. She said, "I love you, baby."

She stood up and moved to stand over him as she spoke. "Oh mighty and honorable Death, keeper of the dead, hear my plea. Before you now lies the body of Michael Lanesra, whose life was recently taken away while he attempted to save the lives of people he never knew. His reward should have been something far more than just dying."

A few minutes passed. Judy took a deep breath and was about to continue the ritual, when a voice spoke: "Then what does your champion and lover deserve, if not death? Immortality perhaps?"

The loud, booming voice caught her off guard and sent a shiver down her spine. Her heart started pounding wildly. She thought of running away. The voice was so loud and terrifying that she expected something to jump out and grab her. The spell book didn't mention Death giving a reply.

"You have nothing to say? Perhaps you did not think you would receive an answer," the voice said as sweat began to build up and drip from Judy's face.

"H-he died in a fire," she stuttered, not knowing what else to say.

"Champion or hated bastard, everyone must die! There are no mortals exempt from this law! If you attempt to break this, you will anger me immensely, human. None could stop my wrath," the voice declared as the room grew cold.

Gaining a little courage, Judy asked, "But why would returning him to life be such a crime? If it's so wrong, why is there such a thing as a resurrection in the first place?"

"Don't worry. The warlock who wrote that incantation is paying for it at this very moment. In years to come, when you get here, I will be sure to introduce you to him!" the voice said.

"Then I offer my life for his," she said quickly.

"Oh really? Now, why would I want your life? What could I do with it? As pathetic as it is, I cannot live it, though it was a noble offer. Your hero is dead and will remain that way! Now, leave the room so that I may claim his soul," the voice commanded.

Remembering what she'd read about finishing the ritual, Judy ignored the voice and attempted to complete the spell as she tried to control her trembling.

"What have I ordered?" the voice said. "Leave the room, lock the door, and give thanks to your pantheon of gods. Be grateful that I did not claim your soul for your ignorance as well as such brazen actions!"

With that command, Judy stopped what she was doing, quickly rushed out of the room, and locked the door, just as she'd been ordered. She didn't look back and never noticed the purple glow emanating from under the door.

# CHAPTER 10

Quarrel stood on the dike near the Carey Avenue Bridge, looking toward center city Wilkes-Barre, thinking about the destruction brought about recently by unknown forces. She thought about her recent battle in Japan with crime boss Taguchi Soto. If she hadn't been victorious, she wouldn't have been there now.

Looking across the river at the Lance Colliery, she wondered how protected it was. The Dorrance Mine just behind the courthouse was still filling with billions of gallons of Susquehanna River water. It had been the beginning of the carnage that had set all of the chaos in motion. If unknown forces had been able to get in there and cause that destruction, what was keeping those forces from doing something similar at that end of the city, in the mines around there?

*The bridge would definitely go*, she thought. *The canal rejoins the river down around the bend. The Lance buildings will probably go just to cover their tracks. To make an even bigger impact, they'll target the Loree, just around the corner in Larksville. But it's not a heavily populated area compared to the northern section of the city, and in the other two areas, there are a few businesses, but they're sort of stretched out along Route 11, with houses on the other side, going up the hill.*

Deciding to take a closer look, Quarrel wished she'd brought her motorcycle instead of walking. Several steps later, she caught a glimpse of Power of Justice following behind. Turning around, she waited for him to catch up as she asked, "You're not following me, are you?"

"Sort of," he answered, adjusting his mask. "Star had to go to the bathroom, so I told her to just stay there and keep an eye on Judy."

"You're out here all alone?" she asked, teasing. "Can you handle that?"

Taking a quick look around, he answered, "No, not at all, though I'd like to use this chance to get to know you a little better."

"Oh, in what way?" she asked. "Not interested in your girlfriend anymore?"

"No, it's not like that," he replied. "You've been fighting crime a lot longer than the rest of us. I'm kind of wondering why you joined up with us rookies in the first place."

"Are you implying that I'm too good for you and the others?" she asked as she started walking across the bridge.

"Not at all," he answered, following her.

"I heard what you said to Star. Shockwave is just as green as you are. He's got his reasons for doing this, just as you and I do. I'm not here to question that; he's quite welcome to join up with me or go it alone if you don't want him. You just seem to get further and have better results when you've got more people working with you than against you. Right now, with the way Wilkes-Barre is under attack, we've got to stand together, or these masks don't mean a thing."

"I think you're right about that," Power of Justice said, looking down at the river below. "They've already taken one of us. I don't know what Judy is thinking; she claims that Michael is still alive and needs medical attention. I know that she said she's also a nurse, but he needs to be in a hospital, not at home. She also said she knows magic. I've seen that hocus-pocus stuff on television. Saving Michael is going to take more than sleight-of-hand parlor tricks. Judy needs to come to her senses and do the right thing."

"You were surprised that Michael was Arsenal," Quarrel said as they reached the Larksville side. "How did you know him?"

"I met him in high school at the state wrestling tournament. We were in the gold-medal match. Up until that time, nobody had beaten me or even come close to it. I was that dominant. Until Michael put my shoulders to the mat, I gave him my best, and I think he toyed with me during the entire bout."

"Did you get the gold the following year?" Quarrel asked, standing on the bridge and looking to her left at the layout of the Lance mine complex.

"No," he answered, "Michael Lanesra beat me all three years. I got three silver medals. Back in high school, some people in the school district called Mike the Grappling Assassin."

"The Grappling Assassin?" she repeated. Then she said, "So as good as you were, Michael was better."

"Yes, he was in a league of his own. In fact, he had the state record for least amount of points scored against him. I think I put a total of six points up in three years against him, whereas each year that I faced him, the assassin put twenty points on me," he said as they started walking. "So what are we looking for?"

"The first bomb went off in the Dorrance Mine, underneath the river, which I think was nothing more than a distraction to get the crowds there to see the carnage. Getting emergency management and the others down there to set up where that natural gas was being piped was the plan all along. That was the blast that took down the bridge, leveled most of the buildings in the area, and killed the majority of the people. The third attack took place later behind Denny's in Parsons, when they went into the Mineral Springs Mine. We've got the same setup here at the Lance Colliery, a mine that definitely runs under the river. A blast would take this bridge down easily, and there are houses and businesses nearby—everything but government buildings. Right down the road less than half a mile is the Loree Mine complex. I'd bet these two mines are linked together somewhere. That only adds to the destruction and death that strategically set bombs could cause. Since you've decided to tag along, I'm going to take a look around this area to make sure nothing is about to happen."

"Ever been down in the mines?" Power of Justice asked as they made their way up Chestnut Street in Larksville.

Looking back toward the river and the largest structure across the street, she answered, "No, but I've got a funny feeling that might change soon."

"You think we're going to find something that warrants us going in?" Power of Justice asked as they watched three white vans drive past.

"There's a good chance of that," she answered as they reached the top of the hill. "But you never know. We've got a pretty good view of the city and surrounding area. We'll head up Broadway and then down to Nesbitt Street and over to the Loree for a look around."

"And that's down around the corner?" Power of Justice asked, making sure he understood.

"Yes," she answered. "Rumor has it that a lot of the mines are connected somewhere below ground for safety reasons, so in theory, we could enter the shaft at Loree and come up at Glen Alden, Empire, or Baltimore. We probably even could reach Plains, Pittston, or somewhere else on this side of the river, like maybe the Harry E."

"So with enough explosions, Wilkes-Barre could be in a lot of trouble," Power of Justice said, trying to envision the destruction something like that would cause. "And nobody has come forward to take credit for this?"

"Not that I'm aware of," Quarrel answered as they reached the top of the hill on Broadway, in between the two large culm banks. "Unless it happened while we were with Judy, none of us thought to put the television on and check the news. On the way back, we'll stop to pick up the *Wilkes-Barre Record* and see if we can use anything in there to break this case."

Nodding in agreement, he asked, "Do you carry money with you?"

"Yes," she answered. "I'll buy the paper."

The walk to the Loree through Larksville didn't bring them in contact with anyone suspicious. It was a calm, warm, and sunny day. By the time they reached the entrance to the Loree, they had built a following of neighborhood children.

"Do you see that?" he asked, referring to the children following behind.

"Yes," she answered without turning back. "If you want to go sign autographs and shake hands, go ahead, but that's not what I'm out here for."

Looking back a second time, he replied, "Yeah, it's not like they know who I am. They just see the mask and flashy costume."

After a quick look around and a fifteen-minute conversation with the security guards, Quarrel came to the conclusion that nothing was going to happen and decided to leave.

"So why didn't we talk to the guards at the Lance Mine?" Power of Justice asked as they walked back toward Nesbitt Street.

"Because the miners were still working," she replied. "Tonight we'll come back and do a follow-up."

"At both places?" he asked, thinking he and Quarrel would definitely be going underground. "You think the terrorists will come back here?"

"I don't know where they'll strike next," she answered. "You know, in this line of work, you constantly have to check and recheck things. They went into the mines twice already and haven't been caught, so why would they change the game plan?"

"True," Power of Justice said as they came out onto Route 11. "Are we going to head back to Lance and head into Wilkes-Barre, or do you want to go the other way into Kingston?"

"We're going to Kingston," she answered as they made their way across the street. "But we're going to take the railroad tracks near the river."

Several minutes later, they passed through the parking area of the Lance Mine and reached the tracks near the river. Looking in both directions for oncoming trains or any sign of danger, they saw nothing but a group of children. When the kids saw the heroes, two of them ran toward them.

"Hi, kids. What's up?" Power of Justice said as they came to a stop in front of him.

"It's Andy. He's gone," one little girl answered. "The monster chased him out to the island in the middle of the river."

"Monster?" Quarrel said, wondering what the girl meant. "What kind of monster?"

"It looked like a Frankenstein monster," she answered, pointing out toward the trees on the island in the middle of the river.

Kneeling down next to the girl, Quarrel said, "You know there's no such thing as a Frankenstein monster. Where is Andy really?"

"I told you," the little girl said, looking toward Billy, another of the children. "He went out to that island."

"By himself?" Power of Justice asked, looking out at the island known as King Richard Island.

"Because of those bombs, the river's not that deep," Billy answered, looking to the little girl.

"Do your parents know you play down here on these tracks near the river?" Power of Justice asked, looking back at the others. "With all of the trouble going on, this could be a very dangerous place to be."

"We're not supposed to," Billy answered, shrugging, "but we don't tell nobody."

"This is why you shouldn't come down here without an adult," Quarrel scolded as she looked out toward the island, hoping to see Andy.

"The monster chased after Andy, and we ran the other way," the little girl said, pointing to where they'd fled.

Looking at her partner, Quarrel said, "What do you think?"

"Where is the monster at?" Power of Justice asked, hoping to not get wet. "Can you show us?"

Nodding, the little girl took Quarrel by the hand and escorted her and Power of Justice to the place where they'd walk out to the island.

To their surprise, the river didn't go more than a few inches above their ankles, which made Quarrel wonder just how much river water was going underground and where exactly it was ending up. As she stepped onto the island, Quarrel could hear the voice of an older man with a heavy German accent. As far as she was concerned, it didn't sound like a monster.

Another man came into view. He looked to be in his late forties, and she realized that man could be the monster the children were referring to. His face was severely disfigured, and by the way he talked, she knew he suffered from some type of severe mental disorder.

"Ouch! Ouch!" the handicapped man cried as the older man pulled on his ear.

"What did I tell you, Thomas? You never listen. I told you not to stray from me! We have a job to do, and we must keep our schedule," the man said. Suddenly, he noticed Quarrel and the others approaching.

"Who are you?" Quarrel asked, stopping a few yards from them.

"Von Kragen," he answered, taking off his wire-rimmed glasses and cleaning them with his shirt. "Dr. Helmut Von Kragen."

*A doctor?* she thought. Then she asked, "Is this man a patient of yours?"

"No," the doctor answered, returning his glasses to his face. "Thomas is my son. As you can see, he is severely challenged."

Nodding, Power of Justice said, "That solves most of our problem."

"Your costume," Von Kragen said to Quarrel. "I have seen it before. You are the fräulein archer, are you not?"

"Yes, I am," she answered, getting an eerie feeling.

"Long ago, my superiors dreamed of creating a master race of super soldiers," he said, recalling the events as if they were yesterday. "But those follies were brought to an end in April of 1945, and the world—I can only dream of what might have been. Now, come, Thomas. We must be going. Say goodbye to the fräulein superhero and her partner."

Watching as they walked out to the place where they'd crossed, Quarrel couldn't help but wonder if that man could have been a Nazi. She heard footsteps from behind and saw Billy running up. Right behind him was another young boy.

"I found Andy," Billy said with a smile.

"I can see that," Quarrel said as she knelt down. "Let's stay away from this place for a while."

"Okay," they said together.

Watching to make sure the doctor and his son were far enough away, they escorted the children back to the mainland and sent them off in the other direction.

# CHAPTER 11

Tired from all of the events that had befallen her in the past thirty-six hours, Judy collapsed on her bed and drifted off to sleep. Her desire for a good life had come crashing down two days ago with the painful death of her boyfriend and her failed attempt to resurrect him.

Sometime later, she found herself alone in a flower-covered field. She wept while she sat on a large, flat slate rock. In her hand was a crinkled, faded picture taken back when she'd first spied him on a Wednesday night, his first night as Arsenal.

Suddenly, a warm, gentle breeze blew through the field and pulled the picture from her hand. The loss of the picture caught her by surprise, and she watched as it drifted aimlessly through the air, moving farther and farther away. She suddenly realized it was all she had of him, and she immediately gave chase. A few moments later, she was lucky enough to wrestle it away from the wind. Attempting to flatten the picture and remove some of the wrinkles, she discovered she was no longer standing in the flower field, and everything was becoming a little darker.

A rickety, rusty black metal fence now stood behind her and spread out for an unknown distance in both directions. Looking down, Judy saw high grass and partially covered unmarked graves. Immediately, her heart began pounding wildly at the thought of her decomposed boyfriend rising up out of the ground and crying, "You did this to me!"

After a few seconds, she was able to convince herself Michael wasn't going to rise up and claim her. She began to read the graves to see if he was really buried there. Fives markers later, she found his gravestone and knelt down in front of it. She read, "Here lies Michael Lanesra, beloved of Judy Monteno, 1970 to 1991."

As she looked over those words, she began to cry. "Sweet Michael, I'm sorry I failed you. I wish I'd been there watching over you like I had done so many times in the past. I wish I could hold you one last time and feel your lips pressed against mine as your kiss takes my breath away. I will count out the days until we see each other in heaven. Please don't be upset if I arrive early. I love you."

Laughter was the response she heard, but it wasn't that of a man; it sounded demonic or at least not human.

Terrified, Judy sprang up and moved backward away from Michael's grave, thinking that the laughter had originated there.

"So you've lost a loved one," the raspy voice said. "And now you are all alone!"

"Who is this?" she yelled, wondering if this voice had anything to do with the voice that had kept her from completing the resurrection spell.

Whirling around, Judy looked in every direction as she tried to see where the voice was coming from, and without realizing it, she backed herself out onto a cliff. Suddenly, the voice made itself known; rising up out of the grass approximately twenty yards directly in front of her was a dark brownish beast.

It stood on its hind legs, and Judy was baffled as to how something so enormous could hide in grass that wasn't any higher than two to three feet. Its facial features made Judy think it was some type of dragon. She noted the way its jaws and teeth extended out from its face.

"Don't be afraid," the creature said as a smile stretched across its face, allowing Judy to see the rows of jagged teeth glistening in the sunlight. "You should be terrified if you wish to please me. I like the way it makes your heart feel as I pluck it from your chest."

Leaning in closer to enjoy the sweat blending with her scent, it licked its lips and allowed its massive tongue to stretch out and touch Judy's cheek. Pushing it away from her, she moved back and closer to the edge of the cliff. At that instant, both of them were caught off guard by the yellow golf ball that rolled to a stop in between them. The creature looked around with a puzzled expression on its face.

Judy too was confused, but she recognized the meaning of the golf ball; it was Arsenal's calling card. Even though Arsenal had died and this was her dream, she in no way was responsible for it being there. The creature's large, leathery wings sprouted up from their resting place on its back as it turned and gazed back at who or what had rolled the ball.

"I'm not interrupting anything, am I?" a voice that was recognizable to Judy said. "I didn't want to disturb you while you were out walking your pet!"

"Pet?" it repeated in a loud, booming voice. "I am nobody's pet! No human possesses the power to control me. You make better snacks than masters."

"I wouldn't just tame you; I'd break you until you knelt before me," Arsenal said. "My punishments would be so severe they would burn your fear of me into your DNA! You and your species would be so terrified of me that your offspring would die just by being in my presence."

"Bold words," the creature replied. "I think it's more like the other way around. You and your species fear me. I am the power. I am your every fear!"

"Fear is not a problem," Arsenal said. "Come see!"

Arsenal pulled his war hammer from its place on his utility belt and held it by the chain. As he began swinging it in the air over his head, he said, "I break the jaws of the wicked and pluck the spoils from their teeth. Come and see."

Rising up into the air, the creature smiled and said, "Very well, snack. Hammer and all, I will consume you."

A grin stretched across Arsenal's face as the creature moved into position to bite Arsenal. He ran at full speed toward the creature, and when he got in range, the hammer struck the right side of its face with a loud cracking sound.

The blow from the weapon left the creature not only in pain but also humiliated. Nobody, not even its master, had used something as archaic as an iron weapon on it. This dream-state hologram was not going to get away with it either; the beast would regroup and kill it.

That place was just a dream plane created by Judy, but the creature was an interloper, and it was there to induce fear and terrorize Judy. In the real world, her magic could stop it. If it could be victorious in the dream world, she would think twice about crossing it in the real world. That was the plan. The creature had never expected any kind of resistance, nor had it expected its target to have Arsenal on her side.

"How dare you use an iron weapon against me!" the creature yelled. "How disgusting, you weak fool."

"Must have hurt," Arsenal replied as he lifted the hammer and began swinging it over his head again. "I am Arsenal, the Wicked Breaker and, well, the Iron Weapon. You know, he shall flee far from the iron weapon, or maybe you don't, but it's right out of the Bible. Job 20:24, to be exact."

The beast was about to respond; however, the moment it tried to speak, Arsenal threw his hammer, and it hit the creature in the mouth, causing it to choke. Unsheathing the sword from his back, Arsenal rushed in to finish off the monster, only to be knocked to the left by the creature's tail.

The impact left Arsenal breathless just long enough for the creature to spit out Arsenal's war hammer. Arsenal dropped the sword as he hit the ground, and the creature moved in to finish Arsenal off by leaping through the air and landing hard on his chest. As Arsenal struggled to breathe, the creature laughed and leaned in to comment on its foe's demise.

"You are pinned and about to be consumed. Say goodbye to your woman," it said. "But don't worry; she will be joining you in my stomach shortly."

"I hate to tell you, but this is her dream, not yours," Arsenal replied, holding his arms straight up and ejecting his mantis poles directly into the creature's eyes.

The monster fell backward as blood and puss splattered out in every direction. Arsenal was able to get to his feet and retrieve his sword. As the creature tried to focus past the pain, regroup, and deal with Arsenal, it felt something slice across its chest. It was sharp, and the creature felt more blood pour from its body.

Taking to the sky to get out of range of Arsenal's sword, the creature was finally able to get vision in one of its eyes. Instead of flying off and saving that fight for another dream, the creature sailed up higher, turned, and went right at Arsenal.

Looking up at the charging beast coming at him full speed, he kept his eyes locked on it. Arsenal raised his sword above his head and prepared to swing. Suddenly, a large burst of light struck the creature on its right side and sent it crashing into the ground. As it hit the ground, Judy hit it with a second burst of magic. The creature slowly stood up and realized victory was out of reach.

"You've shown me that you are more of a threat than I first anticipated. I suspect it's because this is all a dream," it said, returning to its place in the air.

That time, the creature didn't mount an attack; it kept flying and didn't look back. Whatever it had thought of, the creature was going to use it in the real world, where it was positive it would face them again. For now, it would study its mistakes and failures there in Judy's dream.

Making sure the creature had gone and wasn't circling around for another strike, Arsenal kept his eye to the sky as he returned his weapons to their locations. When he turned to look for Judy, he was swept off his feet and lost in the warmth of her kiss. The touch of her lips and the pleasure of her smile made him hold her tighter, and he wished the moment would last forever.

"Is this really you?" she asked as tears rolled down her cheeks.

"Yes," he answered, "it's me. I don't fully understand how, but it's me. This is your dream, but you didn't summon me; I came of my own accord when I sensed you were in danger. I love you so much, Judy, and would never let any harm come to you."

"But you died in my arms," she replied. "I tried to save you with my magic and failed."

"I don't know where I was. I assumed wrongly that I was in the afterlife, but that doesn't explain the pantheon I was standing before. I don't know if they were angels or unknown gods, but they told me their plans for me, and I accepted the offer they gave me."

"What offer?" Judy asked, puzzled.

"I'm going to be their Arsenal, their protector of … everything," he answered, unsure what that meant.

"Will you be there when I wake?" she asked, hoping he would say yes.

"No, as much as I wish I could. I will not be there when you wake, but don't be discouraged by this. We will be together soon, and I will never leave you again like this." He kissed her again.

As his lips touched hers, she began to fade.

"Michael, something's wrong," she said, panicking.

"Don't be afraid," he said. "You're just waking up."

"I love you," she said as her dream disappeared, and it all went black.

"I know," he said as he too vanished. "I love you too."

# CHAPTER 12

A little more than fifteen hundred years ago, Xenyzyon had arrived on Earth after being forced from his home world. He was genetically created as the ultimate killing machine. His name meant "Destroyer"—a job he'd done all too well until a more efficient and all-around superior breed had replaced him. Now Xenyzyon and the rest of his kind served as nothing more than food and practice for their more powerful replacements.

During the onslaught, Xenyzyon managed to escape and stow away on a cargo ship to evade his hunters. Once the ship was out of the planet's atmosphere, Xenyzyon went on a killing spree that destroyed the ship's controls in the process. His savagery almost got him killed, but the ship collided with a lake in the mountains, which helped him survive the impact. Xenyzyon was now trapped on a planet he knew nothing about, yet he was free from the hunters that had murdered the rest of his kind.

Xenyzyon's favorite source of food was the American Indian. At first, they believed their gods had sent the beast to punish them. They quickly concluded the gods couldn't be so cruel and began plotting his demise. Another forty-six Indians would die before shamans from the twelve nearest tribes united to deal with the problem. They elected not to kill it, fearing that whatever had sent it would be angered and come to wreak punishment on them. Instead, they trapped Xenyzyon in a cave and contained him there with powerful magic, hoping there weren't others who'd come to help.

As powerful as their magic was, fifteen hundred years later, the magic began to weaken. In less than a month, it would cease to hold Xenyzyon at all. Even though those who'd imprisoned the beast had been dead for centuries, he still wanted revenge. Exploring the dream plane was something new, and Xenyzyon hoped he could use it for just that purpose.

It wasn't until a few months ago that Xenyzyon had fully entered that reality and begun exploring it with his newfound powers. That was when he'd first sensed the power within Judy and sought her out to understand what magic really was.

However, the plan didn't go as expected, and now Xenyzyon was going to have to deal with her and her boyfriend. He believed Judy's magic could reinforce the prison and keep it locked away in Wilkes-Barre Mountain.

At the same moment, standing in front of the mirror in the room where Judy had attempted to resurrect Arsenal, Jack Beighn was looking over Arsenal's body. According to the agreement he'd made with the voices in the light, he was to be in control. Because of Jack's abilities, it was his job to repair any type of damage that had contributed to the demise of Michael Lanesra.

Both Michael's and Jack's souls were to inhabit the same body, and the deities in charge, known as the Powers That Be, were going to make sure this Arsenal was better off than any of the other previous Arsenals. As long as Michael wore the costume, he would be immortal, and Jack, now going by the name Kidneybean, would heal him and prevent further damage to their prized possession.

Shadow, Judy's familiar, was sitting on the window ledge. He was more involved in the grand scheme of things than anyone could possibly have imagined. Shadow wasn't only aware of the conversation that Michael and Jack had had with the voices; he'd taken part in it because he was one of those powers.

Because of the way things originally had gone in that existence, the powers had voted to scrap it all and start over. This time, they vowed to make things different, and merging Michael and Jack into one being was one of their changes. Adding Judy as Michael's girlfriend was the other.

"What do you think?" Jack asked, looking at his reflection in the mirror and then turning toward Shadow. "I mean, besides the fact that the body is completely cooked, though it does have a nice purplish color to it. Makes me think of a pickled egg—you know, like the kind you make with the red beets?"

Shadow's only response was to move his tail slightly, which didn't please Jack at all.

"I can read your thoughts," he said. "I know you are fully capable of speech and can communicate if you so choose."

For a moment, Shadow remained quiet. Then he said, "You are correct to say that. You will return Michael's body to its proper state, along with the costume as well."

"Of course, I will," Jack said. "Is there a time limit?"

"Yes, there is," Shadow replied. "Forces are at work, and situations are building that will require Arsenal's presence in the city."

Looking out the window toward central city, Jack said, "The city has changed. It's been awhile since I've walked those streets, so for now, that's where I think I'll be."

"You have a job to do," Shadow scolded. "Healing Michael is your priority. Don't go out there seeking to do anything that would hamper or prolong it."

"Relax. It's all under control," Jack said as a small purple sphere of energy appeared at waist level in front of him.

Besides having purple skin and strong telepathic abilities, he was gifted with the ability to create gateways he could use to travel. He could open a portal that would take him anywhere he desired, whether or not he had ever actually been there. What surprised Shadow was how well he seemed to have mastered that power while being dead.

The purple sphere grew to be slightly longer than Jack, and glancing into it, Shadow could see the other side. It was a rooftop, and he could hear the sounds of the city below.

As Jack was about to enter the gateway, he asked, "Do you want to come along to keep an eye on me? Or am I okay to be out on my own?"

"Whatever you do, I can undo it if I believe it would go against the design of the grand scheme," Shadow answered. "As powerful as you are, your powers are feeble compared to mine."

As Jack stepped out onto the roof of the south-side YMCA building in downtown Wilkes-Barre, his mind was flooded with the thoughts of everyone within the city. Many of them held little interest, and quickly, he put them out of his mind, except for the woman in the alley below—the one who was struggling and resisting her attackers with all that she had but not doing a very good job of it.

The leader—a tall, fairly muscular Latino named Raphael—was eyeing what he saw between her legs, and he thought he was going to get it. That all came to an end when Jack decided to make his presence known.

None of the attackers noticed him, though his purple shadow did cause them to stop and wonder what was happening.

"So what do we have here?" Jack asked, unsure of what he should say.

When the five attackers saw what was speaking to them, they couldn't respond. Terror kept them silent and unable to do anything other than tremble. One of them even wet himself. The moment he sensed it, Kidneybean had to keep from laughing and spoiling the fear he was trying to generate.

"You coward," Jack said, whirling around to face the attacker who'd relieved himself. "You soiled yourself. Go home and shower, you pathetic idiot!"

The man, Justin, didn't say anything; he just put his head down and walked away. Once he got around the corner, he took off running as he swore to himself he was never going to associate with people like Raphael ever again.

"Now, as for the rest of you," Jack said as he turned to face Raphael, "why do you think I should allow scum like you to exist?"

Before Raphael could answer, Jack spun around to face the man behind him, who was in the process of pulling out a pocketknife. Jack said, "That won't harm me, Tomas."

Surprised Jack knew what he was going to do, Tomas, startled and confused, looked to Raphael for some kind of help.

"No, he won't give you any," Jack said, using his psionic abilities to keep Raphael from responding in any way. "In fact, he isn't going to be able to do anything at the moment. His thoughts betray him, and I don't like how he thinks he could take me out in a fight either."

Sweat began to trickle down Raphael's face. He couldn't see his face turning purple, but his face hurt, and he knew that freakish person was doing it. All he wanted to do was get out of there; he was being humiliated in front of his crew, and he didn't like it. Everything from his neck down felt okay; his brain, however, felt as if it were being crushed inside his skull, and that terrified him. It wasn't until the man thought of his twin baby girls that Jack eased up.

"Next time you feel that way, it will only be because you remember it as a flashback on your way to the afterlife. Raphael, go home, and take care of your daughters, Tina and Alicia, and your girlfriend, Rene. If you don't use this opportunity to change your life for the better, I will know the moment you take a step onto the wrong path, and I will clamp the Mind Helmet on your puny brain so tightly your head will explode!"

Raphael nodded, and as tough as he was, he apologized, looked down at the girl, and then walked away. His partners saw what he was doing and followed. Jack didn't do anything to them; he knew Raphael had such a strong presence that they would do whatever he did.

"Now, Natalie, get up," he said, extending his hand. "Everything is okay now. You are safe, and as long as I'm around, you'll never be in danger."

"What? Who are you?" she asked, getting to her feet on her own.

"You fear me too?" he said. "Perhaps if you saw me in a more recognizable form?"

In the blink of an eye, Jack's appearance went from the decayed, burned dark purple skin of a dead man to a fully healed superhero wearing a brown trench coat with a black-and-yellow costume underneath.

"Arsenal?" she said, mystified.

"Yes," Jack said in a voice that sounded more like his. "Everything is okay. Go home, and take care of your grandfather."

A short time later, Jack elected to fly. Since Arsenal couldn't fly, Jack waited until Natalie was out of sight before he took his first leap into the air. It took a little concentration, and after a few minutes of looking wobbly, Jack appeared as if he were a natural.

As soon as he had reached a decent height, he looked down at the city below, and he felt a sensation. It was a detected brain wave Kidneybean knew shouldn't have been on Earth. The creature was trapped inside

Wilkes-Barre Mountain, where fading Indian magic wouldn't contain it much longer.

For a brief instant, Jack thought of facing Xenyzyon and killing him before he could get free, thus saving the city from more danger. With all of the things that had befallen the city, allowing that thing to get out wouldn't be a wise choice, but it would bring the eight-member team together he saw in his visions. It would also bring out the evil that was working to ruin the city.

*Even with all of my abilities, I can't see the face of the one orchestrating this crime*, he thought, flying in the other direction. *There are powerful forces involved in this, and I am not happy.*

Jason Ostren parked his car, grabbed his freshly opened bag of Middleswarth sour cream potato chips, and closed the door. He walked up the slight hill and entered his cousin's house. Just as he closed the door, he heard the words "You aren't going to believe what I found."

Recalling all of the times he'd heard that, Jason knew where the next sentence was going to lead.

"Probably not," Jason said, playing along as he sat down on the couch.

"Well, I need you to go to the library with me," Ben said. "I found something on the mountain I need to research. I copied down the symbols and need you to help me."

"What kind of symbols?" Jason asked, opening the bag of chips and offering him some. "Alien? Indian?"

"Not sure," he replied, taking a handful. "I'm thinking Indian."

"Is that where we're headed now?" Jason asked as he started eating too.

"Soon as we finish lunch," he answered as he handed Jason the notebook.

Thinking there would only be one or two symbols, Jason was surprised by the number of pages Ben had filled. Briefly, he thought his cousin might have finally stumbled onto something, but then he thought, *Naw, he's been all over that mountain more times than I can recall. I know because I've been a few steps behind him each time.*

"I'm surprised you made it up there with the martial law imposed on the city," Jason said, taking another handful of chips. "I had to drive all the way past the Woodland's resort to get here."

"We can get out of Parsons the way you got in here, head up Jumper Road, go through Bear Creek, and take the long way around to get there," Ben suggested as Jason handed the notebook back to him.

"The same way we went when we were searching for those Indian relics," Jason said, recalling the trip. "Not knowing there was a lake out there, and we didn't have a boat."

"Yeah, but you've got to admit that was one hell of a bike ride," Ben said, recalling the ride. "And an awesome ride down the side of the mountain too."

"We had to be going at least thirty-plus miles an hour coming down that," Jason said, thinking about the rush he'd felt during that ride.

Several hours later, the four reached Wilkes-Barre Mountain, and by three o'clock, Jason was pulling off to the side of the road. They saw construction vehicles parked nearby and wondered what they were there for. As they started taking out their camping gear, Jason was the first to see the sign: Future Home of Dyna Cam Industries. He read it aloud.

"What?" Ben said, walking over to read the sign for himself. "When did this crap start? On my mountain!" *Not on my mountain*, he thought. Then he said, "Better get these symbols translated before they plow and bulldoze everything."

With a little less than an hour before the sun fully set, Ben, Michelle, Jason, and Amanda his girlfriend were on their way to the cave. Looking down the mountain, Amanda said, "Well, at least we'll get a good view of Wilkes-Barre tonight."

"You really think we'll have time to look down at the city?" Michelle asked, setting down her backpack. "You know we're going to be doing something we'll be complaining about until next time we come up here."

"Speaking of coming up here," Amanda said, "when are you and Ben going to buy land up here?"

Laughing, Michelle replied, "Jason and I were just talking about that earlier, and he said we ought to buy a double. That way, he could save on gas money."

Once they'd laid out all of their gear and set up the tent, Ben walked back to the cave, and just like before, it was blocked by the illusion. As he'd been the last one to trespass, Ben's footprints were still visible. He turned back to the group and motioned for them to follow.

One by one, each of them approached the illusion, and strangely, only Amanda was able to see through it.

"And you were in there?" she asked, sticking her head inside the cave.

"Yes," Ben said. "That's where I was when I discovered the symbols."

Pushing past him, Amanda said, "Jason, grab a flashlight. I've got to see this."

Doing as his girlfriend told him, Jason returned a few minutes later and followed her in for a look. He said, "Wow, there sure are a lot of these symbols. How long did it take you to copy all of this?"

"Same as it did the last time you asked," Ben replied. "A couple of hours. Hopefully with the books we got today at the library, this won't take us very long."

"And you brought your camera?" Michelle asked. She leaned in and kissed his cheek. "Good job, dear."

By midnight, Ben was the only one awake and still working to decipher the symbols. Jason wasn't sleeping but likely would be any minute. Stepping back to look over what he had completed, Ben thought he had enough of the symbols figured out to make an attempt to read them.

He was about to begin, when he heard both girls screaming. He dropped his tablet. Both men rushed to the tent and saw their girlfriends sitting up, trembling and terrified.

Rushing to Michelle's side, Ben asked, "What happened?"

"Ben, we've got to get out of here," she said, breathing hard. "You've got to stop what you're doing."

"What? Why?" he asked, looking over at Amanda, expecting to see her laugh.

"This stuff isn't meant for you to decode," Amanda said, shaking her head. "It's a prison. If you don't stop, you're going to let out an ancient evil, and we'll all be dead before we can get off this mountain."

"Ben, leave this stuff. Take me home," Michelle pleaded, taking his arm.

Looking at her and then out toward the cave, Amanda said, "Jason, let's go. We've got to get as far away from this thing as possible."

Jason didn't know what to say. In all of the times they'd gone out on expeditions, it was the first time something like that had occurred. He looked at his cousin and then at Amanda and said, "Come on. We're going home."

He knew Ben wouldn't like hearing those words, but Amanda was more important than his fame. He watched for a moment as Ben stood up and said, "Give me a moment to grab the library books, and we'll head out."

"Thanks, Ben," Jason said as he reached for the bucket of water to extinguish the fire.

Ben didn't reply as he helped put the fire out.

*Another dream dies hard*, he thought, walking back to Michelle. *And in my mind, the laughter continues.*

# CHAPTER 13

Dyna Cam Industries, Wilkes-Barre's and Luzerne County's largest employer, was founded in 1901 by Anderson Hampton and his three brothers. The company began in a small room in the back of Cyril Hampton's grocery store on Public Square, just down the road from the current thirty-five-story corporate building built after the 1972 flood. The brothers not only took and produced pictures at their father's grocery store but also designed and built their own camera to rival Kodak.

By 1906, the brothers had hired four other people: three to assist with the camera business and one to help run the grocery store. Together the seven men were able to build thirteen cameras a week, which they sold for 50 percent less than their competitors charged. In less than a year, the brothers hired another six people, and they began discussing expanding the business to meet the needs of the public. At that time, they moved out of the grocery store and into a larger warehouse just a few blocks away, south of Public Square, and hired thirty-five more people.

Once the warehouse was fully operational, Anderson took on the role of president and performed administrative duties instead of building the cameras. His brothers Levi and Eugene became vice presidents, while Chester Grant and Milton Kincaid, two of the first employees hired, became working foremen. Their jobs involved overseeing the work of the others and training new employees. Abe Linney, the third original hire, passed away in 1909 from a heart attack at the age of thirty-seven.

Another tragedy to strike the company was the death of Eugene Hampton, the second-youngest of the four brothers. His life ended at the hands of the Germans when they sank the *Lusitania*. Instead of taking over as president of the company the brothers elected to pass it on to his son. Eugene Thurman Hampton, at age of twenty-six, was in charge of Hampton Cameras, and he would continue in that role for the next thirteen years.

Cyril remained owner of the locally successful grocery business, which became known as the birthplace of Hampton Cameras. The original store operated on the corner of North Washington and Union Street, next to the high school. The newer second store opened on South Main Street across from Planters Peanut, another business that would become successful and known worldwide. In 1928, Cyril died at the age of sixty-one from lung cancer, and his two nephews, Matthew and Lucas, took over, with each of them running one of the stores.

As successful as Hampton Cameras was, the cameras were only sold in Pennsylvania, New Jersey, and New York. When the company stretched its business and bought property in Ohio, Illinois, and Tennessee, they really saw profits soar. By that time, the company, making more money than ever before, sought to expand all the way to the West Coast. The day before the stock market crashed in 1929, they opened their largest plant in downtown Los Angeles.

The following day, Eugene Thurman Hampton committed suicide when he learned that he'd lost more than $125,000, a little more than half of what he owned in the company. A week later, the new Los Angeles plant mysteriously caught fire. Before rebuilding could take place, an earthquake struck the area and destroyed the remaining segments of the building.

Without money to start a second rebuilding, the company struggled to sell the land, which took more than five years. It would be thirty years before Hampton Cameras was on the West Coast again.

Truman Caldicott became the next president; he had been with the company for the past eleven years and was the first college graduate with a business degree to reach the top position. Instead of trying to establish the company nationwide, he focused on keeping it in the Northeast, where it beat all other competition. The company also began designing movie cameras, and as the rumor went, they did so because the company itself couldn't be in California.

World War II brought Hampton Cameras out of the Depression just in time to go overseas with the fighting soldiers to record the countless deaths and atrocities committed. By January 1942, Hampton Cameras was the only company under contract with both the United States Army and the British Army. Toward the end of the war, a rumor circulated that a Hampton Camera had taken the first picture of Mussolini hanging with his lover and their driver after they were caught by the Italian mob.

With the invention of the television, Hampton Cameras branched out and began building their own sets after they bought a small company in Kentucky in 1953. Carl Lace, the new president, believed that one day televisions and cameras would be linked in a yet-to-be-discovered way.

Carl worked at the Pennsylvania School of Electrical Engineering and helped to build and design the Electronic Numerical Integrator and Computer, known as EINAC, shortly after the end of the Second World War. Besides the television, Carl was interested in having Hampton Cameras develop new technologies, such as the computer, though it would be more than ten years before his company built one of their own.

In 1965, Hampton introduced their first computer to the world, which didn't do what they expected. In 1967, they reintroduced the computer, which was smaller in size and twice as efficient. The second model was something the business world needed. When the United States landed on the moon, Hampton technologies helped get them there, take pictures, and record video. Shortly after that, Hampton Cameras began working on a smaller home version of their computer, and people flocked to the stores to purchase it in 1971.

A year later, Hampton Cameras bought out Dynamic Camera Industries. It was a move that would have caused Anderson Hampton to roll over in his grave. Carl Lace retired the day after the deal was finalized, and Gino Tarento, the former CEO, took over the new company. He didn't last more than a few years; the FBI had him removed when they learned he was linked to organized crime.

For the next ten years, the company had three CEOs, two of which died from health issues, while David Brandt Morris stepped down for undisclosed reasons. Kyle Brock took over operations soon after that, and by 1983, the company's profits doubled. In the early part of the century, most people in Wilkes-Barre worked in the region's mines; in the latter part of the century, nearly double that worked for Dynamic Camera Industries.

Dynamic Camera shortened its name to Dyna Cam Industries and designed more than just cameras. They designed computers, telephones, surveillance, and other electronic devices, passing Kodak as the leading company. The reason for the change, as the story went, was that the major stockholder wanted change—more money on his investment—so he installed a sapient dominant as CEO. Kyle's only power was that he was a business genius. The major stockholder's name was Lt. General Mason Colts.

A majority of top-secret government projects were awarded to Dyna Cam, who constructed six large warehouse-sized buildings in Wilkes-Barre to accommodate everything. The largest of the buildings was to be built just outside of the city, on Wilkes-Barre Mountain, where they could field-test in a more open area. There were also plans to renovate the Mineral Springs Mine complex as an underground testing facility.

Despite all of the good things Dyna Cam was doing for Wilkes-Barre and the surrounding communities, if the truth got out, it could ruin everything. The city had been shocked when Gino Tarento was removed from power. If Kyle Brock's secrets got out, the area's economy would collapse.

Making his way down the hallway was another off-the-books employee of Dyna Cam Industries, the elder brother of the president, Reverend Bradley Brock. Bradley was paid directly by Kyle. That was also how Bradley got the financial backing to do what he was planning for the city.

Bradley was the oldest of the four siblings. William Marcel Brock and Anna Setter Brock were his parents. They met at an early age and were married at fifteen. Two years later, Bradley and Selma, twins, were born first; however, Selma died at birth. Kyle was born twenty years later, and Susan came along nine years after that. Susan worked two jobs to put herself through school to become a journalist.

Reaching the lobby, Bradley saw two young people off to his right. They were having a discussion about seeing his brother. Taking a second glance, Bradley saw something unique about the woman's aura. Besides being a priest, Bradley also had practiced magic for most of his life, without one getting in the way of the other. Fewer than ten people living knew Bradley practiced religion and magic together.

"You think he's going to believe what we're going to tell him?" Ben asked as he stopped pacing.

"I'm not sure if I even believe you. We don't know how long we'll have to wait, if we even get to see him," Judy replied. "We've been waiting here most of the day. We don't have an appointment, and most likely, we'll be told to leave at five, when Mr. Brock leaves for the day, if he hasn't already."

"We've got to talk to him," Ben said, still hesitating to tell her about the voice that had suggested he speak with Brock. "Try the desk again," he said, shrugging and looking in that direction.

"Can I help you?" the priest said, walking up to them.

Startled by his sudden appearance, neither spoke as they looked at him.

"My name is Reverend Brock. You look as if you need help," he said, keeping his eyes on Judy.

Turning toward Ben, she replied, "Maybe we should tell him; he might be able to help us."

Ben didn't know how to respond. Telling a suspected crime boss about a monster in the woods was going to be hard enough. Trying to tell that same story to a man of the cloth who talked to God on a daily basis would be even harder. The priest would think he was a crackpot and have security remove them from the building.

"Father, Ben discovered something on the mountain that we think Mr. Brock needs to hear about," she said. "But because we don't have an appointment, we haven't been able to speak with him."

"What exactly did you discover on the mountain?" he asked, wondering how important the matter truly was.

After thinking about how he could say it properly, Ben just started speaking and hoped the story would sound right as he said it. "I found a cave—more like a tunnel—up on the mountain. I've been going up there since I was a kid, but oddly enough, I'd never been to that particular place before. When I was able to get a light on, I discovered strange symbols on the walls, and I returned later to decipher them."

"Were you able to understand any of it?" Father Brock asked. "Do you have any way to prove this?"

Reaching into his jacket pocket, Ben pulled out his folded papers, and he rummaged through them to show what he had discovered. "If

I had a table, I could organize this stuff a little better and give an easier explanation," he said, pulling out pages and handing them to Father Brock.

Looking at a few of the pages with some interest, Father Brock replied, "Is any of this related to the Indians who once lived in the area? I know that several tribes lived here at one time or another."

"I found a few books at the library that allowed me to decipher the symbols," Ben said. "You'll have to excuse me; all of this came about so fast that I didn't have any time to prepare anything official."

Nodding in an understanding way, Father Brock said, "This is very interesting. Are you here to tell my brother that you want the cave excavated for study purposes? Were there any artifacts discovered within?"

"No, there's something evil trapped by the Indian magic inside that cave. I know that's hard to believe, especially for a man of God, but I didn't come here to lie to a man like Kyle Brock," Ben said. "The reason I'm not up there now is that my girlfriend had a nightmare the first night we were camping. Her fear of the dream and its warning brought us here today."

"I must admit your story does have a fanciful ring to it, but I do believe that you aren't lying. Looking into your eyes, I can see the truth within your soul, and I agree that you wouldn't come here to lie to my brother," Bradley said. He looked toward the receptionist's desk and gestured. "Helen, phone Kyle, and tell him I'll be coming back up to see him, and I'm bringing company. And tell him it's urgent."

"Yes, Father," Helen replied, picking up the phone.

# CHAPTER 14

For the last thirty years, Bradley Brock had given his love to one woman: Astanna Syznchalla. To say the heat of their passion was like no other wouldn't have been exactly the right words. Astanna Syznchalla, in her true form, couldn't exist on the physical plane of Earth; it was too cold.

However, Bradley had figured out a way to change that. Then they would be together at last, and once he accomplished his goals, they would rule over the earth.

Astanna Syznchalla was a demoness who had been cast out of heaven with the rest of the angels when they lost the war. Just like the others, when she fell from the celestial place, she burned. Unlike the others, her flame was never extinguished, which kept her from walking the earth as her kin did. As burned as she was, her beauty was still far more than any human had ever seen.

Bradley had met her in Spain during World War II, when his plane was shot down over the coast. Astanna wasn't the woman he met who nursed him back to health; she came into his life later on. Sophie was the Spanish rebel who stole his heart, and for the first few months, they were in love.

She introduced him to magic, and they began working on a family, all of which ended badly. They planned to get married, but Sophie and his daughter died in the delivery room. Shortly after that, Astanna came into his life.

When the war ended and he returned to the States, Bradley traveled the country, spending time in Kansas City, Baltimore, Denver, San Diego, Carson City, and Tallahassee before making his way back to Wilkes-Barre. It had been a long time since he had seen anyone in his family; Kyle had been only a child when he'd left to fight in the war.

His little brother had grown to become a successful businessman, running Dyna Cam Industries, and from what he was told, he had a sister named Susan. Having never known her, Bradley didn't reach out to her when he returned. Kyle's money, power, and contacts called his name and seduced his greed.

By the time the two brothers finally met, Astanna had taught Bradley everything she thought he needed to know to be one of the strongest practitioners of magic in the world. During that time, she told him the tale of a man named Anton Gregor Lafosse.

Just like Bradley, Lafosse had sought the power that magic held; however, being nothing more than a sideshow magician, he'd failed to achieve it. The magic he'd yearned for and the power that came with it had taken control of his life and consumed him in ways that mortal man could never understand.

As Bradley recalled the stories, he remembered meeting him briefly in France at the airport. They'd spoken no words, but each had been aware of who the other was because of the forces teaching them.

"Lafosse was the only fool I've ever known who was beaten by this way of life. From whatever afterlife you're suffering, Anton, pay attention because this is what you do with true power. Learn from it!"

Whether or not Anton Gregor Lafosse was able to hear, Bradley never got a reply.

Bradley walked away from the window, reached the elevator, and pushed the button for the ground floor. Moments later, when he reached the lobby, he saw Wes standing at the receptionist's desk, trying to get a date. As he caught sight of Bradley, Wes gave her a wink and walked over to him.

"Took longer than expected," Wes said, slipping his tablet back into his pocket. "Everything okay?"

"Yes, it is," Bradley replied as they started walking toward the front doors. "But there's something else I've got to do."

"Yeah, I'm working on the speech for that," Wes said, stopping to open the door. "What's the something you've got to do?"

"I'll tell you in the van," Bradley answered, looking around for Ben and Judy. "Something that may be able to help our cause, but first, I need you to drop me off at the church. Pick me up in about an hour, and then take me up to the new Dyna Cam site in Wilkes-Barre Township."

"Wilkes-Barre Township?" Wes repeated. "What's up there?"

"Help," Bradley replied. "If all goes well. No more questions; I need to think."

The church, located not far from downtown Wilkes-Barre, had nearly been shut down due to lack of worshippers and money to maintain it. All of that had changed when Bradley borrowed the money from his brother. By 1986, it was fully restored, and an average Sunday service consisted of no fewer than two hundred people.

The majority of them had made their way through the prison system and were now working to have society forgive them of their sins. That was how Bradley had met Wes. Wes had been one of the first people to come to the church. Actually, he had been living there illegally when Bradley had come to look the place over.

Because of what they'd been doing to the city, the ten-minute drive took almost three times as long. Bradley didn't notice; he was deep in thought. Wes, however, knew the delay was keeping him from what he needed to do. That night, before the eleven o'clock news, Wes, in disguise, would come on television and announce to the world who they were and why they'd targeted Wilkes-Barre.

Making his way past all of the equipment, Bradley made his way up the back stairs to the small room at the end of the hallway. Once he entered, he locked the door and then took off his clothing. Once he was completely naked, he climbed the ladder in the left corner. Bradley pushed on the hatch at the top, entered the small room, and made his way over to the table in the center.

He took a match from a box, struck it, and then lit the white candle in the center of the table. As the flame heated the wick, Bradley knelt and waited the brief instant for the face of Astanna to appear. Seeing the details of her face emerge aroused him, and though he wasn't there for that, he couldn't control the feeling and wouldn't have turned her down.

"Focus past your desires, Bradley," Astanna said, looking directly at his rising organ and then at his face. "What is it you are contacting me for? Are your plans ahead of schedule?"

"No," Bradley answered. "They're moving accordingly, and the shield will soon be in place. In no time after that, the fires will be set to bring you here."

"And why are you here now?" Astanna asked. "For the other reason?"

He wanted to say yes—her touch and her kiss were perfect—but he knew he hadn't had time to fully heal from their last romantic encounter. Even with the protective spells and magical creams covering his body, a lot of his body hair had burned off. Creating the illusion of still having hair was becoming more and more burdensome, but he knew he couldn't stop it now that he was so close with his plans to rule Wilkes-Barre. He couldn't risk it.

"No," he answered. "Though I am not rejecting you, there is a beast trapped within a cave not far from here, and I seek to use it for our plans."

"And what would you have me do?" she asked, reaching out her hand and gently caressing him.

"Help me break the spells that keep this thing contained," Bradley answered, trying to remain focused.

"Let me think on it," she said as she slipped her arms around his waist.

More than an hour passed before Bradley made his way back down the ladder. As he recast the illusions on his face, Bradley did his best to ignore the pain from the first- and second-degree burns he felt on his lips, face, and other parts of his body she'd touched. Ten minutes later, he reached the van and heard Wes practicing his speech.

Opening the door, Bradley asked, "How's the speech going?"

"Just as long as I'm ready for tonight," Wes replied, starting the van.

Bradley and Wes weren't the only ones involved in the scheme to destroy the city; they were just the leaders out in the field. Kyle Brock was the money and the technology behind the plan, but he had a secret group he was answering to. Mason Colts and soon-to-be CIA director Siegfried Lauren were two of the names Bradley had heard whispered from time to time. He could have learned the others, but why? They would all bow and burn before Astanna anyway, so why bother?

Bradley had been brought on board to add mysticism and do what Kyle's hired assassins couldn't get away with. He'd then recruited a lot of the ex-convicts who came to his church. Just as Kyle had members behind the scenes whom he discussed matters with, Bradley did the same with Astanna, and none of them knew he intended to usurp Kyle's scheme. With Wilkes-Barre on its dying knees, Bradley would take over.

There was a reason Astanna Syznchalla sought Wilkes-Barre. She'd been one of the first fallen angels cast out of heaven. Lucifer, the archangel who'd led the revolt, had been the last one to fall, though he'd fallen the quickest and burned the brightest.

His impact was rumored to have been in the mountains just outside of Wilkes-Barre, at a place called the Seven Tubs Nature Area. Celestial beings calling themselves Die Veilen Augen meaning the many eyed ones, had told Astanna that Lucifer had bounced on impact and caused the creation of the seven waterfalls before making his way to the Garden of Eden.

Any scientist would have theorized that the tubs had been carved out by the last ice age, but on the other hand, had any of those scientists been alive to witness it? The followers of Lucifer who were higher up in the chain of command knew where the true impact had occurred. Whether or not it was true, Astanna wanted Wilkes-Barre for her seat of power. From there, she would expand her domain until it stretched across the entire American continent.

Bradley knew he and Astanna would have to deal with Kyle's forces as well as local superheroes, such as Quarrel and those rookies she'd been spotted with, but they weren't the true threat. More experienced heroes, such as the government-backed group the High Lords and a few out of New York, were more of a concern. At the moment, none of them had taken notice of the events unfolding in Wilkes-Barre.

"Where do you want me to drop you at?" Wes asked, driving up North Hampton Street.

Watching as they passed underneath the Interstate 81 bridges, Bradley answered, "On the side of the road, near the construction entrance. Drop me off, and I'll walk back."

"I can wait," Wes said, glancing at his watch. "I still have time."

"No," Bradley said. "In case things go wrong, I don't want you around. I left instructions back at the church. You'll need to contact my mistress and tell her what happened."

"Your mistress?" Wes repeated while thinking, *He's got a woman.*

"Yes," Bradley answered. "You have yet to meet her."

Pulling off to the side of the road, Wes said, "How long should I wait before I contact her?"

"Twenty-four hours," Bradley answered, opening the door. "Get the message out; let television spread the word."

After closing the door, Bradley watched as Wes drove off, and then he cast a few spells to locate the route Ben had described. Since Ben had been there the night before, nobody else had passed through the area, and Bradley had no problems in his search. While walking, Bradley noticed the mine fire burning near him.

*Something like this,* Bradley thought, walking toward the smoke rising out of the ground. *I can use this for my needs.*

What should have been a fairly quick walk took a little longer as Bradley investigated the burning ground. Stopping and kneeling down at the white-hot dirt, Bradley knew that this creature had to be included in his plans. Looking around, Bradley discovered a bent aluminum pole which had need for.

Bradley walked back over to the burning dirt, slammed the pole down, and spoke an incantation. As he finished, flames swirled out of the ground, and he watched with a smile as the fire covered the pole. Then he continued his walk to the cave.

Coming to a stop at the trail where Ben had jumped from the dogs, Bradley looked down at the pit and didn't see anything out of the ordinary. However, he was able to sense a little of the fading Indian magic within.

Making his way down the other side, Bradley saw the inside of the cave where Ben had done his work. Thinking back over what Ben had told him and his brother, he was surprised that someone without any type of true power would get that close to something so dangerous.

*His face has a familiarity to it*, Bradley thought. *Only brazen stupidity or a fearless desire to be recognized would cause someone like Ben to come to this area. The woman named Judy—I sensed she knew magic. How strong, I don't know, yet I'm not sensing any of that now, so why was she with him there and not here? Why didn't she come here and deal with this creature? Perhaps the answer is that she can't; she's not strong enough. Or this is a trap, but what would they gain from this? Who would suggest they set this up, and what if they failed to achieve their goal?*

Stepping in front of the entrance, Bradley cast a spell that allowed him to see things as they truly were through the illusion and look at what was within. The second spell he cast allowed Astanna to see through the heat within his aura. Her presence provided him with security. If things got out of control, she would be there to protect him.

Xenyzyon's scaly brown skin, which once had held muscle in place, now seemed to keep old age and flab poorly packaged. His wings looked as if they would tear in flight the moment Xenyzyon leaped into the air. However, the eyes—when they locked on Bradley, he saw there was still a fire burning inside. Xenyzyon needed to get out and prove he was still up to the task.

Bradley knew the magical cords holding the creature to the cavern wall wouldn't last more than a month. He also knew the creature might be too weak and useless by then. As he pondered his next move, the creature spoke, and saliva dripped from the three rows of teeth in his mouth.

"Are you a sacrifice?" Xenyzyon asked, reaching out to touch Bradley's face with his tongue.

Moving away, Bradley said, "No. How is it that you speak a language I can understand?"

"I am an ancient killing machine; adaptation is my best feature. Your language is quite simple. I have come to master the various Indian dialects," Xenyzyon answered. "After that, it was easy to hunt and feed, until they grew wise and trapped me within the soil, using some kind of trickery or strange technology. Had it not been for that, I would rule this land. As to what put me on this rock you call home, my masters chose to hunt my kind after they designed the next generation of my species. As superior as they were, we didn't go down easily. A planet-wide war raged on for our survival. As to who won, I don't know."

"Then can I assume there are others of your kind here?" Bradley asked, thinking that if he had to release all of them, his conquest of Wilkes-Barre would be over quickly.

"Thousands of your years ago, there might have been many of us," Xenyzyon replied, "but I fear that I am the only one of my species left, unless others found ways to escape or turn the tide of the war."

"How is it that you are still living?" Bradley asked. "Was this war fought on Earth?"

"No," Xenyzyon answered. "Your planet couldn't handle that level of genocide. The technology of my former masters is something your kind would not comprehend. I live because I took the opportunity to hide on board the flagship of my former masters, and once we reached the safety of space, I slaughtered them. My only fault was that I didn't know how to operate the craft, and after drifting aimlessly through space, the ship crashed here. I could have gone anywhere, but I sensed residue power residing in the seven waterfalls not far from here and chose this place to learn where it had originated. After several years of my freely hunting and killing the so-called top of the food chain, the Indians, working together, caused me to fall into this trap where you find me now."

"I know the power that you speak of," Bradley said. "It is something you could never understand. In time, I can change all of that. Because of your past, he will welcome you among his ranks. I have no doubt of that. My mistress is in league with Satan himself, and an introduction wouldn't be out of the question. But first, I have a request to ask of you."

"A request?" Xenyzyon repeated. "After you let me out, you want me to do what?"

"What you do best. What you were made to do," Bradley answered. "There is a large city not far from here. Go there to feed and regain your strength. After you've seen the sights and sharpened your talons, return here, and I will discuss what we can accomplish together."

Xenyzyon nodded and replied, "I will seek out the city and feed. During that time, I will think over your offer. If I don't return, then I never will. Much change has occurred since my imprisonment began."

"One more hell spawn unleashed upon the world," Bradley said, turning away from Xenyzyon. "Remain still; it's going to get hot in here."

"Fire?" Xenyzyon said. "I do not fear fire."

"This fire you will," Bradley said, walking away from the cave. "This fire is unlike anything you've ever seen or experienced before."

Returning to the bent aluminum pole he'd left in the ground, Bradley rubbed his hands together, and upon kneeling, he said, "My dear mistress, I am ready to take your power into my hands."

The flicker of white light that flashed across the orange flame informed Bradley that Astanna had heard and answered his prayer. Showing no fear or hesitation, Bradley pulled out the burning-hot pole, and though there was warmth, his body suffered little damage. When he reached the front of the cave ten minutes later, Bradley struck the barrier.

The explosion knocked Bradley back into Ben's camping area, while Xenyzyon was violently shot out the other end of the cave. The magical barrier created by the Indians was no more, and their enemy Xenyzyon was now free. Stretching his wings for the first time in centuries caused Xenyzyon great pain. Gazing at the man who'd set him free, Xenyzyon lifted off of the ground and got his first glimpse of Wilkes-Barre.

# CHAPTER 15

Shortly after Bradley freed Xenyzyon from the mountain, Wes and his men began their broadcast. The room they were using was located in a vacant building not far from Old Public Square. The last tenants of the building, which had been built in 1910, had been a toy store and an upstairs dentist office, both of which had gone out of business more than a decade earlier.

Prior to being homeless and addicted to various drugs, Wes had served in the United States Army and been stationed in West Germany. It hadn't taken him long to learn to speak German and become familiar with the customs as well as the histories of the various terrorist organizations operating there.

The one that caught his attention the most had started out as a small-time group. They deceived the public into thinking they were nothing more than a day care service, taking care of the children of rich diplomats at the Guten Tag Gang day care center. When they made their move, the Guten Tag Gang took the children hostage.

The politicians immediately paid the ransom, and as promised, the gang returned their children. However, less than twenty-four hours later, the children were all dead from poisoned food the gang had fed them. By the time the authorities moved in, the gang had split up and gone underground.

Though none of the members were ever captured, Wes was confident that none of them had gone into hiding in the United States. Originally, Wes and his superiors had discussed using a Middle Eastern group like those in Iran that had been involved in taking American hostages. However, since he couldn't speak Farsi or any Middle Eastern language, they chose the German group. Because Wes had learned enough of the German language to develop an accent, he knew he could dress and play the part.

Throughout Luzerne County, every channel showed the same thing. The regular programming faded out, and a man named Heinrich Waffen stepped into view and began speaking. "*Achtung*! *Achtung*, citizens of Wilkes-Barre! Because of the actions of the United States, Wilkes-Barre has been chosen as the location of the first of many battles in your country. We are like the werewolves of old. Though the head of our leader has been removed, we are still a deadly threat. Guten Tag is fully prepared to cause the death and destruction of all those in our way. We intend to bring America to its knees, and your blood will write the first chapters in this war!"

# CHAPTER 16

Susan K. Thomas sat up, stretched, and looked around the empty theater. She had come there to see a movie, and just like last time, she'd slept through it.

"Definitely too many late nights as Quarrel," she said, sitting up even more as she heard a man snoring.

Getting up from her seat, she picked up her backpack and said, "I wonder how he spends his nights."

She took three steps, when another man came running in. She watched as he approached the sleeping man and called out, "Marc! Marc, you aren't going to believe this. You've got to get up."

Sitting up, the muscular man stretched and looked back as his brother reached the section where he sat. "Believe what, Dan?" Marc asked.

"Marc, you've got to see this," his brother said, pointing. "This is what you were looking for. You said a bank robber wasn't good enough to start your career. Well, this is big."

"What are you talking about?" Susan K. asked, stopping next to Dan.

Looking at her and then back to his brother, Dan said, "There's a monster flying around the parking lot. I know that sounds fake, but take a look around the room. How many people were in here when you walked in?"

Shrugging, Marc answered, "I don't know. There were a few people in here—maybe ten or fifteen."

"What do you mean a monster?" Susan K. asked. "Are you serious?"

"Yes, dead serious. Look, lady, if I were you, I'd stay in here," Dan said. Then he added, "Marc, this is your chance. Are you ready for this?"

"Yeah, we're professionals," Marc said. "We've been doing this for a while."

"Professionals, huh?" she said, creating her energy bow. "Do you have any names?"

"Uh, um, Splitscreen and Duplex," Marc answered, stunned by what he'd just witnessed. He pointed to his brother. "I'm Duplex, and he's Splitscreen."

"Boy, I gotta tell you," she said, "ever since my return from Japan, superheroes have been popping out of the woodwork. Well, let me get into costume. I can see by the looks on your faces that you already know who I am."

Her energy bow disappeared, and the brothers stood there watching as she ran off to the women's restroom to assume her crime-fighting identity. Slapping his brother in the chest, Marc said, "Quarrel! Can you believe it? We're going to fight crime alongside Quarrel. Dan, this is it—the big event you've been waiting for!"

"Ouch," he said. "Watch it. I know, I know. It's Quarrel."

Marc flexed his muscles, and his skin took on a silvery metallic color. He said, "Guess I'd better get ready too—ready for the debut of Duplex."

"Yeah, well, we're using my power to teleport," Dan said. "I haven't come up with an idea for a costume yet, so we're going to use my way of teleporting."

"Why not just go out through the fire exit?" Duplex asked, pointing it out. "Where is this thing at?"

"Near Sears," Dan answered. "The other side of the mall. But it was also flying."

"This thing can fly?" Quarrel said, returning. "I've got to see this thing."

"Well, I was going to use a computer monitor in Radio Shack to teleport," Dan said, "but I'll use one of the video game monitors here."

"Teleport?" Quarrel repeated. "You mean like on *Star Trek*?"

"Yes," Splitscreen answered. "Besides illusions, I can teleport through any monitor, whether or not it's turned on. Marc can teleport too, but not in such an awesome manner as me."

"You have the awesome teleporting ability and I have the muscle," Marc added, as he flexed his arms.

"How far can you go?" she asked.

"Not sure," Splitscreen answered, shrugging. "I never tried to find out."

"Well, now's not the time," Duplex said, eager to get out. "This thing had better be what you said it was."

"Marc, I'm telling you. I'm not lying," Splitscreen said as they stopped in front of a Galaxian video game. "So get ready."

The light from the video game spilled out of the monitor, and as each color surrounded them, they began to fade out. The pull into the machine was like that of a gentle breeze, and the moment they disappeared from the theater, they materialized in the parking lot on the right side of the Giant Market building, where they got their first glimpse of the creature.

Even though he was in the air and more than fifty yards away, Xenyzyon still had the appearance of a deadly killing machine. As old as he was, Xenyzyon was still more fearsome than what the people shopping ever would have expected. In the fifteen minutes he'd been attacking and feeding, many people foolishly had flocked to watch.

Traffic on Mundy Street and Kidder Street had become blocked by curiosity seekers, who ended up becoming Xenyzyon's next snack. Falling half-eaten bodies added to the chaos among the people who sought to get away but couldn't because of the traffic jams on both roads and in both directions.

"This has to stop," Marc said, taking steps in the creature's direction. "Splitscreen, keep Quarrel close. I don't want to see either of you get hurt."

"What?" Quarrel said, shocked by his statement. "What do you mean keep me close? I've been doing this a lot longer than you. Thanks for being worried, but maybe you ought to keep an eye on your brother."

"Hey, wait a minute," Splitscreen said. "Neither of you has to keep an eye on me. I'm not sure if my illusions will work on a creature like that. But I can make sure fewer people want a better look at it."

Quarrel and Duplex left Splitscreen to do whatever he could to keep Xenyzyon from killing any more people. Quarrel released five bolts of energy in the hopes of getting Xenyzyon's attention.

Spinning around in midair, Xenyzyon spotted Quarrel as she fired. Seeing the white bolts of energy coming at him, Xenyzyon attempted to swat them, but he missed and was surprised when each of them bounced and popped against his leathery skin.

"Let me try this," Duplex said, picking up the nearest vehicle.

As Xenyzyon sailed toward them, Duplex threw the car and was surprised when Xenyzyon knocked it away. Stopping just yards away, the creature flapped his wings and scanned the two.

"New participants," Xenyzyon remarked, licking his lips. "Food that fights back—how interesting."

Moving in closer, Xenyzyon intended to use his mouth to rip Quarrel in half; however, Duplex stepped in the way and struck him as hard as possible in the left side of his jaw. The force of the blow knocked Xenyzyon to the ground, and he tumbled to a stop several feet away.

Stepping in front of Quarrel, Duplex said, "I'm going to take care of this thing once and for all."

Before Quarrel could comment, Duplex reached out to grab Xenyzyon, but the creature moved at a speed that surprised him. Duplex's ability to teleport left Xenyzyon equally surprised. Duplex landed in a position that enabled him to maintain his grip on Xenyzyon's right wing, which allowed him to use all of the force he could.

Stumbling backward, Xenyzyon struggled to break free of Duplex as both tumbled through the parking lot. Vehicles and streetlamps became their victims, falling over and bending upon impact as the two collided with them.

"This is Susan Brock, reporting to you from the Wyoming Valley Mall, just above the second Mundy Street entrance. What you are seeing is real, but exactly what you are seeing, nobody seems to know. Whether or not this is connected to the pirated broadcast is also unknown. Witnesses say a creature came from the mountain shortly after an explosion occurred there. On the scene, battling this monster, as much as they're trying to help, they're basically doing nothing more than crowd control, the exception being the armored hero. Thanks to his metallic skin and strength, he has been able to stand up to this monster. Standing here with me now is one of the team's newest members. Splitscreen, where were you when all of this began? Were you out shopping or driving by?"

"I was shopping in Hess's, when I saw that thing fly down off the mountain. I just happened to be walking past the doors and saw it,"

Splitscreen replied. "That's when I went back to the movies to find my brother."

"Is that where he works?" Susan asked, holding the microphone out to him.

"No, he bought a ticket," he answered, leaning into the microphone. "But he was sleeping when I got there."

"And the rest of the group?" Susan asked. "Where was Quarrel?"

"She was at the movie with my brother," he answered, wondering if he should have said it that way.

"Are you saying that Quarrel and your brother are a couple?" Susan asked, looking at Duplex. "And is Duplex your brother?"

"Yes, he is," Splitscreen replied. "And no, they are not. I went to the theater to get my brother, and Quarrel just happened to be there out of costume. That's how we met her."

Watching as Quarrel limped over to the shelter where they were standing, Susan turned to her and asked, "Quarrel, Susan Brock here. Can you tell us what happened?"

"We're attempting to take on a lot more than we can handle," she answered, leaning up against a taxi as sweat poured off of her face.

"How did you injure your leg?" Susan asked, looking at Quarrel's injury.

"I was diving behind a car to get away from that thing," she answered. "I'm lucky Duplex was there to save me, or it would have been a lot worse."

"It's happening," Ron said, turning the volume up on Judy's television.

"Now what do we do?" Ben asked nervously as he watched Xenyzyon circle the mall.

"This is your monster, Ben," a voice at the top of the stairs replied. "You found it; you brought us together; and now you must face it, be there, and kill it."

"Fight that?" he said, looking back at the television. "That thing is out of my league."

"Then I suppose you could stay here," the voice suggested. "Give up the name, and let somebody else save the world as Shockwave."

"Mike?" Ron said, moving toward the stairs. "Is that you? Are you fully healed?"

"I am not who you think I am," Kidneybean replied, "but you will have your leader soon. The process is almost complete. When it is done, both of us will arrive to clean up this mess."

"Both of you?" Star asked. "Who else is up there?"

Shrugging, Ron looked up the steps and saw a purplish figure move just out of his sight. The figure said, "Go now. The city is expecting you to protect them. The others are in need of your help."

"What about Quarrel?" Ben asked, pulling his mask out of his pocket.

"I don't know," Star answered, shrugging. "I guess it's just the four of us."

"No. According to the news, she's already there," Ron said, picking his mask up off the coffee table. "Who knows? Maybe the military will be there too by the time we get there, and we'll just have to do cleanup."

"No," Kidneybean said. "The military has been ordered to stand down. Though I cannot see the forces at work behind this, strong magic is at work."

"Strong magic?" Ron repeated. He looked at Judy. "That's why you're on our side."

"Yes," Kidneybean answered, "she makes your leader a stronger Arsenal—in most cases. While he'd still alive."

*Lucky him*, Ben thought. *I wonder where I could get help like that. Who makes me a stronger Shockwave?*

"Synapsis," Kidneybean answered in response to his thought. "But the rest of that explanation won't be given today."

Judy's magic brought the team into the mall parking lot alongside a Long John Silver's located across from Sears. After a few moments of regaining their composure, they were startled by all of the people standing and watching.

"People!" Power of Justice yelled. "Evacuate the area! This thing isn't a publicity stunt."

Most of the people ignored him and continued to observe the fight between Duplex and Xenyzyon. No matter what he said, they all believed they were far enough away and that the creature couldn't get every one of them.

Judy was the only one there who'd faced Xenyzyon before, though only in a dream. His large, pointy football-shaped head and three rows of razor-sharp teeth were just as terrifying in person. She tried to be as brave as she had been in the field as she ran through the spells she knew. The burst of energy that flew from her fingertips struck Xenyzyon's left wing, knocking him from the sky.

Screaming from the flames, he struggled to put out the fire as Duplex jumped on him and started punching. With each blow, Xenyzyon saw stars. Using as much force as he could muster, Xenyzyon grabbed Duplex and threw him, yelling, "Enough! Get off of me!"

Using all of his strength, Xenyzyon managed to throw him down the hill into the parking lot of Pine Mall, the shopping area nearest to the main mall. Seeing Judy dressed in black and standing next to Power of Justice, Xenyzyon flew as hard as he could to reach her.

"Heads up!" Shockwave yelled, seeing Xenyzyon moving quickly toward them.

Showing no fear, Judy stood her ground, preparing to strike him with another spell. Power of Justice didn't let her finish, as he rushed in and pulled her out of the way.

"What are you doing?" Judy yelled, looking up at him. "You ruined the spell! I had it!"

Coming to a hard stop, Xenyzyon whirled around and said, "Quarrelling with your protector—interesting. He is not the one from your dream. Where is your Iron Weapon now?"

Popping out of nowhere, Duplex appeared just off to Xenyzyon's left and said, "You mean me? I'm not finished with you yet."

Even in his armored form, Duplex's endurance was beginning to fail him; he was sweating and breathing hard. With all of the training he'd done, he'd never expected anything like this. Xenyzyon could see he was tired, and he intended to use it to his advantage; however, after being trapped in the mountain for such a long time, he wasn't in the best shape either.

Rising up into the air with his wings fully extended, he was disrupted by a strange noise and looked over his shoulder along with everyone else. It was as if the sound was meant to be a distraction. But who or what had the power to get everyone to stop and look?

It was Kidneybean, levitating in the air, rising up over Sears. He looked down at Xenyzyon and the rest of the team. His mind scanned the thoughts of all those in the vicinity, and he knew the fear and grief of those who'd died at the hands of the creature. The fight had brought the team together, and now, as the core members of the Knight Shift, they could work to bring the problems in Wilkes-Barre to an end.

"Xenyzyon, your attack is over!" Kidneybean said in a voice that sounded like a mixture of his and Arsenal's.

Swatting Duplex out of his way, Xenyzyon yelled, "Nay!" He lunged at Judy, picked her up, and rose up into the sky as he kept his eyes locked on his purple foe. "This woman is the key to your power, and now you all can watch as I kill her."

Judy screamed as Xenyzyon attempted to squeeze the life from her body. He raised her up to his mouth, and his tongue touched her face. Resisting as much as she could, Judy mentally ran through her spells. When she found the one she believed would save her and do the most damage to Xenyzyon, she cast it.

His jaws stretched back, and as his foul breath filled the air, she spoke words that sent a chunk of ice the size of a baseball deep into his mouth. Xenyzyon choked as he dropped Judy, and Kidneybean hit him hard with a burst of purple energy.

"Attention, Michael Lanesra. This is Captain Kidneybean, signing off. Please report to the helm," he said as his body began to vibrate. "Arsenal, I'm signing off. The helm is yours. Don't screw it up any time soon."

Kidneybean kept his focus on holding Xenyzyon in place as his body separated from Arsenal's, causing him to land on the ground moments before Judy did. Seeing her fall, he rushed to catch her, and as he slid on his knees underneath, she landed in his arms. At the same moment, Xenyzyon managed to break free as Duplex appeared on his back, and with a boost of energy fueled by anger and rage, Duplex started pounding until he saw blood.

Each of Duplex's blows was to the back of Xenyzyon's head, and the hits added to the pain and throbbing he was already suffering from. As Xenyzyon reached for Duplex, Kidneybean struck him directly in the face with a second burst of purple plasma.

"Can you feel it?" Kidneybean asked, applying more pressure. "It's called the Mind Helmet. It's pure psionic plasma squeezing and burning your mind until I've squashed the damn thing into nothing! Know me for what I am: Kidneybean, your destroyer!"

Xenyzyon wrestled with the pain as he fought to break free, but the more he fought, the harder Kidneybean applied the psionic weapon. Adding to Xenyzyon's problem were the bolts of energy Quarrel was firing at him. Xenyzyon knew they were harmless, but they kept him from dealing with the one crushing his brain.

Falling from his position on Xenyzyon, Duplex landed on the pavement. He grabbed the nearest lamppost and hurled it at the creature. The lamppost struck Xenyzyon in the back of his neck just as Kidneybean's Mind Helmut caused his brain to explode.

"It's all over, Judy," Arsenal said as he held her face. He gently kissed her. "Now we can go home."

"But if Kidneybean is gone, why are your eyes still purple?" she asked in between kisses.

Reaching into his trench coat pocket, he pulled out a pair of sunglasses and said, "Almost forgot. My eyes are purple because it's a reminder that he's in there watching."

# CHAPTER 17

In the small pocket dimension of hellfire located deep within the sun, Astanna Syznchalla paced as she looked over the city of Wilkes-Barre. Bradley's plan to use the beast Xenyzyon to wreak havoc on the city had failed. The heroes operating there had united and won a major victory. It was the first serious setback in their planned takeover. To make sure that was the only setback, Astanna decided to search the city and enlist others to her cause.

The first of the recruits was a man who'd served in an army more than forty years ago, when his führer had attempted to take over the world. Astanna had been well aware of Helmet von Kragen since then; she thought him interesting and a unique murderer. His experience at world conquest didn't interest her; it was his ability to manipulate and corrupt human flesh that she sought. Helmet von Kragen was one of the oldest known sapient dominants in the world, and his power impressed her.

When the Nazi war machine had been defeated in 1945, a large group of high-ranking members had been put on trial for what they'd done. Helmet Von Kragen was not part of that punishment process, nor was the doctor part of Paperclip or any of the other secret projects that brought German scientists into the United States.

Helmet was part of something a lot more secretive, and what he'd done to the Jews was wicked. The United States military was interested in using his unique abilities to battle the threat of Communism.

To make ends meet, Helmut often performed abortions on the city's hookers, and from time to time, he would also claim one for himself. His twisted perversions were only fulfilled when he used his abilities to keep screaming and resisting to a minimum. Often, when he was through, he would simply kill off the woman and dump the body in the river.

Astanna had been watching Helmut for quite some time, and when he came to Wilkes-Barre, she knew he was the soldier she would need to achieve victory. Bradley had the magic, but Helmut was the one she would enlist to create the army for her conquest.

The woman lying on the table had been sedated through the powers of Von Kragen. She needed his help in getting rid of a pregnancy she didn't want and couldn't afford. The old German, who sounded crazy at times, always agreed to help any of the streetwalkers. As far as she knew, he never asked for money.

Unzipping his trousers, Helmut was about to climb on top of her, when he spotted what appeared to be a feminine image forming in the candlelight. At first, he didn't pay much attention to it, thinking it was just a trick in his mind, but then it started growing. As it fell across his right shoulder, he stopped his movement. The image took on a more feminine form.

"Is that how you fulfill your desires?" Astanna asked as the rest of her form stretched out of the flame. "Remove the remainder of your clothing, and take a real woman—if you can handle the heat."

Doing as she said, Helmet undressed and approached as sweat and body heat steamed up his glasses. He took them off and reached for Astanna's body. The heat her body generated didn't weaken his determination to have his pleasures released into her. The intensity of the heat caused some discomfort but didn't take away from his size. Even when he could smell the hair in that region burning, he kept pushing. Minutes later, when Helmut finished, she made the offer to him.

"There was only one man I ever took orders from, and may Der Führer rest in peace," Helmut said, giving the Nazi salute. "With that being said, I would never dream of doing what we are doing with Der Führer. Times have changed. I will now swear allegiance to you and only you."

"Understood," she said, looking at the woman lying on the table. "Get rid of that filth, and I will know that you are faithful. Do not look for scum like that again, or I will send you to a place where suffering is the devil's pleasure."

"Yes," he said, reaching for his glasses.

"From now on, Helmut von Kragen, I am your mistress," Astanna declared, watching as he reached for his clothing. "You will obey no others but me!"

"Yes, Mistress," Helmut said as he saluted her.

"Very good," she said as Helmut put his pants on.

# CHAPTER 18

In the vastness of space, there existed an unknown substance that appeared to be holding the universe and everything within it together. It had come to be called dark matter, though for a long time, scientists had been unable to prove it actually existed.

Proof of the substance finally had come in the care of a meteor that Dyna Cam scientists had discovered five years ago on an ice shelf off the coast of the South Pole.

Though the scientists had known dark matter existed, they'd never suspected to find it in the form they did. They'd discovered the substance within the stone and taken it to Wilkes-Barre for further research. After five years of heavy research and millions of dollars, Mason Colts had confidence that it could be injected into men to transform them into living weapons for the military to use in dealing with any futuristic threat to Earth or the United States.

The scientists also learned that certain sapient dominants were born with that same dark energy running through their DNA. Shadow Master was one of them. Rachael Lepanto and Larry Stontz had that same genetic imprint in their DNA, but it had yet to manifest itself. They were part of Lt. General Mason Colt's 109th, stationed in Wilkes-Barre at the Kingston Armory.

The first project, Nightbringer, involved the matter being injected into human test subjects. They injected seven candidates, all of whom were members of the 109th and known to Mason Colts. Each of the seven had within his or her DNA the cells that would create the same dark energy, but for some unknown reason, the matter had yet to manifest itself. According to Colts, Nightbringer was going to change that.

Iron Man was the second project, which came about by accident. Inside the meteor, the scientists also discovered a strange new metal that was the by-product of the dark energy. Whether or not all of the dark energy in the universe was capable of producing the by-product was unknown, but the metal within the meteor was stronger than steel and appeared to be quasi-sentient as well.

After research, the scientists decided the metal should be used to create a new class of indestructible weapons to battle any futuristic threats. They conducted tests to find a way to replicate the material so they would have enough of it. One day an accident occurred: a scientist spilled the scalding liquid on his foot.

As expected, the liquid burned off the skin, and the scientist died as he watched the scalding metal consume the bones of his foot. When the others arrived, they saw how the super steel had covered all of the bones of his foot. That discovery changed their concept of weapons. Instead of creating unbreakable machines, they would use the super steel to cover the bones of the test subjects. They just needed to find a process to apply it safely and keep the subjects alive.

From the start of the projects, the top scientist was Dr. Arab Shpagh, a Middle Easterner who was born a sapient dominant. As the story went, by the age of five, Arab's IQ registered at three hundred, with the potential of going three times as high. Most, however, believed he was not a genius but more of a mad scientist, and several countries treated him as such.

If caught in China, he was to be executed on sight. In Russia, they threatened to send him to Siberia. The United States did not agree with that and refused to let such talent go to waste. Just like Helmut von Kragen, Dr. Shpagh was brought in secretly by Mason Colts to work at Dyna Cam Industries.

By the time both Iron Man and Nightbringer were ready for human testing, the seven people Colts had selected had been whittled down to Larry Stontz and Rachael Lepanto. Allan Phile, Gregory Elking, Danielle Zmythe, Hector Chavez, and Cecil Karr all had been killed in classified combat missions in the Middle East within the span of three years.

"Here we are in the Coal Street Park Field, home of the Wilkes-Barre Giants, who are playing host to the Wilkes-Barre Marauders," Marc said, tossing a football into the air.

"Yeah, and this time, the Marauders will win," Ben declared as he and his two partners took to their side of the field.

"Which of us is going to run it?" Larry asked, looking to his left at his partners.

"I'll take it," Dan said, patting his chest.

"Good, 'cause here it comes," Ben said, watching as the ball sailed through the air.

"I've got it!" Dan yelled. He caught it and took off up the field.

He managed to get fifteen yards before his brother and their friend Floyd Lymans tackled him. Slowly, he got to his feet and made his way over to where his partners were waiting in a huddle. He said, "Here's the plan. I'll quarter. Ben, you go five and cut left. Larry, you go long and cut at the fifty. Whoever is open will get it."

***

"Which one is he?" Ace asked, looking down at them from the top of the hill.

"He's the one wearing the Houston Oilers jersey," Majestic Beauty answered, pointing him out.

"Larry's the only one we're taking, right?" Razor asked, cracking his knuckles.

"Yeah, he's the only one. Do what you like with the others; just don't let them scream too loudly," she said, eager to fight. "Remember, they've got to think we're German terrorists, so try to act German—whatever that means."

"Don't worry about them screaming; they'll be too scared for that when they see my trolls," Troll King remarked, unbuttoning his trench coat jacket.

"Just don't make too many of those creepy things," Ace said. He got a strange feeling from them.

"Too many of those creepy things? I'll make just enough to get the job done, whatever that number might be," he said. He thought, *Which will be enough to make you crap your pants.*

"Well, if everybody's ready, let's get the party started," Majestic Beauty said, getting in the van.

"I'm ready. Let's do it," Razor said, following Ace into the back of the van.

"Hey, you can't drive that through here!" Dan shouted to the driver as the van drove out into their play area.

"Oh, sorry," he said, sticking his head out the window. "I'm kinda lost and thought you guys could help me."

Larry immediately recognized the voice and knew the man wasn't somebody who was lost and looking for directions. The driver was someone he knew, and most likely, his other former partners were either in the van or nearby.

"This isn't going to be good," Larry said, taking the ball from Jason.

"What are you going to do?" Jason said, letting go.

"Save our lives, especially mine," Larry answered, throwing the football at Troll King.

"Larry!" Floyd yelled as the ball struck Troll King in the face.

"Everybody run!" Larry ordered. "Get the hell out of here! This is a trick!"

Suddenly, the doors of the van slid open, and Majestic Beauty and the others stepped out.

"Guten Tag. *Geben sie uns* Larry Stontz, and we'll allow you all to live," Majestic Beauty said in her best German accent.

"Larry?" Marc said, looking at his friend as he stepped closer to the van. "All of this for Larry? When did you join the circus?"

"You're very funny," Razor, the big, bald, muscular brute, said, springing from the van. He struck Marc with his razor-sharp fist, knocking him to the ground.

The force of the blow left cuts on Marc's face, and his head spun as he slowly struggled to his feet. He said, "I hope you're ready for what's coming next."

The words fell on deaf ears. As Razor took another swing at Marc, Marc's skin took on a brick-red color. Though Razor's punch would have dented a tank, Duplex didn't think Razor was a real problem. Unlike during his battle with Xenyzyon, he didn't believe he would need to use his hardest form. Also, his red-brick form was the one he'd been training with most.

"Makes things a little fairer. Don't you think?" Duplex asked, catching Razor's fist.

"Doesn't even out the sides at all. We're taking Stontz, and that's final," Razor said, pushing the hero back.

"Glad you think that way," Duplex said as he disappeared.

Whirling around, Razor looked to see where his opponent had gone, and in doing so, he became disoriented.

"Looking for me?" Duplex asked, reappearing behind him. He knocked Razor into a grove of trees. "Like I told you, this won't be easy. Our strength appears to be equal, but our powers are vastly different, and you won't be taking any friend of mine!"

"Guten Tag. You are the one called Shockwave, are you not?" Ace inquired, closing in on him.

"What's it to you?" Ben nervously asked, realizing how outmatched he was.

"Very important. Allow me to introduce myself. My name is Ace, and from this point on, you and I are adversaries," he said, shooting reddish spade-shaped energy from his hands at Ben.

Stumbling backward, Ben tried to figure out how his foe knew his secret identity.

Ace continued his taunting attack. "With a name like Shockwave, I was expecting you to be a force to reckon with. I guess that would be asking too much from a guy who no doubt took his name from a comic book character."

"Why don't we go fist to fist? I'd be glad to explain it to you," Ben said, trying not to show how surprised he was.

"This is much more entertaining," Ace answered, taunting Ben, knowing he was the better man.

*This isn't looking good*, Dan thought as he moved toward a group of trees. *Especially since I have to go to the bathroom at a time like this.*

Moments later, when he stepped out, ready to fight, his thoughts immediately went to his illusory powers. Creating the illusion of being invisible, Dan quietly moved toward the van, where a redheaded female acted as if she were in command.

After listening for a few minutes, he concentrated on creating three police cars coming down Coal Street toward them.

The ugly man in the trench coat was the first to notice the cars. "Majestic!" Troll King yelled, pointing. "Cops!"

"It's not real," she said, not hearing any sound coming from the direction of the police cars. "Find the illusionist; he's behind this."

"You got it," Troll King said, creating more trolls with the intention of finding Larry.

"Guess that wasn't such a smart thing to do," Dan said as she made her way toward him. He stepped back into the bushes. "Well, whoever this woman is, she won't be using those sai on me. Need to find a way to take her out quickly."

His thinking worked out, and Majestic Beauty stopped dead in her tracks as she and Arsenal stood face-to-face.

"You," she said, stepping back away from Arsenal. "The press says you're the man to beat. Well, I don't buy that. Bring it on!"

As she took up a defensive position with her sai, Dan struck her from behind and took her out with a single blow to the back of her head.

"That ought to tip the odds in our favor," he said, kneeling down and removing her bootlaces, which he used to tie her up.

"Fleeing?" Ace asked, taunting Larry, who was trying to escape.

"Fleeing? I dropped out. I want nothing to do with the agency anymore," Larry answered, walking backward at a quickened pace.

"You can't drop out, Larry. Once you're in, you're in," Ace said. "The boss has one last job for you."

"Let him get somebody else!" Larry answered, not knowing that Troll King and his trolls were starting to circle.

"Tell him yourself," Troll King said as three of the trolls grabbed him and carried him back to the van.

Larry resisted and struggled to get free, but because of the strength of the trolls and their grip, there was nothing Larry could do other than hope one of his friends would help. He had no such luck; the trolls got him into the van and kept him there as Troll King called to his partners.

"Where's Majestic at?" Ace said, quickly getting into the van.

"Can't find her," Razor answered, slamming the side door shut. "Let's just get the hell out of here. She can take care of herself."

"Let's hope so. Brock will be pissed if she can't," Troll King said, driving off.

"Hey, Officer, over here!" Dan yelled as he motioned to the policemen.

"Dan!" Duplex yelled, running over to him.

"Not all of them got away," Dan said, pointing to an unconscious Majestic Beauty.

"Who are you?" Detective Julius Arbinovawitz asked, looking Dan over.

"He's my brother," Duplex answered, remaining in his form.

"And who is she?" Julius asked, picking up one of Majestic Beauty's sai.

"I don't know. I've never seen her before," Dan answered, shrugging. "But I bet she's working for Guten Tag."

*Guten Tag?* Julius thought, recalling the broadcast he'd seen. "I'm not sure about that since I've never seen any reports on them. When we actually have proof that they are involved in all of this, then we'll take it from there."

"What if she has a German accent?" Duplex asked. "Can we then assume she is proof Guten Tag is involved in all of this?"

"It will put us a lot closer to getting the answers we need," Julius answered as Majestic Beauty started to come around. "And put an end to all of this."

As Majestic Beauty opened her eyes, she recalled what Julius had said and what her orders were, and she said in her best German accent, "*Wer bist du?*"

"Who are you?" Julius asked as she touched the back of her head.

"Part of the group out to *gib mir meinen Anwalt*!" she said, sitting up.

"That's what I thought you'd say," Julius answered, taking out his handcuffs. "For that, you are under arrest."

"Who do you think she's really working with?" Ben asked as the police drove off.

"She said Guten Tag, but who knows?" Duplex said. "I just know that we'd better let Arsenal know. This wasn't just an abduction; they had superpowers."

"Yeah, they did," Ben said. "Why did they want Larry? Did he work with them?"

"I've known Larry all my life," Duplex said. "I don't know what happened after he went into the military, but he never appeared capable of something like this."

"Maybe he chickened out," Ben suggested, guessing. "Maybe that's why they're after him—he knows too much."

"In any case, we'd better call Mike and Judy to let them know what just happened," Ben said, digging into his pocket for change. "Let's hope the pay phone is working."

"Morning," Judy said as Karen sat up.

"Morning," Karen replied, stretching. "What time is it?"

"Eleven thirty," Judy answered. "How are you feeling?

"I'm still a little sore," she replied, rubbing her right forearm.

"Hungry?" Judy asked, heading toward the kitchen.

"I'll have whatever you're having," she said, watching for a moment and then following.

"I'm thinking of running to the store for breakfast," Judy said. "There's some stuff here, but there are five of us."

"I'll go," Karen said as Judy took the keys from her purse. "If you don't mind me driving your car."

"No, not at all," she replied, tossing the keys to her. "Are you going alone, or are you taking Ron with you?"

"I'll take him along for a ride," Karen answered as they walked up the stairs.

Judy knocked on the door, opened it, and said, "Mike, Karen's off to the grocery store. Do you guys want her to pick up anything special?"

"Nope, I guess just lunch meat and bread," Michael answered, taking forty dollars out of his wallet and handing it to Karen. "Maybe soda, or do you guys want coffee too?"

"Soda's fine," Ron answered, looking around at the others. "I mean for me."

"Yeah, I can do soda. Had coffee this morning for breakfast," Quarrel said, stretching. "Some kind of food would be nice."

"Are you ready?" Karen asked, looking at Ron. "I'm going to need help with this stuff."

"Well," he said, looking at the map, "yeah, I'm ready." Walking out with his girlfriend, he told the others, "See you guys in a few."

After having fallen back asleep on the couch, Judy woke and made her way back up to where the others were. When she opened the door, they were still at work, looking over the same map. The topic of conversation was Guten Tag, and knowing what those words meant, she couldn't help but wonder about the name.

"Why would a terrorist group out to cause fear and terror call itself Hello, or Good Day?" she asked, kneeling down next to Michael.

"They took the name because originally, they were a day care center in Berlin. They were taking care of the children of rich politicians and took the kids hostage. The parents then paid to get them back, but within twenty-four hours, the children were all dead. Guten Tag poisoned them. None of them were ever caught because they all went into hiding," Quarrel said, looking at Mike and Judy. "Nobody expected to see them pop up in Wilkes-Barre and cause all of this. They've got to be working with somebody else."

"Well, we've got to stop this before they strike again," Arsenal said, looking up from the map.

"Doorbell," Judy said, turning toward the hallway.

"Judy!" Marc said as he opened the door. "We've got trouble. Where's Mike?"

"He's upstairs. What's wrong?" she asked as he and the others walked in.

"Guten Tag," Ben answered. "We've had our first run-in with them."

"Mike!" Judy yelled. "We've got company!"

She led the three of them upstairs, and Arsenal stepped out into the hallway and asked, "What's going on?"

"We've got trouble, boss," Marc answered, coming to a stop in front of him. "We just had it out with Guten Tag at Coal Street Park. They took a friend of mine."

"Who?" Quarrel asked, coming out of the room and standing behind Arsenal.

"Larry Stontz," Marc answered. "I don't think either of you know him."

"Larry Stontz," Arsenal repeated, gesturing for them to come in. "You're right. I don't know him. So why would they take him? What's Larry done for Guten Tag to take notice to him?"

"I don't know," Marc answered as he saw the map of Wilkes-Barre lying on the floor. "Didn't act like a terrorist in any way that I can tell. Hadn't seen him in a while. He stopped over this morning and brought up the idea of playing football, not blowing up Public Square."

"I would certainly hope not," Arsenal said. "At least you're here instead of hunting them on your own. We'll have to find out what Larry was into since you don't know. Who else can you think of?"

"Besides Dan, I don't know," Marc said, thinking. "He was in the army, so I guess we could start there."

"The good news is, we got one of them," Dan said. "A redhead martial artist carrying a pair of sai."

"Sai?" Arsenal repeated. He looked at Quarrel. "Do you know anybody who fights with those?"

Shaking her head, she answered, "Not offhand. Did you get her name?"

"Majestic Beauty, I think," Dan answered, looking at Ben.

"The guy I fought was Ace," Ben said. "And there was an ugly guy—I think his name was Troll King. It looked like he was creating little creatures, as if he had magic or something."

"Magic?" Judy said. "My trouble. I suppose that only adds to the problem. That has to be how they get around without being seen. I've been trying to locate them with my magic, but it felt like I was being blocked. It has to be him."

Looking around, Marc asked, "Where are Ron and Karen?"

"They ran to the grocery store for food," Arsenal answered. "Sticking around for something to eat?"

"Not a bad idea," Ben answered, kneeling down as he looked over the city map. "But we have to figure out what their next move is. Apparently, they went from blowing things up to kidnapping."

"Was Larry the first person they took?" Judy asked, standing in the doorway.

"I've no idea," Marc answered, glancing up from the map. "He's the only one I'm aware of. The courthouse, Parsons, and now Coal Street—is there any connection?"

Before anyone could give an answer, the front door opened, and Ron called out, "Food's here!"

"Lunch meat, bread, and soda," Arsenal said as they made their way out into the hallway. "Help yourselves."

"Where's Karen?" Marc asked, stopping at the bottom step.

Laughing, Ron replied, "She stepped in something. She's out there cleaning it off her shoe."

"I'll help her with the bags," Marc said, stepping outside.

# CHAPTER 19

Stepping out onto the porch, Duplex couldn't help but smile and laugh as he watched his teammate clean off her shoe.

"Karen, what did you do?" he asked, teasing. "Is that gum?"

"I wish," she replied, standing up and turning around. She dragged her foot across the sidewalk. "Gum doesn't stink. What brings you here today? Did Arsenal call you?"

"No," Duplex answered, walking down the stairs to pick up the groceries. "Guten Tag attacked us at Coal Street Park, and they took a friend of mine, Larry Stontz. Now we're trying to figure out why."

"How well did you know this guy Larry?" Karen asked, following Duplex onto the porch.

"We grew up in the same neighborhood," Duplex answered, running his fingers through his hair. "He's a few years older than me. Other than that, he was fine; he graduated from Nanticoke and went into the army. I didn't see him until yesterday; he said he wanted to get in a game of football, so that's what we did."

"Do you know any of the guys who kidnapped him?" she asked, watching him pace the porch. "I wonder why they took him. Did he know anything? Was he anyone important?"

"Well, he was in the military, but I don't think he was anyone important, just a soldier. They all were wearing costumes and knew him by name, so the random-abduction scenario is out of the picture. They had to know him in one way or another."

Before Karen could ask another question, a loud explosion in the direction of Kingston disrupted the conversation. Quickly looking that way, they saw a large mushroom cloud rise up into the air, and they wondered if this explosion was nuclear.

Without hesitating, Duplex opened the door, tossed the groceries inside, grabbed Star's hand, and said, "Come on."

The next things Star saw were burning trees and small fires burning at the bottom of the hill. A strong smell of oil was in the air. Falling to her knees, she immediately began vomiting. It had been her first time teleporting with him, and the sudden change of scenery caused her sickness. The second and third explosions were almost on top of each other, as if they were one enormous explosion. She wondered what they'd gotten into.

Struggling to stand, she cried out, "What the hell did you do to me? Where am I?"

"I'm sorry," Duplex said, putting his arm around her and helping her stand. "We teleported. I should have warned you about it first. My teleportation is harder than Judy's. I'm sorry."

Leaning back over, she emptied the rest of her stomach. Then she replied, "Just don't go rushing off. I need you here with me, at least until I can stand on my own."

Keeping his arm around her, he said, "It won't last more than a few seconds. Normally, I'd say just take deep breaths, but with that burning oil, I don't think that would be a very smart idea."

She nodded, and within a few minutes, the queasiness slowly passed. From their position on Route 11, Star and Duplex could see the fires and black smoke rising into the air. When the fourth explosion occurred, the darkened skies made their search-and-rescue objective even harder.

"Let's head up this road and see if we can get a better look at what's going on," Duplex said, helping her to walk. "Hopefully the air up there will be a little better."

"I'm doing okay now," she said shakily as she pointed down the road. "You check the marina."

The Edwardsville Marina had been built and designed to house the boats using the river and canals in Wilkes-Barre. It was situated behind the Edwardsville shopping district and was filled by Toby's Creek. The marina often served as a parking area for boat-riding shoppers.

Located next to the complex, just a few hundred yards away on the other side of the dike in between the shopping areas, was the Kingston Oil Company. There were nine large tankers filled with oil, which had become a target like everything else in the area.

Just across the river, in South Wilkes-Barre, the blackening skies and strong odor kept most locked in their homes, praying for safety. Others believed the end was coming and felt that theft and vandalism were the way to go, giving the police more than they were prepared to handle.

Duplex could see this wasn't going to be an easy battle; just being able to breathe was a major concern. At the thought of facing off with Guten Tag again, he reverted back to his armored form, hoping he wouldn't have to fight under those conditions. He wasn't afraid; he just wasn't looking forward to choking to death as he fought for his life.

*Wasn't a good idea to bring Karen over here like this,* he thought, *and then leave her alone. I hope it wasn't two stupid ideas on top of each other.*

"You head up the road," he said, pointing. "Stay alert in case Guten Tag is still in the area. I'm going to investigate the marina."

"Be careful," she said as he vanished.

As Duplex disappeared, she heard and then saw police cars speeding up Route 11 toward her. Moving to the side of the road, she pulled her mask over her face as five police cars came to a stop in front of her.

From the first police car, she heard the comment "It's one of those from the mall."

*Yes,* she thought, and she asked, "Is that a good thing?"

"You know who did this?" the cop in the passenger seat asked, looking over at her. "*Sprechen Sie Deutsch?*"

"What?" she asked, familiar with the phrase. "No!"

"Then what are you doing here?" the cop asked as he opened his door and partially stepped out of the vehicle. "Who else is here with you?"

"Duplex. Big and muscular, with metallic steel skin," she answered, pointing. "He went down that way to the marina."

"Down to the marina?" the driver said, looking in that direction.

"Well, we're here now," the other cop said. "We don't need anything else to make matters worse. Just stay out of the way."

*Wow,* she thought, stepping away from the car. *Guess these guys won't be on my Christmas list.*

She moved back as the cruisers drove past. The final one remained, and when the window rolled down, Karen was looking at a Spanish policewoman.

"What do you know about this attack?" she asked while taking a closer look at Karen. "Did you see or hear anyone speaking German?"

"No," Karen answered quickly, not wanting to mention that they'd teleported there. "My partner and I just arrived minutes before you showed up."

"The mine underneath the Gateway Center has collapsed, and fifteen miners are trapped," the Spanish cop said. "Things don't seem to be getting any better; they're just getting worse around here."

"Are you asking for help?" Karen asked, stepping up to the car.

"I would if I knew your name," she replied. "I'm Patrolman Rita Martinez."

"Star," she answered. "You can call me Star."

"Well, Star," Rita said, looking at her, "yes, unofficially, I'm asking for your help. We can't put the general public in danger, but that costume means you're willing to do that on your own, making my answer yes."

"I understand that," Star said as she started walking up the road. "And I'll do my best not to let you down."

When they arrived at the mine entrance a few minutes later, a few other police cars were arriving from Courtdale, Pringle, and Edwardsville, pulling in from a secondary road, followed by news reporter vehicles.

*There's got to be at least fifty people here, not counting the people gathering around the gate*, Karen thought, watching as the police made sure that was where they remained.

The Woodward Mine, like all of the other mines in town, had been open for business for nearly a century. It was one of the top-ten coal-producing mines in Luzerne County. Their area of mining was located under what was now the shopping area. By the time businesses had started popping up in the late '50s and early '60s, the region had been covered with tunnels.

In some areas, the tunnels were less than a hundred feet below the surface. Back when construction had begun, there'd been no drilling. The land had been leveled, and construction had begun on the homes and businesses that now populated the danger area. There'd been no major problems reported until the attack that had begun a little more than an hour ago.

The large wooden structure was the place of business for two hundred people working above and below ground. When the first explosion occurred, all of the teams below ground were immediately ordered out, for fear it could become another Wilkes-Barre incident. Kingston police were quickly notified of the collapsed shaft and immediately took action.

Listening to the mine foreman, Gene Patsimmons, Star looked over the map and was surprised by what she was learning.

"I knew there were still mines open, but I never thought it was anything of this scale. My biggest fear is that one of these tankers is going to collapse down into a tunnel and spread burning oil, making things a thousand times worse."

"Well, we're keeping our fingers crossed. So far, there's only one incident we are aware of," Gene replied. "And hopefully Chet Hill and his team aren't in need of first aid. Where's that partner of yours?"

Appearing on the walkway, Duplex was stunned by the destruction he saw. Several bodies were floating in the water, two of which were burned badly. Along with the bodies, there were several large pieces of debris and three partially sunken boats. On the good side of the dock were five boats trying to get out to the river and downstream before they became the next victims.

Seeing that the back end of the complex was burning, he knew there wasn't a lot of time. After ripping off the front door, he stepped inside and quickly yelled out for anyone within to get out. With no reply, he moved as close to the fire as possible to check for injured individuals.

"So far so good," he said, moving quickly along the main aisle in front of the restaurant.

Looking through the kitchen door, he again called out with no reply. Then he spotted an open exit door.

As he headed for it, he said, "They're all out."

Checking the area out back, he saw that Kingston Shoes and Jim Dandy's Restaurant had their doors open also. There was silence. He heard only the roof of Kmart burning.

"Only one left," he said, teleporting.

Reappearing in the laundry aisle, Duplex looked around and called out, "Is there anyone in here?"

He made his way back out of the aisle and stood in front of the meat counter. Looking at the meat sitting there and slowly spoiling upset him, and he wished he could prevent it. He even briefly contemplated taking some of it with him but reminded himself that wasn't his reason for being there. Shaking his head as he started walking away, he noticed a young girl at the far end of the building, near the offices.

"Hey!" he yelled. "You've got to get out of here!"

As he came into her view, he could see she was nervous, but she wasn't alone.

"Who's here with you?" Duplex asked, slowly approaching her.

"Who is that? Is that the police?" a male voice asked from within the office.

When Duplex stepped in front of her, she dropped to her knees and said, "Don't hurt me."

He looked at her and then into the office, where he saw a bald middle-aged man cleaning out a safe.

"Robbing the place?" Duplex yelled, blocking the doorway.

"Who are you?" the bald man asked, turning to face him. "You're not getting this money. See, Catherine? I told you we couldn't leave it."

"Couldn't leave what?" Duplex said. "The money stays. Close the safe!"

"I'm the day-shift manager," the bald man said. "You're either killing me, or I'm taking this to the bank."

"Taking it to the bank?" Duplex repeated. "I'm supposed to believe that?"

"Where else would I be taking it?" he asked. "My brother-in-law is the general manager."

"And the girl?" Duplex asked. "Who is she?"

"My daughter," he answered, zipping the money bag. "My name is Dale. I saw you fight that thing at the mall the other day."

"Yes, that was just the beginning," Duplex said. "Things have spiraled out of control. There's been another attack, and the oil tankers are burning. Staying here isn't safe; the air will become toxic. If you're actually stealing that money and lying to me about taking it to the bank, I will hunt you down!"

"You've got my word, sir," the man replied, looking toward his daughter. "Come on, Catherine. Let's get to the bank and then to your uncle's to let him know it's safe."

Deciding they weren't going to steal the money, Duplex teleported to the other side of the oil fire. Looking toward it, he could see that the air was slightly better because the wind was blowing the smoke in the other direction.

*This isn't getting any better. The light is totally gone from the sky, and I'd say the body count is on its way up,* Duplex thought as he put his hand over his mouth to try to block the strong odor.

His armored form would protect him from fire, but his lungs were a different matter. The smell of burning oil was strong, and seeing the flames rise into the air, he knew he needed to go inside to check for survivors.

*All of this water, and none of it's good enough to use against this oil,* he thought, entering the mall.

"Is there anybody in here?" he yelled, walking down the corridor.

Once he reached the main walking area, he peered into the toy store just as the lights shorted out. With no reply, he continued on toward the Rite Aid. Coming to a stop, he looked around and called out again. Suddenly, he heard bullets ricocheting off of his body. Looking around, he saw a man with a mask over his face crouched down near the entrance to Radio Shack.

"The place is on fire!" he yelled. "And all you can think of is getting your hands on a computer? Really? Then, to prove how stupid you are, you're shooting at a walking tank."

Storming over, the masked man fired four more times without Duplex taking any damage. As he attempted to drop the gun and run, Duplex grabbed him and teleported. They reappeared two hundred yards away at a command post at the gas station across the street from the mall, where paramedics were taking care of the injured.

Dropping the vomiting gunman at the feet of a policeman, he said, "My name is Duplex. I'm with the Knight Shift. He was caught trying to rob Radio Shack."

Not waiting for an answer, Duplex teleported again and reappeared at the entrance to Hills Department Store. As he stepped up to the door, he saw two women getting onto motorcycles that matched the colors of their costumes. Had he decided to investigate instead of watch them drive off, he might have learned they were the newest members of Guten Tag.

Slaughter and Massacre had been adversaries of Quarrel for the past several years. Had it not been for Wes's speech putting the blame for the Wilkes-Barre attacks on Guten Tag, the present event wouldn't have been happening. As a result of the speech, Conquest, the leader, had gone into hiding in Wilkes-Barre and decided to take action. He'd offered the sisters membership into Guten Tag.

Of all of the possible targets in and around the city of Wilkes-Barre, Conquest concluded that the oil tankers in Edwardsville would be the best demonstration. If the attacks in the city were to be blamed on Guten Tag, hiring the top two known freelance criminals in the city was his best course of action.

Closing his eyes, Duplex walked right through the glass doors and entered the snack-bar area. Gazing into the partially darkened building, he yelled, "Anybody in here? You need to get out because you're in danger! If you need assistance, my name is Duplex! I'm here to help you!"

Each time he called out, there was no reply. Minutes later, he arrived at the entrance to Walden Books. Looking into the darkness, he saw only books scattered about the floor and concluded that anyone inside must have gotten out.

Stepping outside at the Burlington Coat entrance, he smelled spray paint and then noticed the words *Guten Tag* on the wall.

"They're here," he said, looking around the parking lot. He clenched his fists. "I wonder if those two biker chicks are involved. Where's Arbinovawitz? I've got his proof."

Returning to the command area, Duplex looked for a cop to inform about the message he'd seen. Instead, he saw a large gathering of people on the road, standing where the residential section of the street began.

As he stood there observing, he saw an ambulance pull into the gas station at the corner of the block. Behind him, another oil tanker exploded, making the situation even worse. The darkening skies brought people out of their homes to the streets. Those gathered prayed for anyone trapped or injured.

Making his way over to the ambulance crew, he caught a glimpse of the two women on the motorcycles. Stepping out onto Route 11, he pondered teleporting after them but decided the task at hand was more important. If he'd read the papers and watched the news, he would have known they were the criminals Quarrel had faced off against many times.

"Duplex!" a young teenage boy called out as he came running across the street.

Surprised that somebody recognized him, he spun around and said, "Yeah? What's wrong?"

"A large sinkhole just opened behind the stores in the inner parking lot left of the west-side movie theater," the boy replied, pointing in that direction.

"Any injuries? Anybody fall in?" Duplex asked, taking steps across the street.

Looking over his armored form, the boy answered, "I don't know. Can you check it out?"

"Yes," he answered. "Come on. Show me."

Entering the inner parking lot of the Gateway Shopping Center, Duplex saw a large sinkhole with five cars partially sticking out of it.

"So now there are problems below ground," Duplex said, leaning over as he put his hands on his knees. "And there are no doubt miners trapped in here too." Turning to the kid, he asked, "Where's the nearest mine?"

After thinking for a moment, the boy answered, "The Larksville and Plymouth area. I'd say the one on the hill behind the marina is probably the closest."

"That's where I left my partner," Duplex said, thinking of Star. *I wonder if she found anything.*

After pulling the five vehicles out of the hole, Duplex reappeared several feet from where he'd left Karen. Surprised she was gone, he remembered what the boy had said and walked up the road to the mine entrance. While watching the oil burn uncontrollably below, he hoped Star was on the surface when the mine collapsed.

Picking up his pace, he thought, *I'm already in trouble for taking off with her. If she's injured, I'm going to have hell to pay, and I'm not ready to face off with the team over it.*

Just as he reached the top of the hill, a young female Spanish cop approached and said, "I know you. The fight at the mall—you fought off that creature. We need your help. Some miners are trapped inside the mine. Can you get in there and rescue them?"

Knowing he couldn't say no, Duplex shrugged and answered, "Sure, I'll see what I can do. You didn't happen to see my partner, Star, did you? I'm hoping she came up this way after we split up."

"Yes," the cop replied. "She's up here."

*Well, that's good. At least she's okay,* he thought as they walked up the steep road and made their way over to the growing crowd of police, reporters, and onlookers.

Reverting to his human form, Duplex was caught off guard and hit with a right cross. He stumbled backward. Power of Justice said, "That was my girlfriend you yanked off the porch."

"Ron!" Star yelled, rushing over.

"Step back," the Spanish cop ordered, putting her hand on her weapon.

Shaking off the blow, Duplex reverted to his brick form and replied, "It's okay. I've got this. The first one was yours because I didn't think my decision through. If you hit me again like that, I won't think twice about tearing you apart."

"You don't see me walking away, do you?" Power of Justice said, throwing his hands up as he stepped closer to him.

"Gentlemen!" Arsenal yelled, trying to get in between them before the reporters could get a story. "This isn't how a team operates. We'll discuss this later."

Arsenal turned to look at Power of Justice and said, "If it happens again, I'm out."

"It won't happen again," Duplex said, walking away.

"I never expected that," Judy said, approaching Splitscreen.

"Maybe I'll go talk to him," Dan said, taking a step toward Power of Justice.

"No," Arsenal said, overhearing him. "Leave your brother alone."

"I meant Ron," Dan said, pointing to him.

"I don't think that will work either," Arsenal said, noticing that Susan Brock had been watching the fight.

"Can I get a few minutes of your time, Arsenal?" she asked, looking at him as she motioned for the cameraman to follow.

"Well," he said, hesitating, "what's your question?"

"According to the illegal broadcast from the other day, Guten Tag is claiming responsibility for what's going on in Wilkes-Barre. Do you think this is just another attack by them?" she asked as the cameraman came to a stop.

"So far, it looks that way," Arsenal replied, turning to face the camera. "I didn't see any of that broadcast, so I'm not really sure what the actual problem with the United States is, but I intend to put a stop to all of this as quickly as possible. I know that at the moment, it doesn't look that way, but earlier in the day, we managed to catch one of them, and as far as I know, she's still being held by the Wilkes-Barre police."

"Hey!" Splitscreen called out, ignoring Arsenal's words and following Power of Justice. "Is that vandalism?"

Turning to look, Power of Justice replied, "Does it matter at a time like this?"

Approaching the wall, Splitscreen said, "Wait. Guten Tag—they were here."

Looking around, Power of Justice said, "How do you know it was really Guten Tag and not just someone painting that on there?"

# CHAPTER 20

John Radner stood up, tossed a wrench onto the worktable, and reached for the once-white hand towel lying there. As he attempted to remove some of the grease from his fingers, he walked out of the garage and looked around. He'd opened the Diamond City Garage, where he worked, a little more than eleven years ago. He looked out at the city.

Three years after opening the garage, John had bought the adjacent scrapyard, and the Diamond City Scrapyard had become part of his business. One of the first things he'd done was secure the city's towing contract, and then he'd expanded into the outlying towns. In a matter of a few months, John had become a player in local politics as well.

Things really had taken off when his cousin Tommy came to town and convinced John to start his own motorcycle gang. When younger, they both had ridden for the Scorpions until the FBI had broken up the gang. He'd thought that lifestyle was behind him but concluded there could be a motorcycle gang in Wilkes-Barre, provided it wasn't an outlaw gang.

Ever since the age of twelve, John had been on a motorcycle of some kind, and even now, it was his preferred means of travel. Tommy had led the Diamond City Riders until he'd lost his battle with cancer two years after the gang was formed. In the short time that he'd been leader, he'd made a lot of friends, and when he'd passed, out of respect, his friends had come to Wilkes-Barre and joined the Riders.

All of the new members had taken up residence in the Laurels, a collection of seven skyscrapers built fifteen stories high to house the majority of people from the town of Laurel Run. Nearly a hundred years ago, a mine fire had begun burning under the town and been left unchecked for nearly sixty years, resulting in the destruction of more than one hundred homes and businesses.

The Laurels had been built to help those in Laurel Run who couldn't afford to or chose not to rebuild elsewhere. Most of the buildings had remained vacant after former Laurel Run inhabitants moved out years ago. The closeness of several mines made it the perfect location for miners to live.

For a while, the housing project had seemed like a modern version of a coal-mining patch town. After fifteen years, the Spanish moving into the area had begun take it over. By 1980, there were very original tenants living there.

As the times had changed, so had the appearance of the Laurels, which had gone from a clean and modern residential area to a high-rise housing project in less than twenty years. Security had become an issue, and as the complex was so close to John Radner's business, he'd created the Diamond City Security Service, which was nothing more than armed bikers from his gang watching over the Laurels and dispensing justice in their own way.

Over the following months, the Diamond City guards had gone from being honest serve-and-protect-style guards to having their hands in everything illegal in the complex. By 1988, each of the so-called guards had been making money off of one or more illegal enterprises.

"It's three thirty, John," Alice, John's wife, said as she walked into the garage and opened a bottle of Diet Coke.

"Okay," he said, tossing the towel back onto the workbench. "Father Brock is coming over here to talk. My guess is it's about starting a church group or something."

"Are you looking for God, John?" Alice asked as she walked over to look at the work he was doing on a bike.

Smirking, he didn't respond as he took the bottle from her and took a drink.

"No," he said, handing it back to her. "Apparently, he's been having trouble with some of the people around here, and I'm guessing he wants to talk about that."

"Your guards can't get the job done 'cause most of them are on the other side of the law," Alice answered. "This might not be the type of visit you're expecting. He might even say that you're part of the overall problem."

"So you think he's coming here to put the fear of God into me?" John asked, reaching for his cigarettes.

"I've known John Radner for years," Wes said as he and Father Brock reached the intersection of Coal Street and Route 315.

"And talking him into joining our cause?" Father Brock asked, fiddling with his prayer beads.

"The Diamond City Riders won't say no to the right price," Wes replied. "I get a lot of my supplies from Hades."

"What?" Bradley said, surprised by his answer.

"Not that Hades," Wes said. "Hades Krohn. He's a Diamond Rider. I've known him for almost twenty years. We served together. He gets me the military-grade stuff I've been using. Hades had, even done some time bringing out the beast, but he wasn't in control, and it bit him, he got burned bad."

"Why isn't he working for us now?" Bradley asked as Wes stopped at the intersection.

"You weren't paying enough," he answered, waiting for the light to change.

"So offer him more," Bradley replied. "If he's got the skill you think he does, give him what he wants."

"Then you're going to give me a raise too?" Wes asked. "If you're telling me to give him what he wants, that's more than you paid me."

"But now you're getting more," Bradley said. "So, talk to him about our cause. Talk to him while I talk to John Radner."

As Father Brock entered the garage, Wes thought of all of the other people he would need to pull this operation off. He hoped that meeting would go better than the one he'd had with the Spanish gang on the bridge. The money he'd lost wasn't going to be easy to replace, and he was lucky the people he and Bradley worked for hadn't had him killed because of it.

Hades Krohn had been a fire bug since the age of seven. He'd set his first major fire when he was thirteen while hiking with the Boy Scouts. Decades later, fire scars were still visible in a large section of Larksville Mountain.

As he'd grown, so did had fires and the number of people who'd suffered and died because of his actions. However, Hades was never caught. He'd gone from being an Eagle Scout to a second lieutenant in the United Sates Army, where he'd learned about demolition and how to improve his craft. Hades was the one the other members paid to take care of problems that wouldn't go away.

"Hello, John," Father Brock said as he walked into the garage.

"Father," John said, shaking his hand as Walt closed the door. "You know Walt, don't you?"

"Yes," he answered, glancing back at him. "He sits in the front row during church."

"Is that why you're here—to increase membership?" John asked as the three of them sat down.

"No, the one I serve has asked me to come here," Father Brock replied. "The work of the devil is at hand, and if we don't do something, he and his forces will overrun the place, and there won't be any place left to hide. It will open the gates of hell and unleash forces that will bring about the end of days."

"Is it really going to be as bad as you say?" Walt asked, thinking about how far-fetched that sounded.

"The truth is often far stranger than you would believe, gentlemen. With the way things are going in the world today, you don't think it's going to go on like this forever, do you? The Lord has spoken to me, John; he has specifically asked me to start with cleansing the evil from this city. I believe the only way to stop hell-spawned fire is with the Lord's fire of creation," Father Brock said, locking eyes with John.

"What do you want from me?" he asked. "Protection?"

"Paid protection," Father Brock answered. "You and the Diamond City Riders will be paid for your services, and getting John into heaven will be a lot easier."

"How long do I have to think over your offer?" John asked, reaching into a small refrigerator and taking out a cold bottle of beer.

"I'll give you till the end of the week," Father Brock answered as he got up from his seat.

The conversation lasted another twenty minutes before Father Brock and Wes left the garage. To think things through, John hopped on his bike and took a ride through the city. He came to a stop at the top of Coal Street and gazed down into the downtown area below. A little more than a month ago, a massive grass fire had left most of Coal Street Park in ruin. The arsonist hadn't been caught, and John wondered if Guten Tag had been behind it in some way. He wondered if he should take the offer.

After pulling over, he stepped off the bike and looked at the burned grass and playground equipment as he thought, *This town has superheroes, yet they can't get this taken care of. Something is going on, and if it isn't stopped, there won't be anything left. They're blowing up the ground I walk on, and everything else they're burning. The money is the only reason I'm going to get involved; it's going to help patch things up with the Assassins up in Scranton.*

John got back on his bike, pulled out into traffic, and continued his ride down the hill. Reaching Canal Street, John looked over at the water as he waited at the light and wondered if anything was going to happen in the water. As the light turned green, he continued on his ride, and moments later, he reached the Veterans Bridge and headed to Kingston.

Off to his right were the mostly destroyed North Street Bridge and the rest of the destruction caused by the first attack on the city. The recovery crews were still pulling bodies from the rubble while cleaning up the millions of dollars' worth of damage.

"They'll be cleaning that mess up until next spring," John said, turning his attention back to the road. "I wonder if the government is going to do anything about this crap."

Minutes later, John reached the Kingston Post Office and turned onto Route 11, heading toward Edwardsville. Suddenly, he caught sight of a bright orange fireball shooting into the sky, and a large blast followed. The force of it knocked John from his motorcycle and into the windshield of the taxi behind him.

The taxi driver slammed on her brakes, which started a chain reaction with the next fifteen cars. The destruction was similar to the North Street Bridge attack; the only difference was that fewer buildings collapsed, and no important officials were killed or injured.

John feared it might be a nuclear attack of some kind; his heart pounded as he struggled to get off of the taxi. Minutes later, with the help of the taxi driver, he was lying near the curb in pain, looking at the devastation caused by the blast and the black smoke rising into the air.

# CHAPTER 21

No sooner had Duplex taken Star's hand and vanished than Quarrel and Shockwave stepped out onto the porch as the fourth tanker exploded. Neither had seen their teammates disappear, and they assumed they were still in the area as they looked at the black smoke rushing skyward.

"Whoa," Shockwave said, seeing the orange glow.

"Great. Just when it seemed like things were starting to settle down," Quarrel said, watching as the fifth fireball shot into the afternoon sky. Looking back toward Shockwave, she said, "Tell Arsenal I'm going to check this out."

"I'm going with you," he replied, following her to her motorcycle.

As they got on and she started it up, she said, "They must have hit Edwardsville Oil, and that's going to make thing a hell of a lot worse."

As he put his arms around her waist, he imagined what the scene was going to look like and said, "We're going to need to get a lot of help on this."

"Help? You mean like outside help?" she said while speeding down Hazel Street toward downtown. "The only way we'll get help is if somebody takes notice of what is going on here, and then seasoned groups like the High Lords and the League of Knights will show up."

*The League of Knights and the High Lords in Wilkes-Barre?* he thought, and he asked, "Aren't the High Lords with the government?"

"Yes," she answered, pulling up onto the sidewalk to avoid a red light. "Which means the government would have to send them in."

"What are the odds of that?" Shockwave asked as Quarrel turned onto Route 11.

Coming to a stop, they were both amazed by the damage on the road and the black smoke rising into the air. Whoever was at fault for this disaster knew exactly what they were doing. It looked as if they were in a war zone. Both had seen pictures and news reports of the destruction caused by the bombs that had taken down the North Street Bridge and the judicial sector of the city.

This attack didn't cause a high death toll like that one had; this one was meant to show the world that fear and anarchy ruled the day. With the bent and mangled oil tanks burning, the heat in the air made it feel a lot warmer.

As Shockwave stepped off of the back of the bike, a strange feeling came over him. An event this big was something he'd never expected when he'd chosen to become a superhero. Having nothing more than dumb luck on his side made him wonder if fighting crime was something he should be doing. He'd been right that to win this war, they were going to need help, but none of them had the contacts to make those calls.

*Keep calm*, he thought, feeling sweat building up within his costume as he looked around, wondering where to begin.

As he regained control of his nerves, he caught sight of a man leaning up against a Klein Candy delivery truck. Moving in closer, he saw that the man was holding his wrist, and he asked, "Are you all right?"

The driver nodded and, as he looked Shockwave over, said, "I'll make it, but the people ahead of me look worse off."

*Guess I'd better head that way*, Shockwave thought, looking at all of the injured people nearby and still inside their vehicles. *And a lot to choose from. If only I knew first aid.*

Quarrel watched as two men pushed an elderly woman down and forced their way inside her apartment. Quarrel immediately created her energy bow and followed the attackers inside.

The first—a tall, thin man who couldn't stand up straight—was pulling out a blackjack, when Quarrel struck him with a bolt from her energy bow. The stunning shot caused him to make a strange noise as he dropped to the ground.

His Spanish partner jumped when he saw the man collapse, and he threw up his arms to surrender. Seeing the elderly woman on the ground,

Quarrel didn't buy the man's gesture, and she put two shots into his chest. As he collapsed, she turned to the old woman and asked, "Are you okay?"

Stepping away from the two men, she answered, "Yes. Thank you, Quarrel."

After tying up the two men, Quarrel escorted the woman out of the apartment, thinking, *Where's my partner?*

Stepping out onto the stairs, she called out to Shockwave but didn't get a reply. Seeing her motorcycle still in its parked location, she knew he hadn't taken off on it.

*But then again, I don't think he knows how to drive it*, she thought, helping the woman to the sidewalk.

Off to her left, Quarrel caught sight of two motorcycles speeding in the other direction, and just by the color alone, she knew who they were. Coming to a stop, the two riders dismounted their bikes and unsheathed their weapons. They were her biggest threats: Slaughter and Massacre, sisters and former members of the military.

That day, their job was to add to the terror, chaos, and fears of the people, all thanks to Wes's speech making Guten Tag the culprit. He was going to put the blame on them, thinking it was a lie he could get away with.

The first explosion flipped the lead jeep and killed all four of the soldiers within, causing the six vehicles behind to immediately stop. The soldiers jumped out and quickly took cover as Slaughter and Massacre continued throwing grenades. Even before their commander gave the order, the soldiers opened fire.

Gun or no gun, neither of the sisters showed any fear, and they quickly moved to put as many of the soldiers down permanently as possible. The sisters had military training and the sapient-dominant powers of stealth and kinetic reflection, meaning bullets and any kinetic projectiles would bounce harmlessly off of their auras.

Most of the soldiers who fell by their bladed weapons never knew death was coming. Had Slaughter and Massacre been born in the feudal period, they would have easily been the equivalent of top-tier ninjas.

"Just what I need at a time like this," Quarrel said. "Let's hope they don't stumble upon my partner; he wouldn't stand a chance against them."

Crawling as quickly as she could along the ground, Quarrel hoped Shockwave would stay wherever he was and not jump in, because it could be the last thing he did. Peering up several cars later, she saw a group of soldiers directing their gunfire toward the side of a house and a black pickup truck.

"They've got to have them pinned down over there," she said, looking over the area. "If they didn't find a way out through the backyard."

"Get that manhole cover up!" Slaughter yelled, watching as her sister forced her fingers into the grooves.

"I'm working on it," Massacre said, "but it's heavy. I could use some help."

Looking at the manhole cover, Slaughter pulled the last grenade off of her belt and yanked the pin. Without looking, she tossed it. Grabbing the small opening, she forced her hands in next to her sister's, and they managed to lift the cover as the grenade went off.

Both sisters quickly scurried into the hole but didn't get a chance to pull the cover over it. Black tar covered their bodies.

Quarrel reached the opening at the same time four soldiers did, and as her energy bow dissipated, she said, "I've got this. Get your men to watch the other covers in the area; they've got to come out somewhere."

Nodding, the lead soldier motioned for his men to do what she'd suggested. As Quarrel bent down to enter the hole, she noticed a small trace of what appeared to be oil and wondered what the chances were that it would have splattered that far from the explosion. Hopping down into the sewer, she found out what it really was, and before she could scream, Blackball covered her face with his tar.

# CHAPTER 22

The sun beating down on the forehead of Cam Egavas made him wish for a long, cold rain and something cold to drink. He was returning to Wilkes-Barre, a place he hadn't seen since he was fourteen. Twelve years later, Cam wanted answers to his past and the truth about his father and two cousins, all of whom were wanted for various murders.

Cam was the only male in his family who hadn't followed that career path, and some of his family members hated him because of it. Instead, he'd become what some people considered a vigilante or a superhero. The name his opponents called him had come from his fighting style: a savage, berserk rage.

His fingernails hadn't extended to talon length in more than half a year, and he hoped to keep the streak alive. As he walked down Route 315, he looked out at the view of the city below and watched as the black smoke from Edwardsville rose into the air. As he watched the smoke, he cleared his throat and concluded that his streak was on its way to an end.

The gob of spit that hit the pavement was his body's way of telling him there was going to be trouble—something that would require Cam to assume his role as Savage—but whatever the trouble was, it would have to wait. Cam was more than ten miles away from Wilkes-Barre and a lot farther from the fire.

Reaching the parking lot of the Bear Creek Tavern, he saw a large racing banner and said, "Welcome, NASCAR fans. It isn't my favorite sport, but I do like watching the King win, which I think happened at the last race I was at."

Cam walked into the tavern and glanced around the bar for a place to sit. Three men were sitting at the left end of the bar. Cam suspected they might be the reason his danger sense was flaring. Swallowing the spit building in his throat, Cam sat down and ordered a beer.

"How about a bath and a shave?" one of the men said, looking down the bar at him.

Ignoring the comment, Cam told the bartender, "Whatever you just poured, I'll take one of those."

"Gibbons," the bartender said, leaning over the bar.

"Guess that's what I'm drinking," Cam said, attempting to ignore the three men as he reached into his pocket and pulled out a crinkled five-dollar bill.

The moment the bartender took the bill, three other men entered the bar and sat at a table behind Cam on his right. Turning back as the bartender placed the bottle of beer in front of him, Cam felt the mucus building quickly in his throat. He took a fast drink, hoping it would push some of the mucus down, while he felt his fingernails slowly start to grow.

To Cam's surprise, the three men behind him weren't interested in him. They were from a rival biker gang and were discussing the black smoke rising over Wilkes-Barre and everything else going on in the city. Catching a glimpse of one of the biker jackets, Cam couldn't make out the name, but he was confident the Hell's Angels didn't operate in the area. It was a group he'd had troubles with in the past.

*Trouble is trouble*, Cam thought, taking a second-long drink from the bottle.

The other three men appeared to be from a different biker gang, and as Cam sat there, he realized the trouble brewing probably wasn't going to involve him directly. He was going to get caught in the middle. However, with the way the group to his left had made comments about him, they would be his first targets if and when a fight broke out.

As the minutes passed by, Cam wondered if his senses were deceiving him, and with one final drink, he finished his beer. Motioning to the bartender for a second beer, Cam watched two bikers get up from their tables and enter the men's room. Both men had similar builds and looked as if they could have played professional football.

The second man had barely stepped through the door, when he came flying out, crashing into the jukebox. All of the bikers sprang up from their seats and drew their weapons as they waited for the other biker to come out. That didn't happen; instead, they heard the muffled screams of the first biker.

Cam's danger sense was going wild. He cleared his throat, turned his head, and spit as he stepped away from his barstool. The first biker, encased in a tar-like black substance, landed with a thud in view of everybody else. As the room fell eerily silent, Cam knew that wasn't good, and as an all-black figure stepped out of the bathroom.

It didn't matter to Cam that he was the only one without a firearm; his talons were just as deadly. Judging by the look of the thing they were facing, Cam's weapons would do more damage than their guns would. After a brief moment of Cam and Blackball sizing each other up, Blackball lunged at him.

Talons extended, Cam did the same, and the foes met as the bikers opened fire, not caring which of the two they struck. One of theirs was already a victim, and they didn't intend to be next, so they did what they thought best: they shot to kill. They asked no questions; they just pulled the triggers, and the first few bullets struck Cam's legs, causing him to stumble.

His talons managed to reach their intended target, digging deep into Blackball's body, but they caused no noticeable pain or damage of any kind. When his talons penetrated Blackball's skin, Cam couldn't believe what he was feeling, and if he hadn't seen it, he would have thought he was fighting a creature made out of black jelly.

Collapsing to the ground, Cam cried out from the pain in his legs, and even though he did his best to ignore it, he had a hard time standing. Blackball took advantage of that, swinging his large fist and knocking Cam back to the ground.

Circling around them, the bikers took aim and fired at Blackball as two of them attempted to rescue the biker encased in the tar-like substance. Blackball figured out what they were attempting to do but showed little concern. They could try to free their friend all they wanted, but they wouldn't be able to stop his plan of capturing the sapient dominants in the room.

The bullets passed through Blackball's body, and the only harm done was to the objects surrounding him—including Cam. He took several shots to his upper body as Blackball lunged at him. Blackball slipped on a piece of debris on the floor and fell on top of Cam as the bikers continued their attack.

The bikers could see Cam struggling to breathe and get free, but each gasp of air enabled more of tar-like substance to enter his lungs. After a few moments, the struggle was over, and Cam slipped into unconsciousness.

While Cam was fighting for his life, a woman named Laura Tonal was slipping into her blue-and-silver costume for the first time. She had recently been let out of the Tollhouse Institution for hearing voices. She'd realized on her own that she was hearing them because she was sapient dominant.

Until that episode had occurred, she'd wanted to follow in the footsteps of Karen Whitehal and train to be an Olympic-level gymnast. Now, six years later, at the age of nineteen, Laura knew it was too late for that dream. She'd read about Quarrel fighting crime in the streets of Wilkes-Barre and concluded that her telepathic powers had been given to her for that sole purpose. She was going to take to the streets to fight crime as Wildstar and be part of a team.

Her teammate was going to be a man named Disc. He too was a sapient dominant, with the ability to create black or white energy discs similar to the bolts created by Quarrel. Laura knew she could trust him because Walter Reedley was her cousin and had been her best friend since they were six.

Since Walter was on the Meyers High School track team, his costume resembled his track uniform. He wore an all-black costume with white high-top sneakers, gloves with the fingers cut off, and a white tank top with the mask sewn onto it. It had taken him ten tries to get the sewing right.

"I can't believe we're finally doing this," Walter said as he looked over the work he'd done on the mask.

*I know what you mean*, Laura replied telepathically from the bathroom, where she was getting dressed. *Night one, and we're about to go out the window.*

"Any idea where we're going to start patrolling first?" he asked, slipping the tank top and cowl over his head. "Downtown?"

"Kingston," she said without hesitation. "Everybody is watching downtown Wilkes-Barre; it's probably the safest place to be, and we don't want that on our first night."

"Nope," he answered. "So what's going on in Kingston?"

"Trouble," she said. "Mentally, the name Guten Tag keeps coming up."

"Guten Tag? Isn't that German?" he asked as he tied his shoes.

"Yes," she answered, stepping out of the bathroom. "Well, what do you think?"

"Whoa, I like it," he said. He pointed to her desk. "It's just like you designed it. So does this mean we're going to be investigating this Guten Tag thing?"

"Yes," she replied as she began stretching. "Hopefully with my telepathy, we'll find out who is behind all of this terrorism and get popular really quick."

"And the world will know who Disc and Wildstar are," he said as he too began to stretch.

Climbing out the window and down the tree wasn't as difficult as they'd thought it would be, and within minutes, they were walking the streets of South Wilkes-Barre. Most didn't pay any attention to them, and those who did simply asked, "Who are you?"

"Disc and Wildstar," Julius repeated after overhearing their conversation as he walked up the steps to his house.

Watching as they continued up the street, he thought, *Just what this city needs—more heroes. With all of the crap that's going on in this city, one of the amateurs is going to get killed like that Arsenal character did.*

His shift had just ended. Julius hadn't been out of work for more than twenty minutes, when the first explosion rocked the tranquility of the day. Something in the direction of Kingston had just blown up, and judging by the size of the fireball, the explosion wasn't an accident.

*With all of these heroes popping up, I wonder if I should keep an eye out for the four horsemen,* Julius thought, speeding through Wilkes-Barre to the police station.

"Maybe we should start looking to the skies for the four horsemen," Wildstar said as they jogged down Old River Road toward the trestle at the river.

"What?" Disc said, slowing up so she could keep pace. "What are you talking about?"

"It was a random thought I picked up," she answered. She pointed to the rising smoke and added, "Let's hope they're not waiting to join the fight next."

Ten minutes later, they were stepping off of the trestle and entering the Wilkes-Barre Zoo, which came to an end on the other side of the street, where the Kingston oil tanks were burning. They climbed over the fence and stopped at the bottom of the embankment just as a group of kids came out of the tunnel. With the aid of her telepathy, Wildstar learned that the four of them were from a school in Berwick, in town on a field trip. As she received the information, she wondered why they would come to Wilkes-Barre with all of the trouble going on.

The two heroes led the children to their bus and the rest of their party. They noticed that the black smoke was getting worse, and the local people started to panic. Adding to the chaos was the gunfire they could hear off in the direction of the fire.

"It's the military," Wildstar said, looking to Disc. "And they're chasing Guten Tag."

"Well, let's go," he said, eager to get involved.

"Not so fast," she said. "It's in the sewers."

"In the sewers? And we're going down there?" he asked. "On our first night, we're going into the sewers. Man, we're going to stink and probably have to make new costumes. I hope we get our man."

# CHAPTER 23

"How does Majk sound?" Arsenal asked looking to her while standing on the ledge, then down and watching the firefighters struggle to extinguish the burning oil below them.

"I think Majk fits," she replied, stepping away from her boyfriend. "You know, when I fell in love while watching you roam the streets of Wilkes-Barre, I never thought I'd be your partner in all of this."

"Not only are you my partner; you're part of the Knight Shift," Arsenal said, watching as she used her magic to slowly rise up off of the ground.

"I love you too, dear," she said, levitating out over the ledge.

Floating higher into the sky and closer to the burning oil below, Majk knew she had to do her best before the fire got out of control. The smell alone would kill, and she intended to stop the disaster before anyone else died because of it. She reminded herself to concentrate; if she looked down at the fire or succumbed to the odor, she would fall to her death.

As long as the spells held up, Judy didn't have to worry. Her uncle Ramsey had taught her, and as far as she was concerned, there wasn't anyone better. Her parents had been adept at magic but not on the level that he had been. Ramsey had been her inspiration and the one she'd looked to the most for guidance.

*Uncle, I wish you were here now*, she thought, glancing down at the chaotic, hellish scene below.

She could feel the heat from the burning oil at that height, and she knew extinguishing the fire was going to take strategy. The Susquehanna River was close, but even all of that water wouldn't contain the blaze.

*Dirt doesn't burn*, she thought, looking around and seeing coal deposits. *But coal does, and that's all I see.*

"I've got her in my sight," the man in maroon armor said, speaking into his commlink.

The armored hit man known as Mercedes, one of Kyle Brock's mercenaries, flew up from his hidden location. He was also an employee working for Dyna Cam's military armored-defense division, a job he'd held since graduating from MIT and the 109th five years earlier.

*This is going to be interesting*, he thought, scanning her aura. *Technology versus magic. Let's see how well my armor holds up.*

The first burst of energy tore through her black robes, just barely missing the left side of her body. His second shot struck her back as she spun around, leaving her too stunned to move and sending her falling toward the burning oil below. Arsenal saw what was going on, but his best weapon was useless. As he watched, panic and anger built up inside; he knew he was helpless to save her.

Judy screamed as she fell toward the ground. Arsenal watched, speechless and stunned.

Suddenly, Duplex caught her in his arms as he teleported underneath her.

"I've got you," he said as they continued to fall. "Hang on for the ride of your life."

Before she could utter a word, they vanished and left Mercedes searching his onboard sensors for answers.

*And what about her armored savior? Did he jump that high?* he thought, looking down at the fire. *If so, where did he go?*

Several moments later, Mercedes learned the answer when Duplex reappeared on his back and began pummeling him. Each blow hit with such force that it pushed Mercedes closer to the ground. Mercedes hoped he'd built the suit to withstand attacks of that magnitude, but by the fifth blow, he realized that wasn't the case.

Rolling over, Mercedes struck back, and after three strikes, he managed to knock Duplex off. As Duplex fell toward the ground, Mercedes fired a shot and hit him in the chest, pushing him closer to the ground and hopefully farther away. However, the instant it looked as if Duplex were going to slam into the ground, he vanished.

Rolling back around, Mercedes returned to his search for Judy only to have Duplex hit him feetfirst. The blow hit Mercedes in the center of his back with such force that he felt as if he were going to be snapped in half. Struggling to maintain his position in the sky, Mercedes feared this attack might put him out of the fight permanently.

When Duplex reappeared on his back a third time, Duplex said, "I don't know who you are or what your reason is for taking the city to its knees, but you're not going to get away with it!"

Mercedes answered, but Duplex didn't hear him because his attack had broken Mercedes's mic. Even if Duplex had heard his response, it wouldn't have changed things; Mercedes still would have been knocked out of the sky. With his helmet malfunctioning as the minutes went on, Mercedes became less of a threat to Duplex and more of a problem for the ground he was about to collide with.

The police and firemen watched as the battle raged on above them, knowing there was little they could do against the armored warriors. They'd put in a call for helicopter assistance, but they didn't know whether or not it would get there in time and be of use.

Arsenal rushed down the embankment as quickly as he could just as Troll King pulled up in his white van. With everything going on, nobody paid any attention to him, until Power of Justice saw the trolls appear out of nowhere. The sudden appearance of the creatures caused the police to open fire, and reporters and onlookers ran for cover.

Motioning for her cameraman to start filming, Susan Brock began reporting on what was unfolding. "This is Susan Brock, reporting to you live from Larksville, just behind the Kingston Marina and the burning oil tankers. I haven't had the chance to ask questions because we've come under attack by creatures that I can only describe as monsters out of a horror movie. As to how or why they are here, I don't know, but they came from the white van that pulled up a few minutes ago. I've concluded they are linked in some way to Guten Tag."

The red spade-shaped bursts of energy that sailed through the air ended the broadcast when they caused the camera to explode. The cameraman collapsed to the ground, and Susan saw a large chunk of metal sticking out of his cheek. Dropping her mic, Susan ran for cover as Ace looked for his next target.

Several feet away, he saw a police officer. As Ace's energy spades struck the officer in the right leg and shoulder, the policeman dropped his pistol, which Power of Justice dove for and obtained. Moving back behind the door, Power of Justice looked around for Star and caught sight of her putting up her best against two of the troll-like creatures.

Taking a step in that direction, he pulled the trigger and managed to remove the right leg of the creature to Star's left. As the creature fell to the ground, it disappeared, leaving all who'd seen it confused. The sudden disappearance caused Star to pause in her attack, which gave the remaining trolls the opportunity to strike her in the face.

Ace too saw the troll disappear and fired a volley of spades at Power of Justice. All four of the shots hit the car, shattering the glass and damaging the door. Power of Justice took the opportunity to fire back, and two of the five bullets struck Ace in the chest, putting him down permanently.

Power of Justice looked around for another target, when he saw Splitscreen being attacked as he tried to help Star. Unfortunately, his pistol was empty. He threw it at the nearest troll and charged the pack, hoping to do whatever he could to help.

He didn't get more than three steps before Troll King yelled, "He's the target!"

In the seconds it took Power of Justice to realize what was happening, seven trolls tackled him and dragged him toward the van. The remaining police saw what was going on and began shooting at the trolls, but for each one they hit, Troll King created another. After seven minutes of fighting, the trolls managed to get the struggling Power of Justice into the van. Once the back door was shut and the trolls had Power of Justice secured, Troll King drove off.

Falling down the hill at the edge of the marina, Arsenal came to a stop just prior to hitting the water. As he stood up, he looked to the other side and could see the oil burning. The strong odor made it hard for him to breathe even with his mask on, but he knew he couldn't stop searching for Judy.

Making his way over to the walkway, Arsenal looked out over the water and boats; he could see at least five bodies floating face down in the water. Luckily, none of them had blonde hair and black robes.

*She's got to be here somewhere*, he thought, crossing his fingers. *I hope I'm wrong and she used some kind of magic to whisk herself away.*

Reaching the other side of the marina, Arsenal made his way up the stairs to the dike and walkway, taking the same route Duplex had earlier. Standing on the top of the dike and walking trail, Arsenal tried to locate Judy. With all of the smoke filling the area, it was hard for him to see any true distance. After calling out her name a few times, he wasn't sure what to do next.

*She can't be dead*, he thought. *I refuse to accept it. Her magic had to have saved her.*

"Help me!" a woman cried out from back at the marina.

"Judy!" he said, whirling around and rushing back down the steps. "She's alive."

When he reached the platform, he yelled, "Judy, where are you?"

"Help me!" she replied. "I can see you. I'm the fifth boat to the left of you. Hurry!"

Counting out the boats, Arsenal ran, but when he reached the fifth boat, Judy wasn't there. It was a woman with bright reddish-orange hair, partially covered by debris.

He stopped suddenly as his heart sank. He asked, "Are you okay?"

Looking him over, she asked, "Are you a hero?"

"Yes. Yes, I am," he answered. "I'm Arsenal."

*Boom.*

The explosion threw Arsenal off of the boat and onto the walkway. The sudden rush of pain through his body caused him to open his eyes. When he looked around, he discovered he was lying on the dike. To his surprise, he was able to not only sit up but also get back to his feet. Pulling up his mask, Arsenal spit out the blood in his mouth as he tried to figure out what had happened.

With his head still spinning, he turned in the direction of the boat and saw it sinking. As he wondered if the explosion had been a bomb or something else, he heard a woman call out, "Are you okay?"

Running toward him was another woman with similar features, and Arsenal at first assumed she was the other woman's twin. Spitting out more blood, Arsenal did his best to regain his composure, and as she got closer, she asked, "Who are you? Are you a hero?"

After hesitating for a moment, Arsenal replied, "Yes."

*Boom.*

The second blast threw Arsenal down the walkway and left him with a broken collarbone. His head was pounding, and he felt the pain of a broken bone. He forced himself to stand as he looked around for another similar-looking woman. This time, when he saw her approaching, he knew something was dangerously wrong.

Taking a defensive stance, he waited for the question, and as she asked it, Arsenal took out his war hammer.

Swinging it over his head as she approached, he said, "Yes, I am a hero. Come and see!"

*Boom.*

That time, Arsenal didn't get up. The blast threw him down the embankment into the Kmart parking lot.

The woman who'd taken out Arsenal was Kelsie Steedman, known as Bombsquad, who had the ability to create explosive duplicates of herself. Kelsie was nearby, watching her clones take down the leader of the opposition: Arsenal.

Her partner, Lightwave, rose up on his self-created light energy board and said, "Contact the others. Tell them we got their leader, and uh, tell them it looks like Mercedes is dead."

"Are you sure he's dead?" Bombsquad asked. "Their metal strongman and his teleportation hit him hard, but I don't think Mercedes is dead."

"Well, I don't like him much, so searching this inferno for him isn't something I intend to do," Lightwave said, moving to retrieve Arsenal's body. "If he's alive, then his armor saved his ass."

Lightwave and his brother, Shadow Master, were usually a two-man team. They were former bounty hunters who had been operating out of Kansas City. In the beginning, they'd been successful, but years into their career, they'd ended up owing money to various criminal organizations because of their gambling.

If things in Wilkes-Barre worked out, the brothers would be paid enough money to clear all of those debts, provided they survived and didn't incur the wrath of their teammates and newfound enemies.

"Is he truly dead?" Bombsquad asked. "We don't have a body, and even if we did, the doctors working for Brock are in a league of their own."

Lightwave didn't respond; he knew the three doctors she was referring to were all extremely gifted. One, Jane Kelmore, was a sapient dominant with the ability to heal others by touch. No matter the ailment, disease, or injury, Jane could manipulate the person's flesh and bone.

Unlike the other two, she was there against her will, as her brother was in debt to Kyle Brock for an incredible amount of money. She was more or less a slave, and Mercedes was her handler. Because of his armor, she couldn't touch his skin and was unable to command his body.

Nygen Trungpa was one of the best scientists in his field, but compared to his mentor, he was nothing. Nygen had been accepted into college when he was fifteen, and by the age of thirty, he had received seven degrees: two in Japan and five in the United States. He could have worked anywhere and made top dollar at any company, but instead, he'd come to work at Dyna Cam for Kyle Brock.

His life had ended during a humanitarian trip to the Middle East, when a terrorist group known as the Waffen Handschar had shot down his plane. Dr. Shpagh, a man whom most of the world didn't know existed, had given him a second chance at life. Those who were aware of Arab Shpagh considered him to be insane.

The truth was, Arab was a sapient-dominant genius who'd reinvented the term *mad scientist*. He'd taught Nygen things nobody else could understand, and in return, all he wanted was his loyalty. Arab had given

Nygen a second life, and Nygen knew Arab could take it away in an instant.

Duplex returned with Majk just as the police were taking control. Splitscreen rushed up to them to explain what had occurred and tell them Power of Justice had been taken.

Clenching his fists, Duplex replied, "Who are these clowns?"

"I don't know, but Ron managed to shoot and kill one of them this time," Splitscreen said, pointing to the paramedics pulling a sheet over Ace.

"Good," Majk said. "Does anybody recognize him?"

"Not that I know of," Splitscreen answered. "But there's one less threat to worry about."

Shaking his head, Duplex said, "Two. Somebody wearing armor went after Judy. He won't be a problem either. Whether or not he survived the fall, he got his ass kicked."

Star joined the others and learned what had occurred and where Arsenal had gone.

Susan Brock then asked if they intended to go after the trapped miners. As much as the group wanted to say no, the responsibility of being a superhero meant that wasn't an option.

# CHAPTER 24

"What do you think they're discussing in there?" Val asked as she leaned up against the wall.

"How bad things are getting in the city," Julius answered as he watched the armed guards at the door change their posts. "Why do they need us here if the military is here too?"

"We did bring Mayor Hart IV here," Val answered, "which makes him our assignment. They're here to protect the area, not just one man. Let's hope they take care of things quickly. Wilkes-Barre has been all over the news for the past few months, and it's not good. People have been leaving the area in droves. The only people coming to the city are reporters doing stories on the terror. Wilkes-Barre hasn't had trouble like this since the Pennamite Wars, and that was over two hundred years ago."

"Wilkes-Barre hasn't seen trouble like this since that war, and like it or not, I don't think it's going to be over any time soon," Julius said, glancing at his watch. "We haven't caught anybody yet who can provide us with answers as to who's behind it and why Wilkes-Barre has been put center stage like this."

"It's spreading to the west side," Val said. "That oil fire wasn't easy to put out; seven firemen were taken to the hospital after fighting that."

"With the exception of the hotel fire, all of the other attacks were on some type of energy source: the oil field, two coal mines, and the natural gas line by the courthouse."

Several people were sitting at a large table: Mayor Daniel Hart IV of Wilkes-Barre, Mayor Steven Linde of Wilkes-Barre Township, Mayor

Donald Hoskins of Kingston, Mayor Arthur McAdams of Nanticoke, Kyle Brock, Dr. Nygen Trungpa, Siegfried Lauren of the CIA, and Lt. General Mason Colts.

"Afternoon, gentlemen," Mayor Hart IV said as he sat down next to Mayor Hoskins. "Have we made any arrests in all of this? How is it that Wilkes-Barre is supposedly under attack by a Middle Eastern group, yet nobody has seen a person of Arabian descent in the city?"

"Because it's looking like they're German terrorists, and whoever made that broadcast on television has to be working with them," Siegfried Lauren answered. "Our contacts ought to be making arrests by the end of the week."

"Our contacts?" Mayor Linde repeated. "How many operatives do you have working in the city?"

"The official number is classified," he answered as he cleaned his glasses. "Some of our agents are in deep cover."

*Indeed, they are*, Kyle thought, looking toward Nygen. *And my wallet is lighter because of it.*

"We can have a team in place by the end of the day," Nygen said. "The technology we've been working with at Dyna Cam will make it possible to bring this to a quicker conclusion."

"What kind of technology?" Mayor Hart IV asked. "Do you mean like a superweapon of some kind?"

"Well, yes, a three-man team from two of our latest projects, Nightbringer and Iron Man," Nygen said. "They will be working with the deep-cover agents to eliminate this threat and restore peace."

"What proof do you have that this is going to work?" Mayor Linde asked. "This area can't take any more of this; people are leaving like it's the Exodus, and I doubt they'll be coming back."

"The United States military runs on Dyna Cam technology. There's nothing better in the world—period!" Mason Colts replied. "Our enemy has run out of resources; their days are numbered."

"I'm not worried about the world," Mayor Hart IV said. "This is small-town America, not the Middle East. This wasn't one horrific event; it was a series of attacks that I believe are acts of war and that took place in the United States, in Wilkes-Barre, at the feet of the offices of Dyna Cam.

The only way it could get more notice would be if it were to take place at the steps of the White House."

Jane Kelmore had lived in London all of her life, and since the age of ten, she'd had the strange ability to heal other people by touch. Several years after discovering the ability, she'd been told she was sapient dominant. Her parents had suggested she go to school to become a doctor, but she'd known she had to do more to heal than any school or person could teach her.

At the age of sixteen, Jane had run away. She'd fled to South Africa with her brother to heal the sick. The first several months had gone as expected, but as word got out, Jane had become a target of the enemies of her brother, Nigel. The one with the longest reach was Dyna Cam. Word had reached the ears of Kyle Brock, who'd sent an operative named Superior Justice to collect her.

With the aid of technology designed by Arab Shpagh, Kyle was able to keep Jane in line. Mercedes, the only armored agent at Dyna Cam, had been assigned the responsibility of keeping an eye on her. Now that he was missing and presumed dead, that task fell to Razor, Kyle's newest thug, bodyguard, and team leader.

The flesh on Arsenal's leg had slowly separated, allowing Jane to see the muscle, tendons, and bones within. Arsenal felt no pain; Susan's flesh-manipulating abilities prevented that. His right leg from the knee down was the first segment of the operation. If anything went wrong, Jane was positive her powers could deal with it.

Shpagh stood in the corner, using sign language to communicate with Nygen. He was eager to see how the alien metallic bacteria worked on Arsenal. All of the tests had been positive, and now they had the perfect subject for it. Watching as the metallic substance jumped around in the test tube, Nygen thought it looked like silver soda.

"The subject is ready," Jane said, looking toward Nygen.

He nodded in reply and stepped forward with the first syringe filled with the sentient super steel bacteria. He glanced over for final approval from Arab, who gave a quick nod, and Nygen injected Arsenal with the first dose. One of the five people in the room enjoyed the procedure the most, because when all was said and done, this was being done for Kidneybean, because Arsenal's body with or without Doctor Kelmore's assistance.

None of them detected the presence of Kidneybean, though if it hadn't been for him, the operation wouldn't have gotten under way. Jane's powers opened Arsenal up, but Kidneybean's mind over matter did the hard part. In his opinion, the operation wasn't needed, but on the other hand, when he looked at the big picture, having bones of that caliber would make him a tougher Arsenal. An upgrade like that would please the Powers That Be, and that was something Kidneybean hoped to be rewarded for.

Just as they began moving the flesh off of Arsenal's skull, a purple snot bubble popped out of Jane's right nostril. As she reacted to it, she heard a male voice in her mind say, *Hmm, metallic bones—how interesting. You do good work, especially under these circumstances. I've been rummaging through your memories and learned how you came to be here. Imagine the good you could do working for the right people, the Knight Shift.*

*Who are you?* Jane thought as she wiped the strange purple substance off of her face.

*For now, that's classified information, but keep doing what you're doing. I'm going to investigate the mind of Mr. One Million Six. Who is that, you ask? That's what the good doctor's name translates to. Luckily, I'm familiar with Arabic.*

*He wasn't sapient dominant when he was tested,* Jane thought. *Could this experiment have altered his DNA? Could our entire conversation have been a test by Shpagh? I'm not sure.*

Nygen Trungpa looked over Arsenal and was impressed by Jane's work. Her flesh-manipulating talents had left no marks or scars on him anywhere. Other than an increase in his body weight, Arsenal would have no knowledge of or side effects from the procedure.

Jane didn't realize she had taken Kidneybean's subliminal suggestion. She'd unknowingly altered his bone structure, enabling him to be triple-jointed in certain regions of his body.

When Arsenal woke, the only difference he felt was the sensation of being heavier. As he struggled to sit up, he glanced over his body, wondering what had caused the heaviness. There were no signs anything had been done to him, and since he was alone in the room, there was no one to ask.

*Hey, Mike, how's the body?* Kidneybean asked.

"Jack?" he said, looking around, thinking he was in the room with him. "What happened to me? Where am I?"

*Kidnapped by the people trying to destroy Wilkes-Barre. Apparently, you're going to be part of the city-saving soldier program sponsored by Dyna Cam. Kyle has selected you and Ron to be part of a three-man group genetically altered to be stronger in a variety of ways to stop the threat to the city,* Kidneybean answered. *You're part of a government black-ops project called Iron Man.*

"Iron Man? What's that?" Arsenal asked. "Am I getting armor?"

*You already did,* Kidneybean answered. *Thanks to Jane Kelmore, you've got alien steel covering your bones. Head to toe, all of your bones are unbreakable.*

Hopping off of the table, Arsenal touched his face and arms and said, "How did she do this? I feel like I gained a lot of weight."

*Relax, Mikey. You weighed this much on the wrestling team the last time you pinned Ron Powers,* Kidneybean answered. *The metal only made you fifteen pounds heavier. Watch your step when you walk.*

"Why?" Arsenal asked. "What else did they do to me?"

*My gift in all of this,* Kidneybean said, *is that you're triple-jointed. Once you learn martial arts, you'll be very dangerous.*

"Really? I can bend my fingers in the other direction?" he said, trying it. "Whoa, this is cool."

*Yeah, your knees bend in the other direction, as do your elbows and fingers,* Kidneybean said. *But don't worry. I'll help you move until you can figure it out on your own.*

"Good, 'cause we need to get out of here, find Judy and the others, and try to stop this before it gets any worse," Arsenal said, feeling his toes move.

*Not so fast. You're supposed to be under their control*, Kidneybean said. *They're going to give you a headset to wear that will keep you under their control. But don't worry. I managed to fix all three of the headsets so they don't work.*

"So we can leave right now?" Arsenal said, looking toward the door.

*If you want, but you'll have every one of Kyle Brock's assassins after you*, Kidneybean said. *Stick around until the time is right. Then we'll make a run for it.*

*Bastards left me*, Majestic Beauty thought, staring at the ashtray in front of her.

While she sat there, she recalled all of the events that had led up to that moment and wondered how much worse it was going to get before she saw the light. Since she was still undercover, she knew she had to keep her answers to a minimum and not let out anything that could blow her cover. However, the more she thought about it, the more she felt betrayed.

*I need to contact Lauren. He'll know what to do*, she thought. *But if I tell them, will they believe me? What am I being charged with? Probably nothing more than kidnapping, and if I told them who Larry Stontz was and his role in all of this, they'd drop those domestic terrorist charges.*

Rachael Lepanto had been a model since the age of thirteen. She'd put that career aside to join the military when she graduated from Wilkes-Barre Area High School. After her basic training, she'd been selected for a top-secret program with the CIA that would wake her dormant sapient-dominant genes. That was when she'd met Larry, and after five years of training, neither had shown any signs of releasing sapient-dominant genes.

When the scientists working at Dyna Cam had started searching for candidates, Mason Colts had suggested Rachael and Larry. Also during that time, Siegfried Lauren had brought them into the CIA to work for him. Dyna Cam had been involved in quite a few black-ops projects, but with rumors circulating that they were involved in something else, Lauren had wanted to know what.

In response to the destruction of Wilkes-Barre by unknown terrorist forces, Dyna Cam and its investors would come in and buy up the destroyed, ruined regions of the city to use for their own needs. The people who lived there would be forced out until there was nothing left of the original Wilkes-Barre.

The other superpower-wielding enforcers working with Dyna Cam were there to make sure there was no resistance. Kyle was well aware of Quarrel, but as far as he was concerned, she posed no threat to him or his plans; Arsenal and the other new heroes presented the biggest problem.

*Boom.*

The loud explosion rocked the Wilkes-Barre police station, knocking Rachael out of her chair. Val and Julius were on their way to question her when the attack occurred. They both pulled out their weapons and rushed outside to see what the commotion was. The police station and city hall, located in front of it, were now under attack.

Outside were Razor, Bombsquad, Shadow Master, Lightwave, Arsenal, Power of Justice, and Larry, known as Operative Three. To keep from being recognized, they all wore white jumpsuits and masks, though they used the same code names. Arsenal, Larry, and Power of Justice had the numbers 1, 2, and 3 painted across their chests.

Bombsquad's clones led the attack, and Razor's strength allowed him to throw any parked vehicles in the way. A white van parked around the corner in front of the *Sunday Independent* building, and the group stepped out with no passersby taking notice.

Cracking his knuckles, Razor walked across the street and picked up a green Dodge. Turning toward Bombsquad, he nodded, and she created three clones that ran ahead and spread out into the parking lot. A few seconds later, the clones detonated in unison, giving the impression of one large explosion.

Just as the clones blew up, Razor threw the car, which struck the front stairs and left them impossible to use. The first few police officers who charged out the doors were injured when they fell down the stairs. Several rushed out the garage door and managed to pull out their weapons, but they were at first unsure who the opposition was.

From what Val could see, there were seven attackers, and due to their clothing, she had no idea who they were. She stepped out onto the street, saw the destructive force approaching, and pulled her pistol out. She took aim at Shadow Master when he rose up into the air.

As Shadow Master rose up and began creating weapons out of dark energy, Larry did the same. His white jumpsuit slowly turned black and took on the appearance of black robes. While the jumpsuit transformed around Larry, Val fired at both of them.

The two shots that struck Shadow Master did no harm thanks to the bulletproof padding he wore. Though he felt no pain, he didn't ignore her attack; he created three black energy shaped diamonds and hurled them down at her. Two of them struck the wall of the police station, while the third broke the knee of another police officer.

"Hold your attack!" Larry ordered, spinning around to face Shadow Master.

"What?" Shadow Master yelled, turning toward him as he created another black energy diamond.

"They are not the one we are here for," Larry replied. "She is inside."

"And how do you think we're going to get her, Operative Three?" he asked. "Just walk in and ask?"

"My transformation is complete," Larry said with his arms extended. "The gift forced upon me is now mine to command. There is a flaw in your plans, and it is called Shadowspawn!"

"Shadow what?" Shadow Master repeated, watching as Larry pulled off his headset.

Dropping it to the ground below, Larry replied, "Shadowspawn. That is who I am, and from now on, you will address me as such! But know this: though I am a spawn of the shadows, you are not now, nor will you ever be, my master!"

Knowing what he was referring to, Shadow Master said, "Oh yeah? We'll just have to see about that!"

Hearing the commotion between his brother and Larry, Lightwave got involved, creating a baseball bat out of white energy.

"I still do not fear either of you," Shadowspawn said. "I don't consider either of you a threat. You are fodder under my feet! Come. Bring your attack. I will show you the fear I will induce and the pain I will inflict!"

Larry Stontz and Rachael Lepanto had trained together and gone undercover together to take part in Project Nightbringer and Project Iron Man. During the course of his preparation, Larry had begun having dreams warning him of the problems that would occur when Dyna Cam began injecting him with the dark energy.

Larry had the ability to take full control of his dreams, and he organized them into a world where he could mediate and study. When he entered the temple, he immediately began to pray and contemplate how he could deal with what he knew was his destiny.

That was when the darkness within the dark energy began communicating with him. In his dreams, in meditation, Larry Stontz learned of his true destiny: the darkness told him to become the Shadowspawn. As much as it looked like Larry was in control, it was actually the darkness within the dark energy doing all of the talking.

"Go back to the van!" Lightwave ordered, commanding his energy board to move in front of Shadowspawn.

As he came to a stop, Shadowspawn asked, "Are you speaking to me? You should be telling that to your brother. It would keep him alive."

Shadowspawn's grip on Lightwave's face was firm and tight, leaving Lightwave unable to give an answer. As Shadowspawn squeezed harder and harder, Lightwave could feel blood oozing where Shadowspawn's fingernails were digging into his skin. He also felt a burning sensation that was the equivalent of acid.

"There is no tomorrow for you!" Shadowspawn said, continuing to squeeze. "Your life ends today!"

Tilting his head toward Power of Justice, who was completely surprised by what was going on, Shadowspawn said, "Ah, I sense the darkness flows through you as well. You were a chosen alternate in all of this, and just like the rest of these fools, you are not in my league either. But we, on the other hand, are teammates, and that has advantages all its own." Tossing Lightwave to him, Shadowspawn added, "Deal with this, and you will be free!"

Power of Justice didn't argue; he had been injected with the same dark energy, and he too wore a headset, which he knew, thanks to Kidneybean, was designed to keep him controlled. However, Shadowspawn had removed his with ease, and there didn't seem to be any backlash because of it.

*Let's hope the system is down*, Power of Justice thought as Lightwave fell through the air toward him.

Hitting the ground hard, Lightwave felt his right hip pop, and he screamed out from the pain. Struggling to stand, he created a bent version of his energy board and used it like a seat. Willing it up into the air, he then created a light energy mace and began spinning it over his head.

*You can't fly*, Power of Justice told himself. *He's got the advantage, but if you concentrate and focus your power, with any luck, you'll hit him. One shot. Hit him hard, and run like hell.*

Val watched as the four men broke off from the group and started fighting among themselves. Whether or not they were in agreement wasn't a concern of hers; she still had to defend the police station. Julius had gone to check on the woman they were about to question.

*She's got to be the reason for all of this*, Val thought, taking aim at Shadow Master. *Maybe she's their leader. Either way, they won't be around to rescue her. Two and Three are fighting against the other two. They must be new recruits along with One.*

The first bullet struck Shadow Master in his left calf, and as he reacted to it, Shadowspawn hit him with a burst of dark energy. Both men had the same substance flowing through their molecular structure, but by the way Shadowspawn used his, it burned like heated acid. The second shot just missed Shadow Master as fell he from the sky.

Shadow Master never hit the ground; Shadowspawn teleported below and caught him. He didn't give Shadow Master time to recuperate; he immediately teleported seven times to steeper heights. Each time Shadowspawn reappeared, he punched Shadow Master in either the face or the chest. The blows were hard enough that Shadow Master wasn't able to mount a defense. Shadow Master formed a spiked club in his right hand, but lack of concentration made it appear as if it were melting. Shadowspawn saw that, and as he dropped him, he laughed.

"My time here is done," Shadowspawn said, reviewing the carnage below. "Now I must make myself scarce."

"No!" Lightwave screamed as his brother hit the ground.

Lightwave commanded the board toward Shadowspawn as he disappeared. He intended to strike with his energy mace but was too late. The swing was a miss and left him open to being shot at by Val and Power of Justice.

*One shot*, Power of Justice thought as he released a burst of dark energy from his right hand.

The force of the blast knocked Lightwave off of his energy board and through the third-floor window of city hall.

*Now, run*, he thought, turning toward the parking lot across the street and running hard.

# CHAPTER 25

Watching as his partner fled the scene, Arsenal took aim and fired as many distraction shots as possible at the police. A few of the policemen managed to get off several shots at Arsenal, but nothing came close to hitting him. As Arsenal disappeared from view, three officers gave chase.

Knowing he'd made himself a target by doing that, Arsenal quickly retreated to the end of the parking lot and took each of the officers down with a stunning shot. Making sure no others followed, Arsenal disappeared from view and took off running down Pennsylvania Boulevard.

Once he reached the underside of the Ellis Roberts Bridge, Arsenal heard Kidneybean telepathically: *You're clear. Head to the back of the parking lot.*

The parking lot belonged to the George Caitlin Art Museum and Institute, which had been built in honor of George Caitlin, an artist who'd painted scenes and portraits of American Indians. Those portraits had been stored and viewed within since the museum opened to the public in 1938.

"What am I doing?" he asked, moving cautiously.

*Getting out of that ugly white jumpsuit*, Kidneybean answered. *A little secret: we don't have a link if you aren't wearing your costume. Just for future reference.*

"Yeah?" Arsenal said. "Whose idea was that?"

Laughing, Kidneybean replied, *Mine.*

"So you're saying if I drop dead, I need to make sure I'm dressed as Arsenal?" he said, coming around the back of the building.

*Pretty much*, Kidneybean replied. *If you want to live forever, it's going to be in that costume.*

Arsenal stepped behind a Dumpster and said, "How could I forget? I wouldn't have wanted it any other way."

Lightwave opened his eyes and tried to focus past the memory of what had happened to his brother. The pain in his hip kept him from concentrating on his brother's memory.

"Dammit, Lance," Lightwave said, holding back his tears. "Now what am I going to do?"

Clearing the blood from his throat, he stood up and immediately leaned back against the wall. No sooner had his shoulder hit the wall than the door to the room he was in opened, and a bald middle-aged man peered in.

"Are you okay?" he asked, looking Lightwave over.

"Get out," he answered, struggling to stand. "I'm fine. I can handle this."

"Who are you?" the man asked as he watched Lightwave create an energy board.

"One of your worries," he answered as he sat on it and flew out the window. "Flee while you can."

Following him, the man stopped at the window and watched as Lightwave disappeared into the chaos. He wondered what was happening outside. Police were shooting, and bombs were bursting all around. Was the person he'd just seen one of the heroes the city was in need of?

Creating another baseball bat out of energy, Lightwave randomly selected a direction to begin his search for Power of Justice. He should have stayed and assisted his partners in getting Majestic Beauty out of jail, but being the weakest of the three and having an injury, he knew he would be a hindrance. The sight of his dead brother lying on the ground below the window wouldn't have helped either.

Making his way up North Main Street, Power of Justice reached the walking entrance of the Ramada Hotel parking lot. Lightwave moved into position to swing his weapon, only to have Power of Justice lean over to pull the top half of his jumpsuit off. The noise the weapon made when it hit the wall was loud enough that Power of Justice heard it and knew it was an attack.

Almost falling over, Power of Justice spun around to see Lightwave regrouping to swing again. The burst of black energy that Power of Justice struck him with knocked him off of the energy board and sent him crashing into the ground five feet away. As Lightwave rolled across the ground, the injury to his hip felt worse.

Cursing and screaming from the burn as he reached for the energy bat, Lightwave got hit again by Power of Justice. The dark energy shredded his costume, and he screamed from the heat.

Power of Justice yelled, "You made me! Now deal with the consequences!" He kicked Lightwave in the ribs. After three shots, he said, "If you attempt to follow me, I'll kill you!"

Just then, two fairly built college-aged men, thinking they were doing something good, knocked Power of Justice to the ground. Each had the build of a football player or a wrestler, and Power of Justice knew this wasn't going to be easy.

"Get off of me!" Power of Justice yelled, pushing the taller man in the gray sweater and raising his right fist.

"We're not letting you do any more shit to our city!" the second guy said, not backing down.

"Your city?" Power of Justice yelled, taking a swing. "I'm the goddamn good guy!"

The fist struck the second guy, who was closer, and knocked him backward. Power of Justice felt his jaw crack.

*Wow*, he thought, *I think I just broke his jaw. Guess he should learn to mind his own business. I'd better watch my strength from now on. Maybe that shot taught them a lesson.*

Falling backward, the second man made a painful noise as he hit the ground, grabbing his jaw. The first man saw his friend lying on the sidewalk and looked back at Power of Justice, who was ready to swing again. Thinking it had been just a lucky punch, the man pushed Power of Justice, raised his left hand, and swung at him.

Catching the fist in his hand, Power of Justice said, "Not a smart idea."

As he squeezed the man's fist, he released a small amount of dark energy and burned it. As the man screamed, Power of Justice kept his grip and said, "When I let go, take your friend and run away. If not, I'm going to beat you until you learn to mind your own business."

The man nodded, and as Power of Justice let go, he shook his hand as if the pain would ease up, looked at his friend, and ran off. Watching as he fled, Power of Justice said to the other man, "You're still here?"

As the second man left, Power of Justice saw Lightwave lying there and was tempted to hit him again with his dark energy, but with all of the other people around, he didn't want to make things worse. Jogging up the street, Power of Justice hoped to find a place where he could lie low and think things over.

Two blocks later, he came to his apartment, and as he looked up at it, he briefly pondered going there. Returning home to Karen would be a good way to end all of the madness he'd suffered through.

*But would she be there? She's probably out with Judy and the others, searching for me.* He thought about how good it would feel to return there just to relax.

After thinking the idea over, he concluded that it might not be a wise choice. *Dressed like this, people might think I'm someone else, like those two guys did. Better stay away. I think I'll go to the cemetery.*

The ten-minute walk from where he was to the cemetery gave him time to think. However, when he got there, something strange was going on. From where he was standing, Power of Justice could see that more than thirty graves had been dug up. Curious as to what was going on, he made his way in through the front gate.

*I wonder if this is in any way related to what happened at the mine down on the corner,* he thought, looking in that direction. He could see the destroyed buildings and hear the workers. Upon entering the cemetery, he took several steps in that direction, thinking the bodies possibly had fallen into the mine below and needed to be returned.

*All these holes. How many people were digging here?* he thought, looking at the closest holes. *Are they done for the day? I don't see anyone working, let alone any equipment.*

Deciding to investigate the destruction of the mine complex, Power of Justice put everything else out of his mind. Walking through the Connecticut section of the Wilkes-Barre Cemetery, he could hear equipment running, but he didn't see or hear anyone near the river.

*This is getting strange*, he thought, moving a little faster. *The trolley tracks and the canal are down here too. I wonder where they rerouted the trolley.*

Just as he reached the end of the cemetery and a large hole in the fence, Power of Justice heard gunfire. Crouching down, he heard people panicking in the direction of the bridge collapse.

"Are they attacking the same area again?" he said, trying to see who was doing the shooting.

Making his way along the narrow ledge, he was finally able to see a little more of what was going on. He hopped into the canal, swam to the other side, and, after a few minutes, found a way out on the railroad tracks on the other end.

A group of mostly dirt-covered, slow-walking people were moving toward a group of armed security guards and policemen. Power of Justice was about to fire his energy at the people, but he decided to watch and wait. He wasn't sure why he hesitated; then he saw the old German he'd encountered with Quarrel.

He was acting strange and appeared to be cheering. Power of Justice thought, *Maybe he's just gone nuts with all of the stuff that's going on. Then again, how did he get down here? This area is closed off to the public. There's a cleanup and investigation going on. Unless he's giving them advice on how to fill those holes in the river, I'm going to conclude that he's part of the problem.*

Coming closer, he could see dirt and dried blood on the man's clothing. He didn't see or hear anyone else who might have been working with him, but Power of Justice didn't want to take a risk. His right fist was instantly covered with dark energy.

The old man saw the energy form on Power of Justice's hand and knew he was in trouble. He quickly clasped his hands and started pleading, watching as Power of Justice clenched his fist. He then took aim and prepared to fire at the six attacking men. However, none of them appeared as if they were hampered by what was happening.

As they beat on him, one of them made the comment that Power of Justice shouldn't have touched his friends. The six men weren't under the control of the old man; they were friends of the two men who'd jumped in during his fight with Lightwave. They'd followed him, and they intended to get payback for what he'd done to their friends.

None of the six men had any intention of stopping as they kicked and punched him. At first, they didn't notice the old man touching them one by one. When the old man touched the third attacker, the three who remained untouched saw that the others were acting differently and jumped back at their sudden alteration. One of the men thought Power of Justice was behind it. He learned the hard way when his three former friends took him down.

Screaming as the old man touched him, he felt his skin shifting and his brain being twisted. The other two men took off running, and Power of Justice fired his dark energy and knocked one of the men into the river. Power of Justice concluded that the man on the ground had died when the old man touched him.

*Maybe in his next life, he'll learn to mind his own business*, Power of Justice thought. *But he's got to be the last who dies by my hands today.*

He clenched his fists and focused his energy to fire on the old man. Instead, he started to levitate. At first, he didn't notice, until he was more than three feet off the ground. The old man saw him rise up and commanded two of the remaining men to pull him down. As Power of Justice struggled, he realized he had no idea how he was able to levitate, and he had to break his promise—he fired energy from both fists, killing both men.

"This ends now!" Power of Justice declared, lifting both hands up to fire.

No energy came from his hands; three policemen did it for him, seven shots tore through Shadow Master's body and put him on the ground permanently. Looking back, he saw the policemen running toward him, and at first, he thought they were going to arrest him. He was surprised when they inquired if he was okay.

# CHAPTER 26

Deep down under the city of Wilkes-Barre and its deepest mines was Lake Wilkes-Barre, a place that had never seen the light of day and had been created through accidents of man. During the various floods that had struck the Wyoming Valley over the last 150 years, the water had covered the land but disappeared quicker than expected.

Where did it go? As one would suspect, it went into the mines, and according to the theory, it filled a cavern below the city. The billions of gallons of river water that gushed into the Knox Mine in January 1959 had added considerably to the lake.

Recently, two escapees from the top-secret Copper Farms military instillation had discovered a way down to the lake. Both men were born sapient dominant but were disfigured by it and, as a result, were thought of as being more alien than human. That was one of the reasons Mason Colts was in Wilkes-Barre: to try to locate the two test subjects.

One of the two was named Slayer. Despite his normal facial features and upper body, his lower body resembled that of a spider. He was also a cannibal and had a particular taste for sapient dominants. He would drain away their abilities, flesh, and mind to increase his own telepathic abilities. However, his diet had caused him to become extremely overweight.

The other man, known as Blackball, had a body that looked as if it were completely covered in tar. His abilities included creating duplicates of himself and using the substance on his body as a weapon. He could also teleport and would bring sapient dominants to his smarter partner to feed upon. The substance that covered Blackball kept him from having the need to eat, sleep, or relieve himself.

The Martz bus came to a stop, and Kim Downey stepped off in what she hoped would be her new hometown of Wilkes-Barre. Her intent was to forget about her life in Boston and the years of drug addiction she'd suffered through. With just one suitcase to her name, Kim didn't know what her next step would be. She hoped it would be a good one.

As the bus pulled away, she heard a loud crushing noise and concluded that an accident must have occurred. Kim wasn't the only one who heard the sound and saw the cause. One of the nearest to the accident was Blackball, the same Blackball clone who'd claimed Cam earlier in the day.

The one Blackball had taken down was Marcus P. Wedler, a Wilkes College student who was born sapient dominant. Marcus had an increased intellect and superspeed, as, thanks to his intelligence, he'd created a set of metal legs that made him three times faster. He was in the process of field testing the legs, and thanks to Slayer's mental link with Blackball, they knew where to attack.

Springing up from the sewer, Marcus, who'd decided upon the name Roadkill, had been about to step on the grate, when he'd been knocked into the air. That was the crashing noise Kim and the others had heard: Roadkill hitting the ground at more than four hundred miles an hour. The pain he felt from the impact left him unable to get up, and the injury to his right lung only aided in his passing out.

In the minute that it took Kim to reach him, Blackball was merging with him and preparing to teleport. Just like Marcus, Kim was also a sapient dominant; her unique ability was to weaken the powers of others and gradually turn them off. Blackball never had encountered anyone like her, and if she'd had more experience, she could have reclaimed Roadkill, wiped away Blackball's tar-like skin, and forced Blackball to retreat.

But that was not what happened. Blackball fought back. He not only created several weaker copies of himself but also made more targets to distract Kim and keep her from defeating him.

*Does this kind of stuff happen here all of the time?* she thought, glancing at the bystanders scattered up and down the street.

Kim was aware of her abilities, but past drug use had kept her from practicing and taking them to the level she could attain. Still, she was going to do her best to keep the guy covered in black from taking the guy with the metal legs. Granted, she didn't know if he was a good or bad guy, and she didn't know who the other guy was either.

Focusing on the black figure, Kim made Blackball operate at a slower pace, which made him feel as if he were sticking to the ground. As for the clones, she tried to get them to do the same and felt the effort taxing her. It was as if she had a heavy weight on her back. The feeling made her feel almost as weak as Blackball. The man with the metal legs wasn't moving and would be of no help.

Thinking of her friends back home, she wished they were there to help; their powers would have been useful against the black thing. Then she thought about how they'd been when she'd left them, and she realized that as interesting as their powers were, they probably would have been too stoned to react to this situation. Her friends were sapient dominant just as she was, but none of them used their powers to fight or support crime in any shape or form.

"There's got to be some kind of help in this city," she said. "Doesn't the guy with metal legs have a partner or a team?"

Looking down the road, Kim saw no other heroic-looking people approaching and thought, *Nope, I guess I'm his only hope.*

Hearing a noise behind her, Kim turned to see Blackball lunging at her. She was unable to dodge, and he claimed her, along with the man she'd tried to save.

Mason Colts sat in his office, watching surveillance video. The destruction of the Kingston Oil Company hadn't been part of the plan. He didn't object to it, but if Guten Tag was going to take part in this war, then operatives might have to be scrambled to deal with them.

*Then again, if this all falls apart,* Colts thought, *they could be the scapegoats. Rachael and Larry worked for me in Iran, and now they're working with the Germans. How many of Brock's men speak German? With Rachael sitting in jail, I'll send in a lawyer to provoke her into speaking German and then get him to accidentally suggest a link between her and Guten Tag.*

The objective was to simulate a terrorist attack on an American city to measure the response of the local government and police force. Because of the power players involved in the criminal black-ops project, they'd selected Wilkes-Barre. If they'd had to give a grade thus far, it wouldn't have been good.

The money that the power players were going to make off of the attack was in the billions. The lives lost and property destroyed didn't matter because those factors would be figured into their winnings. Wilkes-Barre was going to be a battle zone, and regardless of what occurred, it was all about profit; contracts for and against the survival of the city were in effect.

Mason Colts had spent most of his military career on the wrong side of schemes like this. When the idea to change the course of history in the '60s was conceived, he was left out on the deaths of John F. Kennedy, Martin Luther King Jr., Malcolm X, and Robert F. Kennedy, which was hard to believe since he'd taken part in the death of General George S. Patton Jr.

The Gulf of Tonkin and Pearl Harbor were two other interesting incidents that Colts was not linked to. Those major events had changed world history and America. Attacking a city in that manner and at that magnitude beat out a plan for a three-city attack, a plan that involved hijacking five jets with the intent of crashing two of them into the World Trade Center towers in New York City; two in Washington, DC, with the White House, Capitol, Pentagon, Washington Memorial, and Lincoln Memorial as suggested targets; and a fifth one into the heart of Wilkes-Barre, to strike the Public Square Plaza Hotel.

Wilkes-Barre was also involved in that criminal black-ops project, but it wasn't the only target. The chaos and carnage would have been spread across the eastern United States. The damage would have been centralized to the impact site, whereas in this case, it was directed at an entire city, presenting more of a problem.

Assisting in this operation was Bradley Brock, Kyle's older brother, a longtime priest who had studied black magic since World War II. Bradley's two professions were at opposite ends of the spectrum, yet for most of his adult life, he had been able to mix magic and religion with no problems.

Due to the explosions that had torn through the bottom of the river, the water of Lake Wilkes-Barre was rising quickly. Slayer had moved his residence to higher ground, but even that cavern wasn't going to remain dry for long.

The collected sapient-dominant humans were safely stored at the far end of the cavern. His hunger was growing as he looked over the people Blackball had recently collected. Their souls, auras, and flesh would be consumed little by little. The ones he sought to taste the most were Laura and Cam.

Lately, he'd become interested in tasting something new, something that humanity called magic. Both Judy and Bradley were on his list to be collected and consumed. His only problem was he didn't think Blackball would be capable of capturing either of them.

When Blackball returned with Kim and Marcus, a strange image began forming in front of Slayer. Even in the darkness, his eyes had to focus, and what he saw led him to believe the image was an illusion that his mind created. As it became easier to see, Slayer concluded it was a sapient dominant in astral form, working for the military.

The forming figure was that of an attractive woman. Slayer knew she wasn't someone they were allied with, which led Slayer to believe he was being hunted. Her long, flowing black hair and see-through white gown made his male organs swell in ways he'd never experienced before.

Slayer had decided long ago to give up the ability to speak, believing that it prevented him from using his abilities to their fullest extent. Now, as he looked at the beautiful woman before him, he knew that choice had been a big mistake.

Forcing out the words, his dry, shriveled vocal cords managed to ask, "What do you want?"

For Astanna Syznchalla to appear in a place that far from a true heat source meant she had to concentrate all of her power to make her presence known. Slayer and Blackball were standing before her, both were important enough that she believed she had to be there. Astanna believed they were the missing pieces to her army. With Von Kragen dead, Slayer was the perfect fit. Instead of building her an army, they were already eliminating the sapient-dominant opposition.

"An offer for better things," Astanna replied. "I'm building an army. All of your problems on the surface will be eliminated. The forces hunting you are soon to be eliminated, and you will be free to feed upon any sapient-dominant human you desire without consequence or retribution."

"Colts," Slayer said. "I want to feed on Colts."

"Very well," she said, coming closer to him. Slipping her arms around his fat, sluggish frame, she said, "Swear your allegiance to me, and I will personally feed him to you."

The kiss that sealed the deal spread third-degree burns all over the front of his body. The sensation was in no way pleasant, but it was his first kiss, and in light of the release that followed, he briefly ignored the pain.

The night sky spread across the Wilkes-Barre skyline as Bradley Brock made his way to the top of the Public Square Plaza Hotel. Being the tallest building in the state outside of Pittsburgh and Philadelphia, it was the perfect place for Bradley to bring his plans to a finale and open the portal to bring Astanna there.

Bradley was finally going to be with her and experience all of her love. The magic he was going to use would cover the city with a barrier that would trap the heat from the soon-to-be ignited fires and keep the place from cooling down. Wilkes-Barre was basically going to become a giant oven that Astanna would live inside once it was hot enough.

The atmosphere that he would rip from the sky would cover all of the city, with the exception of Kirby Park. Its exclusion was due to the Susquehanna River being in the way. Everything else would burn, and in time, the barrier would be expanded until all of the American continent was consumed.

As Bradley spoke the cantrips that would hold the barrier to the ground, Wes gathered his minions to do their work. The fires they started would be looked upon as offerings to Bradley's mistress. He had done everything to bring her there; all that was left was to reignite the fire in the hotel.

Astanna Syznchalla was coming; there was nothing on Earth that was going to prevent that. In Bradley's mind, it was all going to burn.

"Now is the time to make your money," Wes said, looking out over the crowd. "There are too many things wrong in the world today, and this is our time to change all of that. It's a change we can make right here in our section of the world, right here in Wilkes-Barre. It'll be a fresh start, and when historians look back, they'll see that the ashes ended the threat of terrorism. Their guns, bombs, and hatred are not strong enough to prevail against our fire, which is the same fire that forged creation. You can't see them, but they are here, and only the fire will know. Listen to the monster. Set it free, and it will save us."

The monster Wes referred to was what the arsonists called the fires they would set. Most of those in the crowd were aware of the monster and had been burned in summoning it, yet they all respected it. They loved it and enjoyed watching it grow as it consumed and destroyed, which was no different from what Bradley sought in seeing Astanna.

The red Pontiac pulled into the parking lot at Turkey Hill in the Miner's Mills section of the city. With all of the turmoil spreading throughout the rest of Wilkes-Barre, the store was empty. The man working that night had been employed there for the last three weeks and was preparing to end his shift.

The three people who entered the store didn't look any different from any others who had entered prior. Two men and a woman spread out and proceeded to shop. The tall man made his way toward the first-aid section and took a bottle of alcohol off the shelf.

"What are you doing?" the cashier asked, watching as the man opened the bottle.

"Taking a look at it before I spill it all over the floor," he answered. "Tell me—how long do you think it will take to burn? I already know because I'm an arsonist. I like to feed the monster."

"What?" the cashier yelled. "Get the hell out of here! I'm calling the police!"

Stepping up to him, the tall man grabbed his name tag, and as he read it, he said, "Thomas, you're not getting out. It's hungry."

Pulling back, Thomas was about to speak, when he felt something sharp pierce his left lung, making it harder for him to cry out. He collapsed to the floor, and the tall man poured a second bottle of alcohol over Thomas's head. Screams filled the room as the three people robbed the store.

"And now you burn," the tall man said, taking out his lighter.

Struggling for air and pleading for his life, Thomas watched the flame appear on the lighter. His heart pounded wildly as the two seconds he had left of his life came quickly to a close, and the fire touched his head.

At the upper end of the city was the Wyoming Valley Sanitation Plant, which took care of all of the sewage in the area. The large, grassy fields behind it that stretched to the river and wooded area just to the south became the next area to be victimized.

The Wilkes-Barre police had been alerted to the situation, and to assist them, the Plymouth police were sent in. However, the two patrol cars never reached the scene; they were the first to discover Bradley's magical barrier. Neither car made it across the bridge. The first was sliced in half and continued moving for another fifty feet. The second car slammed into the barrier and killed the police officer instantly when he slammed his head into the windshield, breaking his neck.

The barrier didn't stop at the bridge; it sliced straight through and down into the water. The Carey Avenue Bridge and the smaller Breslau Bridge were no longer useable. The people walking on the walkways were just as surprised. Those who saw the car accidents rushed in to help, thinking the bridges might collapse.

The other cars traveling on the bridge were lucky enough not to be cut into sections by the barrier, but they did cause a pileup that led to several injuries. Any ambulances that were contacted now had only one way to arrive. Half of the injured were sent to the Nesbitt Hospital or the Nanticoke City Hospital.

Thanks to the ambulance services, the outside world was now aware of the barrier and how serious the terrorism had become. However, that didn't do much to help the people who were stuck on the other side of the barrier. Even though the electricity for the city was still working, the light from the Public Square Plaza Hotel burning up the inside of the barrier lit up like a giant nightlight.

Just across the Breslau Bridge, in that section of town, a group that had started the massive grass fire at the sanitation plant was now seeking to burn people's homes. The first house to go up in flames was a vacant house, but when the neighbors rushed to investigate and extinguish it, the arsonists struck a second house.

A family of six owned the second house, and as it burned, others grabbed their weapons and started searching for those responsible. The first arsonist shot was a woman attempting to start a car on fire. The shooter didn't own the vehicle, but he knew he had to stop her from adding to the chaos and fear.

By the time the police were on the scene, eleven people were dead. The two squad cars screeched to a stop, and the shootout lasted another fifteen minutes before one of the police officers and the remaining four arsonists were dead. Three of those arsonists were eliminated by Raphael's Spanish street gang, which turned the neighborhood hatred and fear into something good.

The large wooden structure that made up the South Wilkes-Barre Mine lit up the night sky in the same way the hotel did at the other end of the city. The top of the roof ignited just as the barrier destroyed the Plymouth police cars. Wes and his three-man group also managed to set explosives in the mine below, farther down underneath the houses, churches, and businesses.

From the street entrance to Schiel's grocery store to the front doors of Meyers High School, there was a fifty-foot-deep trench. Thirteen houses collapsed into the hole, nineteen people were injured, and two elderly twin brothers died. Three houses exploded when the gas line ruptured and added to the chaos.

With the fire department already spread thin, people knew there wasn't any help coming, nor would anyone be coming to prevent the fire from growing and spreading to the nearby woods as well as the homes across the street. People were gathering and using garden hoses, but aside from keeping their homes from burning, their efforts did little. As good as the idea was, it didn't prevent the blaze from forcing the elderly out of the retirement complex.

# CHAPTER 27

"We're out," Razor said as his face appeared in the shattered brick wall.

"It's about time," Rachael said, getting up as she looked at the cuffs. "Now, if you could get these off."

Pushing the broken cinder blocks out of the way, he made his way in and easily snapped her handcuffs. "Let's go," he said, pointing. "Little resistance. Bombsquad's outside taking care of the Wilkes-Barre police force."

"What about the others?" Rachael asked, climbing through the hole.

"They're dead," Razor answered, following behind. "Apparently, Brock's idea was a big mistake, and those witch doctors he paid a fortune for, Trungpa and Shpagh, are going to pay."

"Never did trust them. I don't understand Arabic, let alone sigh language," Rachael said, moving quickly down the corridor.

When they reached the street through the indoor garage, she got her first glimpse of Bombsquad's devastating powers and the battlefield she'd turned the city hall area and police parking lot into. Rachael had seen her powers at work on training missions, but that level of carnage was something she had never seen before, and she knew her teammate possessed real power.

*I wonder where Colts and his troops are. Why are they standing down?* she thought, following Razor up the street toward James M. Coughlin High School, which was located across the street. *Bombsquad might have taken down the police like that, but if Colts were here, things would be different.*

She was right. Most of the police were either injured or, like Val and Julius, were helping others who were. None of them attempted to give chase, until the police helicopter unit arrived. It was located at the Wilkes-Barre

Township station and had been in service since 1970. Donations from Dyna Cam Industries funded it.

Razor and Rachael made their way to the front of the older high school building, trying to think of a way to get away from the helicopter. Razor picked up a trash can stationed at the front door and threw it, but it missed. He smashed the glass front door.

"This way," he said, ripping the door off its hinges.

Stepping inside, they looked at the office to the right and the classroom to the left. Moving to the hallway, they looked at the stairs in front of them and then in both directions. Rachael asked, "Which way?"

Coming around the corner, Arsenal stopped in the Hazard Wire complex, wondering what his next move would be. Ahead of him was the intersection of Ross Street and Pennsylvania Boulevard. The post office and the Flat Irons building were two major concerns, as they were prime targets for possible future attacks.

As he walked, a loud blast from the third-floor window just above him threw him to the ground. Glass and brick went flying everywhere as Arsenal rushed to get out of the way, and as he looked back, he saw two motorcycles coming around the corner.

A second blast sent a chunk of brick down onto the front of the second biker. Arsenal watched the accident occur as the first driver stopped almost alongside Arsenal. As he stepped off of his bike and looked at his girlfriend, Hades went berserk and screamed out her name. He took a quick glance at Arsenal and ran to her side. Though she was wearing a helmet, there was blood flowing down onto her face.

Arsenal took a step toward her, and Hades pulled out a pistol as he said, "Don't! I mean it!"

"I'm here to help," Arsenal said, holding his hands up where Hades could see them.

"I don't like your kind," Hades replied. "This city is falling apart, and you're the reason for it."

"I didn't just blow up the building," Arsenal answered as something within the building crackled and popped. "But I'll look past your comment and help you."

Raising the pistol, Hades replied, "One more step, and I'll blow your head off!"

Remembering what his dark side had told him, he kept his hands up and said, "And how far do you think you'll get? My death won't be what you think."

"Publicity doesn't make you immortal," Hades said, taking a shot at him.

The bullet didn't hit Arsenal; it barely missed his left side as it tore a hole through his trench coat. Stopping in his tracks, Arsenal said, "Your partner is dead if I don't help you."

Hades was about to fire again, when he was thrown onto his back. As Arsenal took the steps to reach him, he saw a bullet hole in the center of Hades' head. Puzzled as to who'd shot him, Arsenal looked around and saw a military jeep approaching. Keeping his hands up, he moved to the sidewalk as the jeep sped through the intersection.

Seeing four armed soldiers in the jeep, Arsenal kept his hands up. They stopped in front of him. He wasn't afraid, but one of them had just shot his opponent, and he didn't want to be next on the list. Motioning toward the injured biker, Arsenal said, "The other one is still alive and in need of a doctor."

"Keep still, masked man," the driver ordered, "and you'll be allowed to live."

The four men were part of the 109th. Though their commanding officer had yet to give them orders to intervene, the four men had an agenda all their own. Their city was falling apart, and they weren't going to wait any longer to act. If they were looked upon as going AWOL, then they would deal with that later, when they were discovered.

While he stood there with his hands up, Arsenal watched two of the soldiers rush over to help the injured woman. There wasn't much they could do, but they did their best. None of the five men noticed that Hades was starting to move.

It wasn't until a small flame appeared where the bullet hole was that Arsenal and the driver took notice. Jumping from the jeep, the driver kept his rifle on Hades as he sat up.

"Gaffney," the driver called out, knowing that his shot had been the one to take down the biker.

Gaffney lifted his rifle to fire again as flames covered more of Hades' body. The soldiers wondered if he was sapient dominant or something else. In either case, the flames kept them from reacting, whereas Arsenal tackled and knocked him back to the ground. Hades' body had been altered by the monster that sought to destroy the city, but thanks to Arsenal's dark side, Kidneybean, his plan backfired.

Even though Arsenal's body was heavier, his dark side helped him move, and he'd become used to the extra weight. The moment he landed on Hades, Arsenal used the extra weight to pummel him. The fire continued spreading, and Arsenal recalled how he'd died the last time he'd been so close to heat of that magnitude.

Just as the fire was about to ignite his costume, he rolled off, and Gaffney fired again. Two shots struck Hades in the head, and the third tore through his chest where his heart should have been. That time, Hades stayed down as the fire slowly extinguished itself.

Before Arsenal could react, a loud explosion in the air directly above got their attention. As they looked up, they saw two more helicopters explode in the same manner. None of them had seen anything fly through the sky and strike the helicopters, which left them wondering if the explosions had come from within.

"What the hell?" Arsenal said, talking to Gaffney. "Did you see that?"

"Yes," he answered, looking through the scope of his rifle. "Something took them out. The debris is stuck in the air."

"What? How?" Arsenal said, squinting to look. "Are you sure?"

"Positive," Gaffney replied. "It's just sitting there in the air. I don't know what it is, but none of the stuff is falling."

Looking at the driver, Arsenal asked, "Any idea what could be causing that?"

"No," the driver answered as they carried the female biker to the jeep. "But I'll be sure my superiors know about this as soon as we get to First Hospital."

*That's just around the corner from where we're at now*, Arsenal thought. *Let's hope his superiors act as quickly as they should.*

Razor and Rachael found their way down into the basement of the high school. They knew the pilot had seen them enter the school as he spun off, but they hoped to be gone before others showed up to pick up the trail.

"This place is over a hundred years old, which means it's got a fallout shelter somewhere in here," Razor said, coming to a stop in front of a large green metal grate. "And I know it's right here under out feet." Reaching down, he pulled up the grate. "They'll never think to search down here. That helicopter is most likely searching the back of the building and streets behind us."

"Farther and farther into the ground we run," Rachael said, recalling a movie she'd seen. "Deeper and deeper down the rabbit hole."

Making sure she was down far enough, Razor climbed in and dropped the grate. The moment he let it drop, he realized there was no light. However, as he was just about to curse and pick the grate back up, Rachael found the breaker.

"Good," he said, walking down the ladder. "Let me guess. The door is locked."

Turning the handle, she answered, "No, but it is rusty."

Leaning over her, he gave the door a hard shove, and as it flung open, he pushed past her and said, "They thought this would save them from a nuclear attack. They were wrong."

Rachael didn't respond; she knew he was right as she made her way through the large room. Razor walked up to the wall, smashed through it with one punch, and then stepped into the Wilkes-Barre sewer system.

Looking up and down the line, he pointed right and said, "This way to Dyna Cam."

Arsenal stood alone on Hazard Street, wondering where he could go next. His thoughts were of Judy and returning home. Deciding that was the best thing to do, he began walking. He made it to the parking lot of Nardone's Pizza, when he noticed the fire on High Street. The trees and grass on the same side of the road as the mine complex and high-rise retirement center were burning.

The elderly were being herded out of the building as quickly as possible and escorted down the street to the church on the corner of Dana Street and to the slightly farther First Hospital up the road. The people who lived in the homes and apartments on the other side of the street were there to assist.

Some helped with the elderly, while those who had garden hoses attempted to extinguish the fire. Farther up the road, Arsenal saw that all of the buildings in the South Wilkes-Barre Mine were burning. The fire stretched so high into the sky it allowed Arsenal to see the light reflecting off of the force that held the helicopter fragments in the air.

"God help us all," Arsenal said, watching as the fire easily consumed the building and trees. "There's no end to this, and I don't know what to do next. Dammit, Mitch, I wish you were here. I could sure use your input. On the other hand, if it wasn't for you and this damn silly idea to be better than Quarrel, who knows where I'd be?"

Moving back toward the crowd, Arsenal wondered how much more of that section was burning. Following the fire down the hill, Arsenal saw that the fire stopped where there was nothing to burn. However, across the street, on one side of the road were railroad track and plenty of burnable items, such as trees, grass, and trash—enough to stretch the fire to Ashley.

On the other side of the street was Vulcan Iron, the country's oldest company for building trains and engines. If the large complex were to burn, the fire could stretch into Lee Park and easily reach the greyhound racing track, another business that had been around for a long time.

*I wonder if they got the dogs to a safe place*, Arsenal thought. *There's got to be a way to stop this, but I don't know how.*

With everything going on, Arsenal hadn't realized he'd walked completely away from where he intended to go, which was to Judy. A loud explosion not far from where he stood brought him out of his distraction. Less than one hundred yards away was Schiel's grocery store. Arsenal at first thought the sound might have been a car exploding, but as he thought about it more, he realized the explosion had been too loud.

"A bomb?" he said, rushing to the parking lot. "As if there wasn't enough to worry about."

When he first entered the parking lot, Arsenal couldn't tell what had just exploded. The people gathered there, who had no idea where to flee, pointed it out to him. They also mentioned the large, gaping crater that was once Hanover Street, and Arsenal was able to see the fires burning because of it.

"Wow," Arsenal said, stunned by what he saw. "Wilkes-Barre has become a battlefield."

"But, mister," a young girl said, looking up at him, "you're a superhero. You have to save us. My mommy said you're better than Quarrel."

The young girl's words gave Arsenal something to think about. Suddenly, out of the corner of his eye, he saw his teammate. Star was about a 150 yards down the street from him and was facing off against a figure clad in all black.

Unfamiliar with the person she was facing, Arsenal rushed to her side. Making his way over the debris, he saw Judy lying unconscious across the front of a light blue jeep. Scanning the ground, Arsenal took the quickest route to get to them. In the few minutes that it took, he never took his eyes off their opponent.

"Hey!" Blackball yelled as Arsenal tackled him.

To Arsenal's surprise, he went straight through him and landed in front of him as his opponent split in half. Rolling over, he watched as Blackball split into two separate beings, and he knew this wasn't going to be an easy fight. Due to the speed at which Blackball moved, Arsenal was able to reach Star's side.

"Michael, you're still alive," Star said, surprised.

"I could be better," he answered. "Wilkes-Barre is falling apart. What happened here?"

"We were out looking for you and the others," she answered. "Shockwave went back to watch out for his family. Duplex and Splitscreen are out there somewhere also."

"What happened to Judy?" he asked as the two Blackballs fully reformed.

"This thing caused the explosion, and Judy was thrown into the jeep," she answered, taking a fighting stance as Blackball moved toward them.

"Are you part of this attack on the city?" Arsenal asked Blackball, stepping in front of Star.

"He's not going to answer you," Star replied. "At least he didn't say anything to us."

"Did he cause this?" Arsenal asked, keeping both Blackballs in front of him.

"I don't know," she said, "but he was stalking us."

Arsenal threw the first punch, and to his surprise, he felt as if he were hitting a large gummy bear. His fist seemed to bounce back, and Blackball didn't appear to feel any type of pain from it. Arsenal noticed small bits of the black substance on his knuckles. The second Blackball moved to deal with Star, and she kicked him in defense, but unlike Arsenal's attack, her foot went through his chest.

Falling down, she noticed the same sticky black substance splattered across her right leg, and she wondered if their opponent was even human. Her kick at least should have knocked Blackball backward. Her leg had passed almost completely through him—where was his inner structure? There were no bones or muscle noticeable, let alone any blood loss.

Arsenal saw what had just happened and wasn't sure what his next move should be. His blow had been deflected, yet Blackball's body had reacted differently.

*Maybe because she's a woman, her body had a different reaction to this thing*, Arsenal thought. *Could it be targeting women?*

"Star, get out of here!" Arsenal yelled. "I think it's after you. I'll keep it distracted until you're clear."

"Where am I going to go?" Star asked. "Is there a place I should go where we can meet up? What about Judy?"

*What about Judy?* he thought. *She's right. Damn, I can't deal with this craziness anymore.*

Putting his fists up in front of his face, Arsenal prepared to face off with both Blackballs again. Meanwhile, Star got to her feet and prepared to move backward and retreat. Suddenly, the first Blackball disappeared, and as Star spun around to run, she stepped into Blackball. Arsenal called out to her. He knew she couldn't respond, and he felt helpless as she struggled to breathe.

Looking around, Arsenal found a small shard of glass, and he used it to try to slice into Blackball. The second Blackball saw that, his fist swelled up, which he then used to knock Arsenal down, preventing him from cutting his other self. Stars spun around Arsenal's head as he dropped the glass, and Blackball raised his hand up to strike a second time.

Judy's eyes opened, and she slid off the front of the jeep. The phrase she spoke ignited her fingernails, and as she spoke the rest of the incantation, she hurled a large fireball. Blackball saw it coming and couldn't react fast enough; the fireball hit him, and he exploded into a thousand black droplets.

"Star!" Judy yelled, seeing Blackball disappear.

"She's gone!" Arsenal cried out, spinning around. "You've got to track her."

Climbing up the ladder, Razor pushed open the door leading to the subbasement of Dyna Cam.

As Rachael climbed out, he said, "Hit the shower. Mr. Brock wants to speak to you."

*This hopefully will go smoothly*, she thought, heading to her locker for a change of clothes and a towel.

The sublevel above them was the training facility, which consisted of a specially made weight room to accommodate Razor's super strength, a wrestling and martial arts area, and a shower room. After locking the door, Rachael stepped into the shower, adjusted the water, and pulled the handle.

As the water ran over her body, she recalled the events that had brought her to that point: deep-cover work for Siegfried Lauren and the CIA, who had been investigating Dyna Cam's other business investments. She'd been an intended recipient of Project Nightbringer and Project Iron Man, until Splitscreen had taken her out.

"According to Razor, that program ended up being a bust," she said, recalling the conversation. "I'd probably be dead by now if I'd taken part in it. Probably would have died in the lab."

Several minutes later, Rachael dried off and got dressed. As she tied her boots, she glanced up at the clock. She made her way over to the elevator, pushed the button, and waited for the doors to open. As she waited, her mind drifted back to her escape, and she wondered if the police were still searching or were doing other more important things.

*If I don't get to turn things around, eventually, they'll find me,* she thought, stepping into the elevator. *And hopefully I'll have my superiors there to keep the handcuffs off this time. Speaking of superiors, why hasn't Colts sent in his troops?*

When she got off the elevator, there were no guards waiting, and she wondered where they had been reassigned. She knew there was little chance they'd been allowed to go home to be with their families during all of the chaos. Shrugging it off as not a concern of hers, she stepped up to Kyle Brock's office and reached for the handle.

After knocking, she slowly opened the door and walked in to see Razor standing across from Kyle Brock, who was sitting at his desk. On the left corner of the desk was a black leather briefcase with gold trim, and as she saw it, Kyle pushed it toward Razor.

"Ms. Lepanto," Kyle said, turning toward her, "I see you are well and in good health."

"Yeah, well, I could be doing better," she answered. "Not too thrilled about having to go through the experience of being arrested, but I'm grateful I was let out by my employer."

"Yes," he answered, "and now I need answers. I need to know what you told them."

"Nothing," she answered with a shake of her head. "I never got the chance to. They never questioned me. Razor broke me out before it happened."

Nodding, Kyle slid his chair back and stood up. "You'll have to convince Razor."

Cracking his knuckles, Razor said, "And the money in there is going to be mine, so make sure I believe what you tell me, whether or not it's what actually happened."

Ignoring Razor's words, she tried to plead with Kyle, but he didn't want to hear it. He walked out of his office, saying, "Oh, and, Razor, any damage done in my office comes out of that money."

"Yes, sir, Mr. Brock," Razor replied as the door closed.

Seeing the door close, Rachael took two steps back, took a quick look around the room at her surroundings, and hoped for something she could use to her advantage. The door wasn't far from her, and if she ran for it, there was a chance she might make it, unless Kyle had locked the door.

*There's only one way to find out*, she thought, preparing to test her theory.

As if he could read her mind, Razor turned and forcefully pushed Kyle's desk. As it slid into the door, he said, "Don't even think of it."

"Think of what?" she asked, surprised he'd caught on that quickly.

"You're not getting out of here, not without telling me what happened," Razor said. "And I plan to let my fists do the talking."

Knowing the dangerous amount of pain he could inflict, Rachael reminded herself to stay away from him. Besides having fists that could easily dent steel, the small, thin hairs on his body were extremely sharp, and a glancing blow could cause her to bleed to death.

*Keep him at a safe distance*, she thought, moving toward the windows. *I don't think there's a way out in that direction.*

In the brief moment that she looked out the window, she didn't see Razor pull the carpet out from under her feet. As she flipped through the air, Razor moved to her side by the time she landed, and he struck her, which sent her head spinning.

He didn't give her a chance to speak, electing to hit her again. Spitting the blood from her mouth, she kneed him as hard as she could and managed to crawl away. Getting to her feet, she timed her kick and hit him in the jaw as he was preparing to stand up.

Even though she struck him with her hardest kick, his strength and endurance allowed him to ignore her attack. Stepping back, Rachael gave her best and struck with three more kicks, all of which hit in the same general area and ended with the same minimal effect.

Shaking his head and shrugging off her attack, Razor wiped his mouth and said, "That's not the story you ought to be telling. I don't believe you so far, and I find that very little you say and do is going to change my mind."

"I'll remember that when I'm walking out of here with that briefcase," she said as she continued moving back to keep her distance and avoid being struck again.

Her plan worked, until she tripped on the carpet, and Razor took advantage of her stumble by striking her square in the jaw. Catching her as she fell backward, Razor backhanded her and knocked her into the glass. She hit so hard that the impact caused the glass to crack. Moaning from the pain, she leaned up against the window, trying to stand as Razor moved in.

She struggled to speak as the glass cracked, and she fell onto a small ledge. Convinced she deserved the beating he was giving her, Razor moved to help her; he knew that if she fell into a public place, the police would be there to ask questions, especially since she'd just escaped from their jail several hours earlier.

"No," she said in a pain-filled tone. "This is my end. You're all gonna pay!"

"No!" Razor yelled, lunging for her.

His timing was off, and instead of grabbing her, his hand accidentally assisted her in getting off of the roof. As the ground came up quickly, Rachael said a quick prayer and hoped to be forgiven as everything went black.

# CHAPTER 28

The teleportation-tracking spell that Judy cast impressed Arsenal so much that it gave him a small glimmer of hope. Her magic could turn the battle in their favor and bring the chaos to an end. He also hoped she could do something to prevent any more deaths during the war.

The instant Arsenal and Judy arrived at their new location, Judy created a ball of fire in her hand that enabled her to see a few feet around them. She hadn't thought they were going to appear in total darkness. Her secondary reason for creating the fire was to use it as a weapon against Blackball.

"Can you get that a little brighter?" Arsenal asked, squinting. "I can't see much of anything in here. Where are we—at the edge of space?"

"I don't know," Judy answered. She took a step and fell into water.

"Judy!" he called out as everything went black.

"Michael, I'm here, and I'm okay," she said, reaching out for him. "The water is cold."

Feeling around for his girlfriend, Arsenal also fell into the water. Jumping up, he grabbed on to Judy, and as they clung together, he said, "Wow, you're right; it is cold."

"Yes," she replied, rubbing her hands together. "Let me try to dry my hands, and I'll get the fire back."

"I can't help but think this is some kind of trap we fell into," Arsenal said, pulling his gloves off and shoving them into his pockets. "I don't want anything large and creepy looking popping up out of nowhere and eating us, as silly as that might sound."

"Trust me, Mike. Nothing sounds silly and far-fetched anymore," she said as he put his hands over hers. "I think we ought to leave and find another way to find Star," she added, pulling away and recasting the fire spell.

"I can see," he said, looking around into the darkness. "Still don't know where we are. Give me a few minutes to see if we can get a sense of direction. If not, we'll leave and find another way. Do you think you might have cast the spell wrong, or is that not possible?"

"To be honest with you, a lot of these spells are new to me. I've read over a lot of stuff, and some incantations are a mixture of spells, so yes, I could have cast something wrong. We could be in some weird dimension with no way home," she said as she started to shiver.

Helping her back onto dry land, he said, "Don't worry. We'll find her."

Looking around at the darkness, she said, "I don't know where they're at, unless that thing brought her here and ran off to somewhere else in this limbo-like place."

Blackball was watching from the darkness. As Judy attempted to increase the light, he sprang up and pulled Arsenal down into the water. Had it not been for the stars Arsenal saw spinning around his head, he would have been in total darkness.

"Michael!" Judy cried out, watching as he splashed and struggled to get free.

"Get back!" Arsenal cried out, fighting to stay above the water. "I don't know what this thing is. Stay out of the water."

"I can put you into a shield when you get out of the water!" she yelled, trying to increase the light from her spell.

"No!" he yelled. "This creature might get in. I can't risk that. You might have to leave me here."

"I can't do that!" she yelled as Blackball pulled Arsenal back under. "Michael!"

Raising his fists, Blackball, who didn't have to breathe, had no problem pounding on Arsenal and forcing the air from his lungs. Choking from the water, Arsenal tried to fight back but couldn't get his footing. The struggle didn't last long, and Arsenal's body went limp and floated to the surface.

Blackball watched. He was about to move for Judy, when he saw the body start to shake. Even in the darkness, Blackball caught sight of strange purple liquid seeping from Arsenal's body. Unsure what it was, he moved to investigate and was surprised when Arsenal opened his purple eyes.

"You have done something you will never be able to comprehend," Kidneybean said, coming face-to-face with Blackball. "I too can breathe underwater, but that's where our similarities end. You've been collecting sapient-dominant humans for quite some time. Well, your harvesting is over. You ought to consider yourself lucky. You killed the Protector of Existence, although technically, he hasn't been given that title yet."

Before Blackball could react, a burst of purple energy struck him in the face, and as he had no defense and the brain of a child, it killed him. The explosion caught Judy's attention. She hoped it was something Arsenal had done, and she believed the figure floating out of the water had to be him.

"Michael?" she called out, trying to brighten her light.

"I am here," he said in a deep voice. "Look around you. There are cocoons. Break them open. They're the Knight Shift."

Turning around, she said, "I see them, but, Michael, there aren't that many members on our team."

"Use fire to get them out of that stuff," Kidneybean said. "Whatever that sticky substance is, it melts."

Nodding, she said, "Okay, I'll do it."

Fifteen minutes later, Judy had melted enough of the substance to see their faces, and in two instances, she had to use CPR, first on Roadkill and then on Massacre. She failed to bring Massacre back; Slayer had been feeding on her and her sister.

When she came to Cam, the small flame she used to melt the substance appeared to also be taking care of the wounds on his face. Cam was the first one fully awake, and he wanted to know where he was.

"That I can't tell you," Judy said, shrugging as she turned away from him. "Because I don't know either. We tracked him here using my magic. My boyfriend, Arsenal, is out there in the water."

"Arsenal? So what name do you go by?" Cam asked, sitting up. "I've got one I was born with and a code name, which I don't have much use for."

"Which one would that be?" Judy asked, moving to her next patient. "Majk is the name Arsenal gave me. Judy is the name I was born with."

"Majk," he repeated, as if impressed. "Well, you can call me Cam. Cam Egavas. The Savage."

"The Savage? Does that mean you're a fighter?" she asked, stopping in her task. "Are you one of those guys who will just jump into a fight to kick ass no matter what the odds are?"

"Why? You know my family?" Cam asked, struggling to get his arms free from the remaining residual substance. "'cause if they're involved in your problem, honey, I'm all yours."

"Well, I don't know who your family is or if your family is involved in this," Judy said, returning to the melting. "Wilkes-Barre is in trouble, and we're its only help."

As she pulled the substance away from the next face, Judy recognized her friend and cried out, "Quarrel!"

Upon hearing her name, she began to cough, and Judy turned her onto her side as she spit out the substance from her mouth. Leaning over, Cam watched as the woman cleared her throat and stomach.

"Is she okay?" Cam asked, trying to figure out if he knew her.

"It looks like it," Judy answered as Quarrel spit and looked over at Cam.

"What's with your boyfriend out in the water?" Cam asked, looking in that direction. "Did he lose something? Does he have some kind of supervision?"

"No, I don't know what he's doing," she answered. "Possibly keeping watch in case anything comes back."

As if standing next to him, Kidneybean replied, "You are correct, Cam. I am out here dealing with problems that came up since our arrival here. I will join you onshore shortly."

An hour later, all of the heroes were free of their cocoons. Slaughter, Massacre, and the biker were the only three Judy couldn't save. Quarrel was the only one who'd known the sisters, and she was relieved she would never have to face them again. She didn't hold back her feelings about them and the troubles they'd put her through.

"You've been fighting crime in Wilkes-Barre for over five years, and I have to say, all of us who live in the city are doing this because of you," Wildstar said, approaching her. Pointing to Star, she continued. "And I tried to follow in your footsteps and be an Olympic gymnast."

Puzzled, Star asked, "How did you know?"

"My name is Laura Tonal. I'm a sapient-dominant telepath. I took the name Wildstar without knowing you used the name Star. Besides, the mask you use doesn't really hide your face much."

"Can you read all of our minds?" Roadkill asked, "or do you have to probe a person's mind?"

"Both. If I don't focus, they can overwhelm me," she answered. She looked out toward Arsenal. "Judy, what did you say your boyfriend's name was?"

Judy did not respond. When Wildstar looked at her, she collapsed, and because she couldn't read Judy's mind, she knew something was wrong. She took two steps and saw the hideous form of Slayer as Judy's light spell began to flicker. Cam's senses failed to detect Slayer, but when it all went black, he was the first one to attack.

Following their new teammate, Disc and Quarrel used their energy weapons and fired in the direction of Slayer while trying not to hit Cam. Seeing Savage charging, Slayer swung his two front right legs up to deflect his attack. His other front legs were occupied by holding Judy, whom he intended to feast upon.

Looking down at his metal legs, Roadkill felt helpless. He wanted to run and do something to help, but the darkness was like nothing he'd ever experienced prior. Quarrel's energy bolts gave him brief glimpses of his surroundings, and after the third one, he felt he should at least try.

*Just a step*, he thought, *and I could knock that thing back.*

The attack never came. As Roadkill slowly stood up, Slayer claimed his mind. There was no screaming or sign of struggle; he just stopped, as if the light to his mind had shut off and left his brain as dark as the cavern.

Slayer then claimed Quarrel and Disc together, which slowed his physical movement slightly, allowing Cam to get past his front legs. The talon attacks did serious damage, and even without his sense of sight, Cam knew exactly where to strike. Out of all of the heroes, Cam was the hardest for Slayer to collect.

The amount of water it took for Arsenal to drown was just enough to fill his lungs and stomach. At the instant his life faded out, Kidneybean took over. After scolding Arsenal on the meaning of life, he went about restoring him to the land of the living. At the same instant, he took the time to scan the entire area for any other threats.

*The city is directly above us*, Kidneybean thought. *A mile perhaps. So, this is where all of the mine water ends up, in what I would guess is the largest underground lake in Pennsylvania. The fools who are working to burn this city would be drowned out with all of the water that's here. But that battle is yet to come, and if I'm part of it, then they'll all drown.*

Arsenal opened his eyes and was back in the cavern, surrounded by total darkness. He could hear the fight between Slayer and Savage going on but didn't know who was who. Even though Arsenal was without a weapon, he wasn't defenseless, and he felt along the ground for a rock to use. Moving as quickly as he could, Arsenal joined the fight, and once he knew he could avoid striking Cam, he let Slayer have it. The two men fought Slayer, making it harder for him to fight the battle on the astral plane, where he was struggling to pull them. With all of them out of their bodies, he could feed on what he sought from them.

Out of the three of them, only Slayer could see in that level of darkness; his two foes were fighting on instinct. All of the others were in the astral and confused as to how and why they were there.

Another member sitting in the dark was Kim Downey. She had no idea what had happened to the others, but she could hear the fight going on. Reaching out and feeling the darkness, Kim wondered if her power could help her new teammates in some way. Focusing, she concentrated on the hideous face of Slayer and hoped to contribute to the team.

The strain Slayer felt was as if someone were pushing down on his body, as if his power were in some way being squeezed. For his power to work, he had to focus harder. Unfortunately, Kim didn't have as much practice and experience in aiming her power, and Cam suffered just as much as Slayer did. Luckily, Cam was a fighter and in a lot better shape than both Arsenal and Slayer.

Those in the astral plane were not affected by Kim's power dampening and were unaware of the struggle Slayer was going through. Wildstar sensed only his power and knew that defeating him wasn't going to be easy; Cam was still fighting Slayer in the physical world.

*That has to be helping in some way because now he's fighting us on two fronts*, Wildstar thought, watching her teammates. *Or at least it's helping there. It's here where we're going to need the extra help. I've only been on the astral plane a few times; trying to explain to the others where we're at won't be easy.*

Lumbering forward, Slayer advanced at a speed that seemed to upset him. His nearest target was Star; she had no abilities that would be a challenge or threat. Claiming her as a quick energy boost would do a lot to help him deal with the others. Sensing that they had no experience in the astral plane, he believed it would be an easy feeding.

He'd deal with the three not on that plane after he increased his energy levels. Those he would torture slowly and use to feed his physical body. He could no longer sense Blackball and knew that these heroes had to be responsible for his demise. However, as strong as he was, he couldn't detect who had the power to kill him.

*It's not wise to enter here.* An alien voice echoed through Slayer's mind. Wildstar heard it as well.

Neither of them knew what it was or the cause of it, and both wondered who the new player in the war could be. Slayer wasn't worried about an ally or an adversary; he was most worried that his feeding would be prolonged, which would prevent him from gaining levels of energy he hadn't experienced in quite some time.

"Who are you?" Slayer asked, looking the heroes over as he stopped several feet away from Star. "I know there's a telepath among you, but even she is not that powerful."

The eerie grayness of the place had a light source that nobody could identify, but as they looked at it, the grayness slowly developed purple strands in it. Out of all of them, Judy was the only one who recognized it for what it was, Slayer sensed her relief and pushed past Star to attack Judy before she could make any contact with the new threat.

"I would rethink your current idea," Kidneybean said as the purple strand began to take on a human form. "Your hound managed to kill my former host, and now I intend to make repayment!"

"I will kill them all!" Slayer declared, raising his front legs to strike Judy.

"If you weren't fat and lazy, I might be worried about facing off against someone of your psionic discipline," Kidneybean said as he completed his purple form. "But I am the new player on the block, and my powers are far greater than anything you can understand or have faced in the past. You might wonder what my name is. Because I was hated for being a genius-level sapient dominant with purple skin, they taunted me. The name they chose for my humiliation is the one that will be burned into your mind: Kidneybean. They called me Kidneybean! Fear me!"

All but Majk and Star were confused by his statement, but because he was within each of their minds, they knew there was power backing up his words. However, even as Slayer reached out to grab him, they weren't sure if he was trustworthy or allied with them.

Killing one of them became his plan. The swelling within his mind made him feel as if his head were going to explode. If he could kill one and consume what he needed, Slayer believed the tide would change in his favor.

Kidneybean's response to that thought was "No!"

As Arsenal kicked Slayer in the face, all three of them heard Kidneybean loud and clear as he said no. The instant Arsenal's boot hit his face, an unseen purple ooze seeped out and exploded, throwing all three into the water.

Kim screamed as she hit the water. Cam swam to her aid as Slayer's headless body ceased moving. Arsenal sprang up out of the water, ready to continue, as he heard Wildstar coming around. Looking in her direction, he saw only darkness. Then he heard Kidneybean tell him that the threat was over and that he was leaving. His last words were "Wilkes-Barre is burning. Go save it."

As Majk's light spell illuminated the area, Wildstar asked, "What happened?"

"Kidneybean," Arsenal replied. "A name that at this moment doesn't induce fear, but I suspect that will change one day. Wilkes-Barre is in trouble, and it seems like we're the only ones who can stop this madness. My name is Arsenal, and thanks to my other half, I know who all of you are, and all I can say is, welcome to the Knight Shift."

"Is your other half the reason why you call yourself Arsenal? 'cause I don't see any weapons," Savage said, squeezing the water from his clothes. "Were you in the military?"

"No," Arsenal answered. "It just happened to be the name I chose—because of my father."

"Was he a soldier?" Savage asked. "The one who pushed you?"

"No," Arsenal answered. "His drunken misadventures put me out on the streets searching for him. The variety of weapons I picked up along the way were the reason for the name. They ended up helping me in fights against those who wanted my father's head on a platter."

"Then your father was no different from mine in some ways," Savage said, recalling the beatings he'd taken in his life.

"Yeah, we walk in our own footsteps," Arsenal said. "As for my weapons, they're sitting at Dyna Cam until I retrieve them."

"Dyna Cam? So what are we waiting for?" Cam asked. "I've heard of Dyna Cam before. Is that where we're stationed?"

Arsenal said, "No, Dyna Cam is linked to the problems going on in the city."

"I thought Guten Tag was?" Cam asked, confused. "How long have I been out of the picture?"

"Guten Tag, Dyna Cam—who can be sure anymore," Arsenal answered. "They're probably connected. Wilkes-Barre is burning, and that's what has to stop!"

# CHAPTER 29

Images of the casting out filled her mind. The war for control of heaven had failed. It didn't end with their defeat. They were in front of the gates, when the Lord spoke the unforgettable phrase: "Get out!"

One by one, they fell through the clouds, down through space and the atmosphere, until they hit the earth like meteors. Astanna Syznchalla was no different in that respect; she was, however, one of the most attractive of the female angels as well as one of the few angels who truly understood the meaning and pleasures of sex.

She was facing off against a principality when the phrase was spoken. She'd ripped off half of his left wing, and she was about to claim his right eye, when she began her descent. Just like the other fallen angels, Astanna burned on her way down, but she believed the Lord was jealous of her beauty, and she burned at a hotter rate than the others, the only exception being Lucifer. He was the last to fall and the first to hit.

Whether or not jealousy played any part in her burning, she would have to wait until apocatastasis to learn the truth. However, that end-time moment wouldn't come to pass for at least another thousand millennia or longer. Of all of those who fell, Astanna was the only one whose flame never went out, which convinced her of her jealousy theory. As a result, she could never walk the earth alongside the angel she followed, because it was too cold.

The closest she could get to Earth was to live within the sun, and through heat and flame, she was able to make allies and contacts on Earth.

During World War II, Astanna had found a man named Bradley Brock and taken the time to teach him and mold him into the soldier she sought—one able to walk among her kind.

Recently, she'd added the demented German doctor Helmut von Kragen and the freakish spider-looking human called Slayer, but they'd both failed to keep their promises. Now only Bradley remained, and she was close to walking and ruling over Wilkes-Barre.

"Hang tight, folks," Majk said as her fingers moved through the air. "We're about to teleport into Wilkes-Barre."

"Let's hope there's something left to fight for," Star said as light began to crackle around Majk and her hands.

"Shockwave, Splitscreen, Duplex, and your boyfriend, Power of Justice," Arsenal said as the portal Majk created started to expand. "Those are the members you've all yet to meet. I hope they're still alive."

"Amen to that," Disc said. "Well, what are we waiting for? Let's go see Wilkes-Barre."

The swirling colored lights stretched out around them, and the moment the light touched their feet, they disappeared. The group reappeared on the grass at the front entrance of Meyers High School. The destruction of Hanover Street hadn't changed; the strong scent of things burning was a lot stronger, and they could see traces of smoke forming in the air.

The sky above was dark, but the fires in Wilkes-Barre made it feel like a hot afternoon in the middle of August. Stretching as he struggled to get a breath of fresh air, Roadkill looked around and said, "I'll scout the city, and I guess Wildstar's telepathy will be how we keep in touch."

Caught off guard by his statement, she said, "Um, yeah."

As Roadkill took off running, Savage's senses were going haywire. He cleared his throat and said, "Lots of trouble brewing around here."

"Try to stay focused," Arsenal said. "We've got a lot of combat coming up, but we need to make sure we're dealing with the big picture and not the little danger spots that will pop up."

Looking up Hanover Street at the South Wilkes-Barre inferno, Quarrel said, "Let me guess. This isn't the worst of it."

"No, the worst is yet to come," Arsenal answered. "But we do know that Dyna Cam, on some level, is involved in this, possibly in a way similar to the way Ford and Citibank were with the Nazi party."

"Let me guess. That's one of the buildings that isn't burning," she said. "You know, in all of my years fighting crime in the city, I never really faced off against Brock, yet as a crime boss, he managed to pull this off."

"Adding to this is the invisible dome over the city," Arsenal said, gesturing up at the sky. "I don't know how it got there, but I'm guessing that's why it's so hot here."

"Can't your magic take care of that?" Quarrel asked looking at Majk, gazing up at the sky.

"I'm working on it," she answered, thinking.

"So this is Wilkes-Barre," the woman in a black leather costume said, looking at a map of northeastern Pennsylvania, which was marked with a red pin. "I've never been there, and you're telling me it's under attack by an unknown group of terrorists. Where is this group located, and who do they know that they can get financing like this?"

"I don't know, Wind Rider," said the leader of the group, a woman named Algae, shaking her head. "I've read the reports and watched the stories on the news just like you. I don't know, but someone out there isn't telling us everything."

"And we're going there to put an end to this?" asked Triphammer, the man with a large hammer strapped on his back.

"Yes," Algae answered. "Wilkes-Barre has become a battle zone, and we've got to stop it before it gets worse."

"High Tide and Blitzkrieg are on their way," Triphammer said. "I don't know about Stone Fist or Arachnoid. Haven't seen them today."

"We're all going," Algae said. "The jet will be ready in fifteen minutes, and we'll be there in two hours."

The entire group had, at one time, been in the military and part of the government project that trained sapient dominants to use their abilities to serve and protect the United States. They'd trained and been given the code name the High Lords. Financed by the government, their group went into hot spots around the world to deal with threats others couldn't deal with.

"Another mission? We just got back from Alaska three days ago," High Tide said as he undid his tie.

"We're getting the big money," Blitzkrieg said as he sat on a bench around the corner from the lockers, waiting for his partner.

"Lucky I don't have a family to spend it on," High Tide said, taking off his unbuttoned shirt and leaving his light blue spandex top showing. "No worries about in-laws I don't like or taking the kids to the dentist. Just me and a lot of money that I don't have time to spend."

"Well, I plan to find a woman to settle down with," Blitzkrieg said, smiling. "Who knows? Maybe she's in Wilkes-Barre, waiting to be rescued."

Laughing, High Tide replied, "Yeah, maybe she's waiting to rescue you."

"If you don't hurry, we won't get to see which of us is right," Blitzkrieg said, using his superspeed to quickly change into his orange-and-white costume.

"Why don't you just run there, scout out the place, and report back to tell Algae what you found?" High Tide suggested as he slipped his shoes on.

"Dressed already?" Blitzkrieg asked. "You mean you're not going to sit in the shower to juice up?"

"No, Wilkes-Barre is near a river," he answered. "There will be more than enough water for me to use."

The swirling fires danced around as if they had minds of their own. The fields of grass that once had covered the southern end of the city were now burning, and fire spouts were forming. As they moved and came in contact with the others, they formed into a larger one, growing in dimension and intensity.

The Wilkes-Barre Area Sanitation Plant was lost as the fire ravaged the entire complex, and the foul odor coming from the place only made things worse as it cooked in the heat. The flames reached higher and higher into the sky; some appeared to bounce off the barrier.

Astanna Syznchalla had arrived. The heat and flame generated by Bradley and his forces finally had reached a level she could tolerate.

"Bradley, my love!" she screamed. "Where are you? The fire of passion is spreading! Where are you? I am in need of you, my love."

All of the Knight Shift heard her words, which sent shivers up their spines. This was no terrorist group out to destroy the Great Satan once and for all. This looked more like the return of Satan himself. With the way things were burning, the city looked like hell on Earth.

Hearing the screams of more than five hundred people flooding her mind, Wildstar fainted.

"I've got you!" Savage called out, catching her.

"The Breslau area," Wildstar said, opening her eyes. "Down near the bridge and sewage plant. That's where the fire is spawning."

"What do you mean spawning?" Arsenal asked, gazing in that direction.

"There's a great evil here," she answered, trembling. "It's the reason for all of this. She's not with them. I don't think we can beat it."

"We have no choice," Arsenal said. "We're stuck in here. The city is counting on us to put an end to this chaos, and so far, we haven't done a bang-up job."

As the heroes looked around at the carnage, Savage asked, "Do the hydrants work? How far is the nearest water source?"

"The river is on the other side of the barrier," Arsenal answered, pointing. "It's just a few blocks in that direction."

"So what about the place we just came from?" Disc asked. "That was water, right?"

Arsenal shrugged as he looked at Majk and asked, "Well, would it work?"

"Never thought of it, but yeah, it should," she answered, thinking. "I just need to find a spell that can shoot the water into the city, and we could use it to fight this."

"Well, if we can't control it, then the water is going to be wasted," Arsenal said, putting his arm around her. "You'll figure something out."

The fireball struck the taxi on Coal Street Bridge, sending the first explosion echoing off the barrier above. Five more vehicles followed. Bradley's magical assault caused chaos and a massive fire on the bridge. After watching briefly as the fire spread, he looked toward Public Square. He watched as the top third of the Public Square Plaza Hotel burned and illuminated the barrier above it.

"Wilkes-Barre is soon to be a thing of the past," Bradley said, looking down at the canal. "And the hotel will be the palace of my mistress."

While he gazed down at the carnage and dreamed of his future as ruler of the city, a bullet grazed his leg. He had cast a spell of protection, but it didn't apply to physical attacks. It was meant to deal with the heroes, who, as far as he knew, didn't carry firearms.

"A foolish mistake," Bradley said, launching three fireballs down at the gang gathered on Canal Street.

At the same time, Bradley noticed three tanks traveling down the boulevard toward him. As he looked them over, he couldn't help but notice that the paint scheme wasn't right. They looked more like tanks from World War II.

Squinting, he tried to read and identify the writing. Then he decided to just attack and deal with the threat. Bradley hurled three more fireballs at the lead tank and was surprised when they struck the ground and did damage to the cement and pavement. The explosions the fireballs caused did no damage to the tanks, nor did the tanks fire back at Bradley, which left him puzzled.

"I think he's onto your illusions," Duplex said to his brother as he reverted to his armored form. "Keep still, and if he sees us, stay behind me."

Remaining crouched behind a tree, Splitscreen watched as Bradley looked around for a clue as to who or what was behind the tanks but saw nothing. Stepping out from behind the tree to keep his brother safe, Duplex made his presence known and walked out into the open. His shiny metallic skin caught Bradley's attention, and as their eyes met, both wondered who the other was.

"Who are you?" Bradley asked, forming a fireball in his hand as Duplex walked out onto the railroad tracks.

"I intend to stop you!" Duplex answered. "I represent the Knight Shift, and as for who I am, you can call me Duplex."

"Duplex?" Bradley said. "I am unimpressed, but if that is what you wish to have etched on your tombstone, so be it. And as the Father of the Flame, I can assure you that nobody will care if you scream in hell. Your friends will be there with you. Victory will be mine. Wilkes-Barre is going to be burning ash under my feet!"

"The only victory you'll have is the one you dream about. I'm going to break your neck," Duplex declared, reaching down and ripping a chunk of the sidewalk out.

Taking two quick steps, Duplex threw the cement chunk with so much power and anger that it caught Bradley by surprise. His first reaction was to move to his right, not to block, deflect, or return fire. Taking advantage of that, Duplex teleported right next to him and struck Bradley with his fist.

Duplex struck him with such force that Bradley felt his jaw crack and screamed out from the pain. Then the clothing Bradley was wearing began to catch fire. However, the flames didn't seem to be consuming the clothing; it was as if the flames were spreading like some type of pyrokinetic armor.

As Duplex landed back on the ground, his first reaction was that of joy, as he thought Bradley was burning. Then he realized he hadn't set Bradly on fire with that punch; something else had caused the flames. Taking a second look, he realized the fire seemed to be covering his body without burning him and looked similar to samurai-style armor.

Retreating toward the railroad tracks, Duplex caught sight of his brother still hiding and said, "Why are you still here?"

"Safer under the illusion than trying to run," he answered. "The tank idea didn't work, and I don't want to attempt to run and have this guy see through the illusion."

"Then stay put. I'll draw the fight away from here," Duplex said as he continued moving. "When I head toward those people watching, try to get them out of here too."

"Okay," Splitscreen said, looking up at Bradley as he moved around the tree.

Reaching the railroad tracks and the nearest boxcar, Duplex took a moment to look back and see if his brother had made a run for it. As Splitscreen took off toward the other people hiding in the trees, Bradley launched another volley of fireballs at Duplex.

None of the six fireballs struck him. Duplex assumed Bradley was trying to spread the fire and get more of Wilkes-Barre burning rather than hit him. The last fireball landed inside the boxcar and quickly caught it on fire. Knowing he couldn't put the fire out, Duplex knocked the car off of the tracks and quickly flipped it onto its side. Then he jumped on top of it in an attempt to close the door.

Seeing his opponent had his back turned, Bradley hit Duplex with a second volley of fireballs. The first two knocked him off of the boxcar as the fire spread. Feeling the sting as he stood up, Duplex saw the flames quickly spreading and converging with what was already burning.

Teleporting, Duplex appeared next to Bradley and swung. He was several inches too far away, but he grazed the left side of Bradley's face just enough to add to the pain he felt in his broken jaw. Screaming from the pain, Bradley switched from casting fireballs to hurling lightning bolts. Instead of burning the city down, he was going to electrocute Duplex.

The electricity crackled as it formed into a bolt in his hand. Duplex saw what was coming and quickly looked for a place to hide. With nowhere to go as he ran, he realized that to avoid being electrocuted, he needed to do two things, and as he reverted to his brick form, he teleported.

Reappearing next to Bradley, Duplex hit him with his shoulder and knocked him out of the air. Struggling to regain control, Bradley hit the ground a split second after his heavier opponent. The prior injuries to his leg became more of a problem, and upon landing, he collapsed to the ground, screaming from the pain.

Duplex landed with a loud thud, and as he took steps toward Bradley, Bradley began praying. As Duplex reached out, a white flame stopped him from grabbing Bradley. Pulling away quickly, Duplex felt the immense heat, and as it scarred the ground, it rose up to block his view of Bradley.

Looking at his brick-red hand for any signs of injury, Duplex heard, "Who was that?"

Thinking it was his brother, he turned around and was surprised to see the metallic legs of somebody else. Looking him over, he said, "And you are?"

"Roadkill. I'm with the Knight Shift. Who are you?" he asked, keeping his eyes on the white fire.

"Knight Shift?" he said, startled. "Really? Are you with another branch of the group?"

Putting his hand to his head, Roadkill looked as if he were in deep thought. Then he nodded and said, "I told Wildstar to let Arsenal know I found you."

"Wildstar?" he repeated. "You mean Star?"

"No, but she's there too," Roadkill answered as something began to move in the flames. "We'd better move."

"Go get my brother," Duplex said, pointing toward the people off to his left.

Turning back toward the fire, both men watched as a fire spout formed with Bradley inside. Pondering what to do, they watched as he disappeared with a pop of the flame. Taking the several steps to the now extinguished spot, they wondered where he'd gone and what was coming next.

# CHAPTER 30

Stone Fist stood next to Algae, knocking on the magical barrier as they looked through it at the city beyond.

"So that's Wilkes-Barre," he said. "And we can't get in."

"So far, no," Algae answered. "I can't even communicate with the plants. We're stuck out here until we can find a way in. Triphammer and Wind Rider are on top of it. Hopefully his hammer has the power to crack this thing."

Watching the river run behind them, Stone Fist saw High Tide standing in the river, shooting bursts of water at the barrier. The water simply bounced off of it. The barrier ended at the edge of the shore where it met the Susquehanna River, and even though Kirby Park was part of the city, it was safely located on the wrong side of the water.

The High Lords had set up base at the Kingston Armory, which was just across the street from the park. There, they had been in a classified meeting with Siegfried Lauren and Mason Colts regarding who or what was behind the attack. To eliminate the threat, they first needed to break through the barrier and find those involved.

"Half the city is ablaze. There are masses of people rushing to safer regions of the city," Majk said, pacing as she turned toward Arsenal. "We've got to break the barrier. Where are your weapons?"

"Dyna Cam," Arsenal answered. "Hopefully right where I left them."

"Well, we're going to need them," she said. "I'm going to use your sword to break through that barrier."

"This ought to be interesting," Arsenal said as he stood up from the tree he had been leaning against.

"Do we have time for this?" Disc asked. "Shouldn't we be dealing with the force behind the fires in Wilkes-Barre?"

"Do you know where we could get a sword at this time?" Majk asked, looking around at the group. "We don't have a weapon locker lying around."

"Are we all going to break into Dyna Cam?" Star asked "Or should some of us stay here until you get back?"

"I'll stay here," Kim said. "I think I can do better helping the people here."

The team was hiding out at the dam just below the Woodlands Resort, at the edge of the barrier. It was the safest place Arsenal could think of to regroup and plan. It was also a wooded area Arsenal knew well, as he'd been up there countless times since he was a kid.

"So who is going to be on this team?" Savage asked, approaching Arsenal. "I mean, besides me?"

Thinking as he looked around, he was about to answer, when Majk said, "Wildstar, me, and Arsenal."

"What about the rest of us?" Duplex asked. "What are we going to do?"

Shrugging, Arsenal replied, "You're in charge. You figure it out."

"Me? You're leaving me in charge?" he said, surprised, looking for his brother. "Wow."

Surprised by what she'd heard, Quarrel said, "You won't be gone long, will you?"

"Not sure," he answered, "but you're also in charge."

"Are you done?" Majk asked. "How many people are you leaving in charge?"

"Just two," Arsenal answered, turning away.

Arsenal, Majk, Wildstar, and Savage appeared in town in front of the Dyna Cam Industries building on Public Square as the Public Square Plaza Hotel behind them burned. The group was about to enter the building, when Wildstar looked up into the sky and saw Wind Rider and Triphammer. She read their minds.

"Arsenal," she said, pointing, "look up there, on the other side of the barrier. We've got help. They're trying to break through."

"Do you know who it is?" Arsenal asked as the rest of the group looked up.

"They're with the—oh, wow. The High Lords," Wildstar said. "And they're hoping to break through the top. Changing the subject, there's a woman being held inside. Her name is Jane Kelmore. She's the one who operated on you."

"Yeah," Arsenal said, "Kidneybean told me everything. While I get my weapons, look for her."

"She's on the tenth floor," Wildstar said. "Razor told her to stay put. He said if she moves, he'll kill her."

"Where's he at now?" Savage asked. "I take it he's the reason you brought me along. Is he the one with the knives?"

"He's a lot tougher than you think," Wildstar said, looking at Savage. "He doesn't carry knives; it's his skin you have to be concerned with."

"I know you haven't seen me do my best work," Savage said, clearing his throat, "but don't doubt me. Granted, I'm new to this team, but I think Wilkes-Barre and I will get along just fine."

"None of us has faced Razor before," Majk said, looking at Arsenal. "Except for Duplex, and you left him in charge back at the base, so Cam is the only choice we have."

Putting his hand on Cam's shoulder, he said, "Do us proud, and be the next member of the Knight Shift to put Razor on his ass."

Thinking of his troublesome cousins and family, Savage replied, "I don't think he's going to be the danger you think he is."

Cam Egavas was born in a future not directly connected to this point in time, into a family of criminals and cutthroats. Each of them was taught to kill anyone or anything that challenged or threatened him. His father ran the organization, and his two older cousins were hired killers. Cam never brought down any of them.

He came to be in this alternate past while on the run from his family. The Organization attempted to steal an alternate energy source, but they knew nothing about what they were stealing, and their lack of intelligence made things worse. Then Cam showed up to stop them and ended up killing his sister during the course of it all.

"Are you sure this is a good idea?" Triphammer asked as Wind Rider set him down on the barrier. "I mean, after all, it's about a thousand feet to the ground, and you can't fly."

"Are you talking to yourself again?" she asked as she floated in front of him.

"Yeah, it's the only way to keep my mind off how foolish this idea is," he answered as he reached back and pulled the large hammer off his back.

The name Triphammer was short for Triple Hammer, because when he swung the hammer, it had the effect of hitting three times. His strength allowed him to lift a little more than a ton, and his hammer alone weighed more than five hundred pounds, making him a powerhouse in a fight.

Watching as her partner hefted the weapon over his head, Wind Rider moved back several feet. She'd seen him use the massive weapon in combat before and knew how dangerous it could be. All she had to do was be prepared to catch him when he fell, and thanks to the weight of the weapon, she had to move quickly.

Swinging the hammer as hard as he could, Triphammer concentrated, and in a matter of seconds, his swing was three. Yet when each blow struck the barrier, it bounced off and knocked Triphammer backward. Struggling to keep his stance, Triphammer regripped his hammer and prepared to swing again as he hoped for a different outcome.

The guards inside Dyna Cam had done their best to protect the building, but in the end, they'd concluded their wives and families were more important. Those who remained at the plant were no match for the team when they showed up. They found Susan's and Arsenal's weapons in the subbasement, and just prior to opening the door, Wildstar alerted them that Razor was there as well.

"There are also two doctors in there," Wildstar said as they stopped in front of the door. "Both of them ought to be in jail; they're the ones responsible for the alien metal on your bones. Granted, they were both being paid by Dyna Cam, but they were sinister long before they came to work for Brock. I still don't trust them."

"Who are you?" Majk asked, approaching Dr. Shpagh.

"He won't answer you unless you can speak Arabic," Dr. Trungpa said, stepping up to Majk.

Stepping in front of her, Savage said, "Where's Razor?"

"He just took off up the back stairs," Jane said, pointing to the door as Arsenal retrieved his weapons. "Said he was going to go find Rachael and finish her off."

"Stay here with the others," Savage said, looking to Arsenal. "I'll take care of Razor."

"Who's Rachael?" Majk asked as Savage headed for the door.

"She was running the show," Arsenal answered. "We took her out when they went after Larry. She was the one we broke out of jail. I don't know what happened that put her on Razor's hit list, but that's not our concern. We've got the weapons. Let's cut this barrier."

"What about the doctors?" Wildstar asked, keeping her eyes on them. "Are you trusting enough to leave them?"

"Without resources, they're helpless," Arsenal answered, unsheathing his sword. "Currently, we've got more important things to deal with." Looking at Nygen, he said, "Run while you can. If I hear anything about any trouble involving either of you, then I will use my sword for things you won't live through. Now, get out of my sight before I find a way to deal with both evils at one time."

Majk took the sword from Arsenal and said, "This will only take a few minutes. Get Jane out of the building, but don't take the route where Savage is fighting Razor. Make your way to the top of Coal Street, and by the time you get there, I'll meet you. The spells I'm going to put into this weapon will break the barrier. It shouldn't take me very long."

*I'm getting a magic weapon*, he thought, smiling and recalling his friend. He imagined what Mitch would think. *Yeah, buddy, I feel like I'm somebody now.*

"The only teeth of mine that I'll be putting into a cup are the ones I pull off my fists," Savage said, coming face-to-face with his opponent.

"Talk is cheap," Razor said, swinging and connecting with Savage's jaw.

Feeling the thin hairs on Razor's body slice his skin, Savage hit the wall on the landing and fell backward down the stairs.

Lunging after him, Razor followed headfirst with both fists extended. Savage hit the steps hard, monkey-flipped Razor to the landing below, and then rolled down behind him. Rolling around quickly, Razor was able to slam Savage into the wall. Doing his best to roll with it, Savage sprang to his feet as Razor swung to strike.

That time, Savage's claws blocked while his right hand dug into Razor's ribcage. The depth of the cut caused Razor to scream out as Savage pushed his claws in deeper. Pushing him away, Razor felt the blood quickly seeping out and knew it wasn't going to be long before he was out.

"The city is lost," Razor said as Savage stumbled backward to regain his stance.

"And you'll be dead before the party starts," Savage said, lunging in for another strike.

Moving to his left, Razor was able to dodge the attack and backhand Savage into the wall. Ignoring the pain he felt, Razor moved fast and hit Savage with three shots to his head, the force of which dropped him to the floor.

"I don't know who you are!" he yelled, kicking him. "But my name is Razor!"

Savage mumbled something but was dealing with a fractured skull and blood on his face. He tried to stand. Razor kicked him hard again, and with his last bit of energy, Savage swung his left arm up and struck Razor's inner leg. As he pulled his claws out, the blood flowed, and Razor dropped to one knee.

"Me? As to who I am and what my name is," he said, "I'm the Savage who took you down. Remember my name when you're walking to the gates of hell."

"He took him down," Wildstar said, stopping. "They're both in the stairwell, bleeding to death."

Thinking, Arsenal was about to speak, when Wildstar said, "You go meet up with Judy. We'll get Cam."

Nodding, he replied, "Be careful."

After watching as the two women returned to Dyna Cam, he looked up into the sky and saw Triphammer still working to break through. Then he looked to the top of Coal Street, and three steps later, he saw Judy holding his sword.

After jogging uphill to reach her quicker, Arsenal briefly explained where Wildstar and Jane were. She nodded and replied, "I'm sure they'll be fine. Right now, we've got to concentrate on cracking that barrier."

"I agree," Arsenal said, taking his sword from her. "Tell me what I've got to do."

As Judy explained her plan, she also cast spells on him, and he slowly began to lift up off the ground.

"Hey, I'm floating," Arsenal said, rising several more feet. "Here we go."

"Actually, your boots are attracted to the magic in the barrier," Judy answered, watching.

"What do I do when I get there?" he asked as he slipped the sheathed sword onto his back.

"You'll be stuck to the barrier," she answered. "Once you break it, I'll catch you."

Thinking, he said, "Kidneybean or not, I don't like this idea."

As he got higher in the sky, he jokingly added, "And you promise to catch me after I hit the ground?"

"Yes," she said, watching him drift higher. "Before the second bounce, I'll have the spell ready."

Waving, he said, "I love you too."

Six minutes later, Arsenal touched down on the invisible barrier, and to his surprise, the man with the hammer didn't notice. Doing his best not to look down at the city above him, Arsenal concentrated on the task at hand, which was the barrier and not the surrounding city above him.

Triphammer was in the middle of swinging his hammer, when Arsenal walked up underneath him. Struggling to pull the hammer to a stop, Triphammer forced himself to take a knee, and as he did, he saw Arsenal waving back at him.

"Hello," Arsenal said as he knelt and looked down at Triphammer.

Triphammer looked to his right at Wind Rider, and she pointed down and said, "You're not alone."

"Who are you?" Triphammer asked, gazing down at the upside-down man.

"The name's Arsenal," he replied. "I'm here to break through the barrier."

# CHAPTER 31

Images of the casting out filled her mind, and even after all of that time, Astanna Syznchalla still wanted revenge. She'd followed the ways of her leader, the one who once had been the right hand of the Lord, yet their belief had been crushed, and they'd been defeated during the last great war.

The battle hadn't just ended in defeat; with the simple words "Get out," in an instant, Astanna and her allies had fallen from the cloudy fields of heaven. After all of the time spent burning, Astanna believed her punishment was going to come to an end. The fire that had become permanently attached to her would finally be extinguished.

The heat generated by the fires in Wilkes-Barre would be enough to satisfy her body, and she wouldn't need to have fire surrounding her body. Bradley would be able to look upon her true beauty; it would be her gift to him before she killed him. Once her domain was set up in Wilkes-Barre, she would no longer need any humans to assist her.

"The world is soon to be mine," Astanna said as the fire portal spun open.

"Yes," Bradley replied, kneeling before her. "The flames you provided that enabled my escape also healed me and then fitted me with this armor."

Looking it over, she replied, "Yes, and now you are fully prepared to serve me as the warrior I know you are."

"Yes," he said as he stood up.

"There is one other thing," Astanna said. "A sheathed sword of fire is strapped upon your back to cleanse the rest of this town of the threats attempting to prevent my victory."

"I will eliminate anyone or anything that stands in our way," Bradley declared, pulling the sword off his back.

"Indeed, you will. Now, go seek them out while I set out to find a place for my throne," Astanna said, looking toward the burning Public Square Plaza Hotel.

"As you wish, my mistress," Bradley said, gripping the sword. "Your bidding will be done."

Turning away from Astanna, Bradley looked out over the carnage and already burning regions before him. He saw several people scurrying about, but he felt no reason to worry about any of them and decided it wasn't the time to hunt them down; that was something for later.

"Business first," he said, pondering his next move. "Sport later. If I am to rule by her side, then perhaps I too shall seek out a place to build my sanctum."

The loud thud off to his left startled Bradley as he looked at the stone man standing before him. Immediately, Bradley knew this fight wasn't going to be easy. Killing this opposition was the only way; he had to do it to prove to his mistress he was worthy. Wilkes-Barre was her domain, and it was going to grow with each threat eliminated.

"I am called Stone Fist," he said, approaching. "You are under arrest for what you have done to this city and crimes against the people living here. It would be wise for you to put your weapon down and come quietly, though I suspect if you caused all of this, a fight to the end is your only way out."

"You mean a fight to victory," Bradley replied, stepping back into the fire. "The barrier may have been broken, but the final battle is a victory you will not achieve. Wilkes-Barre will still fall."

It took Bradley only three steps to become one with the fire, and as he faded into the orange monster, Stone Fist pondered his next move. Either magic or born ability meant his opponent was immune to this fire, whereas Stone Fist's skin would protect him only for a brief time. To survive the fight, he would have to be in open air and not inside the inferno, where his senses were his weak spot.

Suddenly, seven fiery clones in the image of Bradley appeared in front of Stone Fist and moved toward him. Sizing up the fire clones, Stone Fist stepped toward the nearest one and prepared to swing. He wasn't sure if he could stop them by sheer force, but he wasn't going to stand by and let the fires spread and increase the size of the inferno.

*The river's not that far from here, but getting the water here isn't going to be easy*, he thought, punching the first duplicate of Bradley.

His fist hit dead center in the clone's chest but passed right through it, causing no damage at all and sending Stone Fist to the ground. The other duplicates then attacked and jumped on him. They did no physical damage, as they were nothing more than quasi-sentient heat and flame; they did, however, make it nearly impossible for him to breathe, and to keep from going blind, he had no choice but to close his eyes.

The water that splashed against his face caught him off guard. His speedster teammate Blitzkrieg had thrown it. In the amount of time it took Stone Fist to sit up, Blitzkrieg hit him again with a second bucket of water.

"My slower partner will be here momentarily," he said, referring to Roadkill.

Three minutes later, Roadkill's bucket of water eliminated one of the duplicates. The sounds of the fire drowned out the loud hiss, but Bradley still sensed the clone's demise. There were now three heroes to deal with. The speedsters would be the hardest, so he would deal with them last. Believing the intense heat would wreak havoc on their lungs, he concluded he still had the upper hand.

The fight was set in front of the creek and businesses on Carey Avenue, the majority of which were burning. The fire had spread to both sides of the street and was threatening the railroad tracks and large grassy field beyond.

There were houses and businesses on the edges of the field, including the largest warehouse in the region, Klein Candy, which transported goods by road, rail, and water. Businesses receiving goods by water used the city's canals and waterways. Klein Candy had been around for more than a hundred years. It had taken up several residences throughout the city before moving to its current three-story structure, which was about to be incinerated.

As Roadkill reached the creek, Bradley could see how fast his opponent was moving, but he was nowhere near as fast as Blitzkrieg, which might work in his favor. The buckets of water the two heroes used to extinguish the fire did little. The heat dried the land and prepared it to burn. New flames emerged quicker than they could prevent them.

The remaining fire clones circled Stone Fist as Bradley spread the fire around them leaving him away from his two partners. Stone Fist didn't realize it at first and reached down, shoved his hands into the earth, and pulled out a large chunk of ground, which he used to knock back the inferno.

To his surprise, the dried soil and dirt had little effect on the fire. However, his senses couldn't say the same and the heat became a serious concern. Roadkill and Blitzkrieg ran for and dumped as much water as they could, but the heat and flames were too strong.

Stepping in with the clones, Bradley swung his sword and sliced deep into the back of Stone Fist's right leg. Stone Fist dropped to one knee and screamed out from the pain as the heat rushed into his lungs. As Stone Fist choked and gasped for oxygen, Bradley took advantage and shoved his burning sword right into his mouth, killing him instantly. Smoke and steam poured from Stone Fist's mouth as he collapsed into the fire.

The loud splashing hiss of water falling from a helicopter above distracted Bradley, and as he yanked out the sword, he looked up. There were three helicopters, all of which were doing the same thing: dropping water to battle the blaze. This was their first batch of water, which they were getting not from the river but from nearby Harvey's Lake.

As the river was so close to the scene of the main event, the military thought taking the water elsewhere made more sense. Concealed within the water was Savage. Wildstar picked up Bradley's thoughts and alerted Arsenal. She then contacted Blitzkrieg and told him to throw Savage into the fire and ask no questions. Arsenal would explain everything later.

Blitzkrieg thought of contacting Algae, but that would only prolong the battle, and there'd been enough death and destruction. If this was their plan, then Savage, if still alive and breathing, would be thrown into the inferno. When Blitzkrieg first reached him, Savage was struggling to stand and mumbling about the fire.

*Don't think about what you're doing*, Blitzkrieg told himself. *Just do it.*

Helping Savage to stand, Blitzkrieg took one step, and as he streaked though the inferno at superspeed, he let Savage go. When he came to a stop in the North End section of the city, Savage collapsed, and the fire covered his body as it began healing.

Bradley saw Savage get to his feet, and just as Astanna's magic healed him, he saw something similar happening with the man standing before him. For an instant, he wondered if her magic healed anything within a certain radius, and he wondered how the fight would end.

*No, I read over all of the files in his pocket,* Bradley thought, sizing up Savage. *He's not with us; he's the enemy—a threat to be terminated.*

Keeping his thoughts to himself, Bradley stepped back, raised his sword, and started swinging. Savage moved to avoid the flaming sword. He had faced that type of weapon and variations of it in his past and always found a way to survive those confrontations.

This was no different, but as Bradley was immune to fire, Savage wondered if he could lose this fight. He had no intention of allowing Bradley to stick him with the weapon and intended to use his razor-sharp fingernails to deflect any future attacks.

The fourth blow nearly succeeded; when Savage stumbled backward over debris, the blade almost sliced into his stomach. However, thanks to experience, he was able to avoid the pain and get in a kick to Bradley's shin. He hit him hard enough to knock him off his feet, and Bradley dropped the sword.

Both men saw the weapon fall away and immediately knew it would aid in achieving victory. Because he was in fire armor, Bradley couldn't cast any spells and needed the weapon to win. Savage knew that, and the quicker he got the sword, the quicker he could end the battle.

Bradley was able to reach it first, but before he could get to his feet and use the weapon, Savage sliced his left wrist. The cut was deep enough to do cause pain, but thanks to the intensity of the inferno, Bradley healed quickly. Not waiting, Savage followed the slice with a kick to Bradley's chest, which knocked him through a burning wall.

This time, as the sword fell from his hand, Savage made sure Bradley didn't pick it up again. He believed the fire didn't just cover Bradley; Bradley was part of it, and the only way to defeat him was to get him out of or away from it.

*Just keep fighting,* Wildstar said telepathically as she watched through his eyes. *Help is on the way.*

*Help? What do you mean?* he thought just as a large burst of water splashed down and knocked both combatants to the ground.

Steam rose off of them as they slowly got to their feet. Both were naked and had trouble standing because of the fresh mud. As Bradley did so, Roadkill knocked him to the ground and took off with the sword.

Seeing the sword disappear, Bradley cursed as he tried to return to his feet. Savage immediately dropped to his knees and shoved his claws into the soft underside of Bradley's jaw. Stunned and unable to scream, Bradley died moments later when Savage's other hand sliced into his heart and killed him.

As he pulled out his claws, Savage said, "One less threat to worry about."

# CHAPTER 32

The five tanks blocking the route into East End were the first to open fire on Astanna Syznchalla. Their opening volley of shots did nothing more than anger her and provide her with more targets to strike. The heroes who could be of assistance to the tanks couldn't do much against Astanna's assault.

Blitzkrieg's water buckets did little, serving as a nothing more than a distraction, despite the speed with which he was running. He switched to attempting to limit her region of the inferno. Duplex used his ability to teleport to the river, and using the back of a dump truck, he was able to drop plenty of water onto the fire. His attacks did more to end Astanna's plans since, thanks to his teleportation, he moved quicker than she could defend. To keep her off guard, he didn't drop all of his water on her; some went toward saving the city.

His partner Power of Justice flew above and fired his dark energy down at her. Power of Justice wasn't sure if it would have any effect on her, but he knew he needed to do something to help the tanks and the helicopters involved in the operation.

His biggest problem was that he still needed to gain control of his flying. Assisting in the distraction was Wind Rider. Had she not been there, Astanna's fire shots would have incinerated Power of Justice.

Algae, Arsenal, Majk, Wildstar, Quarrel, and Lt. General Mason Colts had set up a command center at the Kingston Armory and were now looking over maps and monitors.

"This is where the professionals come in," Colts said, looking directly at Arsenal. "Yeah, this is your city, but I don't know you or anyone else operating in Wilkes-Barre, the only exception being Quarrel. So I will be talking to Algae, whom I consider to be in command of this situation. Whatever you decide to do is up to you, but you'll clear it with Algae first."

*Not in my city*, Arsenal thought, biting his lip.

He didn't say anything as he looked at Majk, Quarrel, and Wildstar. Due to Guten Tag, Wilkes-Barre was being razed. It was under attack by an unknown force, and thanks to Wildstar's telepathy, they knew Bradley Brock was linked to it. There were others, but he was the mastermind.

Arsenal walked away from the table, leaned over, and whispered to Wildstar, "And what do we know about that sword?"

"Nothing," she answered, looking around. "Colts has it, but there's nothing special about it."

"Let's get Judy to take a closer look at it," Arsenal said as the four of them walked out of the building.

"I don't think we've got the time to look at it," Majk replied. "However, your sword has power all its own, and that's where we need to start."

Recalling the painful events in the hotel that had led him to burn to death, he felt hesitant to charge into another inferno. *There's got to be another choice*, he thought, gazing out at the fire consuming his city.

"Judy, what kind of spells can you cast on me that would make me fireproof so I don't burn—again?" Arsenal asked. "Something that would allow me to survive in that inferno."

"I'm not sure," she replied. "I'd need time to study everything—your clothing, the heat in the air, your breathing, and the fact that you'd be surrounded by a raging inferno. Are you sure you want to go charging into another fire after what happened the last time?"

"Believe me," he said, putting his arms around her, "I'm looking for another way, but I'm not sending someone else in to die."

"You won't have to, Michael," Wildstar said. "I'll send someone to pick up Savage. He's fireproof and couldn't be healthier."

"Contact Duplex," Arsenal said. "We'll need him for this too."

John Tide had been fighting for good for most of his military life. He'd discovered and learned to master his ability to absorb and generate water, but this was the first time he'd pushed his abilities like this. He'd gained more than three hundred pounds of absorbed water in less than a few minutes.

If it weren't for Splitscreen and a television monitor, High Tide wouldn't have been much help. Waddling toward the shore was a nearly impossible task, but two minutes later, High Tide disappeared with Splitscreen's assistance and reappeared inside the inferno.

"Yeah, another two or three hours of this, and I might be close to putting this blaze out," High Tide said, looking for a sewer cover, while thinking, *Only next time, remember to clear a way out of here before your water supply is up.*

It wasn't as if he were totally dry and out of water; his body could create it—but not at the speed he would need in order for it to be of any real use. He was pushing his body to take in and expel incredible amounts of water as quickly as he could get to it.

The only manhole cover he was able to locate was fifteen feet from the fire, with several large trees burning on top of it. The intensity of the fire melted pavement, and anything parked was claimed by both the fire and the softening pavement.

*Stay where you are,* Wildstar said telepathically. *Duplex is on the way with a water drop.*

*I'll stay put as long as the fire doesn't return to where it was,* he answered, keeping his eyes on it.

"Ready for your ride?" Duplex asked a moment later as he appeared right behind him. "Gotta warn you: it's a little stronger than a roller coaster."

"As long as I don't burn and live to see tomorrow," High Tide answered. "So how bad could it all be?"

"I'm ready when you are," Savage said as Power of Justice dropped him off.

Turning toward Wildstar, Power of Justice said, "You could have told me he was naked."

"You wouldn't have gone for him," she replied. "Besides, with everything going on, who was going to look up and see him?"

"The female pilot in the third helicopter didn't mind," Savage answered, grinning. "Where's Arsenal?"

"What if we placed a dome over her like the one she put over the city?" Disc asked. "You could do that, right, Judy?"

"I don't know. I haven't tried something like that," she answered, shrugging. "She's going to fight back, so we'll still have to face off against her. The dome would cut off her oxygen, and without it, there's no fire. But she's not going to just stand there and allow it. She's going to fight back, and how many of us are going to get killed in the process?"

"Is she human?" Duplex asked. "Is she the only one left, or are there still others?"

"Her accomplice was Bradley Brock," Wildstar answered, "the brother of Kyle Brock. If we can prove all of this, we can finally take him down and end his reign of crime in Wilkes-Barre."

"Where are those hit men he hired? If we can find them and convince one of them to turn, we've got him," Duplex said. "This could be the final act for that mobster."

"Hey, wait a minute," Splitscreen said. "Jane worked for—well, was held against her will by Dyna Cam."

"Yeah, we'll talk to her," Duplex said. "She's with Shockwave and the others, helping the injured. We need to find her before the hit men do. I don't think Shockwave will pose much of a threat to Razor."

"I don't know about that," Splitscreen said, recalling what he'd heard. "The story is that Savage gave him a good beating, which is how we got Jane on our side in the first place."

"What's Arsenal got planned?" Disc asked as Duplex reverted to his brick form.

"He and I are part of the group that's going to take that fire witch down," Duplex said, walking away from them. "Maybe she'll see how muscular I am and think twice about facing us."

"My troops have been defeated," Astanna said, gazing at the river and the majority of the enemy stationed there. "Claiming this city as my own is now futile. I can only do as much damage as possible and kill as many humans as possible—make them fear my name."

Astanna had come to the conclusion that Wilkes-Barre wasn't going to be hers. Her dream of walking on the ground that her leader, Satan himself, had walked on was not going to come to pass, and at that moment, she wondered if what she'd been told was the truth. The dump truck that knocked her from the pile of rubble caught her by surprise and left her stunned.

"That's right, bitch!" Duplex yelled, flexing. "The Knight Shift has arrived!"

"Give me a lift!" Savage yelled, stepping up next to Duplex, who looked confused by his statement. "Throw me like a spear."

Watching as Savage's claws extended, Duplex realized what he meant.

Duplex picked up his partner and swung back his arm as Savage straightened out his body. The force that Duplex used caught Savage by surprise, and he did his best to compensate as he slammed into Astanna. Two of Savage's claws snapped off on impact, and he screamed from the pain. He'd lost talons in fights prior, but these two had broken off under the skin.

The fire covering Astanna began the healing process as Savage yanked his hands free. In the instant he took to look down, Astanna punched him in the stomach. He collapsed to the ground, gasping for air, and she kicked him and made it harder for him to breathe.

"You mortal fool!" she yelled, grabbing him by the hair. "I am your superior!"

Before Savage could say anything, Power of Justice fired a burst of dark energy that hit her upper chest, causing her to drop his teammate. Dark energy was something she had never felt before, and the pain it caused only added to her rage.

Throwing Savage as if he were nothing more than a doll, Astanna set her sights on the flying threat. As she looked up at Power of Justice, large, fiery wings appeared and spread out across her back. Pure-white fire appeared and spread over her back and then spread to cover her hands.

Seeing Astanna rise up into the air took Arsenal by surprise, and he thought, *She can fly? This has to be the final fight. We need to push ourselves and bring this to an end. We need to be at our best, because she's going to take us out if we're not.*

Pulling the sword off his back, he made sure to keep the weapon ready for the attack he knew was coming his way. For a brief moment, he wished he had a set of wings to take him into the sky to face her. That was when he saw Power of Justice approaching with dark energy flowing from his fist as he fired at Astanna.

The first two shots missed, but the third struck her in the right breast and stopped her in midflight. Screaming from the pain, she created a flaming sword with the intent of decapitating Power of Justice. He pulled up hard, and her weapon just missed removing his left ankle.

Pushing his power of flight as hard as he could, Power of Justice tried to gain distance, but Astanna kept close. Raising her sword high, she was about to strike, when she realized he'd led her over the river.

The drop in temperature caused her to push her speed, and she was able to strike Power of Justice across the middle of his back. Screaming from the severe pain, he fell out of the sky and hit the water below.

The golf ball that sailed past her was the only weapon Arsenal had that could reach her. Had she not picked up his scent on the object, she would have ignored it.

"Land, and face me!" Arsenal yelled, rushing toward her.

Deciding to grant his wish, Astanna created a flaming sword and flew directly at Arsenal, swinging hard. Arsenal's weapon struck hers and sent sparks everywhere. However, that was his last attacking move, and Astanna took the lead. Each of her swings was filled with more and more rage.

*This one with the sword—I sense something within him that is different. His death will keep that secret*, she thought, driving him backward with the force of her attacks. *And that hideous symbol—he will never master its full potential. Killing him, their leader, will fracture their cause and die.*

Judy knew Arsenal needed her help, and she quickly cast a spell to assist him. Knowing they weren't far from the river, she believed the water was the answer. She looked around for Duplex; his strength and teleportation would be the last offense. She thought about what she'd done wrong in using the water from Wilkes-Barre Lake. She believed the water would, if anything, eliminate any ground fires and limit Astanna's area of movement.

Removing herself from the fire and the fight, Judy returned to the shore of the river. The whirlpools were still there and still a problem for the city. She knew where the water was going, but she had the power to bring it all there.

*If I could reverse the whirlpool and do some kind of trick with High Tide,* she thought, trying to imagine how to use the water most effectively.

Duplex had taken matters into his own hands. After filling a dump truck with water, he teleported directly in front of Astanna and dumped it on her. The force of the water and sudden sensation shocked her, but the assault didn't end there; he proceeded to slam the truck over her head.

The force of the blow put a large gash over her right eye, causing a bloodlike substance to ooze out. Feeling it ooze down her face, Astanna exploded with rage, and Duplex became her next target. She hadn't moved like that since before the birth of man and long before the concept of sapient-dominant man, back when the war for heaven had been fought. Even after all that time, her fighting prowess hadn't changed, and her talons dug deep into Duplex's steel skin.

Screaming from the pain, he struck her in the jaw and knocked her through a burning house. Getting to her feet, she picked up a burning metal door, which she attacked Duplex with. Seeing her charging with it, Duplex easily swatted it out of her grasp and continued his attack. Making a second charge, Astanna raised her hands, planning to slice through his skin and do even more damage that time around.

"This time, I will rip your heart out, human!" she yelled, getting closer.

Just before she touched his skin, Duplex vanished, and Astanna stumbled and fell flat on her face. As she slid to a stop, he reappeared behind her and kicked her in the back.

"I am human," he replied, "but as you can see, you are under my boot. I am Duplex, your new master. Remember my name!"

"You're dead!" she screamed, spinning around and lunging at him. "I'm going to kill you!"

As he caught her in his arms, the two of them disappeared. Splashing down in the river, Duplex violently slammed her down into the water and forced her below the surface. Astanna's clawed hands kept him from drowning her, and as the wounds became too much for him to handle, he let go. Screaming out from the cold water surrounding her, Astanna wanted nothing more than to get out of there and back to the fire, where her strength and power lay. The backhand that sent her splashing back into the water prolonged that. Diving at her, Duplex pulled her under the water and pummeled her as fast as he could.

*Duplex, the whirlpool. Take her to the whirlpool,* Wildstar said telepathically, seeing the fight through his thoughts.

"How close am I to it?" he asked, coming to the surface. "I see it." He turned to Astanna. "Come on, bitch. Time to drink the river!" he yelled, grabbing her left wrist.

"Unhand me!" she yelled, struggling against his grip.

Duplex didn't reply; he maintained his grip as they disappeared. Reappearing at the edge of the whirlpool, he yanked her toward him and threw a punch. Astanna sailed through the water and was pulled into the whirlpool. Duplex teleported again. This time, he reappeared on the partial dam created by the collapsed North Street Bridge.

*Wildstar, if you can hear this, she's in the hole,* Duplex thought, hoping his message got through to her.

Since he was unsure if Wildstar had heard him, Duplex started throwing large chunks of cement and debris into the hole to block it and prevent Astanna's return.

"The war is over," he said as he pulled a large chunk of cement from the water and threw it down the hole where he thought she'd be.

# EPILOGUE

The heavy rain summoned by Majk washed away the fires caused by the forces of Astanna and Bradley. It was a welcome relief to the heroes and those who opposed the fires. The sweat and grime of the final battle for the city washed away, but the memories and the traumatic experiences would last a lot longer.

On the top of Palooka Mountain, just outside the city of Wilkes-Barre, stood a lone figure clad in black robes and a cowl. He had been there for quite some time, watching the events unfold. Few people living knew his name or the incredible amount of power he possessed. His knowledge of magic and fear made Astanna Syznchalla look like an amateur.

Though the final battle had taken place at the far end of town, he'd been able to view the outcome. As the forces of fire suffered, he recited a poem by Clayton A. Engle III:

> I felt like Nero as I stood there, laughing at the flames, watching as it all burned. What did I care? The city had to go, no matter what the cost, either in human lives or damaged property. I felt like Nero, as it all started to burn. The only drawback was I had forgotten my violin, so I sang some strange lullaby, as it all went up in smoke.

He looked to the skies and took his first step toward Wilkes-Barre, where he intended to clean up Astanna's mess. He would put the city and the world where it belonged—under his feet.

The story continues in
*The Darkness Afterward.*
Coming soon.

Spearblade,
we're waiting for you.

# ABOUT THE AUTHOR

Clay Engle has lived in the Wilkes-Barre area his entire life. He currently is employed at Core Mark, where he's worked for the last eighteen years. He is the oldest child of Clayton and Janet Engle. He has a younger sister named Shirley and is the father of two daughters, Olivia and Marissa.

Previously, he worked at various restaurants while earning a degree in hotel and restaurant management at Luzerne County Community College, which he received at the age of thirty. Prior to writing his first novel, Engle had poetry published by Quill Books, Sparrowgrass Poetry Forum, and Iliad Books in the 1990s and early 2000s.

*Battle Zone Wilkes-Barre* originally began as a short story about Arsenal and his girlfriend, Majk, in 1988. Thirty years later, Engle perfected the tale and was ready to publish the first of many Arsenal stories.

Printed in the United States
By Bookmasters